Bonnie Duffy's
JOURNEY

D. C. TOWNSEND

PAGE PUBLISHING, INC.
New York, NY

First originally published by Page Publishing, Inc. 2018

ISBN 978-1-64214-566-3 (Paperback)
ISBN 978-1-64214-567-0 (Digital)

Printed in the United States of America

CHAPTER 1

New York

It was Christmas Eve 1885. It was also Bonnie's twelfth birthday. It was cold out, and Bonnie, not having school, spent the day near the register reading a book, *Moby Dick* by Melville, which she had borrowed from the tenement super's wife, Mrs. O'Neal. Bonne really enjoyed reading a good book like this, so she read each word carefully, not wanting to miss one word. A lot of the reading she did was in the school readers, which she could not bring home, or the two- or three-day-old newspapers that were Mr. O'Neal's, the papers that were passed down through several people. Often, parts would be missing, used in the outhouse. For her eleventh birthday and last Christmas, she had received a used copy of *Treasure Island* by Stevenson from her parents. After she read it twice, she traded it for a copy of *The Adventures of Tom Sawyer* by Twain. After two readings, Tom Sawyer was traded for *Huckleberry Finn* again by Twain.

Bonnie knew she was lucky. Her parents had good jobs at the garment factory. They had a nice room in a tenement that had a nice outhouse in the back. It was only two flights of stairs to get water. The heat worked most of the time, and they had a window that viewed the street. The window let air in during the summer. Bonnie knew that she had it better than most of her schoolmates; some had to share a room with no window with many people, and they had no outhouse. They had to use a chamber pot and throw it out a common window. Some had to haul their water from a store, where they had to pay for it.

It was starting to get dark out, and Bonnie realized it would not be long until Mom and Dad would be home. They worked from six to six and had Sundays off. Tomorrow being Christmas, they would have an extra day off. Tonight, they would all go to midnight Mass. Bonnie took a break from reading and added water to the bucket on the register. The water was getting warm, and she would be able to wash up in warm water before they went to Mass.

Bonnie heard a bell ringing and a trumpet blow; it was a fire wagon. Bonnie thought, *Someone will have a very bad Christmas*, as she looked out the window. It was exciting seeing the horses pull the bright-red wagons down the street. The fireman stood proud, blowing his trumpet, warning people to get out of the way. *It must be a big fire. Here comes another fire wagon.*

Bonnie went back to her reading.

Captain Ahab was really scary. Another two fire wagons went by, the sound of their trumpet unmistakable. Bonnie went to the window. The sky was glowing red in the direction of the river. She was hoping her parents would get home soon; maybe she could talk her dad into taking her to see the fire and all the firemen.

The church bell rang. It was six. Bonnie's parents would be home soon; it was only a fifteen-minute walk from their factory.

It seemed to be a long time; maybe they had stopped to get something special for Christmas. Some more fire wagons went by. Bonnie stared out the window. The whole sky was red now, and sometimes it flared up very bright red. The church bell rang again it was nine o'clock. Where were her parents? They were really late. Bonnie was getting scared. They still had to eat, get cleaned up, and dressed for Mass.

Bonnie put on her coat and hat and put her gloves in her pocket. She was going to see Mrs. O'Neal. Bonnie did not know where else to go.

The superintendent's flat was next to the front door. Their flat was big, and it had a bedroom.

Bonnie knocked, and the door opened. Mrs. O'Neal looked concerned and asked Bonnie, "Are your parents home?"

"No. It is getting late. I am a little worried."

Mrs. O'Neal squatted down and put her arms out, pulling Bonnie toward her and hugging her, saying, "Until your parents get home, I want you to stay with us. Have you had dinner?"

"I should go home and wait for my parents."

Mrs. O'Neal said, "I want you to go and get *Moby Dick* and bring it back. We will read it together while we wait for your parents. I can leave my front door cracked open, and we will hear when they come in."

As Mr. O'Neal went out the door, he said, "I think I will go down and see what is happening at the fire."

Bonnie went and got *Moby Dick*. Mrs. O'Neal and Bonnie took turns reading.

After several pages were read, Mrs. O'Neal fixed Bonnie a cup of tea, saying that it would help her relax.

Bonnie awoke in the morning on the O'Neal couch, her shoes off, with a pillow and a blanket. She did not remember lying down. It was Christmas. She had missed midnight Mass, and she had not heard her parents come home. Bonnie felt fuzzy-headed and still tired. She felt weak and unsteady going to the outhouse.

As Bonnie came in from the outhouse, Mrs. O'Neal shouted to Bonnie, "Bonnie, come here and have some breakfast."

"I should have breakfast with my parents."

Mr. O'Neal shouted, "Bonnie, come and have some breakfast. Mrs. O'Neal fixed it especially for you."

Bonnie had a good breakfast, and her head seemed to clear as she ate and drank.

After they ate, Bonnie was anxious to go see her parents. She knew something was wrong.

Mrs. O'Neal held Bonnie by her shoulders and said, "We have to talk. Something really bad happened last night."

"What?" Bonnie inquired.

"There was a fire at the garment factory. Your mother and father are not coming home. They are with Jesus now."

With great anguish, Bonnie blurted, "Are they dead?"

Mrs. O'Neal got on her knees and held Bonnie, and they cried together.

Later, Mr. and Mrs. O'Neal took Bonnie to church. And the three of them kneeled and said a prayer. The Priest gave them Mass and gave Bonnie a special blessing.

Back at the O'Neals', Bonnie was given some more tea and slept most of the day. When she awoke to go to the outhouse, she felt really dizzy.

The next day, Mr. O'Neal went to work.

Mrs. O'Neal took Bonnie to her flat and told Bonnie, "Get what you want. You can only take what you can carry. Everything left will be sold to pay back rent."

Bonnie got the laundry bag and put her clothes in it. There were two dresses, school shoes, underwear, and her mother's favorite scarf, which Bonnie had borrowed. Bonnie went to the loose floorboard and pulled it up, retrieving the money her parents had been saving.

Mrs. O'Neal grabbed the money away from Bonnie and said, "You will not be needing that. It will go toward back rent."

Bonnie picked up her mother's coffee pot and was told to leave it. Bonnie was not even allowed to keep her mother's two special bone hair combs. She was allowed to keep the letters from her grandfather. Mrs. O'Neal made her leave her latest trade, *The Pioneers* by Cooper.

When the church bells rang, it being noon, Mrs. O'Neal took Bonnie to the front door and told her to go with a policeman waiting there. Soon, Bonnie was put in a wagon with bars. There was a man in the wagon who looked to be dead, and he smelled really bad. Then the dead man started to yell, "Stop, stop!" Then he went back to sleep, or he really died.

Bonnie was taken to a police station. They took her bag away and put her in a cell with a bunch of other women. Some of the women were really dirty and smelled. Some had rags for clothes.

A woman came and grabbed Bonnie by the hand, telling her that she was from City Child Services. The lady was taking Bonnie away. Bonnie had to scream and holler to get her bag. People saw the police holding a screaming young girl. Bonnie screamed for her bag, and they gave her the bag to shut her up. She knew that the only things she had were in her bag. Bonnie was then taken to a general mercantile neighborhood store and given to the lady who owned the place.

The city lady told Bonnie, "If you work hard, these people will give you a warm place to sleep and food. If you run away, you will be put in a youth work camp. It is like a prison. There, disobedience is punished with harsh whippings and no food."

Bonnie was shown a cot in the basement and told to relieve herself in a pipe sticking out of the floor. After using the pipe, she was to dump a half-bucket of water in the pipe. Part of Bonnie's job was to put coal into the furnace. Bonnie was told, "Let it get too cold or too hot and you will be whipped on your bare ass." Bonnie soon learned that it was not the amount of coal but how the draft was adjusted, as long as there was a bank of hot coal in the furnace to burn. Her main job was to keep everything clean in the store and keep out of the customers' way; she was not allowed to talk to the customers. Bonnie was occasionally whipped; once was for getting in a customer's way.

Winter turned to spring. Bonnie was never let outside. She ate the old bread, produce that could not be sold, leftovers, and scraps, like pieces of pickles from the bottom of the pickle barrel or cracker crumbs.

Bonnie's father had not liked her mother's father, Grandpa O'King. He was Orange, a Protestant, whereas Bonnie's father was Green, a Catholic. Bonnie's mother never read the letters from Grandpa O'King to Bonnie or let Bonnie read them. Now Bonnie read his letters over and over. Grandpa's wife had died when Bonnie's mother was little. When Bonnie's mother married, Grandpa O'King went west. Grandpa's letters told how he had mined silver near Tombstone and gold in California and Colorado. His last letter said he was in the Black Hills of the Dakota Territory. He had his own mine and was finding some gold. He was not rich yet, but he had his own grubstake. Bonnie kept her spirits up dreaming of going to the Black Hills and finding her grandfather. It was something that Bonnie could hold on to and give her hope.

During the night, Bonnie had the run of the store. She was locked in, and she was expected to clean the counters, sweep the floor, and dust everything. The counters were to be spotless in the morning. The people who lived above had their own steps and entrance.

Bonnie was careful what she took. She had received a couple of strappings for not having everything clean. She knew if she got caught stealing, it would be bad. She was told that if she stole anything, she would be beaten hard and the police would be called and she would be sent to prison. A little here and a little there was blamed on shoplifters. The lady mercantile owner tried to keep track of everything. Occasionally, Bonnie would take a small tomato or small apple when they had a lot and she knew they would not be missed. Bonnie had found a loose brick on the outside of the coal bin, and behind it was her hiding place. The coal bin had a double wall, so there was a lot of room. The store got some maps of America that had the railroads, cities, and major trails on it. One must have been stolen by some boys that came in and were up to no good. Bonnie had a map, some canned goods, matches, a pocket knife, a water canteen, needles and thread, and best of all, some boy's clothes. The store had some books for sale; some were used. Bonnie had time to read the used books, it was the only good thing about the mercantile. Bonnie liked to read Mark Twain, Stevenson, Cooper, and the Wild West stories. In these pages, Bonnie found encouragement, hope, and inspiration. A determination to persevere consumed Bonnie.

Bonnie knew that a girl could not make it on the road hoboing but a boy could.

When they were unloading wagons, the back door was often left open for a short period. As long as the store was kept warm and clean and Bonnie stayed out of the way, she was ignored. Bonnie caused no trouble; she was respectful. She was accepted like a creaky floorboard.

They kept the change for the next day in a small strongbox. They took the extra money to the bank at the end of each day. Bonnie knew where the key to the strongbox was hid. She thought long and hard whether she should take the money. Bonnie thought, *If I take the money, they will hunt me down. The police will not put a lot of effort into finding a runaway orphan, but a thief they would.*

The last things that she would take were an oilskin slicker and a good pair of boots. In a magazine, she had seen an advertisement showing that with an oilskin slicker, one could keep dry in a heavy rain, when walking, sitting, or sleeping in a sitting position.

Bonnie decided to leave on a rainy morning; nobody wanted to be out in the rain. The produce wagon arrived every morning; that would be her time. The postman came in every afternoon and liked to give his weather report, and he was usually accurate.

Bonnie tried to discreetly listen to the customers talk, trying to gain knowledge and read anything that she could get her hands on that helped her make her plan. Bonnie went over her plan again and again. She believed she was ready for her escape.

The postman said there would be heavy rain for at least two days. Bonnie decided, tomorrow was the day. She had put a pair of boots that fit her in the back of the stack so they would not immediately be noticed if they came up missing. They would be missed if counted. She also had a slicker similarly set aside. Over time, when cleaning, she had found a few pennies and two nickels that people lost. She had a total of twenty-one cents. Her three dresses would be left as well as her girl's shoes and underwear. The only girl's thing that she would take was her mother's scarf. Bonnie had made a backpack out of some old canvas; she tried to make it like the one she had seen in an illustration of Theodore Roosevelt. Bonnie had loaded it up and wore it around the store at night to test it. It took several tries to make it work and be comfortable.

Bonnie got her boots and slicker and loaded her backpack. She then thoroughly cleaned the store; she did not want the owners to come looking for her as long as possible. Bonnie had set a schedule where she would not come up early. There was no need, after all, for everything was clean and ready for business, and she would be out of the way.

Bonnie cried when she took a pair of shears and cut her long red hair short like a boy's. She swore she would never cry again; strong people do not cry. She put the shears back where they were kept.

Bonnie put on the boy's clothes and looked at herself in a broken mirror that was stored in the basement. She looked like a boy to Bonnie—oops, Ben. Ben went over it in her mind, *I am a boy. My name is Ben, short for Benjamin.*

There was a knock on the back door. The door was heard opening. There were voices, "Fresh asparaguses." There were wo sets of footsteps into the store. Up the steps, quick and quiet, out the door. As Bonnie ran past the horse hitched to the wagon, the horse was startled and stepped sidewise as it whinnied, startling Bonnie. It was raining hard, and the wind blew down the alley between the buildings. It was a struggle walking against the wind. Nothing could be heard except the driving rain and wind.

As Bonnie turned the corner, she looked back. No one was following. Now the walk to the Brooklyn Bridge and west.

It was hard walking against the wind and rain. Only once before had Bonnie been across the Brooklyn Bridge. She had walked with her parents, then on a nice day. Bonnie's collar and the front of her shirt started to get wet, the pelting rain driving in around her face no matter how tight she tried to hold the slicker hood around her face. The driving rain hurt Bonnie's eyes, making it hard to see. Her feet were getting soaking wet; she could feel the water squishing around her toes. It was hard to see where she was going. She had to look at the street signs. She was glad that she had memorized the street names of her route.

When Bonnie got on the bridge, away from the buildings, the going got easier. After crossing, she worked her way around and under the bridge. There was a crowd of people under the bridge; there was not any room for her there and the people looked scary. She decided to go on. Bonnie did not know where to go, and now she was starting to get cold. After a while, the rain and wind were easing and she could dimly see the sun. Bonnie continued to walk west toward the setting sun.

Getting to the Hudson River, Bonnie was stopped; she would need to get a ferry across. Bonnie was tired, cold, and hungry, but she was not going to cry. She looked across the river, getting across was her next challenge. Bonnie noticed a fire flickering under a nearby pier. There was a group of five people around a small fire. She climbed down, and as she approached, one member of the group waved her to come on over.

"There is room for one more. Warm your bones and try to dry out."

"Hi, I am Ben Duffy. Thank you for letting me join you."

"You have not been on the streets long, have you?"

"No, I want to travel west."

"Brand-new slicker and new boots. I would say you are a rich kid running away from home."

There was an older woman there. She said, "Think twice before going very far. Life on the road is really hard and not a bit glamorous."

One of the men said, "You are lucky we are good people. A lot of people would see your fancy slicker and think you have money. They would leave you stripped and maybe dead. On a rainy day like this, I would like a nice slicker."

Hearing the warning, Bonnie decided to trade her slicker for a heavy old wool coat that had numerous patches, a can of hot hobo stew, and the right to share their camp for the night.

Bonnie said, "The stew is good. It tasted different."

The woman replied, "Rat meat gives it a special taste. New York has a lot of fat rats."

One of the men warned, "Boy, go home while you still can."

Bonnie's street education then started. "If the cops come, run and hide. Otherwise, they will give you a beating with their night sticks and leave you where you fall."

"Look poor, act poor, and be submissive. If you smell bad, people will not want to touch you. They will leave you alone. Do not give anyone any reason to look at you. If children throw rocks or sticks at you, pay them no attention. They will not touch you. They will be afraid of you."

"Some men like young boys like you. Do not accept food, a bath, or a warm place to sleep from a dandy. You will get more than what you want."

The woman smeared some soot on Bonnie's face. She laughingly said, "Looks like a hobo to me!"

"After your boots dry out, smear axle grease on them and your feet will keep dryer in a rain storm."

Bonnie asked, "Where do I get axle grease?"

"From a railroad car axle."

Bonnie then asked, "How do I get across the Hudson River?"

"Do not try to ride on a railroad car. The Bulls, the Railroad Detectives, will get you. They are paid to bash in skulls. Twelve cents on a regular ferry. If you do not have money, grab hold of the horse reins of a wagon and pretend it is your job to lead the horse across. Stay with the horse until you leave the ferry. If you caress the horse's neck to keep him calm, it will help. The teamsters and ferry people know what you are doing. You are doing them a service. The only people that do not know are the ferry owners."

Bonnie wrung out her socks and dumped the water out of her boots. While she was trying to dry her socks on a stick over the fire, one of her socks started to burn. Bonnie's boots were still wet and her socks damp when she put them back on. She then curled up in her big old wool coat and fell asleep.

When daylight started to break, Bonnie was woken by one of her camp companions. The others were already gone.

"I am going across the Hudson this morning. If you are coming, better get up."

Bonnie had to pee really bad, but she could not pee like a boy. "I have a case of the runs. Excuse me a minute."

Bonnie concluded it must have been the rat meat. Besides the pee, she made a stinky deposit.

Then they walked to the ferry dock. Bonnie noticed one of her camp companions ready to lead a horse onto the ferry. They went toward the end of the line. There was a large beer wagon that had a big sign, "HELLS BREWERY," with a team of large draft horses. Bonnie's companion led her to the horse's heads and put her hands in their bridles. These huge beasts terrified Bonnie, but she felt she had no choice. She had to be brave. That was what the heroes in the novels she read would do.

"Hang on and do not let go."

Every time the horses raised their heads, Bonnie's feet dangled. Bonnie held on for dear life. She held on until they were in New Jersey.

The teamster gave Bonnie a nickel tip, saying, "Hell's Brewery likes to put on a show, and you gave everybody a good laugh."

Bonnie's traveling companion then said to her, with a chuckle, "I was sort of hoping that you would get scared and go home where you belong. I am Freddie the Fart. The way you hung on, you got balls. I will ride with you for a while. What's your handle?"

"Benjamin Duffy."

Freddie said, "That ain't no handle for a hobo. It has no grit. Try again."

"How about Bennie?"

"Add an initial to it, like 'Bennie B.' That sounds like a hobo handle."

"Okay."

"That will do until you grow into a good handle."

Freddy the Fart helped Bonnie into a railroad freight car. By noon, they were headed for Albany. Bonnie continued her education. She got out a can of potted ham and chicken and her fork. She opened it up with her patented can opener, took a bite with her fork, then offered it to Freddie. Freddie took it and threw her fork out the open door and stuck his two fingers in the can and pulled out a mouthful, sticking it into his mouth, then he handed the can less than half full back to Bonnie.

After licking his fingers, he said, "How rich is your daddy? Maybe I should hold you for ransom."

Bonnie told the truth. "I am an orphan. When my parents died, they took everything except my mother's scarf and some letters from my grandfather. I got locked in a store overnight and stole everything I have. Now I want to find my grandfather in the Dakota Territory."

Freddie said, "Kid, if you are going to make it to the Dakotas, you are going to have to start acting hobo. No forks or fancy can openers—all you need is a big spoon and a knife. Tell me, the store that you got your stuff from, were they rich or hardworking folks?"

"They were rich and lived in a house, not above their store."

"It is okay to steal from the rich but not working people. That is part of the code."

"What is the code?" Bonnie asked. "I want to learn."

Freddie answered, "The code is not written down. It is how you treat other people. When you shared your tin of meat with me, it showed that you are a good person. I will tell you not all travelers follow the code. Some are bad people—they are tramps or bums. Careful who you camp with or ride with."

Every time they slowed, Freddie would carefully look out the door. Midafternoon, they were slowing down. Freddie looked out and hollered, "Get out and run, Bulls!" They jumped out on what was a steep grade made of rocks. Bonnie lost her footing and rolled down the embankment.

At the bottom, Freddie asked, "Are you all right?"

"I think so. My arm and side hurts."

Freddie felt her side and arm and declared, "You are just bruised. Look up there—a few bruises are better than feeling their clubs up against your head. Those Bulls enjoy seeing brains. They get a bonus for killing trespassers on railroad property. US law lets them kill trespassers. They just say you attacked them, and the law is on their side."

Bonnie looked up, and there were two large men with clubs and guns in holsters.

Freddie said, "Do not worry, they will not follow us down here. It will be too hard for them to get back up to the train. Most Bulls are lazy."

Freddie instructed Bonnie how to go down a steep grade—do not run, small jumps with both feet, try to not go too fast.

They walked around the small town. It had a railroad siding. While they walked, two trains passed going the other way. They got some water from a windmill water pipe pumping from a well into a livestock trough, letting Bonnie filled her canteen. By the time they got to the other side of town, the train they had been on was pulling out after taking on water and coal. They rehopped their ride to Albany. Bonnie had trouble getting into the car; Freddie reached down and pulled her up. They jumped off the train before it got to the railroad yard, avoiding the Bulls. Jumping out, Bonnie lost her footing and did a somersault, making her side hurt worse. Bonnie checked her arm and side. She had a couple of big bruises. Everything moved as it should; it just hurt.

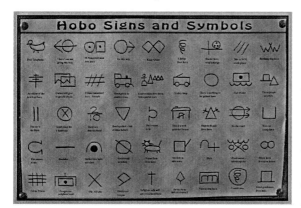

Freddie showed Bonnie some markings on a piling of a railroad truss. Each symbol had a meaning. One symbol meant a lady would give you a good meal for splitting and stacking firewood, a half hour walk, big red barn. Another was of the town where the sheriff liked to beat up hobos. Another directed them to a camp, shelter, a short walk. As they went the short walk, Freddie tried to explain the hobo signs. There were many signs, and he tried to tell Bonnie enough so she could get by. Different small symbols meant distance. A *U* was "camping here." Some were simple, like a series of crossing lines meant "jail bars." Others were complicated.

Freddie asked Bonnie if she had another can of potted meat. She did. It would be their contribution to the camp pot. It was an old shed that was leaning. There were four other people there with an old bucket on a fire. As instructed, Bonnie held out the can and gave it to the elderly man stirring the pot.

He took it, telling them, "Sit down and enjoy the fire. Soup will be soon."

"I am Freddie the Fart." Then he pointed to Bonnie. "Bennie B."

The other people recited their handle, and Freddie shook the hands of several with a unique handshake.

The man that took the potted meat took the top off the can with a pocket knife with one smooth motion. He smelled the meat and dumped it into the soup pot.

Freddie told of their encounter with the Bulls; others had similar stories.

Freddie said, "Bennie B is on to Cleveland and west tomorrow. Any news?"

Bonnie got some advice. "Be aware of the railroad yards at Syracuse, Erie, Ashtabula, and Cleveland—the Bulls are out in force. Word is that the Railroad Barons want to clamp down on free riders. Their passenger revenue is down."

"On the other side of Rochester, there is a good stop for shelter and food, just the other side of the yards. It is a Quaker mission, so expect to listen to a sermon."

The soup was really good. Some of the ingredients were recognizable—carrots, peas, asparagus, chicken. The chicken bones were recognizable; they were in the pot along with Bonnie's potted meat. Thinking of the rat meat, Bonnie did not want to know the other ingredients. Bonnie was hungry; the soup was good.

One of the men gave Bonnie a cup-bowl that he made from a peach can. It had a nice handle made from the lid; he soldered it down to the side over the fire.

Bonnie said, "This is one of the best presents I ever got. Thank you."

The cup-bowl was special to her for he had made it for her, even though he did not know her. Bonnie had not gotten a gift in a long time, not even for Christmas or her birthday.

Bonnie headed the advice she got and slept with her backpack, coat, and boots on.

In the morning, Freddie got her on a westbound freight, for he was headed to Vermont where he had friends and work. Bonnie wanted to give him a hug, but instead, he showed her how to give the handshake of a good hobo.

Bonnie held back the tears as she said, "I will never forget you, Freddie the Fart." It had been a long time since anyone had treated her nicely.

If she could hop a couple of highballs, through express train, get through Syracuse, and avoid the Bulls, she might make Rochester before dark. She wondered what a Quaker was. She guessed some sort of Protestant religion—Christians, she hoped. She had a car to herself, and her train highballed to Syracuse.

Approaching Syracuse, her train took a spur north. Bonnie jumped off when it was going fast, and she did another somersault, a few more bruises. One of the shoulder strap on her backpack was ripped off and her coat got a big rip. She sewed them as she walked to get west of Syracuse to catch a westbound train. It was several miles to the railroad yard. The way the roads were laid out, it was a few more miles to get around the yard. Bonnie struggled to get into the car. Her side still hurt, especially trying to pull herself up. The car she hopped had another traveler in it. It was a boy about her age; he had two black eyes and a fat busted lip. At first, he seemed scared of Bonnie. After a while, they talked, he had run away from home and had been beaten up and robbed. He was trying to get back to Buffalo and his family. His name was Learned Hand. He asked Bonnie for advice like she was an experienced traveler.

Bonnie told him, "I will help you get to Buffalo if you listen to me. There is a place near Rochester where we can get a dry place to sleep and food if we listen to a Quaker sermon."

Learned responded, "I learned my lesson and my grandmother is a Quaker. Quakers are good people."

He had had a fight with his parents. He wanted to drop out of school, and they told him he had to graduate from school and get an education.

Bonnie told him, "My parents were killed in a fire, so I cannot go to school. You are lucky to have parents wanting you to go to school."

Learned started to cry.

"Do not be a crybaby! Go to school and be someone special."

Bonnie amazed herself. Just five months prior, she had been an insecure girl totally dependent on her parents, but now she was on her own, hoboing halfway across the country, giving advice to a runaway boy her own age. But she wished that she were at home instead, waiting for her parents to come home from work, reading a good book.

As the train slowed coming into the yard, they jumped. Two Bulls were watching and saw them, and they were chased into a wooded lot. It hurt as Bonnie ran, but run she did. Learned, the boy, had trouble keeping up. Bonnie had to explain to him what Bulls were.

Evading the Bulls, they walked a few miles, and they noticed a church like building on the other side of Rochester. They were warmly greeted and told to bathe. There were separate bathing stalls each with a basin of cold water, and that made Bonnie happy, for she was trying to keep her identity secret. Bonnie had one change of clothes; the ones she took off were really dirty and smelly. The sisters showed Bonnie how to operate their hand-crank clothes' washer. Her freshly washed clothes were hung to dry. The food was really good. They had fried chicken, corn bread, asparaguses, and bread with quince jelly. Not the kind of food she was raised on, but it was really good. The sisters treated Learned's fat lip. The services were really different than the Catholic services—they spoke all in English—so Bonnie understood what the Priest was saying. The Priest talked of the prodigal son, and Bonnie wondered if it was about the boy with her. The sisters said that it was part of their mission to help travelers, but they did not want to interfere. All were children of God, so they did not judge. There were about a dozen travelers here.

When the sisters were not around, Bonnie asked, "I am going through Cleveland. Is there any news?"

Again, she was warned of the Bulls at every yard and that the Cleveland police were brutal to what they called vagrants.

Bonnie was asked to not call them sisters but Friends. "We are part of the Religious Society of Friends." They told Bonnie that they did not have Priests; they had Pastors that were no more important than any other man in God's eyes. They told her that they believed Catholics and Quakers were all children of God. "All men are God's children." Bonnie doubted she would ever hear that from a Priest or Nun.

Bonnie found it a pleasure to sleep on a cot without her backpack, coat, and boots on. They were served an early breakfast and told that they could stay if they wished and local jobs were available, though the jobs did not pay much. Bonnie and Learned were politely asked and spent a couple of hours helping clean the kitchen.

One of the church ladies said, "You must have a lot of experience cleaning. You have everything spotless. "Cleanliness is next to Godliness."

Bonnie answered, "I use to have to keep a store clean."

They managed to get a good ride. Buffalo was not that far by Bonnie's map. Learned lived on the east side of town, east of the rail yard. They had to make a jump at a fast clip. Bonnie kept to her feet but Learned did a somersault. He was not hurt bad; his ego was hurt more than anything. Bonnie wanted to be on her way, but Learned begged her to stay, saying that his mom was a good cook. Learned's mother hugged him and cried large tears upon seeing him. She was very concerned of his fat busted lip and black eyes.

Learned said, "Mom, this is Bennie B. He saved me and helped me get home. He knows the way of traveling on the rails."

His mom did not seem impressed. Bonnie started to leave and was stopped by Learned's mother. "You brought my son home," she said. "I insist that you spend the night and have a good meal in your stomach."

Bonnie got another excellent home-cooked meal. Bonnie thought, *People here know how to eat good.*

After dinner, Learned was questioned by both his parents to tell the story of his trip. He was totally forgiven, especially when he said that his friend Bennie B had convinced him to finish school and make something special out of himself. His story glorified Bennie B's cunning and daring. This embarrassed Bonnie.

They had a spare room that Bonnie slept in. Bonnie marveled at how really nice their house was. Learned's father worked as a loan manager for a bank. Bonnie worried that they would call the police on her, especially after all the questions she had not answered directly the evening before.

Bonnie got up at the first sign of daylight. She was waylaid in the kitchen on her way out by Learned's mother. "I knew that you would sneak out early. Thank you for bringing my son home. I do not think you are any older than he is, and I cannot fathom being on the road alone at your age. I will not detain you. I believe you are on your way someplace. God be with you and bless you. Here are some fresh-baked cookies for you."

Bonnie got a hug and a kiss on her forehead.

It was several miles to the southbound rails. She had to go south before going west to get around Lake Erie. There were three sets of tracks going south. Which one to Erie? She finally found a mile marker that had some hobo symbols scratched into it. As best as Bonnie could decipher, middle track west to Erie. West track went to a harbor and a factory; east track went to Pennsylvania.

Bonnie hopped a car that had six other riders. One of the men was beaten up badly; Bonnie was told the Bulls got him. Someone said he was unconscious, not dead. Bonnie felt that she was getting better at jumping a car; she was getting practice. But her side still hurt.

It was a long train, one engine pulling and one pushing—long train, long haul. As they approached the Erie yard, half of the passengers jumped and the other half stayed, including the injured man. Bonnie did not want trouble, so she jumped. It was a long walk around the yard, for the yard was large. The train they had been on stopped in the yard.

It seemed a long time until a train headed out of the yard. It was the same train they had been on; only one car had an open door. Bonnie and three others hopped.

In the car were pools of blood—blood spattered on the walls, blood streaks where it looked as if bloody bodies had been dragged out. It was a carnage. Bonnie went to a corner that looked to have only a little blood and threw up. She could not handle this, but she could not walk to the Dakotas. What was she to do? As they neared the Ashtabula yards, she and her fellow travelers jumped. Someone knew that down the tracks was an unused old equipment shed that was used by hobos. There was nobody there; an old pot was found and a fire started. Everybody had something—mainly vegetables, lots of potatoes, and Bonnie donated a can of potted meat. There was an old well pump that took a lot of work to get it pumping. The water smelled a little of Sulphur but was good. At first there was not a lot of talk. The soup was good; as there were only four people, Bonnie gave everybody a cookie. After getting a cookie, everyone seemed to relaxed and the camp talk started. Bonnie learned some more hobo signs from a middle-aged man as he drew some in the dirt with a stick, explaining them to Bonnie.

Bonnie asked, "I am heading west, past Chicago. What is the news?"

She was told, "In Cleveland, take the southern route, the B&O, directly to Gary. That will be before you get into Chicago. You will bypass Sandusky and Toledo. Your route will take you to Defiance, Ohio, then on to Gary, Indiana. In Gary, you will have to choose your way farther west according to your destination."

Bonnie got out her map, and she was shown the way. Six months before, these places were but meaningless names on a map to her. The conversation became stories of special times. Everybody wanted to forget the bloody railroad car.

CHAPTER 2

The Railroad West

Early morning in Ashtabula, Ohio, it was hard for Bonnie to hop the car after all the blood yesterday. What else could she do? It was a long way back to New York. Bonnie questioned herself, could she be brave and strong? She concluded she had no choice but to continue on no matter what she had to face. This was not anything like the novels she had read. All four hopped the same car heading west toward Cleveland. Bonnie was the only traveler going to take the B&O west.

Cleveland was a dirty steel city. Nothing was marked well. Bonnie had been warned of the police in Cleveland that liked to beat up vagrants. Walking to the west side of the rail yard was scary. Bonnie finally asked a couple of boys playing stick-can hockey in the dirt road for directions. One of the boys said that his father worked for the B&O railroad, first set of tracks down the road.

The engine said, "B&O, fourth open door." She hopped. It was a spur that led to a steel mill yard. They hooked up onto some more cars that they were pulling back into the yard. Bonnie jumped out just before entering the yard, hoping that the Bulls had not seen her. It was getting late afternoon. On the next set of tracks over there was a train pulling out. The engine said B&O; it was a huge engine belching black smoke and an enormous tender. They were pulling a lot of cars and pulling hard, gaining speed. This was a train going somewhere far. There were no open box cars; the caboose was coming. She could not hop close to the caboose; they would see her. The caboose was where the Bulls rode. The train was picking up speed; there was a flat car that appeared to have machinery on it.

It was a nice afternoon.

Bonnie ran fast and grabbed a chain holding down the load. Bonnie arm was jerked hard, but she managed to get a leg on the flatbed, pulling herself up. There were two crates that Bonnie squeezed in between. Bonnie's shoulder hurt from the hard jerk, grabbing the chain, and her ribs still hurt from falling down the railroad grade.

The train kept going faster. Bonnie had never gone this fast before. The ground was level and flat, it was late afternoon, and they were going toward the setting sun, west. It was the right direction. As it got dark, Bonnie realized she was on a special highball heading west. It started to rain, and they kept rolling down the tracks. The crates gave her some shelter from the rain and wind, but she was still getting wet. Bonnie could not get off if she wanted to; the train was going too fast. It was dark, and Bonnie had never had this long a ride or gone this fast; she had no idea where she was. She was wet and cold. Bonnie wanted to cry. The last time she had cried was when she cut her hair. She was not going to cry. The strong people in the novels she had read did not cry.

The train had slowed a little for a couple of curves but not slow enough for Bonnie to jump. She was too cold to sleep; she was shivering. It was breaking daylight; the train was starting to slow. It had been a long, uncomfortable, and scary night. Bonnie slid toward the edge of the car so she could see.

"Where was she?"

There was a speed limit sign, so that meant they were approaching a rail yard.

"Where was she?"

The train has slowed enough so she could jump off; it was getting light so she could see.

"Where was she?"

They were slowing and about to enter a yard. There were few trees. Bonnie got ready. There was a good spot ahead, and she jumped off. No bulls in sight, so Bonnie walked along the tracks looking for a clue, looking for a hobo symbol.

"Where was she?"

On a mileage marker, there was a hobo sign—short walk, camping, and shelter. Bonnie was cold, hungry, and wet. Toward the north, Bonnie could see what looked like a tall furnace like the ones she saw in Cleveland. The walk was short. There was a fire under what looked like a log cabin with half of the roof and one side partly burnt out. There was three people there; one was a nasty-looking old woman.

Bonnie said, "Hi, I am Bennie B. I got stuck on a highball out of Cleveland. Where am I?"

After a round of laughter, someone said, "Gary, Indiana, a long way from Cleveland. That train is called the B&O Fireball. It sets the record for distance in hours. It has the newest and biggest engine and tender. It is fired with oil instead of coal. Come and warm yourself. Want some coffee?"

"Coffee sounds good."

Bonnie got out her special cup-bowl. It had gotten partly crushed. With a piece of wood, Bonnie managed to pry on it, straightening it good enough to be used.

"You look young for a rail rider."

Bonnie remembered Freddie's words of advice: "Act like you do not give a shit, just another day. It ain't the time, it's the miles. I do not know about here, but east, the Bulls are busting a lot of heads. I have had to run a couple times, and I have seen some blood spilled."

"Bulls are bad around here and farther west. You sound to be an easterner."

"Brooklyn, New York."

"Where you headed?"

"Black Hills, Dakotas."

"You still got a long way to go, brother."

Bonnie got comfortable and warmed herself. They had a pot on; though it was mainly water, she added her last can of potted ham and chicken. Bonnie still had her twenty-six cents—she was not broke; she might still need it for an emergency. Bonnie was told to take the Union Pacific to Omaha then Cheyenne; after that, they were not sure of the way. They told her of a bypass south of Chicago and warned that Chicago was dangerous.

The others went on their way. Bonnie decided to stay, dry out, and rest up. Between naps, she kept the fire going.

Bonnie pondered, "This was not what I had expected. All of the reading I did had not prepared me for anything. What kind of man is my grandfather?" Bonnie envisioned her grandfather as a handsome, strong, and kind man. She needed something to hang on to; it was her dream that gave her hope.

There was a rain barrel that was full from the recent rain. Bonnie washed out her dirty clothes the best she could and hung them to dry.

Late afternoon, other travelers started to show up. Most brought something for the pot, even a live chicken. Bonnie learned how to kill, clean, and cut up a chicken. The chunks were thrown in the pot, bones and all; the bones added flavor.

Bonnie learned of another route, the Northern Pacific, but that meant going through Chicago. No one knew of a direct route to the Black Hills; no one had been there. One man told her it was still Indian territory. Bonnie's map showed no tracks into the Black Hills. The map did not even show any trails into the Black Hills. However, the map did show trails around the hills.

On a full belly, rested and dried out, the next morning, Bonnie departed. She wanted the Union Pacific tracks heading to Omaha. Getting through Chicago sounded dangerous and confusing, so it would be Omaha. It was midmorning before Bonnie walked around the yard and found the bypass tracks west. She hopped a slow freight that got her to the main tracks heading to Omaha. On the west side of the small switching yard, Bonnie caught a train. She got in an empty box car, hoping it was a long run. There was a lot of small sidings. They stopped often and dropped off cars or picked up cars; it was a milk run. At these small sidings, Bonnie was being reckless and stayed in her car, hoping the Bulls were not concerned with these small sidings.

Late afternoon, her car was dropped off on a small siding, she believed the middle of Illinois. This was a predicament; the through trains did not slow enough to hop, and it might be days before a train switched cars here again. This was farm country. Scanning the horizon, few trees could be seen.

Bonnie headed down the tracks. It was starting to get dark. She found a stack of old railroad tie; they were not stacked neatly. Finding a spot, she crawled into the stack. Bonnie ate her last two cookies and drank the last of her water. She spent the night.

At the break of dawn, Bonnie continued her trek west. At a small siding switch, there was a marker that had a symbol that said, "Food for work, fifteen-minute walk." It was worth a try. Bonnie was thirsty and hungry. There was only one farmhouse within fifteen minutes. It was a large house that was plain, not fancy, with a large unpainted barn. Bonnie knocked on the side door; a middle-aged woman in a long black dress and black bonnet answered.

"Can I help you, child?"

"Food for work, ma'am."

"Yes, I need firewood cut, split, and stacked."

The woman pointed to a pile of logs back of the house, handing her a saw that she kept in the porch. There was what looked to be a large garden and people working in it. In the distance, there were men and horses working in the fields.

Bonnie got a drink of water and filled her canteen from a well pump near the stack of logs. Bonnie went to work. She had seen illustrations of people sawing wood. Bonnie took off her backpack and coat, putting them where she could keep her eye on them. She hoisted a log onto the saw horse, looked at the already stacked wood, and determined the length. The saw was a lot heavier than she thought it would be. Bonnie began pushing the saw back and forth and down into the log. Soon the saw was stuck in the wood. Bonnie struggled to get it out of the cut. The woman showed up.

"City boy does not know how to saw wood."

"Yes, ma'am, I am sorry."

"Let me see your hands."

The farm lady looked at Bonnie's hands.

"Looks like a girl's hands—sure pretty hands, not working hands, city boy."

Bonnie said nothing; she was afraid to speak and did not know what to say.

"That is okay. Bring the saw, and come with me. I have some early spring peas to shuck. Put your coat and bag here on the porch. Do not worry, nobody will steal them here."

"Yes, ma'am."

"What is your name?"

"Benjamin Duffy."

"Roll up your sleeves, wash your hands and arms over there in the sink, wash them good."

"Yes, ma'am."

Bonnie learned to shuck peas; there was a large basket of pea pods. As Bonnie worked, the lady asked her, "Do you believe in God?"

"Yes, ma'am, I am a Catholic."

"That is good. I am Amish. You know what that is?"

"No, ma'am."

"We try to follow the teachings of the Bible without deviation. We try to be devout to God in all things. I notice your accent, where you from?"

"New York, ma'am."

"From what I have heard, a good place to be from. Is it true that it is full of sin?"

"Ma'am, there are good people and bad people there. My parents raised me to follow the teachings of Jesus."

"You look young. Why are you not with them?"

"They were killed in a fire at the factory where they worked."

"Do you have siblings?"

"No, ma'am."

"Why are you out here in God's farmland?"

"I ran away from a store where I had to work. I am going west to live with my grandfather. The people at the store did not treat me nice. They did not even let me go to school, confession, or Mass."

"God has a plan for all of us. Follow his laws and you will have a place in heaven."

Before Bonnie finished one basket of pea pods, a young woman, dressed in a long black dress and bonnet brought in another basket of pea pods to be shucked.

The Amish lady said, "This is Benjamin. He has offered to shuck peas. He is from New York."

Several other baskets of pea pods were brought in. Eventually, Bonnie's hands were getting sore. Other men, women, and children started to come in. The men were all dressed in black and had beards. The large table with many chairs was set, preparing for dinner. Everybody rolled up their sleeves and washed their hands. Bonnie kept shucking peas. Without a word, all gathered around the table. The Amish woman motioned Bonnie to a chair. They all stood and folded their hands and bowed their heads as the oldest man prayed. The prayer was long; it even acknowledged their guest, Benjamin, who today had shared in their work for God and would share in God's blessings. As near as Bonnie could guess, there was a mother, a father, three sons, their wives, and many children from her age to infants. It was one big family that worked, lived, and worshipped together. The food was plentiful and some of the best-tasting Bonnie ever remembered eating; it was a feast.

After the table was cleared, there was a reading from the Bible. It was from Genesis, the serpent, the apple, the temptation, the Original Sin, and being thrown out of Eden. During the prayers and "Amen," Bonnie felt uncomfortable not making the sign of the cross, so she made the sign in her mind, hoping Jesus would understand.

After the Bible reading, Bonnie was escorted to the tack room in the barn by one of the men. Bonnie took her coat and pack. There was a comfortable cot with a pillow and a heavy blanket. As Bonnie went to sleep, she thought of being thrown out of Eden. She thought that now she understood the story. Adam and Eve had survived, and so would she. Nobody in the Bible ever quit.

In the morning, the woman of the house came and woke Bonnie.

"Are you staying another day?" she asked. "You are welcome to stay if you wish."

"I think I should be on my way. Thank you and God bless your wonderful family."

"Come to the house for some breakfast. We do not send one of God's children away with an empty stomach."

Everybody was already busy at work, the men tending to livestock and hitching up horses, the women and children working in the garden. Bonnie said a short prayer out loud, "Thank you, God, for your many blessings," making the sign of the cross in her mind. The breakfast was delicious. Bonnie was given a package of food to take with her, including some more cookies.

The woman said, "May you walk in the path God has given to you and be united with your grandfather."

Bonnie said, "Thank you. You are wonderful people. You have shown me God's goodness. Bless your family."

As Bonnie walked west, several trains sped past her. Midday, Bonnie managed to hop a ride; she tried to get a car near the front of the train. Other hobos had told Bonnie that the engineers did not like the Bulls, for the Bulls tried to intimidate them. She was not real concerned if the engineer saw her hop on; he probably would not say anything. She hoped a car toward the front would not be dropped off early. The cars were organized to make switching easy—first on, last off. It was another milk run; she was making progress west. Bonnie had gotten complacent and was not paying attention. She had been daydreaming.

She heard a voice. "Are you okay in there?"

"Yes, I will get out."

"You do not bother me any. Be careful, the Bulls are working this section of tracks. If you hear three short blasts on the whistle, get out, run, and hide. I hate the Bulls. So I will warn you, remember, three short blasts."

Bonnie got out a cookie and gave it to the engineer. "Thank you. God bless you and your family."

"A little advice, the express trains run at night."

"I got a ride on the Fireball out of Cleveland to Gary, an all-nighter."

"I thought that they locked all the boxcars up on that run."

"I rode on a flatbed between two crates."

"That is a story you can tell that most will not believe. Be careful now, I have to roll. Remember, three short blasts."

The train passed over the Mississippi River. The iron bridge was huge. Bonnie admired the bridge and saw a paddle wheel riverboat down below as she looked out the door. She thought of Mark Twain and his wonderful books. At least the Riverboats are real and look as Twain described.

It was late afternoon when there were three short blasts on the whistle. Bonnie jumped off and quickly found a stack of ties to duck behind. Luckily, there were no Bulls around. Bonnie was near a large yard near Davenport Iowa. She had food and water and felt rested, so why not a night ride? Hopefully, she could hop a highball run.

Bonnie walked around the yard. When it was almost dark, there was a long train with a big engine and tender. It was gaining speed; there was no boxcar doors open. Bonnie could not see any flatbed cars. She saw a door that was cracked open. Bonnie ran; the train was going a little faster than she could run. When the door was going to pass by her, she reached up and grabbed the door sides and pulled herself in. Again, there was pain in her shoulder and side. She made it and was greeted by many moos. It was a car full of cows. As best as she could, she closed the door, leaving it only cracked open. Bonnie had been in some stinky outhouses before, but this topped them all. There was one cow lying on the floor that looked dead and bloated, it had relieved itself and had green goo coming out if its mouth. Bonnie became concerned; what if one of the cows stepped on her! Looking out the cracked door, they were going too fast to jump off. All the cows wanted to stick their noses at the fresh air coming from the partially open door. Bonnie went to a front corner and stood still. She was afraid to sit; she would be stepped on, and the floor was covered with manure and urine.

It was a very long night. They were slowing, and it was still dark out. Bonnie went to the door, having to crowd in with the cows. The moon was out; they were going over a long bridge trestle. Bonnie could see water below. They were slowing, and the speed was slow enough that she could jump but not with the trestle. They were pulling into a railroad yard; Bonnie could not see a spot to jump off. They were in the yard, coming to a stop. There were men walking along the train with lanterns coming toward her; she hid back in the corner. The door started to open, and the cows were pushing to get out. The door slammed shut, and the latch could be heard closing. The vent hatch high in the front was too small for even her skinny body. Bonnie was a prisoner with a herd of cows.

Bonnie could feel and hear that the car was switched from one tract to another. She guessed her car was being put into another train, destination unknown. Bonnie opened all the vents; it was getting hot in the car, and she was beyond smelling. She believed her nose would be dead forever. With a lot of bumps and tugs, the train was being built. Bonnie wondered how long they would leave cows in a car without water. Her water canteen was empty. She had not eaten; she had not been hungry. Bonnie's legs were getting very tired and sore because she had been standing for hours. They were finally moving. Eventually, there was some back and forth. They were putting her cars on sidings.

After what seemed like a long time, Bonnie could hear activity outside the car. Someone opened the doors, and the cows pushed to get out. Bonnie stepped over the dead cow and followed the cows out; running, her legs were numb and stiff. Bonnie was in a large corral full of cows. She ran to the fence, climbing up; on the other side was another corral. She looked around and headed for a fence away from the railroad tracks. As she went over the fence, she was met by several men who yelled, "Get out of here." They pointed toward a gate.

Bonnie ran. Her legs seemed to regain their use; she vaulted over the gate to finding herself on a dirt trail. Bonnie went toward the railroad tracks. She followed the spur toward the main line. Bonnie came across two boys fishing off a small trestle over a small stream.

"What you fishing for?" she asked.

"Trout."

"What is the name of the town over there?"

"Omaha," one of the boys answered. "Are you lost?"

"Yes. Which way to New York?"

This got a giggle from the boys. Bonnie found out what she wanted to know and gave the boys something to talk about. Bonnie went along the creek for a way and found a secluded spot and proceeded to clean herself up, get the manure off herself. She still had a clean change of clothes from Buffalo. The clean clothes were still wet from the rain—better than manure-dirty clothes. It was a nice afternoon. Bonnie washed out her dirty clothes in the creak and hung them to dry on some bushes as her clean, wet clothes dried on her. After having some of her good Amish food and water from the creek, Bonnie lay on her coat, her backpack under her head. Time for a nap. It had been a long night and half a day. She had not slept in over a day.

Bonnie was daydreaming. Omaha was a world away from New York. Everything was different here. Bonnie was aroused by a rustling in the brushes. It was the two boys that were fishing. They were trying to put the sneak on her. Jumping up quickly, she managed to tackle one of the boys. He was a couple years younger than she was. He was at her mercy. His fishing companion dropped her pants, which he had been trying to steal, and ran away. Bonnie let her captive up if he promised to not run away. His father was an engineer for the railroad. He was proud that he knew all about railroads and the railroad schedules. He bragged that he had ridden in the engine with his dad on several occasions. For an Amish cookie, Bonnie found out that there was no railroad line to Deadwood or Lead. He suggested going to Cheyenne and taking a stage or horse north. There were plans to build a railroad, and some lines were under construction to the mine in Lead. There was a through train to Cheyenne leaving at 7:00 p.m. It had one stop for fuel and water, letting an eastbound express train pass. There would probably be no Bulls late at night, he believed. It was half an hour's walk to the westbound rails. Bonnie let her prisoner free; he thanked her for the good cookie. Looking at her map, she thought the boy was telling her the truth.

Bonnie's clothes were dry by then; she headed for the westside of the railroad yard. As Bonnie walked by a house, the boy she had tackled came running out to her.

"The sixth car's door will be closed and latched but not locked. The Bulls will be distracted. Long-short-long whistle is a danger signal. Have a good trip. Thanks for the cookie."

Bonnie said, "Bless you and your family. You are good people."

Bonnie got to the tracks and moved close to the yard and hid in some brush. If she had to open the door, the train had to be going slow. That meant being close to the yard before the train picked up speed. The train was coming. It was coming slow. Bonnie ran out, and as she did, she looked at the engine. She saw a hand waving at her. The sixth car—she raised the latch, slid the door open, and pulled herself in. Her shoulder again screamed with pain. As soon as she was in, she felt the train surge forward, picking up speed. She closed the door, leaving it a crack open so it would not latch closed. Bonnie thought, *Now this is traveling in style. Now for a comfy bed.*

That boy and his dad had helped her out even though they had no reason to help her out.

Riding alone in a box car gave Bonnie plenty of time to think. She leaned back and thought of her trip. Real life was not like the novels of Twain, Stevenson, and Cooper. More like Melville or Poe, strange and scary. One day, she would finish reading *Moby Dick*. She felt all alone in a huge, dangerous world. She had met some good people along her way, though she felt like she had been lucky. Bonnie concluded that there were good people and bad people. Bonnie remembered reading, "Life is what you make of it," though she could not remember where she had read it.

In the middle of the night, they stopped. Bonnie thought about jumping out, but there was no long-short-long whistle. As she waited, ready to jump and run, there was a knock on the door.

"Are you okay?"

Bonnie pushed her last cookie through the door crack, saying, "Thank you."

"You're welcome. My son said you had good cookies. Get off before we reach Cheyenne. I cannot help you with the Bulls there. Remember, long-short-long."

It was not long, and the eastbound train could be heard pulling into the yard. Bonnie sat back and relaxed, a highball to Cheyenne. A week ago, she had never heard of Cheyenne. Bonnie was dozing, dreaming of her mother, father, and her at the park having a picnic lunch. Sitting on the grass, she felt safe and loved; it was a beautiful day. Bonnie's dream was interrupted, hearing a long-short-long whistle. She went to the door. It was still dark with a little moonlight; they had slowed. Bonnie could not see clearly where she was jumping. It looked flat; there were lanterns ahead, so she jumped. She landed, doing a tuck and roll, then ran away from the train through knee-high grass. Looking back, Bonnie saw nobody, so she lay down in the grass and watched the train move into the yard. She lay still and rested, trying to bring back her dream. Bonnie knew that it was just a dream; she could not go back.

At daylight, Bonnie started to walk west on the trail beside the rail line until she came to a small town, there was a crude sign, CHEYENNE. There were no trees except along the river. So this was the Wild West of the novels she had read. Bonnie wondered how much truth there was in the Western novels she had read. Most of the buildings looked like shacks. There was a saloon and brothel with a couple of women dressed inappropriately sitting on a flimsy-looking porch. The women looked dirty, old, and hard, not a bit pretty. The saloon brothel was a shack that looked like it was falling over. Bonnie did not feel comfortable here. Where were the gunslingers, cowboys, and Indians? Where was the sheriff?

There was a woman who was appropriately dressed washing clothes next to a small church, with a graveyard in back with wooden crosses. Bonnie went to talk with the lady.

"Ma'am, I am new here and was hoping that I could get some information. I am a Christian."

"Well, young Christian man, what would you like to know?"

"How do I get to Lead?"

"Take the stage. There are several operators."

"I do not have money for a stagecoach."

"Where are your parents?"

"They died in New York. I want to find my grandfather in Lead."

"How did you get here?"

"I hopped freight cars."

"Lead and Deadwood are rough towns. You sure are a brave little man. Are you willing to work to get there?"

"Yes, ma'am."

"Can you walk a long way?"

"Yes, ma'am."

"You know how to care for and lead horses?"

"A little, ma'am."

"I will talk to the Reverend. Have a seat, and I will be back."

After a while, the Reverend came out of the church.

The Reverend asked, "What is your name, young man?"

"Benjamin Duffy."

"Ah, Irish."

"Yes, Father. My mother's maiden name is O'King."

"Yes, indeed. I am an O'Reilly. What can I do for you?"

"I want to go to Lead."

"Why would you want to go there, to find gold?"

"To find my grandfather. He has a gold mine there. My parents are dead. I have ridden railroad cars all the way here from New York."

The Reverend looked at Bonnie. "That is sure a tall tale even for an Irishman. No blarney now. Can you walk twenty miles a day and sleep under a wagon on the dirt?"

"Yes, sir."

They went into the church.

"Are you Green or Orange?" the Reverend asked.

"I was raised a Catholic. My grandfather is Protestant."

"Do not tell people, but I do both. When you are the only Minister in town, you have to be versatile. Would you like me to hear your confession and receive a blessing?"

"Father, I have sinned." After some hesitation, she said, "I have been living a lie. I am a girl." Bonnie paused, fearful of the Priest's reaction. Not getting an undesirable response, she continued. "I have said profane words and thought bad thoughts and have stolen others' property. I had to be a boy to come here."

"I do not think that they are bad sins, being a child. Say your prayers every morning and night. Bless you, child. Heed the words of Jesus Christ."

Bonnie wondered what kind of a Priest he was, then she remembered, "The Lord works in mysterious ways."

"Come with me, Benjamin."

As they walked, the Reverend gave Bennie advice on the way things were in the hills and Wild West and how to deal with people. Bonnie was warned that there were a lot of evil people in the hills looking for easy money.

He told Bennie, "The Black Hills, with its gold, is the devil's pasture."

Bonnie was then introduced to a large, gruff, and wild-looking man.

The Reverend addressed the mule skinner, "Need an extra set of hands?"

The mule skinner said, "Always need more good help."

"Benjamin, this is Skinner. He drives his mules to Lead with heavy loads. Stay with him, do what he says, and you will get to Lead. Warning—if you do not work hard, he will leave you, and there are bears and lions in the hills as well as savage Indians."

Skinner said, "Benjamin, that ain't no name for a mule skinner! When you work for me, you need a simple name, not a fancy big-shot name."

"How about Bennie B?" Bonnie asked. "That is my hobo handle."

"How about just Bennie? I can remember that."

"Bennie is okay."

Skinner had a large heavy wagon with big wheels and eight mules. They went to the railroad yards, which made Bonnie very uncomfortable. In the railroad yard, they had a hoist that lifted a machine off a flatbed railroad car. They pushed the flatbed car away, leaving the machine hang. Skinner drove his mule and wagon under the machine. They then lowered the machine, placing blocks under it, onto the wagon. Skinner had Bonnie crawl on top of the machine and help him with two big heavy chains, fastening the machine to the wagon. Skinner had Bonnie help lace ropes back and forth, tightening the chains. Even though Bonnie's shoulder hurt pulling and tugging, she did her best. Skinner said the machine was a stamp mill, used to get gold out of rocks.

They stopped in front of a general store, where they picked up eight boxes of supplies that Skinner had ordered as well as ten cases of whiskey. Outside of town, they hooked up eight more mules—that made sixteen, or as Skinner said, eight teams.

Bonnie asked, "Are you going to drink all that whiskey?"

"Maybe one case," Skinner answered. "The extra I sell in Lead for a profit. Sometimes I need it for bribes. The soldiers really appreciate a bottle, and a bottle or two will satisfy the Indians so they let me be."

They headed north to the hills. On top of a ridge, the hills could be seen far off in the distance. They looked black and ominous. Bonnie rode up next to Skinner on the hard-wooden seat. Skinner had a pillow under his rear end that he did not share.

CHAPTER 3

Into the Hills

It was a slow pace; the mules were not fast. Skinner liked to sing even though he had a horrible voice. He could not carry a tune. Skinner said it relaxed the mules so they would be less skittish. As they rode, Skinner taught Bennie how to get his bull whip to snap with the sound of the Devil's sting. After Bonnie felt the Devil's sting on her arm she carefully listened to Skinner, getting the hang of keeping the business end out in front of her. Skinner told Bennie to never whip his mules; it just got their attention if they were not listening. Bonnie did not understand, sing to mules to relax them, then crack a whip over the mules to get their attention, making them skittish. That day, they made it to Fort Russel, just a little up the trail. They camped for the night. Bennie was told to make a fire and cook dinner, but the only thing she knew how to make was hobo soup. She found everything she needed in the wagon, including a slab of salt pork, and some carrots, parsnips, and potatoes.

Two other men showed up and helped unhitch the mules. They were young men in their twenties. One was Kirk and the other Rowdy. After the mules were watered, they were staked out to graze on some grass.

Bonnie was not introduced; she just picked up the names from the men swearing and insulting one another. It seemed that was their way, to curse out each other. Bonnie had made a good-sized pot of soup, thinking some would be left over for the morning. The three men devoured the soup, and Bonnie only got one cup. They were curious about her cup-bowl. Bonnie told them it had been made especially for her by a man in Albany, New York. Bonnie guessed the soup was good the way they ate it, though she never got any acknowledgement.

Skinner got a bottle from the wagon. The three men shared a bottle of whiskey. Bonnie was offered a drink out of the bottle being passed.

Bonnie said, "Whiskey is the devil's brew."

"That is okay by me," Skinner responded. "I will drink your share."

Rowdy added, "If they have whiskey in hell, that is where I want to go."

Kirk demanded, "Shut up, asshole, and pass the bottle."

These men accepted Bonnie as one of the boys. They were very explicit, bragging about their adventures with whores. Bonnie sat quietly and listened, getting an education she did not want. These men were crude and vulgar in ways that Bonnie could not apprehend, and some of what they said Bonnie did not understand. She did not even want to know what they meant.

After emptying the bottle, the men went to sleep under the stars. Bonnie curled up under the wagon in her big old wool coat and went to sleep with disturbing dreams. Bonnie dreamed she was a whore in a brothel.

To Bonnie's dismay, she was awoken at first light.

"Bennie, get your ass up and make some food before I put my foot in your ass."

Rowdy said, "Damn it, where is the coffee?"

Bonnie was able to pull the coals together and get a fire going, coffeepot on. But what to eat? Bonnie was not a cook; she did not know what she was doing. A frying pan and bacon, and as the bacon sizzled, she cracked open and threw in eggs. She put coffee grounds in the pot when the water got hot. The bacon and eggs did not look right, but they were eaten without any comment.

"Coffee won't last with this many ground in the pot," was the only comment.

There were a lot of things hanging from the wagon, and Bonnie soon learned what each was for. Bonnie learned how to chock the wheels, set the brakes, and grease the axles and other moving parts. One of Bonnie's jobs was to grease the axles, brake pivots, and fifth wheel. The axles had a hole in them that grease was spooned in, then a wooden plug was put in the hole and pounded with a mallet. This was repeated until the grease oozed out around the hub and axle. Every morning, the wagon had to be greased. It was a dirty and messy job. At first, Bonnie got grease all over herself; grease did not wash off easily. They did not have any soap. Bonnie learned she could get most of the grease off by rubbing hard with dry grass.

Bonnie learned how to set and tighten brakes, chock the wheels, and harness and handle the mules. Being small, she learned to sing to the mules, look them in the eyes, and stare them down, showing them who was the boss. Begrudgingly, Skinner agreed that the mules liked Bennie's singing better than his. Rowdy and Kirk agreed that they liked Bennie's singing better than Skinner's, prompting a profane and vile lecture from Skinner.

They stopped at most every creek and filled the water barrels attached to the wagon. Bonnie stood on the high wagon, reached down, and grabbed the water bucket ropes, pulling then up and pouring the water into the barrels as the men carried the water from the stream. It was hard lifting the buckets up; her shoulder was getting better.

After a couple of days, Bonnie asked Skinner. "I know that my cooking is not good. If the men would tell me, I will try to do better."

"Bennie, the rule is, if you complain about the cooking, you have to do the cooking. The only man to complain is the man who wants to cook. I am not complaining, but if you cook the bacon first, drain off most of the grease, then cook the eggs separately in some of the grease, it would be nice. A little more meat and vegetables and less water would make a stew. A good cook is treated as a special person."

That evening, Bonnie was told that her stew was good; it stuck to the ribs. She started to realize that these men were hardworking and honest with good hearts. All their profanity and foul talk was part of being tough men. Whiskey sometimes got them talking of their mothers or sweethearts or a favorite schoolteacher or grandmother, and when they talked of these women, the tone of their voices said they had their soft spots; they were not as tough and nasty as they talked.

Bonnie thought they had worked hard, but when they got into the hills, she quickly learned that they had had it easy until now. Luckily, Bonnie's shoulder hurt less than it did. Every foot was gained by hard work. Uphill, the brakes had to be manned, the wheel chocks were dragged by ropes behind every wheel. The mules had to be driven hard. On long grades, they would often stop, rest the mules, and give them water. If their heavy load would break away, it would be a disaster; people and the mules could easily be killed. They had a bell rigged so it would ring, warning other travelers of their presence. On narrow sections of the road, there was no room to pass their large, wide load. Most of the stagecoaches took different routes, though they still had some conflicts with stagecoach drivers. Mostly it would be an exchange of profanity and threats. Nobody could out-curse Skinner. Skinner could be very intimidating.

A steep or long upgrade could take a whole day. Downgrade was harder work; only four mules would be hitched to keep the wagon tong straight and in the center of the road. Brakes were continuously manned; the wheel chocks were constantly eased downhill in front of the front wheels. The wagon continuously moaned, groaned, and squealed under the load. On steep downgrades, two men would go down backward on their knees in front of the front wheels, manning the wheel chocks.

Bonnie tried to do her fair share of the work. Her pants and shirts were being worn into rags, and her boots were nearly worn out. The worst were her knees and hands. Her knees were worn raw, and she had to wrap them with rags to keep going. Her hands were blistered, she even had blisters in blisters, and the parts that were not blistered were dry and cracked. At night, she would put bacon grease on her hands and wrap them in rags.

The men were also wearing themselves out; Rowdy got the honor of the biggest blister. He cheated, though; he had the biggest hands. Everybody took turns at every job. Bonnie learned to handle the reins of eight teams on the mild grades. It took a while for her to get the hang of the bullwhip while holding eight sets of reins. The bullwhip was usually only used to get the mules' attention to get them started. Sometimes they were just stubborn mules and had to be reminded who the boss was.

Handling the reins was not easy. It strained every muscle of the body, especially the lower back and shoulders. Bonnie felt like she was getting stronger and could work harder. The harder it got, the more determined Bonnie felt. She told herself she was not going to give up; she could be tough.

Bonnie did not complain; she knew they tried to make it easy for her. She felt like she was a part of a team, just the weakest member, but she still tried to do her fair share. At night, Bonnie went to sleep sore and exhausted, and morning came early. Bonnie started to have a swallow of whiskey each night; it helped her fall asleep, easing her pains. To the enjoyment of her companions, at first, Bonnie found the whiskey hard to get down. It caused her to lose her breath, and on a couple of occasions, it made her cough and sputter.

After one especially hard day, coming down the longest and steepest grade of the trip, Bonnie got wonderful compliments.

Skinner said, "A toast to Bennie, one hell of a tough boy! He will be something when he grows up into a man." Then he took a pull on their bottle.

Kirk added, "Bennie is not a boy! He is a dammed tough little man." Then he took a pull on their bottle.

Rowdy then added, "I will sign on with Bennie any time," taking his pull.

Bonnie abruptly replied, "You men are full of shit," then Bennie took a pull.

That got a laugh of acceptance. She was one of the crew.

Two more days and they would be delivering their load to the Homestake Mine in Lead, if all went well.

At the last camp before Lead, the main talk was of going to the Gem Theater and getting whores who would do everything. Bonnie listened, trying to understand why these men would work so hard then spend their hard-earned money on a loose woman who did not care about them and would be with another man the next night for money.

Lead, Dakota Territory

They went right down Main Street in Lead; it was a fairly steep downgrade. There was only a short stretch of road that was flat, that was where the mine mill was. The road then went further downhill toward Deadwood. It was midday when they arrived at the mine's mill. It took the rest of the day to unload. Most of the work was done by the mine employees; they had a hoist.

Skinner went into the mine office while Rowdy, Kirk, and Bennie put the wagon back in order including the heavy chains, ropes and chocks. All the mules were watered. All but three mule teams were unhitched, their harnesses removed and placed in the wagon. The extra mules would be led behind the wagon.

Skinner returned to a wagon ready to travel. Each of the crew was given money, and Bonnie received a twenty-dollar gold piece and ten silver dollars. She felt rich. She had never touched a Double Eagle before, twenty dollars in gold; it was heavy. Bonnie did the math and figured, fifteen days—she got two dollars a day. She did not trust her pockets, so she put a couple of silver dollar in each of her pockets. The gold piece was wrapped in her mother's scarf in her backpack.

Homestake Gold Mine and Mill, Lead Dakota Territory

Rowdy and Kirk headed for the Deadwood trolley, whooping and hollering. Bonnie boarded the wagon with Skinner. They stopped and bought a dozen bales of hay and four bags of oats for the mules and went to a bar where Skinner sold his whiskey, except one case.

Skinner said, "I am going back for another load. Want to go back with me and do it again? The money is good."

"What about Rowdy and Kirk?"

"They will take the stagecoach south when they are near busted. I will pick them up on the way back."

"Are you going to get yourself a whore?"

"I am a married man and will send my money to my wife and children in Omaha. What are you going to do?"

"I have a letter from my grandfather. It is from Lead. I want to find him. I do not know where to go here."

"There is a boarding house where you can get a small room, bed, breakfast, and dinner for fifty cents a night just up the hill a bit. Baths are extra. There is a nice woman who runs it."

"Do you think they will let me stay there? I am really dirty."

"They are used to dirty people," Skinner said. "Some of the borders are miners."

As Bonnie exited the wagon, she said, "Skinner, thank you. God bless you. I will never forget you."

Skinner retorted, "You sound like a damn woman."

Bonnie replied, "You are full of shit."

Inside the boardinghouse, Mrs. Johnson gave Bonnie a room for forty cents a night if she helped with the dishes and laundry. Bonnie gave her a silver dollar.

Mrs. Johnson said, "Forty cents a night, two dollars a week, fresh sheets once a week. What would you like? Baths are a dime, with soap and a clean towel."

Bonnie replied, "I will take a week," giving her another silver dollar.

When Bonnie signed the guest register she almost signed Bonnie, but she caught herself, and wrote Benjamin Duffy. "Home address Brooklyn, New York" got Bonnie an inquisitive look.

They had an inside washroom with a pitcher pump, a latch on the door, and a stack of towels. There was a big bar of soap that Bonnie used along with a towel. Her hands were so sore she had to grit her teeth to wash them. The soap stung at her cuts and open blisters, bringing tears to her eyes, but she did not cry; her eyes just got moist. Bonnie cleaned up the best she could. Her face and neck looked mostly clean; her clothes were rags with many sewn patches. Bonnie had managed washing out her change of clothes in a stream the day before, putting them on. They sort of looked clean.

Benjamin was introduced at dinner. There were a couple of engineers that were working at the mine, one salesman, one lady schoolteacher, two geologists, two certified surveyors, and two ladies that owned a mercantile and dry goods store. Dinner was delicious, even with delicious cherry pie, a real treat. Bonnie felt comfortable here. After dinner, she asked one of the ladies that owned the store about clothing, for hers were rags with many patches.

The room she was given was small, with a small bed, and it even had a small window. Only a few times before had Bonnie had a room to herself, and that was just for one night. The basement of the mercantile she shared with several rats and a mangy, smelly cat that often tried to sleep with her and pissed on her stuff.

As she fell asleep, she made her plans: new clothes, bath, bank, and asking about her grandfather.

Bonnie woke up in the middle of the night. She realized she had to go back to being a girl; she could not be a boy forever. Three women lived by themselves in the boardinghouse, so she thought, why not her? Maybe she could tell Mrs. Johnson; she seemed to be nice.

After breakfast, Bonnie helped Mrs. Johnson clear the table, and when they were alone in the kitchen, doing dishes, she said, "Mrs. Johnson, I lied on the guest register."

"I wondered about New York."

"Brooklyn, New York, was true. My name is Bonnie. I am a girl." Bonnie held back a tear; she had gotten good at hiding her emotions.

Mrs. Johnson's look was questioning. Finally, she said, "Drop you pants if you expect me to believe you."

Bonnie dropped her pants and lowered her boy's underwear, with a lone tear coming down her cheek.

Mrs. Johnson looked. "Oh my goodness, pull your pants up!"

Bonnie tried to explain. "I am sorry. I had to become a boy."

Mrs. Johnson and Bonnie sat at the small kitchen table and talked. Bonnie told her story. Mrs. Johnson thought, *What a fanciful story!* yet here she was. She had seen the boy with the mule skinners, and Mrs. Johnson had heard the story of the boy driving the mules. She had been fooled. *Nobody gets hands looking like her playing with dolls.*

Mrs. Johnson asked, "Do you want to be a boy or girl?"

"I want to be a girl again."

"Do you have money for a dress?"

"I have twenty-eight dollars and twenty-six-cents."

They did the dishes and cleaned up the kitchen, then they walked to the dry goods store. Mrs. Johnson went to the backroom with the lady owner. An hour later, they left with a package that contained two dresses, underwear, shoes, socks, a bonnet, and a nice girl's summer coat. Bonnie also insisted on buying a slicker. The ladies questioned this, but Bonnie was adamant. She then asked the lady if she had heard of David O'King, her grandfather.

Mrs. Johnson heated water, and Bonnie took a good bath in warm water. Bonnie had never been in a bath tub before. It felt good, except burning her blistered hands.

Bonnie went in a dirty boy dressed in rags and came out a prim and proper young lady, as long as no one looked close. She had short hair and working hands. The long dress hid her knees, which were covered in scabs.

Another entry was made in the guest registry.

Bonnie gave Mrs. Johnson two nickels for the bath. She was concerned going outside with a dress on, for she was afraid that she would not act appropriately. Bonnie had worked hard to act like a boy, and now she had to act like a girl.

Bonnie went to the bank and opened an account, depositing twelve dollars. She opened an account, being a personable young lady, with a story of looking for her grandfather that had a gold mine. She was told that a Mr. David O'King had an account, but they would not tell her any more, for it was against the bank policy. However, the man at the bank told Bonnie to go the Federal building on Sherman Street in Deadwood and research the mining claims. They were public records, she was told.

At dinner, Bonnie was introduced. There were some strange looks, but good manners prevailed. Bonnie felt good being accepted as a girl. And she endeavored to act ladylike. Bonnie was not going to give up her boy stuff, for she knew if things got tough, she could be tough.

The next morning, Bonnie got on the trollies and went to Deadwood. She found the Federal building. Bonnie was shown the mining claim files. There were boxes and boxes of mining claims. The boxes were by claim number, based on date of the claims, but there was no cross-reference. They had one agent with eight years of backlog. If Bonnie had the claim number, it could be found.

Bonnie met an attorney doing some legal work for a mining company. He too was looking for claim information. He told Bonnie, "Go to the Homestake Mine office. They kept good records. The man who runs the records office has a daughter about your age."

As Bonnie walked back to the trolley, Rowdy passed by, walking the opposite way. He did not recognize Bonnie. She wanted to wish him well but did not dare. Bonnie felt like she was on her fourth life, and she could not publicly connect them. Daughter of Irish immigrants living in Brooklyn, New York. Orphaned and placed in child labor in a New York mercantile. Was a hobo and mule skinner boy. Now she was a young lady in a Dakota mining town on her own.

As Bonnie walked, she thought that her life was all mixed up. She did not fit into any novel that she had read. She concluded she was living her own novel that nobody would bother to read.

At the Homestake office, Bonnie was directed up two flights of steps to a small room in the back of the building. A middle-aged woman greeted her.

"What can I help you with?"

"I am trying to find my grandfather," Bonnie answered. "My parents died and he is my only relative."

"If he is an employee, you are in the wrong office."

Bonnie showed the lady the last letter from her grandfather. "I went to the Federal building, and they could not help me find a mining claim in his name, David O'King."

"The government could not find their own head if they had their fingers up their nose."

The lady made some notes and gave Bonnie back her letter, saying, "Come back tomorrow about this time. I will see what I can find. Do not tell anyone I am doing this for you. My boss will be angry."

That evening at dinner, Bonnie was barraged with questions.

"Where did you come from?"

"Brooklyn, New York."

"How did you get here?"

"Train."

"What route did you take?"

"Albany, Syracuse, Rochester, Buffalo, Cleveland, Gary, Davenport, Omaha, and Cheyenne. From Cheyenne by wagon."

"Did you take that trip by yourself?"

"Yes."

Bonnie wondered what they would think if she told them the details. She hoped they would never know the whole story, not a bit ladylike.

The schoolteacher said, "You should be in school. Did you go to school in New York?"

"After my parents died last Christmas, I could not go to school any longer."

"Why could you not go to school?"

"I had to work."

Mrs. Johnson said, "I think Bonnie needs time to recover from her ordeal. I am sure she will return to school soon. Right now, though, she wants to find her grandfather."

Bonnie helped clear the table and do the dishes. It was worth a dime a day. Mrs. Johnson was the one person Bonnie felt she could trust and confide in.

The next day, Bonnie returned to the Homestake Mine office. The clerk said, "Hopefully this will help you," handing Bonnie a piece of paper. On it was written, "David O'King, claim DK 77-457," the 457th claim filed in 1877 Dakota Territory.

Bonnie returned to the Federal building with the number. She was given a box to look through, but they were not in numerical order, so it took a while to find her grandfather's claim form. Upon finding it, Bonnie copied the information on it.

Name: David O'King

Claim name: The Shirley Bonnie

Location: Southeast of Rochford on Rapid Creek

Description: Pile of quarts' rocks I ½ mile SE of Rochford 200 feet NE of Rapid Creek, than 1000 feet SE to large pine tree blazed, than 450 feet SW to large spruce tree blazed, than 1000 feet NW to pile of shale rocks, than 500 feet NE to beginning, a pile of quarts' rocks

Purpose: Mining, gold, and other minerals

Notes: Upon death, full right to Shirley Duffy and Bonnie Duffy of Brooklyn, New York

Bonnie had the information she needed to complete her quest. On her way to the trolley, she stopped at a hardware store and bought a map of the area. Studying the map, she thought it was about twenty miles to her grandfather's claim from Lead. She knew she could walk that easily in a day. Going back to the boarding house, Bonnie found Mrs. Johnson in the kitchen preparing dinner. She told Mrs. Johnson the wonderful news.

Mrs. Johnson said, "It sounds good! You do know that a lot of miners have abandoned their claims?"

"I know, but I must go and look."

"You will need an escort. That is still wild country."

"I can go by myself. I can be a boy again."

"I do not like that. You are not a boy but a beautiful young lady."

"Just one more time."

Mrs. Johnson sighed. "You do what you think you must do. I am not going to be a part of it. When are you leaving?"

"Tomorrow morning."

"Shall I save your room for you?"

"Not if someone needs it."

"You really scare me. You are braver than most men I know."

"I am not brave. I just learned that I gotta do what I gotta do. Do not worry about me. Nobody has any need to hurt a skinny poor boy. I will sneak out the back door tomorrow morning." After some contemplation, she said, "Can I pay you for some traveling food?"

"There will be a bag of food for you on the table over there. I will worry about you."

"Can I leave a few things here, like one of my dresses and my heavy old coat?"

Deadwood, Dakota Territory

"Of course. Just leave them in your room. I will take care of them for you."

Bonnie packed her back-pack and sewed some patches on her pants and shirts. She would take one of her new dresses, her new bonnet, as well as her girl's shoes. She hoped her grandpa would want to see his granddaughter as a girl. She also packed her new slicker, in case it rained.

Dinner was really good, chicken pot pie and apple pie. After helping with the dishes and cleaning the kitchen, Bonnie said to the guests in the parlor, "I am going away for a few days to see if I can find my grandfather."

CHAPTER 4

Grandfather

Bonnie got up at first light trying to sneak out the back; she was Bennie again. Mrs. Johnson was in the kitchen waiting for her. Bonnie was ordered to sit and have some breakfast, flapjacks with blackberry preserves. There was a package waiting for her containing biscuits, ham, dried apples, two cans of potted meat, and cookies. The cool morning air was invigorating. Bonnie felt good. Her hands were healing, her shoulder had stopped hurting, and she had a spring in her step. She was filled with the anticipation of meeting her grandfather. Optimism was her rule.

Not far out of Lead, a wagon was passing by. It was a man and woman with two boys. They were taking building supplies south, and Bonnie got a ride, sitting on the lumber with the boys.

Bonnie was asked, "Where are you going this fine morning?"

"To find my grandfather in Rochford."

"We live near Rochford. What is his name?"

"David O'King."

One of the boys said, "He is a mean old man."

The woman chastised her son, "Shush, we do not talk bad about people."

The other boy said, "He is mean."

"Boys," the woman said, "enough. Excuse them, they like to tell stories. They hear that kind of story from other children in school. I am sure he is a fine man."

The man then asked, "Where you from? You sound like an easterner."

Bonnie answered, "Brooklyn, New York."

"Wow. You are sure a long way from home. Where are your parents?"

"They died in a fire in New York."

"You have relatives here?"

"My grandfather."

"You traveled all the way out here by yourself?"

"Yes, by the railroad."

"You surely are a brave boy."

That ended the conversation.

The two boys kept staring at Bennie like she was a two-headed dog. When their parents were not looking, Bonnie stuck her tongue out at them. This the boys reacted to, like they were scared of Bennie, and it ended the staring. They finally pulled off the main road, and the man, pointing, said, "Rochford is down the road about three miles."

While walking, Bonnie thought, *Those people seemed friendly at first but were nosy. Grandpa must be there. Even those boys have heard of him. Is Grandpa really mean?* Bonnie started to get scared. *What if Grandpa is mean and does not want me?* Bonnie reassured herself, *I can always go back to work, working as a mule skinner. I can make good money.*

Rochford looked like a hastily built town with a few businesses, a school, a few houses, and many shacks and tents. There was a lot of noise coming from machinery working. After all, it was a mining town. Bonnie recognized a couple of machines as stamp mills, though they were smaller than what she helped Skinner deliver.

A couple of boys were playing hoop sick in the street.

Bonnie said, "Hi, can you tell me where David O'King lives?"

The boys looked at Bennie and shook their heads.

There was a man loading a wagon in front of a store.

Bonnie asked him, "Sir, can you tell me where I can find David O'King?"

"Boy, you do not want to go there. He shoots trespassers."

"He is my grandfather."

"Go down the road a way. After you cross the bridge, take the trail to the left. It is about two miles. Good luck."

Bonnie said, "Thank you, sir."

Bonnie was getting excited and scared all at once. Only a couple of miles to go, after so far. She felt anxious. Why all the warnings? Mom always said her father was a good man.

Down the trail was a crude hand-painted sign with skull and crossbones that said, "NO TRESPASSING." Bonnie walked on. There was a husky-looking man in the creek digging with a shovel, throwing gravel into a sluice box. Bonnie walked to the side of the creek.

"Hi, I am looking for David O'King."

The man swiveled around. Seeing Bennie, he raised his shovel and walked toward Bennie, saying, "Can't you read? No trespassing, get off my property."

"Are you David O'King?"

As he approached, he said, "Yes. Now get off my property."

"I am your granddaughter, Bonnie Duffy."

"I do not want to hear your crap. Get off my property before you get my shovel upside of your head."

"My parents died in a fire. I have been looking for you, Grandpa."

"I do not have a grandson! Now get out of here and leave me alone."

"I am a girl. I just dress like a boy so people leave me alone."

"Yeah, sure. If I dress like a girl, will you leave me alone? Now get out of here."

"I wish that I were not your granddaughter. You are mean! Mom said you were nice. Now I know why my father did not like you."

"Yeah sure, what is your mother's name?"

As Bonnie turned to walk away, she said, "Shirley Duffy. She is dead now."

That seemed to shock the man, he dropped his shovel. "Wait . . . wait, you said she is dead?"

"I told you before, both my mom and dad are dead. They died in a fire. What do you care?"

"Please wait. Do not go. I did not know my sweet Shirley is dead."

Grandfather looked to have tears in his eyes.

"Why, so you can bash my head in with a shovel?"

"You sound just like your mother. How did you get here from New York?"

"I hoboed, riding the rails to Cheyenne, then I worked as a mule skinner to get to Lead." Bonnie held out her hands, saying, "I did not get my hands looking like this doing cross-stitch."

"I made a big, big mistake alienating myself from your mother. I hate myself for that. I am not going to do it again. Even an old hard-headed Irishman can learn. Please, Bonnie, come and let us talk."

"All right, just be nice."

"Are you sure you are a girl? You make a handsome boy."

Bonnie walked into some thick bushes. "I will be right back."

"Where are you going?"

"Girl's stuff."

Grandpa fidgeted waiting for his newly met granddaughter. After a little while, Bonnie reappeared in her dress, bonnet, white girl's socks, and girl's shoes.

Grandpa O'King said, "You are a beautiful young lady."

"Thank you, Grandpa. Nice that you noticed."

"You look beautiful, just like your mother when she was your age, except she had long red hair instead of short."

"I had to cut my hair to be a boy."

"You can go back and forth from girl to boy easily."

"How do you want me to leave, as a boy or girl?"

"I do not want you to leave," Grandpa O'King responded. "I made the mistake of trying to tell your mother whom to marry, and I have paid very dearly for that. I do not care who or what you are. I have become a bitter old man, but please stay, at least for a while so I can get to know you. I want to hear of your mother. I have not gotten a letter from her in a long time."

"I left New York thinking I had to have family. But on the way here, I learned I did not need family, but I want family."

"You are wiser than I am. It took me a long time and much heartache to learn that."

Bonnie answered, "I am not wise. I just had to learn stuff real fast."

They talked and learned about each other. They both told their stories. It was a start of a relationship. Nothing was easy. Everything became a compromise. Six months before, Bonnie would not question the orders of an adult, but now she felt herself as an equal. Bonnie was not going to let anyone hurt her again. She had been forced to confront her own self-reliance and grow up quickly. Bonnie felt the need for family; she did not want to be all alone. She knew what being all alone was like.

Grandpa was set in his ways. He had his regrets, but he hoped he had learned from his mistakes. His heart had been turned cold; now his granddaughter warmed it. Grandpa thought, *If I try real hard, just maybe I can be of some good to her.* Bonnie was his only descendant now that his daughter was dead.

It was not easy for either of them. But they both learned and grew.

Bonnie asked, "Who cooked your dinner before I came? Now you only have to cook half the time, half the work."

Grandpa answered, "Now there is twice as much to cook."

Bonnie said, "I eat less than you do. Hobo food is simpler than what you expect."

This was the way they worked together, the meals were prepared, the floor swept. The production of gold was increased with two working the claim. Life was better, for they both had someone to share it with. Someone to argue with. Someone they knew cared.

The weather was getting warmer. Bonnie found pleasure in working in the creek digging out the gravel and loading it in the sluice box, especially on hot days. The real pleasure came at the end of the day when they fined, with a pan, their daily rewards. The gold was mostly fine flakes with an occasional small nugget.

Most days working together, they were able to get two to four ounces of gold. At eighteen dollars an ounce for unrefined gold, they were becoming well-to-do. A health miner made twenty-three cents an hour at the Homestake mine. Bonnie used her good math skills to figure that if they both worked ten hours a day, they each were making about two dollars and seventy cents an hour, over ten times what a miner made. Bonnie knew she had found a home without people treating her mean and a grandfather that she was learning to love and the love was returned. Grandpa had given up trying to boss Bonnie around. She was just like her mother, grandmother, and himself, strong-willed. Grandpa learned that with Bonnie, he would just have to ask her nicely to do something that was reasonable and look out of the way. Bonnie learned as well that if she asked her grandpa nicely, anything in his power was granted.

In several weeks, they went to Lead for supplies, sell their gold, and deposit the proceeds in the bank. The safest place for their money was the bank, for the area was still lawless. The best way was to let everybody know that your money was in the bank; that way, they would not bushwhack you and search your cabin. The bank had a heavy safe and armed Pinkerton guards. The Pinkertons had a reputation of shooting first and asking questions later, and they could not be bribed.

Grandpa surprised Bonnie and put her name on his bank account. Bonnie refused to look at the balance figures. They came close to having an argument in the bank. Money was a divisive subject to Bonnie. Mrs. O'Neal and the mean woman at the mercantile only cared about money.

They stopped at Mrs. Johnson's boardinghouse, and Bonnie picked up her things she had left and introduced her wonderful grandpa to Mrs. Johnson. Mrs. Johnson hugged Bonnie and told her how happy she was for her and how beautiful she was in a dress.

Grandpa told Bonnie, "Throw that raggedy old coat away. I will buy you a new one."

"It is a good warm coat. I am not going to throw it away. I do not want a new coat."

Going out of town, Bonnie heard the sound of a familiar bell. Bonnie had her grandpa pull their buckboard wagon to the side to let the cargo by. As the heavy wagon stopped at the top of the hill to unhitch some of the mules, Bonnie walked up next to the wagon and yelled, "Skinner, you no-good son of a bitch! What the hell are you doing blocking the public road? Your fat ass should be horsewhipped."

Skinner was ready to give back the profanity upon recognizing the voice, but when he looked, he was dumbfounded, at a loss for words, for here was a pretty young woman swearing in a way that was not at all appropriate.

"Excuse me, miss, are you talking to me?"

"Damned right I am talking to you. Do you not recognize me, you stupid old fart? I am Bennie!" she said with a smile. "Cat got your tongue?" She laughed. "Yeah, I am a girl. Fooled your stupid ass, didn't I? Got you good!"

Skinner said, "It is not nice for a girl to talk like that."

"Listen, asshole, think of me as a mule skinner with a dress on. Can't handle it, can you?"

After the brakes were set and the wheel chocks secured, Skinner got off the wagon, and Bonnie gave him a big hug. Grandpa, Kirk, Rowdy, a young man, and a couple in a buckboard waiting to get by watched in awe. None of them had ever heard a lady curse like a mule skinner. They especially did not expect the hug after the verbal assault.

After the show, Bonnie introduced the crew to her grandpa. They had a new helper that had taken Bonnie's place.

Skinner said, "Put on some pants, boots, and shirt and you can have your job back. I don't care, girl or not. You became a good cook and a hard worker. Nobody will ever believe me that I had a girl working for me that could drive eight teams better than most men."

Grandpa replied, "You cannot have her. She is a very good miner."

Bonnie said, "You are all full of shit!"

They all had a good laugh.

On their way back to Rochford, Bonnie said, "Okay, tell me how bad a girl I am, swearing like that."

"You continually amaze me. You are my granddaughter, and I accept you the way you are. I have no choice. I know that I cannot change you. You would just curse me up and down!"

Bonnie laughed. "I love you, Grandpa."

"Bonnie, I love you too."

* * * * *

The first of September school started in Rochford. Showing up, Bonnie felt uncomfortable. The other students stared at her, but whenever she looked at them, they all looked away. Her hellos were not acknowledged. Quickly, Bonnie realized she was being ostracized. The new kid in school. This school was nothing like her school in New York. There were two teachers and two rooms, older children in one room, the younger children in the other. Bonnie went into the room with the older children and sat in the back.

After, the teacher called class to order.

The teacher addressed Bonnie. "Who are you?"

"I am Bonnie Duffy."

"What makes you think you belong in this class?"

"The students are my age."

"The students in this class have gone to school and earned a promotion here. They have enough knowledge to be here."

"I went to school in Brooklyn, New York, and was in the sixth grade and got all As."

"All right, young lady, who was the fourth President of the United States?"

"James Madison."

"What are the common denominators for fifteen?"

"Three and five."

"Thirteen?"

"None. It is a prime number."

'Who wrote *The Raven*?"

"Edgar Allen Poe."

"There are questions. Are you a girl or a boy?"

"I am a girl."

"Then join our class. I expect you to behave like a girl. No cursing or swearing permitted in class, understand?"

"Yes, ma'am."

Bonnie thought to herself, *My past has given me a reputation. I just want to leave and go home. They do not really know me. They wanted me to leave. They do not like me. But I am going to stay and show them. I am not a quitter. They cannot make me cry.*

Bonnie sat in the back of the class. She did her work, did not raise her hand, and was never called on. She was ignored and gave no reason to bring attention to herself.

At home, Grandpa with Bonnie's help, built onto the cabin two small bedrooms, one for each of them. They put in a big wood stove with a sidearm heater and hot-water storage tank, the latest in innovations. Now they had hot water when they wanted it.

At school, before and after class and at break times, Bonnie overheard the other students talk behind her back. They called her "he-she." When Grandpa asked how school was, Bonnie always said it was good. She decided it was her problem, and Grandpa did not need her problems. Bonnie pondered how the hobos on the road treated her better than her fellow students. The graded papers she got back from the teacher were what Bonnie thought fair; at least the teacher was fair.

Bonnie got into the habit of waiting in the classroom at the end of the day to avoid contact with the other students. One day, coming out of the school, Bonnie was confronted by one of the husky older boys. Several of the students were gathered.

"I want to know, are you a boy or a girl?"

"I am a girl."

He pushed Bonnie backward. There was a boy on his hands and knees behind Bonnie, and she went over backward as two other boys grabbed her skirt hem and pulled her skirt up.

The older boy announced, "It is a girl."

Bonnie was really mad; the Irish Redhead was in total command. She got up and walked toward the older boy. He bent forward at the waist, hands on hips, taunting Bonnie to her face, saying, "He-she." Without hesitation, Bonnie put her fist into the boy's nose. The boy was stunned for a moment, then he grabbed Bonnie with both hands about her neck.

The bully said, "You are going to pay for that, bitch!"

Bonnie quickly rose her knee and made a lucky contact with his groin. The boy released Bonnie and bent over, moaning in agony. Bonnie grabbed the side of his head by the ears, and as she pulled his head down, she again quickly raised her knee. The boy went down on his side in the fetal position, holding his groin, whimpering, blood running from his nose and busted lips.

"Tough guy, pull my dress up, I am going to pull your pants off and see if you are a boy. You cry like a girl."

The bully begged, "I am sorry, please, I am sorry."

All the other boys seemed to back up as the schoolgirls moved closer. Bonnie watched as some of the girls stood over the boy and spit on him. Each girl had a few choice words for the boy as he whimpered on the ground, and a couple of the girls even kicked him. Bonnie realized the boy was a bully that had been intimidating the whole school. Bonnie went home. Bonnie was now mad at herself. She thought, now nobody would ever like her at school.

At home, Grandpa knew something had happened. He noticed Bonnie had wrapped her right hand in her scarf. Her blouse was soiled with what looked like blood splatters on it, and she held her head down.

"What is wrong, Bonnie?"

"Nothing is wrong."

"Do not be fibbing to your grandfather."

Bonnie sighed, "A bully at school pushed me down."

"What did you do?"

"Put him on the ground."

"Did he hurt you?" Grandpa asked. "I see blood on your blouse."

"The blood is his, out of his nose."

"You need any help?"

61

"No, I can take care of myself. I do not want to go to school anymore."

"That is your decision, but if you do not go back to school, the bully will think he won and you were scared away."

Grandpa was concerned. He wanted to do something like beat the crap out of the boy. He knew his granddaughter was tough. He was worried if he interfered, they would take it out on Bonnie. Against his gut feeling, he would watch.

The next day, Bonnie returned to school. Surprisingly, the attitude of Bonnie's fellow students seemed to change, especially the girls. Before entering the classroom, she got "Good morning, Bonnie" several times. The bully did not show up for school.

One of the girls told Bonnie that the bully's younger sister said his father had whipped him for letting a girl beat him up. Another girl told Bonnie the other boys would not stick up for the bully anymore. He cried like a baby when he got hurt; they were not scared of him anymore. A girl had beaten him up. Thus Bonnie was never challenged in school again.

* * * * *

Bonnie bought some chickens, and she and her grandpa built a chicken coop. They had fresh eggs and, on occasion, chicken for dinner. For a while, Grandpa insisted on cooking the chickens. Bonnie wanted to take their feathers off, chop them up, and throw them in a pot of boiling water. Begrudgingly, Bonnie admitted that Grandpa's way was better, either fried or roasted in the newfangled oven attached to the top of their new wood stove. Grandpa had a fish trap set up, and they had fresh fish to eat when a fish was stupid enough to be caught in his makeshift trap. Bonnie also learned to snare rabbits and turkey. Grandpa also taught Bonnie to shoot his rifle; she soon became an accomplished shot. Critters kept trying to steal her chickens, and one shot usually dispatched them.

One late fall afternoon, a cow elk came into the yard.

Bonnie asked, "Grandpa, will you shoot the elk? We will have lots of red meat and its hide for leather."

Grandpa responded, "You shoot her if you want her shot."

Bonnie got Grandpa's rifle from the wall and downed the elk with one shot.

Bonnie said, "Grandpa, now we have to clean, skin, and cut up the elk."

"What do you mean *we*? You were the one that shot her."

"Grandpa, will you show me how?"

"I will help you if you promise not to boss me around and listen to me, at least a little."

"I do not boss you around! I am sorry if I do. Okay, I promise to try to be a mindful granddaughter."

"You are just a typical Redheaded Irish Woman. Let us clean up the mess you made."

The weather was turning cold, and now they would have fresh meat for a while and some good jerky for winter.

The winter was cold, and the snow got deep. Bonnie never missed a school day, though on some days, she arrived at class with only a couple other students and only one teacher for the school. Grandpa made Bonnie a pair of snow shoes and taught her how to walk with them. On real cold days, Bonnie would wear her heavy old wool coat.

Bonnie got her own Winchester repeating rifle for her thirteenth birthday and a double-barrel shotgun for Christmas. Grandpa got a gold railroad pocket watch made by Elgin, with his name engraved on the case.

Winter turned to spring. Life was good. They had plenty to eat, a warm and comfortable home, and when the weather permitted, they worked their claim. They had enough money to live where and however they wanted.

Grandpa hired an attorney and patented his claim, getting a deed for the land. He put Bonnie's name on everything as an equal owner, full rights to survivor.

Spring and summer, Bonnie blossomed into a woman. She gave Grandpa some trying times. He had been through it before with his daughter. His wife had died when his daughter was ten, and he had tried to take on the role of father and mother. This time, he was determined to not make the same mistakes he made before. Grandpa often told himself, *Patience and understanding. She is a good person. She just has to work her way through the changes she is going through.* At times, Grandpa did wish that she was less feisty.

Bonnie often talked about wanting to move to Lead or San Francisco.

Grandpa told Bonnie, "You can live wherever you want. You are the master of your own destiny, and the money in the bank belongs to both of us. It is for you to use as you see fit. But for me, I chose to live here for now."

Bonnie said, "I do not know what I want to do. What do you think I should do?"

Grandpa replied, "Be patient and think about it closely. When you make your decision, I will not stand in your way."

"Sometimes I feel confused, I am still very young and need to be patient. I do not know what else I could want. I have a good home, and everything I want. I feel I want something, and I do not know what it is."

Grandpa thought to himself, *If the door is locked, she will want to unlock it and go through. If the door is open, there is no challenge and no forbidden fruit hidden on the other side. Mother Nature provides Bonnie with enough temptation without Grandpa adding more.*

* * * * *

The narrow-gauge railroad was completed from Deadwood to Rapid City and the standard-gauge railroad completed to Rapid City, with connections to Chicago. A week before Christmas, Grandpa and Bonnie boarded the train destined for Chicago. Grandpa believed it would be good to introduce his granddaughter to the broader world. He himself wanted to experience the big city as a man of means. Bonnie was excited at the prospect of riding in a passenger car instead of a freight car, and be able to look out the windows.

Bonnie, with Mrs. Johnson's help, bought some new fancy dresses, skirts, blouses, a corset, a lady's coat, and new shoes for the trip.

Bonnie told Grandpa, "Last time I rode the rails, I had to watch out for the Bulls so I did not get my head bashed in. Now I have a ticket and can watch out the windows. These seats are a lot more comfortable than the floor of a freight car."

The train stopped at a railroad siding to let another train pass by. Bonnie saw on a mile marker post a hobo sign, a *U* with a line over it and a little *W* beside it. Grandpa noticed Bonnie staring out at a nondescript spot out along a small trail with a blank look in her face.

Grandpa asked, "What are you looking at?"

"Hobo camp."

Grandpa looked and seen what looked like a small old shed with a whiff of smoke rising into the sky. "How do you know that is a hobo camp?"

Bonnie pointed to mile marker post. "On the post, see that sign in hobo lingo—camping, shelter, short walk."

"Do you miss that life?"

"Yes and no, it is part of who I am."

"Do you want to go back to that life?"

"I can't go back."

For the first and only time, Bonnie told Grandpa of her life riding the rails. She told of her escape from the mercantile. Crossing the Hudson River, Freddie the Fart, the Quakers, the bloody box car, a cold and wet night on a flatbed on the Fire Ball Express, and of the Amish family. Bonnie went on telling Grandpa the story, including her time as a mule skinner. It was like Bonnie needed to tell someone.

Grandpa said, "You should write that story down."

"Why, nobody would believe it or understand it. Though it does have a happy ending—I found my wonderful grandfather."

Grandpa pondered. It was an exceptional story. If he did not know his granddaughter, he would not believe it. He knew he did not totally understand it.

Grandpa then told Bonnie, "Your story has two happy endings. You found me and brought joy and happiness back into my life."

Bonnie, holding back a tear, said, "Grandpa, I love you. I do not deserve you, and you are full of shit!"

Grandpa knew "You are full of shit" meant Bonnie did not want to talk about it anymore.

Bonnie wondered if Freddie had made it safely to Vermont and if Learned had stayed in school.

* * * * *

In Chicago, they had a two-bedroom suite in a fine hotel. They went to the theater and an opera, heard the performance of an orchestra, went to museums, dined at fine restaurants, and rode in chauffeured cabs. Bonnie caught the eye of many a young man, and she knew it. They celebrated Christmas Eve at a special performance given by an orchestra and large choir. They performed Handel's *Messiah*. The performances left Grandpa and Bonnie speechless.

After a week of being catered to and seeing wondrous sights, Bonnie asked Grandpa, "When are we going home?" She had seen enough and wanted to go home. Grandpa sensed that Bonnie felt out of place.

On the long ride home, Bonnie met a mining engineer, his wife, and their children. He had accepted a job working for the Homestake Mine. They had spent the holiday in Chicago visiting his parents. Previously, they had spent four years in a country called Chile where he had worked on a project establishing a copper and silver mine. Bonnie was fascinated with the stories they told of such an exotic place. They had sailed on a clipper ship from San Francisco to Chile and then back by steamship.

Grandpa could not help but notice the fascination in his granddaughter.

* * * * *

Returning home, Bonnie often went to the library in Lead to check out books of foreign lands. The idea of foreign travel, ships, and the sea seemed to keep her occupied, along with mining, school, and her regular chores.

Grandpa was glad that at least she had other interests besides boys.

CHAPTER 5

One Spring Day

A few weeks from the end of the school year, on a Monday, Bonnie was walking home from school. She noticed several horses tied up along the road. Suddenly, she was surrounded by men who threw her on the ground and bound and gagged her. She tried to yell and fight them off, but she was overwhelmed. They threw her over a saddle and tied her on. With her hands and feet bound, she was helpless. As best as Bonnie could see, it looked like they were headed southward toward Hill City.

Bonnie was really late getting home from school. She usually informed her grandpa when she would be late. Grandpa headed for town before it got dark. The school was closed. There was a letter addressed to him on the school door.

David O'King

> We have your granddaughter Bonnie. We will return her to you unharmed for three thousand dollars in gold. Bring gold to Hill City on Wednesday, where we will contact you. Do not contact the Sheriff or your granddaughter will be killed. We know that you have the money in the bank.

In the envelope was a lock of red hair.

Grandpa had never imagined anyone would kidnap his grand-daughter. He only thought for a few minutes, and he knew he needed help. Grandpa headed to Thomas Smith's Ranch. Thomas Smith and his wife, a Greek woman, were known for their hospitality. Thomas was known to raise quality horses and was a deputy sheriff that had a reputation for being fearless and a dead shot. They were good honest people, and Grandpa only hoped his own reputation of being a mean old cuss would not lessen his chances of help.

Grandpa was greeted at the Smith Ranch and invited into their home. Thomas and Grandpa had briefly met before.

Grandpa told Thomas, "I have a problem and would like your help. I can pay you. Please read this letter."

Thomas read the letter. "I think we have a problem. When did you get this letter?"

"About an hour ago. It was tacked to the schoolhouse door."

"Do you have that much money?"

"Yes."

"Let us go to Deadwood and get Sheriff Bullock in on this."

"The letter said that if I contacted the Sheriff, they will kill her."

"As long as they have a chance of getting the money, they will not harm her. Sheriff Bullock will keep it quiet. Have you told anyone else?"

"No one."

Thomas said, "The moon is waxing. We should have a couple of hours of moonlight. Let us get going."

Sheriff Seth Bullock was still in his office when Thomas showed him the note and explained the situation.

The Sheriff said, "Mr. O'King, you have a reputation for being a little antisocial, but your granddaughter is known to be a very personable young lady. What do you think we should do?"

"I just want my granddaughter back safe. I do not care what it costs."

"We will see what we can do. No promises, understand? They only want the money. Absolute, no girl, no money."

"Yes, sir."

Sheriff Seth Bullock and Deputy Thomas made a plan. Grandpa listened to it and agreed.

Seth went to the bank president's house in the morning before he left for the bank and filled him in on the plan. After the bank opened, Grandpa went to the bank and asked to see the President. Behind closed doors, he was given 20 twenty-dollar gold pieces and 130 silver dollars. This would be 530 dollars. 150 troy ounces. 12.5 pounds, the equivalent weight of 3,000 dollars in gold. Seth insisted that if things turned bad, he did not want the outlaws getting any more money than was necessary. Grandpa then signed a receipt for 150 twenty-dollar gold pieces, 3,000 dollars. The coins were put in two narrow bags with the gold on top. As Grandpa walked out with two bags of money, the receipt was given to the new tellers to be entered into the ledger.

Grandpa then headed to Hill City with his heavy saddlebags and two Pinkerton guards that were on loan from Mr. Hurst, arranged by Seth. When the bank teller went to lunch, he dropped his handkerchief in the middle of the street. He took his time picking it up; shaking it out almost like he was waving it. One of Seth's deputies watched as a rider, who was watching the street, got on his horse and headed south. A deputy got on a buckboard that had some bales of hay as a load and headed south, following the messenger.

That evening, the bank teller was interrogated in the sheriff's jail cells. He had told two men of the money David O'King had in the bank and of his granddaughter. He had two names for the kidnappers, and he informed them he believed there were four men. He thought they would kill the girl and her grandfather once they had the money. Seth recognized the two names as members of one of the hole-in-the-wall gangs. They were wanted for train robbery and murder. The teller did not know much of the plan. He was paid to watch for a three-thousand-dollar gold withdrawal and make a signal.

* * * * *

Being laid over a saddle and tied up was very uncomfortable. Bonnie's pelvic bones felt like they were poking through her skin.

Originally, Bonnie thought there were four men. But one rode off, so now she had three captors. At dusk, they camped on a trail off the main road. She was untied from the horse's saddle and thrown on the ground. The gag was removed.

Bonnie was warned, "If you talk or try to holler or scream, you will get the gag again and be beaten senseless."

In a quiet voice, Bonnie asked, "Could I please have some water?"

The younger of the three men must have had some compassion, for he held a canteen up to Bonnie's mouth so she could drink.

They built a small fire and fixed themselves some food. Bonnie moved herself around and propped herself against a tree trunk in a sitting position. Her feet and hands were numb from the ropes. Again, the younger man showed compassion and fed Bonnie the remaining few bites of their spicy and oversalted stew and gave her more water. Bonnie remained quiet, not wanting any unwanted attention and to be beaten. Her captors did not talk a lot, but from what Bonnie heard, she concluded they wanted money from her grandfather, and her or her grandfather's life was of no consequence. They just wanted gold.

During the night, Bonnie had peed herself. She had no choice.

In the morning, again, Bonnie was thrown over a saddle. Her wet dress smelling of urine seemed to be of no concern. By noon, they were on a narrow horse trail up the side of a mountain. Again, Bonnie was untied from the saddle and pushed off the horse. The rope around her ankles was cut, and as blood flowed unrestricted to her feet, they stung with pain.

"Walk or we will drag you," she was told.

The younger man helped Bonnie to her feet, and with much difficulty and pain, she walked further up the steep path. They had a concealed camp on a level spot that had a good view of the approach down the hill. Behind them was the steep stone wall of the mountain. Bonnie concluded that her tormentors had chosen the site well; it would be difficult to sneak up here undetected. Bonnie sit in a small alcove, hoping to be out of the way and not bringing attention to herself. The younger man again gave Bonnie some water. The ropes around her wrists seemed to be stretching a little, and she determined to try to pull on them and loosen them. If she could get her fingers to work, maybe she could untie the knot. The feeling returned to Bonnie's feet. During the rest of the day and night, Bonnie tried to stretch the ropes around her wrists. She had to be discreet, doing it slowly and easy, hopping that they did not suspect anything and check her binding. Bonnie again peed herself. She also mussed herself, remembering from her hobo days if you smell bad, people will not want to touch you. Her captors cold camped, no fire. It got cold; again the young man took pity on Bonnie and threw a horse blanket partly over Bonnie and gave her more water. It was apparent he did not like her smell. By morning, Bonnie had the ropes loosened a little, enough that the blood flowed freely, giving Bonnie stinging pain in her hands.

* * * * *

In Hill City, Grandpa had spent the night in a hotel room with the two Pinkerton guards across the hall. Come morning, he got some breakfast in a small restaurant and proceeded to walk up and down Main Street with the heavy saddlebags over his shoulder. Grandpa had been coached as to what to say and how to behave. Sheriff Bullock, Deputy Thomas Smith, and a couple of Hill City deputies were dispersedly hidden, constantly watching Grandpa.

Midmorning, a man approached Grandpa.

"Are you Bonnie's father?"

"I am Bonnie's grandfather."

"Give me the gold, and we will send your daughter to you."

"No girl, no gold."

"I can just kill you right now and take the gold."

Grandpa responded, "The two men following me are Pinkerton. They work for Mr. Hurst. Their orders are 'no girl, no gold.' The bank did not have enough gold. Some of the gold in the bags is Mr. Hurst's gold. Mr. Hurst is the girl's godfather. I cannot call the Pinkertons off, for they do not work for me."

The criminal looked at the two husky men with derby hats, double-breasted coats, and holstered guns. Pinkerton and Hurst were names that even the lowest of outlaws respected. They did not have to face reelection, and their reputation was everything to them. Mr. Hurst had enough money to hire an army of Pinkertons.

Grandpa was given a crude map. He was told, "Go to the location marked on the map with the gold, and when you see your daughter, put the gold down, and back up as your daughter approaches. Do not do anything stupid. There will be guns on your daughter."

Grandpa went to the livery stable to get his horse. Deputy Thomas was hidden there and looked at the map.

On the way, Grandpa was having trouble with his saddle cinch. He had to often stop and tighten it. His progress was slow to the rendezvous spot. The two Pinkertons followed at a distance. Grandpa said several prayers along the way. This gave the Sheriff and his posse time to go ahead and scout out the situation. Grandpa was not a gunman. He only used guns for hunting. He had brought Bonnie's Winchester repeating rifle and her double-barreled shotgun loaded with buckshot.

* * * * *

Midday, the fourth kidnapper arrived at the outlaws' camp, and there was a heated discussion. One of the older men grabbed the fourth man from behind, holding his hand over his mouth as the other older man stabbed him in the chest with a large knife numerous times until he stopped moving.

Bonnie heard, "One less person getting a share. He was useless."

The kidnappers were readying for an assault. They cleaned and loaded all their guns. The younger man had an old Colt Navy cap and ball revolver. He meticulously cleaned and loaded it as Bonnie watched. It was obviously his trusty backup gun. He wrapped it in a piece of oilskin and put it in his saddlebags, which were near Bonnie. With pain, Bonnie managed to pull one of her hands out of one rope's loop. The rope was loose, and the feeling had returned to her hands. She did not know what good it would do. She could not get away running, and there were three of them. Bonnie was facing her own mortality. She had heard their words: no witnesses to identify them. Bonnie said a prayer, asking for forgiveness for her many sins, and prayed for her grandfather.

All three outlaws had their rifles in hand for long-range shooting.

One of the older men had a Sharps rifle. "I see him, here he comes."

The other older man said, "When you get a good shot, shoot the son of a bitch and his horse. Do not miss. We can then pick up the gold."

The man with the Sharps said, "I get the bitch before we kill her."

The man with the Sharps was positioning himself to take aim. The men's attention was on Bonnie's grandfather.

Bonnie thought, *They are going to shoot Grandpa.*

Bonnie slipped her hands from the loose ropes, rolled over to the saddlebags, pulled out the Colt, stood up, held the Colt in both hands, cocked the hammer, pointed it at the man with the Sharps, and shouted, "Shoot my grandfather and I will kill you."

The other older man swung around with his rifle. Bonnie did not hesitate; she shot him in the chest, and he went down. As she cocked the hammer, the man with the Sharps rolled around with his rifle, and Bonnie again did not hesitate and shot him. She cocked the revolver again. The man with the Sharps was trying to raise his riffle, and Bonnie shot him again. The man that Bonnie shot first tried to pull his revolver from his holster as he lay on the ground, but Bonnie shot him again. The younger man was slow to react and was taken off guard. He dropped his rifle and reached for his revolver. Bonnie had her revolver cocked and pointed it at the last man.

Bonnie screamed, "I have two shots left."

He put his hands in the air.

Bonnie had him lie on his stomach, hands on his head. It had all happened so fast without Bonnie thinking, just reacting. Now Bonnie started shaking. She gritted her teeth together, feeling pure rage as her heart pounded in her chest.

It was not long before Sheriff Bullock and several deputies arrived. The Sheriff and deputies were trying to slip up behind the outlaws. Grandpa arrived with the two Pinkertons. He put his arm around Bonnie.

Bonnie asked, "Are they dead?"

Sheriff Bullock answered, "Yes, three of them are dead. This one will be hanged. All four of them are wanted for train robbery and murder. Bonnie, you just made yourself some money. I think there is a hundred dollars' bounty on each of them."

Bonnie replied, "I am sorry, I am sorry. You keep the money, I do not want it."

"As Sheriff, I cannot accept it. It would be unethical. You are the one who captured them. If I took the money, I would be a bounty hunter."

* * * * *

Afterward, Bonnie became melancholy, she stopped going to school. She became negligent in her chores. Bonnie stayed in bed most of the day. When she got up, she only wanted to stare at the horizon. But Grandpa understood. It was a very traumatic experience for a fifteen-year-old girl. His granddaughter had been through more in her short life than most people would experience in a lifetime. Grandpa knew it would take his patience. The one thing he knew for sure was that Bonnie was tough.

In a little over a week, after dinner, Bonnie talked to her Grandpa.

"Grandpa, it seems that bad things happen around me. Is it me?"

"I do not know," Grandpa responded. "Maybe you are being tested. The Lord works in mysterious ways."

"I killed two men, and the one that was nice to me is going to be hanged. Another man was stabbed to death because he did not get the money. They killed him for his share."

"They were bad men. It was not your fault. They reaped what they sowed."

"I am sorry, Grandpa. I should not have come here. I brought all this to you!"

"I learned to hate myself for pushing your mother away. You came and brought me joy. You gave me a reason to enjoy life again. I will stand by you, no matter what. It is not your fault. Let it go. Today is the first day of the rest of your life. Do not let what those bad men did interfere with the rest of your life."

In time, Bonnie came out of her depression with more determination. She seemed to have matured into a strong and confident woman. Less argumentative, with more compassion and understanding, but still feisty.

Deputy Thomas Smith delivered three hundred dollars to Bonnie, the bounty she had earned for bringing train-robbing murderers to justice. The man that was stabbed did not have a bounty on him. The bounty was paid by the Black Hills & Fort Pier Railroad. Bonnie had to sign for the money.

Bonnie said, "If I keep this money, it will be blood money."

Deputy Thomas Smith responded, "Killing a man is a difficult thing. Only a person that is possessed by the Devil finds it easy."

Bonnie donated one hundred dollars to each of two the local churches and one hundred dollars to the Lead public library.

Both Bonnie and Grandpa agreed that they had more money than they needed. So they decided to not do a lot of mining this season. Neither one of them could kick back and enjoy the summer and fall. They started to work an area that was rich in gold. They got gold fever and had the best year ever, mining their claim.

Three more years and they had mined over half of their placer-mining claim. Bonnie had graduated from school. Grandpa was not surprised when Bonnie graduated top of her class, all As. They had developed a relationship with Mr. George Hearst and his family. Bonnie spent a lot of volunteer time at the Lead library. Bonnie and Grandpa rented a small house in Lead so they could spend more time in Lead. Lead had grown up with an opera house and some semblance of modern civilization. With Mr. Hurst's advice, they had invested most of their money in stocks and bonds varying from mining, railroads, steamship lines, manufacturing, oil wells, refining lamp oil and government bonds. Bonnie and Grandpa were planning on going to San Francisco when the weather cleared.

Bonnie tried to dress nice, make herself presentable, hold her tong, and act ladylike. She did not think herself being totally unattractive. On occasion, she noticed men ogling at her. There were a lot of eligible men in the area. None seemed interested in Bonnie. They would casually talk to her but not hold a long conversation.

A young, attractive, eligible attorney set up an office in Lead. He came to the library several times. Bonnie helped him find the information he wanted. They talked. He was real friendly for a while, then he tried to avoid Bonnie. Everybody in the area knew of Bonnie dressing as a boy, driving mules, working as a gold miner, beating up the boy at school, then killing two men. Bonnie concluded that her past made her undesirable; maybe men were afraid of her. She was destined to be an old maid unless she got luck and found a man who was not intimidated by her or her past. Eighteen and never kissed, only a few flirtatious encounters with the attorney, who now avoided her.

It was Christmas Eve, Bonnie's nineteenth birthday. They were invited to Mr. Hurst's house to celebrate with several influential people in Lead.

Mr. Hurst offered a toast.

"Happy birthday to one of Lead's beautiful and charming young ladies. Here's to Bonnie!"

The men all stood. "To Bonnie!"

Grandpa collapsed to the floor.

The Doctor was at the party and immediately tended to Grandpa. The prognosis was that Grandpa had a stroke and died instantly. He did not suffer.

Bonnie just sat with an occasional tear flowing down her cheek. She asked to be taken to her Lead home, and her request was honored.

The next day, many came to give their condolences. Mrs. Johnson tried to console Bonnie, and Bonnie went into her "I am tough" mode, protecting her emotions. In a very businesslike way, she made the necessity arrangements with the Protestant Clergy and undertaker. A couple of days later, David O'King was interred in the

Lead Cemetery. Bonnie had managed to get a man to play the pipes over his grave. A meager Irish farewell—Bonnie wished she could do more.

Bonnie gave a eulogy. "My parents were incinerated in a factory fire in New York. I do not know if they have a grave. I was left an orphan." She paused to wipe a solitary tear. "Then I found my grandfather. Since that time, he has looked out for me and has been my strength, my family. My grandfather was a good man; strong in soul, mind, spirit, and heart. The Lord has taken him away from me, though he will always be in my heart."

After the funeral, Bonnie went to their cabin in Rochford, where she grieved by herself.

Again, she was alone, without family.

CHAPTER 6

San Francisco

As the spring thaw came, Bonnie closed up her cabin. Bonnie found it hard to leave her big old wool coat; it had given her warmth and a secure feeling many a time. It was in a deplorable condition; it was time for Bonnie to move on. At the last minute, Bonnie grabbed her cup-bowl. It was just a piece of junk. But the cup-bowl reminded Bonnie that in hard times, little things can mean so much, giving one hope.

In Lead, Bonnie took care of paperwork. She spent a day on the train to Rapid City, where she verified and updated her deed to her property in Rochford. In Lead, Bonnie got a letter of credit for a bank in San Francisco and arranged for funds to be transferred there. Bonnie visited all her friends and told them she was going to San Francisco to find her way. She then went to her grandfather's grave. He had the tombstone she wanted. Bonnie talked to her grandfather and said a prayer. Grandfather understood, accepted, and was there for her.

Bonnie was introduced to a woman, Georgia, whose husband had been an engineer in the mine. He had died in an accident. Her family lived in San Francisco.

Bonnie, Georgia, and Georgia's children boarded a train, one of several to make their way to San Francisco. Bonnie reflected on her first railroad trip. Then she had little but a naive sense of determination. Now she still had determination, now she had resources, and she could afford to buy tickets and dress in fine clothing. Then she had a goal, to find her grandfather; now she did not know what she was looking for. Now she felt like she was looking for something she had lost, and she just did not know what she was looking for. Perhaps somewhere she felt she belonged or for a purpose and meaning in her life. Bonnie decided to be herself, to not try to be what she was not. People could accept her as she was or move on.

It took several days and a couple of different railroad companies and many different train cars. Georgia was met by her family, and they escorted Bonnie to one of San Francisco's finest hotels where Bonnie got a comfortable room. Bonnie went for a walk in the vicinity and found San Francisco a vibrant place. Everybody seemed to be in a hurry, and Bonnie felt like she was in an alien land, new and exciting to her. She quickly realized that her Lead dress style was not the high fashion of what was known as the Paris of the West. So she went into a couple of dress shops. Bonnie bought one outfit, one she thought appropriate for daily wear. The prices of the fashionable dresses were more than what Bonnie was willing to spend under the circumstances. She was a backwoods girl, after all, and proud of it, not a fashionable, frilly lady.

* * * * *

Bonnie talked to the hotel's concierge, and he said it would be appropriate for an unescorted lady to dine alone in the main dining room of the hotel. Eating in her room with room service was no different from eating in her cabin alone; she had not come to San Francisco to be a hermit. Bonnie had used the library in Lead and Georgia's advice to try to prepare herself for life in San Francisco.

"Table for one for dinner."

"Is madam dining alone tonight?"

"Yes. Table for one, please."

"Right this way, ma'am."

Bonnie was led to a small table that was out of the way, near the kitchen entrance. Her chair was pulled back by the maître d', and she was seated. There was a table that had four young men near her. They were acting a little rowdy, as young men do. Bonnie concluded that this section of the restaurant was for second-class guests, as she thought appropriate for her. She was trying to show her manners. She hoped that after she met other people, she would eat in the first-class area. She knew it would take time.

The waiter asked, "Will madam be dining alone this evening?"

"Yes."

"What would madam like to drink? And would she like an appetizer?"

"A glass of water and a menu please."

"Certainly, ma'am."

Bonnie tried to not pay attention to the rowdy young men, but in her heart, she wished she could join them. They were clearly enjoying the evening.

One of the rowdy young men approached Bonnie.

"A beautiful young lady dining alone is a sin."

"What makes you think that I am beautiful?"

"I am not blind, you are beautiful."

"What makes you think I am a lady?"

"That is self-evident."

This was the first time in a while Bonnie had an opportunity to spar and have some fun with someone. She missed her grandfather; he was a worthy opponent in verbal jousting.

"I do not know you," Bonnie said. "Who are you, sir?"

"I am Joseph Smithfield of San Francisco," the young man said with a smile and a slight bow. "And you, lovely lady, are?"

"I am Bonnie Duffy of Rochford."

"Where is Rochford?"

"Black Hills of South Dakota, one of our newer states."

"Are all the ladies of Rochford as beautiful as you?"

"Joseph, you have a good line, but you are full of shit!"

"Now you have done it, you have captured my interest."

With a slight coy smile, she said, "I am a backwoods girl, not really interesting. Sorry."

"May I please sit with you for a while? I promise if you tell me I will leave. I will. Promise."

"All right, sit down before you embarrass yourself." Again, a coy smile. "What about your companions?"

"We are celebrating. They will not miss me."

"What are you celebrating?"

"In reality, a menial victory of a sporting event."

"It is obviously of importance to you and your friends."

"A handball competition among friends is of no real consequence. Tell me, what do you do in Rochford?"

"Mine gold." With a small smile, Bonnie replied, "See, I am not that interesting."

"You have actually mined gold?"

"A little bit, and I work at the library in Lead. What do you do here in San Francisco?"

"My father is wealth. I mainly spend his money and work at his shipyard."

"I am obviously not of the same social status as you. Can you please excuse me?"

"You are rejecting me because I am rich?"

"Yes. I cannot be bought."

"I am not trying to buy you."

"Prove it, be a man of your word and please leave me now."

With a discreet look of disappointment, Joseph rejoined his buddies.

One of his friend said, "You owe me a twenty. She is not eating out of your hand."

Joseph relied, "Here is your twenty. I am going home."

With a chuckle, his friend said, "She put you in your place."

Bonnie had a delicious dinner. It was charged to her room. Bonnie left a quarter tip, which she had been told was appropriate and generous.

* * * * *

In the morning, Bonnie got a knock on her door. It was a bell boy with an enormous bouquet of exotic flowers. Bonnie had never before received flowers. She read the card.

Please give me another chance.
Will you please join me for breakfast?

Joseph.

Bonnie was surprised. What to do? Her mind raced. Bonnie did not want to accept the flowers; they would only make her feel obligated. But they were so beautiful, and she had never been given flowers before. Joseph was rich, no big deal for him. He had spent the effort and time. He was handsome. He wanted to add her to his conquests. If he said one thing not appropriate, she would give him an earful of her mule skinner language. That would rid her of him. He was handsome and did verbally spar with her. So Bonnie decided to overlook the fact that he was rich and arrogant. At least for now.

Giving the bellhop a quarter, she said, "Tell the gentleman I will see him in the lobby in fifteen minutes."

"Thank you, ma'am. I will inform the gentleman."

On her way down the lift, Bonnie had her mule skinner response memorized. She did not use that language often but found it effective on the proper occasion. It sure got people's attention.

"Thank you for joining me for breakfast."

"Thank you for the flowers—they are gorgeous."

This time, Bonnie with her escort were seated in the main part of the dining room.

Joseph asked, "May I order for you?"

"Why, certainly."

Soufflé, smoked Alaska salmon, oysters, and other delicacies that Bonnie had never heard of before—they were all delicious. After breakfast, they went for a walk; Bonnie got a tour of the beautiful city. They walked and talked. They were not easy on each other; they challenged each other's wit, but they were able to laugh together at their verbal jabs. Joseph gave back to Bonnie what she dished out.

Bonnie did not tell Joseph of her rough past, for she tried to be a lady. Joseph told her of growing up as an overindulged child. He had traveled in Europe and had been to places that were only known to Bonnie in books. To Bonnie, he was like the Pied Piper. Bonnie realized she was being enchanted.

Not wanting to get too involved and misrepresent herself, she said, "Joseph, I must tell you that I am not the lady you think I am. I am the daughter of poor Irish immigrants. I am a backwoods girl who is used to getting her hands dirty. I have shot, skinned, cut up, and cooked my supper and did other things not ladylike. I am stubborn, self-reliant with an awful temper. I am not a lady you can take home to your parents, and I do not want to be one of your conquests."

This surprised Joseph. He was accustomed to ladies trying to be coy and flirtatious, not honest and blunt. He realized his usual lines would not work on this lady. Maybe a straightforward approach. This lady was definitely different and intriguing.

Joseph replied, "I am not asking for you to go to bed with me, nor am I asking you to go and meet my parents. Is it unreasonable that I just want some good company? To me you are real and honest, a breath of fresh air. Money is not the center of everything. So can we be friends? You accused me of being full of shit. Yes, sometimes I am full of shit. But I believe that sometimes you are full of shit too. Also, I like people seeing me with a gorgeous lady."

"You are definitely full of shit!" Bonnie smiled. "On those terms, I can be a friend"

They started to spent time together as friends. They went to concerts and plays and dined together. They had deep conversations during their walks. They could be honest with each other. They developed a standing argument; Bonnie insisted on paying her share. In public, it was not acceptable for an escorted lady to get money out and pay. So Bonnie would discreetly put money in Joseph's pocket. This infuriated Joseph, but he could not protest without making a public scene. It was fun. They enjoyed playing little games with each other. Often, Bonnie would find twice the money she had put in

Joseph's pocket in her handbag. He was clever. They challenged each other, and it was not long until they became best buddies.

Joseph found Bonnie totally different from the ladies he had dated. She was intelligent, witty, interesting, unpredictable, and challenging. Bonnie was not a bit flighty but confident and strong. She was much more than frills and lace; she had substance. Joseph just enjoyed being with her.

Joseph asked, "You do not talk about growing up. You have to have some really good stories growing up in a mining town in the Wild West."

"I am sorry. You do not want to know. Bad things seem to happen around me. I still have my honor and dignity, which I plan on maintaining."

Joseph decided to not push his luck. He believed she was honest with him. She was a lady to him. She was a good person, she was feisty and fun to be with, and he knew she would tell him when she was ready. She had the mystique of mystery about her.

After a while, Joseph had fallen in love with Bonnie, and Bonnie had fallen in love with Joseph. Neither wanted to admit it to themselves. Both did not want to make things complicated and lose a good friend.

* * * * *

Joseph's father tried to discreetly involve himself in his son's affairs. This woman had been taking up all of Joseph's spare time. He was taking long lunches from work to be with her. She seemed to be a mystery. Joseph's father did what all good, rich parents do, protect their children form unscrupulous people. It took almost three weeks for Joseph's father to get a report from a private investigator. It took travel to an out-of-the-way state, several long telegrams, express messages, and the work of a New York private investigator.

Joseph's father managed to accost his son.

"You have been spending a lot of time with this Bonnie girl. What do you know of her?"

"Father, I do not care what your people know! I know what I need to know. Bonnie is a wonderful lady and a good friend."

"Son, this Bonnie Duffy is a very remarkable girl."

"Why do you have to interfere? She is a lady. Bonnie is a good friend."

"For once, just listen. Your young lady friend is certainly interesting. Bonnie Duffy was born on December 24, 1873, to second-generation Irish immigrants in New York City. She was baptized a Catholic, although her mother was Protestant. She is a lone child. In December 1885, Bonnie's parents were killed in a fire at a factory where they worked. She was placed in the New York foster care system. In the spring of 1886, she ran away from her foster parents and was never apprehended. Allegedly, there was some petty theft involved. It is speculated that she dressed as a boy and rode in freight cars and ended up in Cheyenne, Wyoming. There, disguised as a boy, she worked for a freight hauler and made her way to Lead, South Dakota. One man said she can drive a string of mules better than most men. She found her long-lost grandfather in the town of Rochford. Her grandfather had a small gold mine, and Bonnie went to school and helped her grandfather in his mine. Their mine was modestly prosperous. When Bonnie was fifteen, she was kidnapped by a gang of outlaws and held for ransom. These were train robbers, murderers, hardened criminals with bounties on their heads. Somehow, Bonnie got her hands on a gun and shot and killed three of the outlaws and held a fourth at gunpoint for the Sheriff. Bonnie received a reward of one hundred dollars each for three of the outlaws. Last December, her grandfather died of a stroke at a party at the home of Mr. George Hurst, a wealthy and influential mine owner. Bonnie is a respected member of her community. It is reported she is financially comfortable, though not rich. There is nothing in my report that suggests any impropriety, except the occasional use of foul language. I have been told she is a beauty. What I want to know is what a lady like her sees in you."

"Father, you could not resist interfering in my life."

"Do you love her?"

"Bonnie is just a friend."

"Bring her to dinner. I will not say a word to your mother. This young lady might put your mother in her place. At least we might see some fireworks."

"Dad, she is just a friend."

"Bring your friend to dinner."

"What do you think that will accomplish?"

Joseph's dad held up his report and said, "I do not think this is a lady that can be easily intimidated, even by your mother. It might be nice to see your mother challenged."

Joseph now saw Bonnie a little differently. She was a remarkable woman with an interesting past. Definitely not the woman you would want to betray; she might shoot you. Why did his father interfere? His dad asked him if he loved Bonnie. Joseph felt he still had wild oats to sow. Love was not something he wanted to consider, but he had feelings that he could not dismiss. Joseph was thinking, maybe Bonnie had become more than just a friend. Joseph wondered if Bonnie felt the same as he did. Dinner with his mom and dad was not to be taken lightly, especially with his mom. Even if dinner did not work out, Bonnie would understand it was not easy being a rich kid. His mom had never liked any of his friends, especially his lady friends. It was time that he let his mom know he was a man who would chose his own friends.

Bonnie was realizing that Joseph was a special man. He made her feel like she was special. And he was just plain fun to be with. Now Bonnie started to look at Joseph differently. She wanted to spend all her time with him. He was involved in his work and was a dedicated, hardworking man. Joseph was a man to be admired. How was she going to tell him her secrets? Men did not want women that were hobos or mule skinners and especially ones that collected bounties for killing outlaws. Not at all ladylike. Bonnie realized she could not change who she was. She thought back to the basement of the mercantile. She had been lucky and had come far. She was proud of who she was and would not pretend to be what she was not. Joseph was too important for her to deceive. Besides, deception was not in her nature. Bonnie accepted her station in life; she was not a debutante.

* * * * *

Bonnie was nervous meeting Joseph's parents, but he was so insistent Bonnie got tired of saying no. When the carriage pulled up to the enormous mansion, Bonnie wanted to bolt and run. She knew that she did not belong here.

Bonnie first met Joseph's father; it was obvious where Joseph got his charm. Joseph's father reminded Bonnie of Mr. Hurst, a powerful businessman who was also very charming and gracious.

The dining room was enormous, with high ceilings that had frescoes on them with guided trim. It looked like an illustration in a book of a royal palace. Joseph's mother's look and demeanor was what Bonnie would imagine of the matriarch of a royal family, setting at the head of her enormous table. Joseph introduced Bonnie and seated her. Bonnie tried to compose herself, telling herself, *Manners.* The servants were as attentive as Bonnie had ever seen in any restaurant, whether in Chicago or San Francisco. Bonnie was mad at Joseph; he had not warned her. Not an act of a friend. Joseph had said rich—ha, filthy wealthy!

Before dinner was served, the questions from Joseph's mother started.

"You are not from San Francisco. Where are you from?"

"Rochford and Lead, South Dakota."

"I have heard rumors that you are staying at the hotel alone?"

"Yes, ma'am."

"Who supports you?"

"I support myself."

"How do you do that?"

"I own a gold mine in Rochford that has been modestly productive, and I have investments in a variety of industries."

"Where is your family. In Rochford?"

"Ma'am, all my family is deceased."

"You were born and raised in South Dakota?"

"No, ma'am, I was born and lived in Brookline, New York, until I was twelve."

"Your family moved from New York to South Dakota?"

Bonnie was getting a little irritated at the questions, so she concluded that maybe the truth would shut her up. She did not belong here anyway.

"No. On my twelfth birthday, my parents died in a fire at the garment factory where they worked. I was put into a foster work program where I had to work in a mercantile. I was denied the privilege of going to school and church. After four months, I ran away, dressed as a boy, and rode in railroad freight cars. I had some letters from my grandfather from Lead, South Dakota. I managed to get to Cheyenne, Wyoming. There I worked with a mule skinner and made it to Lead. From there, I found my grandfather. He took me in and gave me a home with love."

"That is some story. Is there anything else we should know about you?"

Bonnie was getting angry. She thought to herself, *Okay, lady, chew on this.*

"When I was fifteen, I was kidnapped and held for ransom. My grandfather was bringing the ransom money, and they were going to shoot and kill both of us. No witnesses. I managed to get my hands on a revolver and kill two of the kidnappers. The kidnappers were wanted for train robbery and murder, and I got three hundred dollars' bounty money for the two I killed and a man I held at gunpoint. They later hanged him." Bonnie paused. "Ma'am, I am aware that I am not the kind of woman you would want as a daughter-in-law. Rest assured you and your son are in no danger from me. I am not looking for a husband or lover. I am here because Joseph asked me. He is a good friend."

The questions stopped, and the four of them sat in relative quiet while they ate. Bonnie was surprised she was not shown the door. Joseph actually approvingly smiled at her, which only confused her. Bonnie wanted to be mad at him. Her emotions were stirred up. She did not ask or want any of this.

Bonnie told more than she wanted to. She had lost her composure. The Irish Redhead had come out. Anyway, she realized the questions would have continued until Joseph's mother was satisfied with her interrogation. Now she had no secrets from her friend Joseph or his parents. Either she would be accepted for what she was or she would move on. Besides, this enormous mansion was very uncomfortable for Bonnie. Hell, you could put her Rochford cabin in this dining room and have plenty of room leftover.

After they ate, Joseph's dad finally broke the silence. "Do you know Mr. George Hurst? I believe he lives in Lead, South Dakota."

"Yes. On occasion, my grandfather and I would be invited to dine with him."

"What kind of a man is he?"

"Mr. Hurst is a dynamic businessman and, at the same time, a considerate and compassionate gentleman."

"Tell me about your gold mine."

Bonnie explained that her mine was as a placer deposit where the gold lay in the sand and gravel that were deposited in the stream bed. Gold was heavy and could be separated by washing out the unwanted materials and capturing the gold.

Joseph's father seemed interested.

"How much gold can you mine in a year?"

"My grandfather and I netted a little over two thousand ounces in one very good year."

"How many workers?"

"Just the two of us, we worked hard."

"Two people, forty thousand dollars? I am in the wrong business!"

"Most all that go prospecting for gold end up broke. A person has to look hard in the right places and get really lucky. My grandfather worked hard, studied the geology, and got lucky."

After eating, they retired to the library where their conversation continued. Bonnie now felt these people of high society accepted her. They made her feel welcome; at least they had not shown her the door. They invited her for conversation, and she had not shocked them.

Bonnie found out that Joseph's mother had come to San Francisco as a girl on a clipper ship with her parents. They had come with a cargo of dry goods that they had purchased with a small inheritance, and then they had established a dry goods store.

Joseph's dad came as a cabin boy on a clipper ship. After several trips, he became the ship carpenter's apprentice. He then started a business repairing boats of all size, eventually building ships, and the business evolved into a shipping company. Now the family owned a prosperous steamship company that also built ships. They were also a major shareholder in the largest department store on the West Coast.

Bonnie realized these people knew what hard work was and had lived their own lives of adventure.

Bonnie was full of questions of sailing and sailing ships. She knew the way of the horse, mule, and railroads, but Bonnie was intrigued with sailing ships. She was taken into a study that was full of models of all sorts of boats and ships. She learned that before a ship was built, a model was made to be part of the plan of the ship. Joseph managed the family shipyard. He explained the various details of hull shapes and the rigging that tamed the wind. He showed her a model of a steam engine and explained how it worked.

Joseph said, "I know that I am boring you. What else would you like to see or do?"

"Will you take me to the shipyard so I can see how a ship is built?"

"Are you really interested in ships and ship building?"

"Yes, it sounds fascinating to me. Will you take me to your shipyard, please? Unless I have scared you away with my stories? I told you that you did not want to know."

"You are not scaring me, as long as you are not holding a gun."

With a smile, Bonnie replied, "You are safe for now. I only shoot scoundrels and murderers."

"You are a very amazing lady and a good friend. If I am in a jam, I want you covering my back."

* * * * *

Later, Joseph's mother asked Joseph's father, "I know that you have had your people check that girl out. Do any of those wild stories of hers have any semblance of truth?"

"The only discrepancy between her stories and the report I received is that the Sheriff's report said she shot and killed three men, not two. Also, it is reported she can handle teams of mules and curse and swear in a way that will embarrass most men."

Joseph's mom asked, "What does Joseph see in her? He likes women that have no brains, big tits, and dress in stylish, frilly outfits."

"My question is, what does she see in Joseph? She is as independent as they come. I have been told that she insists on paying her share when they go out."

"Joseph is a very attractive gentleman that will be a catch for any woman."

Joseph's dad stated, "With Bonnie, I think Joseph is going to have to do the catching. I think he will be lucky to catch her. I hope he does not run aground. Bonnie is a very remarkable lady."

"She is the best he has ever brought home, though rough around the edges. Do you think he can find any better?"

"There will never be a woman good enough for your son. I think this lady has grit and brains."

Joseph's mom asked, "Are you saying we should accept her as a daughter-in-law?"

"I do not think it will be your choice. You will be stuck with Joseph's choice."

* * * * *

Early the next morning, Bonnie went to the library and did a little research on steamships. There was an illustrated book on the great steamships of the British Cunard Line. Bonnie checked it out to study. Bonnie's research fascinated her. Ships and the sea were intriguing.

At noon, Joseph picked up Bonnie and took her to lunch.

Bonnie asked, "After lunch, are we going to the shipyard?"

Joseph replied, "I hoped you had forgotten about that."

"I did not forget. I am looking forward to a tour of your shipyard."

"A shipyard is not a place for ladies. It is dirty and dangerous. It is man's territory."

"I told you I am not a prim and proper lady. If you want, I can dress like a man."

"Men there curse and swear, spit tobacco, urinate where they work."

"I promise to keep my profanity to a level that will not embarrass the men, and I promise to not laugh at their little things if they pee in front of me. I will behave."

"You are a pain in the—"

"Go ahead and say it, *ass.*" She grinned at Joseph as she continued, "Take me to the shipyard now, and if I get embarrassed, I will let you buy me dinner for a week and act as a perfect lady with minimal brains. I will even buy and wear a frilly, lacy dress for you."

"Make it a hundred dollars, and you are on."

"Let's go!"

Joseph thought, *This lady has a mind of her own. She is a challenge and intriguing. She is driving me crazy!*

As they walked into the shipyard, the men working stopped what they were doing and stared. If Bonnie had not been with the superintendent, she would have been getting jeers and propositions.

The foreman asked, "Sir, is everything all right?"

"Tell the men to get back to work. I am not paying them to ogle at a lady."

The foreman turned to the workers. "Get the hell back to work and put your eyeballs back in their sockets!" He turned to Bonnie. "Sorry for the language, ma'am."

Bonnie knew if she got Joseph talking about his ship, he would forget she was a girl out of place.

Bonnie replied, "Believe me, you are not going to offend me. How big is this ship?"

Joseph proudly announced, "Six hundred feet long and will displace about twelve four thousand tons fully loaded. It is our latest in steamships. It is designed to take advantage of the expanding trade in the Orient. It will carry high-value cargo and passengers."

"How long to get to Tokyo from here?"

"She is designed to efficiently travel at eighteen knots, and she should make it to Tokyo in two weeks, with a stop in Hawaii for coal. We hope that this new ship will help us corner much of the Asian market."

"Where do I buy a ticket?"

"I will buy you a ticket."

With her defiant little smirk, Bonnie replied, "The hell you will. I can afford my own way. Show me more. What do the boilers and steam engines look like?"

Bonnie started to walk up the stairs to the deck while Joseph tried to dissuade her. Joseph realized he had no control over his lady. He also came to realize Bonnie was his lady; he would have to learn to accept her like his father accepted his mother. Either that or push her out of his life. Damn, why did his parents have to like her? Mom sounded like she was making plans for their wedding. Joseph questioned himself, Why did his parents' opinions weigh heavily on him? He was his own man.

Word quickly spread that the superintendent was giving a lady a tour and all were to be on their best behavior. At each area, a foreman would greet the tour. Bonnie was full of questions about everything from riveting to boiler construction. The huge engines stopped Bonnie in her tracks as she glared at them in awe. The engines were at least three stores high with part of them beneath the deck. After the ship's tour, they toured the design and administration offices. Bonnie had a lot of questions of the interior of the dining room and state rooms. Joseph did not have good answers for some of Bonnie's questions.

* * * * *

After dinner, Bonnie told Joseph in front of the waiter, "Pay the bill with a hundred. I get the change, I will get the tip."

The waiter just smiled. Discretion was part of his trade working in a high-class restaurant.

When Joseph got home, his mother met him.

"What is wrong with you, taking that lovely young lady to the shipyard then taking her into the ship under construction?"

"She told me to take her."

"That is no excuse!"

"If you told Dad to take you on a tour and he said no, what would be the end result?"

Mom asked, "You cannot say no to her?"

"When was the last time Dad told you no?"

"I like that lady of yours. You better take care of her. She has grit."

Joseph's mom always got the last word.

Joseph went into his study and worked on some engineering drawings. Some of the things Bonnie had noticed gave him some concerns. Going from the first-class staterooms to the dining room was not first-class. Changes would have to be made. The real problem was that Bonnie's observations and suggestions were all valid. They built ships the way ships were built; a new set of eyes sees things that are overlooked by tradition. When it came to first-class accommodations, they were exceeding their ship-building expertise.

The next afternoon, Joseph and Bonnie went for a long walk. They both enjoyed their walks, and they talked about a variety of subjects, though up to now, they avoided talking of their feelings for each other.

Joseph confessed, "You are a very important part of my life, but sometimes you make it hard for me. You are really hard on my ego. Do you think that sometimes you can give me some room?"

Bonnie replied, "You are important to me. I know that I have given you some grief. I do not know why, but I like to tease you. I like to see you squirm. I will try to behave. I do not want to hurt you. Can I have a hug?"

They hugged; there was something in the hug. Emotions were strongly felt by both of them, and the emotional feelings could not be ignored. It took a lot of determination for Bonnie to break the trance. Bonnie knew her desires were getting the better of her, and it scared her.

Bonnie changed the subject, with the unspoken approval of Joseph.

Bonnie tried to explain, "I am not criticizing, just discussing with you. Ships are designed by men, including the interiors. What if your ships had a woman's touch?"

"Looking for a job?"

"I am a hobo and gold miner. You need someone with a sense of style and form, someone with a gift for grandeur with class. Why not make your ship a luxury ship, one your mother would enjoy sailing on?"

"My mother's input into ship design, that would be something."

"Yes, it probably would—look at your home."

"I am not going to ask her. You ask her and see what you get."

"I will ask her."

"Dare you, a hundred dollars."

"You are on!"

They got a carriage and talked about how chilly and foggy it had been. Bonnie explained that fog was rare in the Black Hills.

They arrive at the Smithfield mansion and were announced to Joseph's mother. She was behind her own large desk in her own office.

Bonnie told Joseph's mother, "Mrs. Smithfield, Joseph and I were having a debate about the interior design of his new steamship. I said that the interior needed a woman's touch, a ship that you would enjoy sailing on, a true luxury ship."

There was an uncomfortable pause. "I heard that you went for a tour of the disgusting, dirty shipyard. At first, I was appalled. But now you have my undivided attention. What do you suggest?"

"I think with a woman's touch, by a professional designer, the ship could be a splendid ship. Woman will tell their husbands that they want to go on a beautiful Smithfield ship."

Joseph sat and listened. He knew his mother was not happy that Bonnie had toured the shipyard. He now realized he might have to take his mother on a tour. Women, you just cannot win with them. The unforeseen consequence—his mother and Bonnie agreeing, totally the opposite of what he expected. He thought that they would butt heads. Two strong-willed women.

His mom said, "Joseph, are you not needed at the shipyard? I will make sure Bonnie gets back to her hotel safely."

Joseph knew when he was dismissed.

Toward the end of the work day, Joseph got a message from his mother.

"Dinner will be promptly at seven. Bonnie will join us."

Joseph did not want to face Mom and Bonnie; the two of them allied together was a no-win scenario. Joseph promptly headed for the Gentleman's Club that catered to wealthy men who wanted to be entertained. The establishment was known for its discretion.

The dinner discussion centered on the fact of Joseph's absence.

Joseph's dad asserted, "With the two of you ganging up on him, I cannot blame him. If I were Joseph, I would be headed for the hills. Hell, I am heading for the hills too." Dad believed he knew where Joseph would be. He would go and have a drink and a talk with his son.

The two women realized they had overplayed their position. Bonnie returned to her hotel room. For the next several days, she dined alone and walked through the park alone. Bonnie realized how much she cared for Joseph. She had a broken heart, and it was her own fault. She had not given her man the respect due him. She realized she had found what she was looking for, then she had thrown it away for her own self-centered ambitions to be somebody important. Joseph's mother's acceptance had given Bonnie a false sense of self-worth and importance. Bonnie realized she still had some little girl in her with its insecurities and fantasies. Joseph was way out of her class; if she wanted to settle down, she would have to find a man of her own status. Wealthy marry wealthy. It was quite the fantasy.

Bonnie stopped eating in the restaurant. She felt like everybody was looking at her eating alone day after day. She rang for room service; they would deliver her standard breakfast. When she answered the door, she was surprised. It was not her breakfast but an enormous bouquet of flowers with a card.

Can I buy you breakfast?

Joseph

PS: I owe you one hundred dollars.

Bonnie gave the bellboy a quarter and told him to cancel breakfast and tell the gentleman to give her fifteen minutes.

Bonnie took the flowers and hurriedly tried to make herself look presentable.

Again, Bonnie was seated with an escort. Not just an escort but the most handsome man in all of San Francisco. Words were not needed; her smile said it all.

Joseph asked, "May I order for you?"

Bonnie replied, "I think that I will have humble pie."

The waiter inquired, "What can I get for you this morning?"

Joseph answered, "Two servings of humble pie, please."

Waiter replied, "I will check with the kitchen, sir."

The waiter was only a few steps from their table when they could no longer hold back and they broke out in uncontrolled laughter. Everybody looked. They were making a scene.

The maître d' inquired, "Can I be of assistance, sir?"

Joseph, struggling to not laugh, said, "Yes. Can you change our order from humble pie to soufflé with the breakfast sampler?"

"Certainly, sir."

Shortly, subdued laughter could be heard from the kitchen. That brought more laughter to Joseph and Bonnie. The entire restaurant realized it was a moment of youthful romantic play and dismissed the incident.

After eating, they went for a walk through the park.

Joseph informed Bonnie, "Women with an education in engineering and architecture with an eye for aesthetics are scarce. With Mother's help, I have hired two such women. I have a rebellion on my hands. Two of my architects have resigned, and the others are expressing displeasure. I know that you and Mother are right. My mother has even come up with a new name for our ships: *Luxury Liner*. It is the next step in transportation. Change usually comes at a price and is not easy."

Bonnie responded, "I feel that I have brought you much grief, and for that, I am deeply sorry. Whatever I can do to make amends, I will do."

Joseph stated, "There are a couple of European steamship lines presently building passenger ships that are promising luxury to capture the Europe to America market. Thanks to you, we will show them what real luxury is and have the Pacific and Indian Oceans. Let them have the little pond, the Atlantic. Want to help me make the Smithfield Lines the standard of luxury?"

Bonnie decided for once keep her mouth shut; she did not mention the book about the Cunard Lines that she was studying.

Bonnie asked, "What do you want me to do?"

"I have two of the best women architects that I can find that are a little intimidated. Can you help them?"

Bonnie arrived early morning, eager and ready. She was introduced as the accommodations, design, and construction coordinator. The two lady architects were Connie and Rachel. Bonnie asked Joseph to give her a few minutes to get acquainted with the ladies.

It did not take long, and it became apparent to Bonnie that she again had gotten herself in a situation where she did not know what she was doing.

Connie said, "Miss Duffy, when I accepted this job, I thought I was to help out on decorating. I am not experienced or feel competent in designing the accommodations of a huge ship."

Rachel added, "I agree. Tell us what to do. We were given hundreds of drawings and told to fix them, make it a beautiful ship." Rachel pointed to two drafting tables piled high with rolled-up drawings.

Bonnie answered, "Please call me Bonnie, or Shithead might be more appropriate at this time. I am sorry, I made a few comments that the interior could be more luxurious. I have to learn to keep my mouth shut. I am not a quitter, but oh shit, what can we do? Do you want me to talk to Mr. Smithfield?"

Connie said, "I am not a quitter either. It is just overwhelming."

Rachel went and started to roll out a few of the drawings. "These drawings are not that complicated, just a lot of them." The drawings were in no order, just thrown together, probably intentionally.

It was not long before all three ladies were unrolling the drawings and organizing them. Bonnie was taught what was meant by the words in the title box.

Joseph came in. "Need any help?"

Bonnie said, "We are getting organized."

Joseph nodded and said, "I will stay out of your way. Need anything, just ask." He thought, *Three women working together, best stay out of their way.*

Connie and Rachel were trained architects that had done detailing up to now, never trusted with a big project. They immersed themselves in the design of the ship and interior drawings. Bonnie watched and learned, helping out where she could, including a constant flow of coffee.

Joseph came in again. "Ladies, it is seven. Time for dinner."

The ladies all looked at one another.

Bonnie answered, "Give us a few more minutes."

Joseph stated, "Quitting time was an hour ago. Please call it a day and continue tomorrow."

In eight more days of work, the accommodations architects had thrown out most all the interior plans and had even specified some changes in the structural bulkheads moving hatches and the relocation of some service corridors and ductwork. Their idea was to make the first-class cabins like what would be found on a royal yacht, the dining room like that of a first-class hotel, and the game room like a high-class European casino. It became apparent to Bonnie that her job was to make sure what was on the plans would be what was built and to resolve problems between design and actual construction. There were bundles and bundles of drawings, and Bonnie had only a limited idea what they meant. Bonnie got very proficient in sharpening drafting pencils, making blueprints, keeping coffee cups full, organizing, and retrieving drawings.

Bonnie brought Joseph into their drafting studio. The ladies then gave him a presentation of their work in progress. Joseph reviewed many drawings, asked many questions, and asked to see detailed drawings, many of which had not been completed yet.

The ladies waited in anticipation for Joseph's comments. Were they making the right choices? What needed revision and improvement?

Joseph stated, "Looks impressive. Now build it and meet our schedule."

Joseph left, leaving the three ladies looking at each other in shock.

Connie said, "I think he just gave us a go-ahead. What do we do now?"

Rachel spoke. "Designing is one thing, building is another."

Bonnie asked, "Have either of you been on the ship?"

There were two nos.

"Want to go aboard?"

There were two yesses.

There were only a couple of workers on the outside, working on the hull.

Rachel said, "They are installing through-hull fittings."

The three ladies ascended the steps to the ship's deck. A husky man with a pockmarked face who looked intimidating stood on the landing at the top. Bonnie was a few steps away from the top when the worker spoke.

"Sorry, ladies, women are not permitted aboard the ship during construction."

Bonnie continued to the landing, and as she got inches away, the worker backed up a little, letting her stand on the landing.

Bonnie ordered, "Listen, shithead, you have two choices— throw me off these steps and face murder charges or get the hell out of my way. Move your ass now!"

Shocked the worker backed up and let the ladies through, his pockmarked face redder than before.

The passenger hatches were closed, blocking their progress; the eight hatch dogs were all closed on the hatch. One of the architects grabbed one of the handles and, with a healthy jerk, opened it up. They repeated the process seven more times, and they were in the main cabin, main deck. As they walked through the ship's interior, the architects made notes in their notepads and explained the different areas and construction details. They went down into the ship and inspected all the areas. As they went, the workers stopped working and ogled at the ladies. Bonnie was quick to instruct them to get back to work and where they could put their eyeballs. Then they went into the upper decks. They had entered the ship late morning, and by midafternoon, they had toured most of the ship and were going back down the steps.

Rachel asked, "Where did you learn to talk man talk?"

Bonnie chuckled slightly. "I worked as a mule skinner for a while."

Rachel said, "I do not know what a mule skinner is, and I think I do not want to know."

Bonnie stated, "A mule skinner is the person who drives the mules. At one time, I had to get the attention of eight teams of mules. Mules only understand profanity. Mules are sort of like men, you have to get their attention before they hear."

The three ladies reported to Joseph upon their return. The hull, deck, bulkheads, and subdecking were complete, most all the equipment installed. The steel superstructure was finished. But there was little progress on the interior finish. Joseph told the ladies that there was a shortage of labor in the area and progress would be slow. Interior haul painting was holding up progress.

Connie said, "I noticed a lot of men scraping, wire brushing, painting, sweeping, and doing other jobs that do not require exceptional strength. Could those jobs be done by women?"

Joseph shook his head and said, "When you ladies are through, every man on earth will hate me!"

Bonnie said with a wink, "Think of all the ladies that will love you."

Joseph said, "During the civil war, many women had to do the work of the men that were off fighting. All right, we will hire some women, but absolutely no fraternizing between women and men."

Joseph invited Bonnie to dine at the mansion, and she accepted with the stipulation that he would help her understand the architectural drawings. Joseph's parents treated her such that she felt like family. After dinner, they went to the study with all of the ship models. Bonnie had brought a couple of drawings with her. Joseph placed them on a drafting table, and they started going over the details of the drawing. Soon it was apparent to both of them that there was a problem. It was not going to work, their standing close to each other. Soon their faces were close and a kiss was shared with an embrace.

Bonnie said, "Please do not make it difficult for me. I am not ready for this."

Joseph replied, "We cannot continue like this. You are driving me crazy!"

"Me too," Bonnie admitted.

"I will have you taken home."

Bonnie was taken back to her hotel. She did not sleep well, her mind stuck on Joseph.

Joseph went to the Gentleman's Club, but even the ladies there and the alcohol could not distract his mind from Bonnie. Joseph resolved that he was smitten, his days of sowing wild oats over.

At breakfast with his parents, Joseph, a little hungover, announced, "I am getting married."

His mother inquisitively asked, "To whom are you getting married?"

"Bonnie."

"She has agreed?"

"I did not think about that. I think I should ask her."

Mother stated, "I think that would be a good place to start. What if she says no? I do not think she is the kind of woman that will wed you for money. You might want to think what you have to offer her."

"Mom, do you think she will say no?"

"Have you told her that you love her? Has she told you that she loves you?"

"No, but I do love her. I think she loves me. Mom, what do I do?"

"Have you slept together?"

"No, but we want to. She is a real lady."

"Son, you need to pledge your love to her and ask her to marry you. Get on your knees, make it good. You may only have one chance. I wish you luck. She is an exceptional lady."

"Mom, what do I say?"

"Make it from your heart, not your head. She will know the difference. Woman's intuition."

Father interrupted, "See Soll at the jewelers. Remember, it is not the size of the stone but the fire in it."

Mother added, "The Irish have some beautiful traditional wedding bands."

* * * * *

Bonnie was at work early. She wanted to totally involve herself in helping build a great ship. That morning, she had not seen Joseph. She wanted to see him and at the same time, she did not want to see him. Lust was welling up in her, yet she wanted to be a lady, not a woman of sin. The ship was important to Joseph, so it was important to her as well.

The shipyard had added to the "Help Wanted" sign "Jobs for Women." Women started to show up, wanting jobs. All the women job seekers were sent to see the ladies in the new accommodations design department. Connie, Rachel, and Bonnie had no idea what to do; they felt obligated, for they had suggested hiring women.

As the women lined up in the hallway outside their office, Bonnie decided to go see Joseph. She was informed that Joseph had not shown up and they did not know when he would arrive. She was also informed that several men had quit until they were promised they would not have to work with women. Shipbuilding was men's work, not women's work. Bonnie was also informed of the shortage of men willing to work hard; there were several construction projects in the area that were paying top wages.

At that moment, Bonnie was upset with Joseph. Where was he? Why had he given her a job and then abandoned her?

Bonnie asked what they paid a laborer. She was told what they paid men twenty-two cents an hour, but women were worth less.

Then she inquired what a foreman was paid. Foreman's pay started at thirty-one cents an hour.

The three ladies decided to show them what they could do. They would handle the situation. Connie would interview the women, and she asked but one question of the prospective workers: "Are you willing to do hard, dirty work and ignore the men on the job that will probably harass you?"

Bonnie went to the ship and asked a couple of foremen if they would instruct women how to do the scraping, brushing, and painting. They all had feeble excuses. Bonnie observed that a lot of the men were not working hard but seemed to be working in slow motion. She also noticed two young men that appeared to be diligent about their jobs scraping and brushing.

Bonnie asked, "You two also know how to paint?"

"Yes, ma'am."

"Want foreman's pay for supervising a group of hardworking women?"

The two men stopped and looked about at the men that were watching them.

Bonnie said, "Do not worry about them. If they do not get their asses back to work, they will not have a job tomorrow."

A worker said, "You cannot fire us."

Bonnie replied, "You are right. But I work directly for Mr. Smithfield, and if I tell him to fire you, your ass will be gone. Now get back to work and mind your own business."

A couple of the men threw down their tools and said, "I quit!" But the rest went back to work. It was a standoff, and Bonnie was determined enough that she was not going to back down. Joseph could fire her if he wanted to; she did not need a job. Bonnie did not wait for an answer from the two young men.

An hour later, Bonnie returned with twenty women, some in dresses and some in trousers, all appearing ready to go to work.

Bonnie instructed them, "These two men are your foremen. They will show you what to do."

Bonnie left; either they would work together or they would not. She could only give them the opportunity, at least for now, until she was fired. When she saw Joseph, she was going to give him hell.

Several hours later, Connie and Rachael wanted to take some measurements, a good excuse to check up on their new hires, so the three ladies went into the ship. There were two lines of women working hard alongside the two new foreman. They took their measurements and returned to their office. Bonnie felt that maybe she had done something right, and she felt less angry at Joseph.

At the end of the shift, Bonnie went to the ship and handed each lady a pay card to be filled out by them. Those that could not read or write were helped by those that could. Bonnie signed each pay card as well as signing the two young men's cards, writing *Foreman* on their cards.

Bonnie, "Thank you for your good work. Laborers get twenty-two cents an hour, foremen thirty-one cents an hour."

A male worker complained, "That is the same that I make, and I am a man."

Bonnie replied, "You are right. These ladies appear to be working harder than you, so they should make more than you."

Bonnie got no reply.

CHAPTER 7

The Ring

Not hearing from Joseph all day, Bonnie invited Connie and Rachel to dine with her at her hotel. They were seated near the kitchen; they were wearing work dresses, not frilly ones. The three of them were congratulating themselves on how well they had handled the labor problem that had been forced on them.

Bonnie was seated with her back to the entrance. Connie was speaking and abruptly stopped in midsentence; she was looking past Bonnie. Bonnie looked around, and it was Joseph approaching their table.

Bonnie asked, "Where were you today? We had some labor problems and needed you."

Bonnie continued as Joseph knelt on one knee beside her, "We had several men quit, and we hired twenty women. They seem to be hard workers."

Joseph then said the words he had carefully prepared and memorized; he was afraid he would choke. "I pledge my undying love to you and pledge to love you forever. Will you honor me and be my wife?"

Bonnie's mind went blank. She questioned her own ears. "What did you say?"

"I pledge my undying love to you and pledge to love you forever. Will you honor me and be my wife?"

Joseph was holding out a ring of gold with a large sparkling blue stone flanked by diamonds. Bonnie just stared at Joseph; she was concerned with going to bed with him, not thinking of marriage. Joseph took her left hand and slid the ring on her third finger.

Bonnie looked at the ring, then at Joseph, then at the ring, then again at Joseph. Bonnie was emotionally overwhelmed, and large tears flowed down her cheeks as she said in a loud voice, "Yes." Bonnie threw her arms about Joseph's neck, pushing him off balance, and they went to the floor together.

The maître d' came and asked, "May I be of assistance?"

Rachel announced, "He proposed, she accepted, and they are engaged!"

The maître d' then lightly applauded, announcing to the onlookers, "They have just become engaged to be married."

Bonnie did not appear to be in a hurry to get up; she lay on top of Joseph, depositing tears on his face, staring into his eyes. She had a broad grin on her face.

The maître d' walked around them, saying, "Love, what a wonderful thing!" Some of the diners stood, lightly applauded.

Rachel said, "All right, you two, off the floor before you are arrested for obscene conduct!"

As they sat, Bonnie stared at Joseph, and he returned the stare.

"What a beautiful blue stone!" Connie exclaimed, staring at the ring.

Joseph said, "Bright, sparkling blue to match Bonnie's enchanting blue eyes."

Connie replied, "Now you are going to make me cry."

Rachel asked to look at the ring, and Bonnie held her hand out for all to see.

Rachel said, "Beautiful! My grandparents had wedding bands like this, carved with Celtic Knots all the way around, symbolizing never-ending. The knots are an ancient Celtic symbol of the marriage bond."

More large tears flowed down Bonnie's cheeks as she said, "The ring is like my parents' wedding bands, Celtic Knots."

Rachel and Connie felt like they were dining alone, for Joseph and Bonnie kept staring at each other.

After they were served dinner, Connie asked, "Are you two going to eat or just drool on your plates?"

Rachel asked, "When is the wedding?"

Bonnie replied, "Yes."

Joseph echoed, "Yes."

As Rachel and Connie were leaving, Rachel discreetly whispered to Bonnie, "Take him to bed, seal the deal."

That seemed to jolt Bonnie from her trance. Bonnie looked at the ring on her finger, bent over, kissed Joseph on his cheek, and whispered, "Room 405."

Bonnie took the lift while Joseph bounded up the stairs. They nearly collided in front of Room 405. Bonnie could not get her room key to work; her hands were shaking. Joseph was out of breath.

She said, "My key does not seem to work."

Joseph offered, "Let me try it for you, ma'am."

Joseph was the gentleman and assisted the lady as two other guests walked by.

Bonnie said, "Thank you, sir."

Joseph headed for the steps, and when the other couple went into a room, he did an about-face. When Joseph entered Bonnie's room, she had her dress off and was struggling with her corset.

Joseph said, "Let me help you with that. Let us not rush. I want to enjoy every moment with you."

"I am a virgin and scared, and I want you."

* * * * *

As they got dressed in the morning, Bonnie noticed that Joseph was well acquainted with women's undergarments as he helped her with her corset. It took two tries; the first try was emotionally aborted. Earlier, Joseph took time, gently savoring his fiancée's beauty. He knew what to do to help Bonnie with her insecurities as well as what to do and eased her concerns. Everything worked marvelously.

Bonnie softly said, "Thank you! I love you. You make me feel like a woman."

"No. I thank you. You are everything I could ever want in a woman. I love you!"

Joseph went down the stairs and out the rear entrance. Bonnie went down the lift and out the main entrance. They both got their own carriage to the shipyard.

* * * * *

Joseph's mother always read the society column of the morning edition of the local newspaper. "Sounds like he did it!"

Dad asked, "Who did what?"

Mom read, "We were informed from a reliable source that Mr. Joseph Smithfield, son of Harvey and Rebecca Smithfield of San Francisco, proposed to Miss Bonnie Duffy of South Dakota last evening at the Golden Gate Restaurant. We were informed that Miss Duffy exuberantly accepted."

Dad asked, "What do you think they are saying, *exuberantly accepted?*"

"She probably made a scene."

"If she made a scene, are you going to hold it against her?"

Mom laughingly stated, "Matters of love are an excuse for exuberance."

"He did not come home last night, did he?"

"I think he did. That will not be discussed!"

* * * * *

Bonnie arrived a little later than she had planned. There were women lined up at the main gate, wanting a job. Joseph arrived a little after Bonnie. After Joseph attended to business in his office, he and Bonnie took a quick tour of the ship. In the bottom of the bilge, there were twenty women and two men working hard, scraping, brushing, and painting the ship's interior. This work was considered the worst of jobs: it was known to be bad for the workers' lungs but had to be done.

Joseph approached the head foreman. "What do you think?"

The head foreman responded, "I do not like it, but they are working hard and doing a good job. I believe we will have to live with it."

Joseph said, "We are behind schedule, and hardworking men are difficult to find with all the other project in the area. Think we should hire a few more women?"

The head foreman pondered for a while. "I will never admit it in front of the men, but if you want this ship done near schedule, you have no choice. I do not know where you are going to get the men to supervise them."

As they continued their tour, Joseph said, "We should hire more women if we want to stay on schedule. The problem is, the foreman will not supervise them."

In an area where they were unobserved, Bonnie told Joseph, "Some of the women look like they learn quickly. Make them bosses."

Joseph had a lot on his mind. "We need to tell my parents of our engagement. Let's go back and talk to the head foreman."

Joseph talked to the head foreman. "I think we have no choice. Make a couple of the women leaders. I do not think we want to call them foremen. Call them women leaders."

Connie hired twenty more women. Some ladies had to be turned away. The women that were turned away were told to check back in two days, and if more openings came available, they would have preference as their names were taken down.

After the tour, Joseph told Bonnie, "You were very quiet."

"As your wife, I must learn to always show you the respect you deserve and never question you in public."

"I am hoping to marry a tiger, not a pussycat. Please speak up, do not hold back for my benefit. From the stories I have heard, I believe the workers fear you more than they do me. I find it difficult being forceful. I admire your strength. Please do not change for me, I love you just the way you are."

Bonnie, "I love you, even though sometimes you are full of shit."

Joseph, "We make a good couple, we are both full of shit."

"All right, women leaders get the same pay as foremen."

"How about after six months' work?"

"One month."

"Three months."

"Six cents less foremen starting, two cents increase per month until full pay. Deal?"

"Deal, I think I need to make you my negotiator."

Later, they shared a carriage to the mansion.

As they entered the mansion, Mom greeted them, "Is it true that you knocked my son to the floor and kissed him in front of the entire restaurant full of diners?"

Bonnie shyly admitted, "Yes. I was so happy when he proposed that I lost control of my emotions. See the beautiful ring Joseph gave me? I am very sorry." Bonnie was concerned what Joseph's mother thought.

Joseph's mother said, "Beautiful ring. Come and give me a hug, I am so happy for you!" After the sincere hug, Mom added, "It is sometimes necessary to put a man in his place. You got several lines in the social column of the paper this morning."

"The paper said that I threw him on the floor."

Mom, with a smile, explained, "No! They said that you exuberantly accepted. A friend was there and filled me in. She said it was very romantic. Come and let us eat and talk."

From dad, Joseph got a handshake and Bonnie got a hug and kiss on her cheek.

Mom asked, "What are your wedding plans?"

Joseph and Bonnie both shook their heads.

"How soon do you want to be wedded?"

Joseph and Bonnie just looked at each other.

Mom said, "Those are decisions the two of you will need to make together. I will help you make them. That way, it will be done correctly."

Dad responded, "Joseph, Bonnie, do not let my wife intimidate you. You make your own decisions."

Mom continued, "With your father's permission, I think it appropriate if Bonnie would move in here with us. We have lots of room if Bonnie would so like. We can then work together on some of Bonnie's rough edges, making her more sociably acceptable to San Francisco society."

Joseph replied, "I think I will move into a hotel for now. Bonnie and I will discuss our future plans. Bonnie, are you ready to leave?"

Bonnie said, "Yes, I am ready, my handsome man."

Dad responded, "Rebecca, now you've gone and done it. We will be lucky to be invited to their wedding. Anything you children need, just let me know. Your mother need not know. I will feel honored attending your wedding whenever or wherever it is. San Francisco is too concerned with acceptability."

After Joseph and Bonnie left, Harvey and Rebecca had a heated verbal exchange. Harvey went to the Gentleman's Club to escape his wife's ire for the duration of the war between them. Harvey loved his wife. He did not like arguing with her; she could be relentless. He just did not like her meddling and her desire to control.

* * * * *

Joseph rented a room in the hotel down the street. It was in easy walking distance. They kept their distance that night in respect of each other and trying to avoid being the talk of the town. They knew they would be watched.

The next day, they had breakfast together and shared a carriage to the shipyard. One night together, one night apart, and they decided on a short engagement.

Over the next few weeks, the ship was at the stage in construction that required carpenters. They only had six carpenters currently employed. They had started on second-class cabins. Design changes required a high degree of finish work. They would need at least twenty carpenters to make the scheduled completion date.

Mid-morning, Harvey, Joseph's dad, arrived, saying he wanted a tour of the family shipyard. He wanted to check on the progress of their new steamship. He had turned the shipyard over to Joseph a couple of years before. It was a sink-or-swim scenario. Harvey had given his son a chance to prove himself, and as promised, he refrained from interfering, although he monitored the business, wanting no surprises.

Joseph's dad asked, "I have been informed that you and your fiancée have made changes. Some of my associates are concerned that you are ruining the business. I promise to keep my mind open. Can you show me what you are doing? From what I have heard, Bonnie is taking an active role in the shipyard. I would like it if she accompanied us on a tour."

"Father, as you are aware, there is a labor shortage here in the San Francisco area. To keep to an acceptable completion schedule, we have taken some unorthodox hiring practices."

"I have heard about women scraping and painting, taking men's jobs."

"Father, when you cannot hire a man to do the work, a woman that does the work is not taking his job, a job he does not want."

"The question is, can they do the work?"

"Father, let us go and see."

They went to the interior design office to get Bonnie to join them.

Dad asked, "Two women draftsmen."

Bonnie said, "Sir, they are architects, designing the interior accommodations."

Joseph stated, "We are not building just another steamship, we are building a Luxury Liner. The Europeans are building ships to cater to the wealthy. I believe that will be the future of passenger steamships. I hope to build the most luxurious ships on the seas."

Dad asked, "Show me what you have in mind."

Connie and Rachel took over and showed Mr. Smithfield what they had envisioned. They showed him conceptual drawings as well as detailed construction drawings.

Joseph's father stated, "It sounds like a risky gamble. Who would want luxury on a ship crossing an ocean? People just want to get quickly cross with minimal discomfort."

Joseph answered, "If Mother wanted to go to Japan, would she want luxury on the way? What would she be willing to pay for luxury?"

Dad said, "All right, I got the idea. But it is still a gamble."

Dad, Joseph, and Bonnie went for a tour of the ship.

Dad asked, "Do those women work like that all day?"

Bonnie replied, "I believe they outwork the men, and the men know it. It is good motivation for the men. We pay the women the same as male laborers. They are highly motivated. Some are supporting children on their own."

Dad asked, "What are you going to do if this endeavor fails?"

In a slightly sarcastic tone, Bonnie replied, "I will have to teach Joseph how to mine gold. I believe that there is several thousand ounces left in my claim."

Dad replied, "Joseph, I have a lot of confidence in you. With Bonnie behind you, I cannot imagine you failing at anything, even gold mining."

On their way back to the office, Joseph's dad asked, "Can I expect delivery on schedule? I need this ship."

Joseph explained, "We have a shortage of carpenters."

Dad sarcastically answered, "Make those women carpenters. I need that ship. Actually, I could use four more ships right now. The older sailing ships just are not making it, demand it up."

Dad said, "On another subject, your mother will not give any of us any peace until you are married. As soon as you are married, I will finance the next ship—excuse me, Luxury Liner."

After Dad left, Bonnie asked, "Will you trust me to try to solve our carpenter problem?"

Joseph replied, "If it fails, we can go mine gold."

Bonnie went to the carpenters and offered them thirty-five cents an hour to accept women as apprentice carpenters. It ended up a negotiation, and they agreed on forty cents per hour. So the next day, sixteen women would start as apprentice carpenters. It was hard to pick the sixteen women from the many wanting a good job. Literacy and basic mathematics was made a requirement, eliminating almost half the candidates. They ended up drawing straws.

Joseph said, "Women carpenters—if I had any other choice, I would take it. Scraping and painting is one thing, but carpentry, I doubt it."

"Want to bet?" Bonnie challenged.

"You are on. What are we betting for?"

"You lose, you wear a dress. I lose, I wear pants."

Joseph protested, "That is not fair. You have worn pants before."

Bonnie challenged again, "Scared you will lose?"

"You are on."

At the end of the work day, they stopped and talked to the Priest.

Josephs family was a benefactor of the church, and Bonnie pledged a generous gift. They would be married on Saturday morning in eighteen days. Then they went to the mansion.

Joseph announced, "Mom, we are to be married two weeks from Saturday at the Cathedral. We would like to know if you will do the proper announcements and invitations?"

"You do not give me much time. I will need more time than that."

"I really want you to attend and help us. It would mean a lot to Bonnie and me."

"What does your father say?"

"I do not know. You ask him."

"Your father and I are not talking."

"I will stop and inform Dad tomorrow."

In the carriage, Bonnie said, "You seem to be tough on your mother."

Joseph explained, "Some advice, never argue with my mother. Just do what you must and inform her matter-of-factly. Unless you are lucky and she agrees with you. Also, that mansion is hers. Her parents built it, and Mom will defend it with her life."

That evening after dinner, Joseph sneaked into Bonnie's room. They could not wait.

The next day, Joseph went to see his father and updated him. On Friday at noon, before the Saturday wedding, the ship was to be launched. The remaining work would be completed dockside. This would make room for the laying of the keel for the next ship. The steel was already on order as well as the boilers, steam engines, and the many other components. It would be a sister ship to the one that was to be launched. There were four ships of the class planed. The women carpenters seemed to be learning. They had completed a couple of second-class cabins as well as other interior work was underway.

The small simple wedding grew with Joseph's mother's help. Wedding dress, bridesmaids, flowers, rehearsals, and more. It took a lot of head-butting to keep the reception after the wedding small; it was restricted to the people that the mansion could safely accommodate. Not at all small.

Bonnie was not familiar with the launching of ships, and she was too busy to involve herself. She was busy with the wedding and ship's interior work.

The ship would be launched stern first into the open bay. The great engines had been previously tested for a short period, ready for operation. The skid rails were greased, most of the blocking removed. Many heavy ropes were attached to the ship than to shore. Six tug boats had heavy hawsers run to the ship, their bows pointed toward the ship. The area near the shore was roped off with guards, making sure no people would be in the way.

Bonnie was told that she was to Christen the ship for luck. Bonnie did not understand the tradition or know what a big deal it was. She asked what was going to happen.

Joseph said, "The ship will slide into the water. The lines will ensure it moves slowly into the bay. The tugboats will help guide the ship to the dock."

Joseph coached Bonnie, "Your job will be to say, 'I Christen this Ship the SS,' giving the ship's name. Then break the bottle of champagne on the ship's bow, which will start it moving to the water."

Bonnie asked, "What is the ship's name?"

"Ancient Celtic tradition dictates that the name will be revealed as it is launch, look up and see the name as it is revealed. It will be painted on both sides of the bow and on the stern."

Dad, with a crew, was on the bridge to command the ship once it hit the water. There was crew on the ship's deck.

There were many people gathered to see the launch. This made Bonnie nervous. She was not used to dealing with crowds of people watching her. Plus, the wedding was the following day, so more people would be watching her. Bonnie wanted Joseph, not a wedding or ship launching. Bonnie wondered why it took so much for it to be legal to go to bed with the man you love.

A fire was lit in two of the four boilers, giving the ship power. Two short blasts were given on the ship's whistle. Men were ready with sledgehammers to drive out the last wedges holding the last of the blocking.

The Priest gave a blessing of the ship, and the crew and passengers that will sail on the ship.

Joseph said, "At the long blast of the whistle, look up and say your speech and then break the champagne bottle on the bow. Are you ready?"

"I am ready. Now I know that you are full of shit. This bottle will not make this huge ship move."

Joseph gave a hand signal.

The whistle blew.

Bonnie looked up.

The canvas covering the ship's name was released. "I Christen this Ship the SS *Bonnie Duffy*."

Joseph ordered, "Break the champagne bottle."

Bonnie wanted to break the bottle over Joseph's head, but instead, she managed the bow, as the ship started to slide toward the water. As the SS *Bonnie Duffy* slid into the water, the ship's loud whistle blew, and people cheered as other ship whistles could be heard around the bay. It was a birth announcement.

Bonnie was in awe. The huge ship gently slid into the water, not making a big splash but pushing a large wave of water from its stern. As some of the large ropes became taut; they snapped with loud reports. The six tug boats were pulled as they struggled to arrest the ship's movement into the bay. Additional heavy ropes snapped. The SS *Bonnie Duffy* seemed to bob about in the water as it started to turn sideways. Bonnie could see the tips of two of the enormous propellers churn the water into a torrent. The SS *Bonnie Duffy* finally came to a rest out in the bay. Bonnie saw a large Stars and Stripes flag flying from its mast.

Joseph put his arm around Bonnie's waist, pulled her to him, and kissed her. That got another cheer from the audience.

A member of the audience said, "Save that for the altar tomorrow! That is cheating."

Joseph became busy with handshakes, congratulations, and questions from reporters.

Bonnie, in a daze, walked the path the ship had taken to the water's edge, stepping over ropes and around large wooden block and timbers strewn bout. At the water's edge, Bonnie just stared at the huge ship with her name on it in total disbelief.

After a while Joseph came next to Bonnie and held her hand, asking Bonnie, "What are you thinking?"

"I do not know, I must be dreaming."

After several minutes, Joseph told Bonnie, "A lot of people want to meet you. Several reporters want to talk to you."

"Can I just stay here for a while? I feel lost."

Joseph wrestled a couple of large blocks around to make a seat for them and had Bonnie sit; he sat next to Bonnie, putting his arm around her.

Joseph could not understand Bonnie's reaction. She seemed to be in a daze. Maybe talking to her would wake her up. "The ship is sitting high in the water. It has not been completed and is still light, making the launching easier. When brought down to her lines, she will look better, the propellers will be under the water, and she will not bob around like a cork."

Bonnie said, "It is a beautiful ship. You are a gorgeous and wonderful man whom I am to wed tomorrow. You gave me a ring fit for a princess. Now you had me Christen a huge ship named after me. You have overwhelmed me. Please, can I just sit here a while and marvel at your beautiful ship and compose myself?"

"Want me to sit with you?"

"Please take care of business and your guests, I am sorry, I need some time alone."

Bonnie watched as the SS *Bonnie Duffy* was maneuvered around and docked up near where she was sitting. Bonnie wondered what she had done to deserve all this. Now Bonnie wondered, was she worthy of all this? What would be expected of her?

Eventually, Bonnie turned to see if all the people had left. There were three men watching over her. At sunset, Joseph's dad came and escorted her back to her room.

* * * * *

Bonnie was dressed in a gorgeous wedding gown, waiting in an anteroom in the cathedral. Her mind wandered. She was the daughter of Irish immigrants who lived in a one-room tenement in Brooklyn, New York. Then she had been an orphan sleeping on a cot in a basement, working for food and shelter. She had dressed as a boy and hoboed half-way across the country to find her grandfather. She had worked as a mule skinner and miner and was kidnapped and killed men. Now she was a bride to a man whose family was wealthy and respected members of their community. Mr. Hurst, another wealthy and powerful person, had come halfway across the country to walk her down the aisle and give her away. She loved Joseph and wanted to be with him, even though she questioned if she was worthy to be Joseph's wife and part of a great family. She had second thoughts about this wedding. It was like being in a box car on a highball run; there was no getting off. She could not blame anyone. She had hopped this car; she had to ride it to the end of the run. She envisioned it would be a lifelong run with the man she loved. She knew she would have to work hard to be worthy of her husband and his family.

Bonnie's legs felt shaky. The cathedral was packed. All these people standing, watching her walk down the aisle. The organ was playing. Bonnie concentrated on the gorgeous man standing at the altar, waiting for her. That was what this was all about. Mr. Hurst's arm was reassuring, steadying Bonnie.

Mr. Hurst whispered to Bonnie, "I remember your grandfather introducing me to a cute, spunky girl. Now you are a gorgeous and spunky woman."

Bonnie responded, "Thank you for escorting me, the second handsomest man here, right behind Joseph."

Mr. Hurst laughed a little. "To quote a young lady I know, you are full of it!"

A lot of what transpired was a blur to Bonnie, and even the Priest's words were a loss to her. She vaguely remembered saying, "I will" and "I do," Joseph saying "I will" and "I do," the rings slid on her and Joseph's fingers, and Joseph's embrace and kiss.

Leaving the church, they were pelted with rice. The rice worked its way into every seam and opening, and Bonnie could feel rice in her undergarments.

The reception was an event. Gentlemen whom Bonnie had no idea who they were wanted to hold her hand; some even wanted to kiss her cheek. Ladies wanted a hug, some shed tears. Bonnie received "Best wishes!" from all; Joseph received, "Congratulations!" Bonnie had never taken an interest in dancing before, though she and Joseph had practiced a little for their wedding dance. It seemed like every man at the reception wanted to dance with Bonnie, and each of them had a little different step. It was not an enjoyable experience. She had her toes stepped on as she stepped on some toes, and some of the men smelled of alcohol and tobacco. Bonnie tried hard to do everything proper, not for herself but for her husband and his family.

Getting her toes repeatedly stepped on and having to hold her tongue brought back the feisty Bonnie. She was able to put the last two days of bewilderment and confusion behind her.

Finally, Bonnie was paroled, and they were off to the bridal suite at the hotel. An empty carriage was greeted by more well-wishers. Joseph knew what to expect, and they had a plan. They jumped from the carriage as it moved slowly around a sharp curve. Joseph was concerned of Bonnie hurting herself.

Bonnie said, "This is nothing, try to jump from a rail car as it is moving faster than you can run. You learn to tuck and roll, jump up, and run in case the Bulls see you."

Joseph replied, "Sorry, I forgot I married an experienced hobo."

They laughed and giggled as they made their escape. They agreed it was the most fun of the entire day. Joseph had bribed the carriage drivers. They had another carriage waiting for their escape. They went to the shipyard. Several security guards at the shipyard were also bribed. These security guards were armed with revolvers and night sticks; they would not be bothered. No shivaree for them to endure. They were free! They could legally rip each other's clothes off. One of the finished second-class cabins was prepared with everything they needed, including chilled champagne and a change of clothing. They did not rip each other's clothing off, but they slowly undressed each other, toughing, caressing, and kissing at each step. When they finally lay together and joined, they both exploded in a maelstrom of passion. The champagne got warm and was not used; they did not need alcohol. After all they were intoxicated on each other.

During one of their breaks, in each other's arms, Bonnie questioned Joseph, "Where did you hear it was a Celtic tradition to keep a ship's name secret until launching?"

"I do not remember. I think it is a wonderful tradition."

"I love you so much. I will get you back."

Joseph laughed. "I know that I am the luckiest man on earth, with you as a wife."

"I am luckier than you with you as a husband."

"I do not think so. Want to fight about it?"

"It is not proper to dispute your wife's words. Now you will pay."

That started some tickling that evolved into a wrestling match. Joseph soon learned that he had married a woman who was strong and wiry, not easily subdued. Joseph concluded that there were rewards being subdued by his wife; besides, she was wearing him out.

In the morning, Bonnie made Joseph promise her no more surprises; her heart could not take it.

They arrived at the hotel for breakfast. The concierge asked where they wanted the gifts that were sent to the bridal suite delivered.

Bonnie said, "Room 405 please."

Joseph asked, "Is that where we are going to live as man and wife?"

"We can move in with your mother."

"We have an issue to be resolved."

"I will live in the home that my husband provides."

"I will provide a home that will make my wife happy."

During breakfast, they discussed where they would reside. It became a process of elimination. The hotel room was small. A larger motel room would not be private enough and would be too ostentatious. Joseph's mom's mansion came with Mom—maybe in the future, but not now. They could buy or rent a house, but that was more of a commitment than they wanted at the time. They could not decide.

The concierge informed them that the gifts would not fit into room 405.

Joseph asked, "What are we going to do? We should be going on a honeymoon."

Bonnie suggested, "Let us go on a cruise on the first Luxury Liner."

"Are you crazy?"

"We already have the bed broke in, and it is close to work, walking distance. We already have reservations, and the rent is cheap."

Joseph asked, "What will people say?"

"Tell them that you live on a six-hundred-foot luxury yacht."

"Do you think people will believe that?"

Bonnie quipped, "Bring them home and show them."

"You are having too much fun with this,"

Bonnie joked, "What will your mother say?"

"That is a good point."

Bonnie suggested, "It can be temporary until we find what we want. Besides it will be fun. Just so I am with you. Also, remember no more surprises, you promised."

"Whatever my wife desires."

Bonnie stated, "You have a good line of shit. And I love you for it."

Bonnie checked out of her room and instructed the hotel that everything be sent to the shipyard, which got some raised eyebrows.

Being Sunday, Joseph got one of the surveillance workers to use a crane and a cargo net to hoist their things to deck level. They spent the rest of the day moving into a second-class cabin. The other finished cabin was used to put all their things. They had two rooms full of flowers and champagne bottles.

Back at the mansion, it took until late evening for them to go through their gifts. They made a list of everything with the giver's name. Almost everything matched, and Joseph had to explain that there was a registry at his mother's department store. A guest would go and select a gift from the registry and it would be sent.

Bonnie asked, "Your mother selected the gifts we would receive?"

"Welcome to the family! That is the way it works. I am sorry, I should have explained earlier."

"What if I do not like the patterns?"

"You can play my mother's game if you like. Send everything back for exchange."

Bonnie asked, "What will that do?"

"Start a war."

"What do you think we should do?"

"Nothing with the presents for now. Enjoy our life together. I am truly sorry; my mother means well. She just thinks she knows better than others."

Bonnie said, "I think your mother has good taste."

"Now who had a good line of shit?"

"That is not shit, your mother has good taste. She did have you and raise you."

"You do not play fair."

"I do not fight fair either," Bonnie stated. "Want to fight?"

Joseph replied, "Have a little patience. Later, you will get yours."

"I hope that is a promise."

CHAPTER 8

The SS *Bonnie Duffy*

Joseph and Bonnie forgot about moving as the ship continued to competition. They were on schedule. The women carpenters started off slow then picked up the pace. They now had thirty carpenters, mainly women. They had groups that specialized. One group made the berths; they bent and formed the wood into exquisite shapes of form and function. Fit and finish was unrivaled. Others did the paneling, some did the decking, others made built-in cabinetry, and others did the doors. One small crew did the staircases. A couple of ladies made and installed handrails through the ship. No area was without a handrail, for safety. The work schedule was twelve-hour days, six days a week.

Joseph's father selected a Captain, a seasoned sixty-year-old Captain with over fifty years of duty at sea. He had started his career as a cabin boy. He started to hire crew. Joseph's father started to man the ship he would soon take possession of. A head chef was hired, and he hired a few cooks, and they started to organize the galley. Bonnie put two of the women carpenters who were willing, single, and without children on the ship crew roster. Gender was not mentioned, as initials and last names were used. Joseph, Bonnie, and most of the staff and workers were fed by the ship's galley.

In several weeks, the ship was to take its maiden voyage.

Josephs father and mother toured the ship. They were both impressed.

Mom said, "Now I know why you have chosen to reside here instead of my mansion. This is a floating palace. I want to go on a cruise."

Joseph, with a smirk, said to his father, "Dad, what did I tell you?"

Dad responded, "Now you have to fill the ship with paying passengers."

Mom's department store furnished the china, flatware, bedding, and many other items used in the ship. It was becoming hard to complete the construction as things were moved into the ship, furniture, deck chairs, lifeboats, life preservers, firefighting equipment, sailing instruments, and hundreds of other items. A fully equipped infirmary with a Doctor was readied.

The latest in innovation was going into the Bonnie Duffy. Not part of the original design were three generators and electric interior and exterior lighting. Electric navigation lights with oil-lamp back-ups were installed. Several walk-in coolers that were chilled with the electrical system. One of the boilers was kept fired so that electricity was available day and night. Work was being completed with the aid of electric illumination. At dusk, the ship was lit up. People came to look and marvel at Edison's innovation of electric illumination that lit up the *Bonnie Duffy*. The local newspapers had articles of the ship of the future being built in their harbor. They were getting national as well as international attention. People were inquiring about tickets.

Harvey, Joseph's dad, came to meet with Joseph and Bonnie.

Dad said, "We have a problem. The Smithfield Steamship Line is being overwhelmed with requests for ticket information and requests for scheduling for the *Bonnie Duffy*. Some creative reporter reported that we are offering an around-the-world cruise in one of those gossip newspapers. Some people believe it and are asking about tickets and sailing schedule. Your mother thinks it is an excellent idea. She says that the Smithfield name will be the greatest name in steamships. She reads too many newspapers and listens to too much gossip. The two of you have created this problem Luxury Liner, and now you two are going to help me solve it. What are you going to do?"

Joseph, "We still do not have a date for the shakedown cruise."

Dad asserted, "All right, Bonnie, if I remember, you were the one that started this, wanting luxury. Any good ideas?"

Bonnie responded, "People want an around-the-world cruise, give it to them!"

Dad stated, "That would be impossible. The logistics would be overwhelmingly difficult. I need this ship to continue my shipping business. I have commitments. I will lose business in the Pacific market for possible gains in the tentative Luxury Steamship market."

Bonnie answered, "I read your advertisement in the *Los Angeles Daily*, 'Smithfield Lines, coming soon, the most luxurious and advanced ship on the high seas.' Let us show them that we deliver."

Dad paused for a moment. "Bonnie, come up with a plan, and I will consider it." He left.

Joseph turned to his wife. "I cannot believe the way you talk to my dad. You sound like my mother, the only person that dares talk to him that way. What are we going to do now, go and mine gold?"

Bonnie said, "Come up with a plan."

Bonnie went to the Captain, wanting advice. He appeared to be intoxicated. He referred Bonnie to his First Mate, Frank Krupp. The First Mate was hard to find. He was trying to get the ship and its partial crew ready for sea. Bonnie eventually found him in the boiler room. He was talking with a worker that was covered in soot. Seeing Bonnie walking toward him, he held up a hand and screamed, "What are you doing here? Come with me, and I will escort you out! This is unacceptable! A lady in the boiler room!"

Bonnie, in a strong, confident tone, said, "I can go anywhere on this ship I want. Before you drag me out, you might want to know who I am."

"I am Frank Krupp, First Mate of this ship. And I do not care who you are. You do not belong down here."

"I am Bonnie Smithfield. My family owns this ship. Hell, the ship is named for me. Your inebriated Captain sent me to talk to you."

Frank had never had an attractive, well-dressed young lady talk to him like that. Who was she? he wondered. Was she really a member of the owner's family? She was not intimidated and acted like she belonged here.

Frank said, "What do you want to see me about?"

Bonnie said, "Mr. Smithfield has asked me to develop a plan for an around-the-world cruise. I need help and advice."

Frank responded, "I think you will need a lot of help. That is unheard of and not realistic. The logistics will be confounding."

Bonnie answered, "Yes, it is a challenge, I need someone with knowledge of ships and the sea. My father-in-law wants a plan, and I will give him a workable plan. Can you suggest someone with the necessary knowledge willing to work with me?"

Frank asked, "How did you get down here?"

"I came down the forward port, fresh-air intake. It is a shortcut."

"You know this ship."

"I will bet that I know this ship better than you."

While he pondering his next move with this insistent lady, Frank looked around, avoiding eye contact. Frank was not accustomed or comfortable being rudely challenged, especially by a lady. He was looking for a way to rid himself of the lady without being to offensive. Without a lot of consideration, Frank asked, "Where does the hatches go beneath our feet?"

"Which ones? To the ballast tanks, or the bilge, or maybe the freshwater tanks. Also, there is a lamp-oil storage tank and an engine-lubricating oil tank."

Frank realized this woman did know this ship. He could not just dismiss her. "You got my attention. What now?"

Bonnie said, "Let us get out of the here and talk, if you have time."

They went through a hatch up a narrow and tight spiral staircase that the First Mate did not know existed and out another hatch onto the deck.

Frank then said, "I was not aware of those hatches. In case of an emergency, they would be important."

Bonnie explained, "Air intake for the boilers. Two port and two starboard. Seal all of them up, and the boilers will down draft, filling the ship with smoke, a possible disaster."

They ended up in a room that had a bronze plaque, "Passenger Services."

Bonnie informed him, "I made this my office. Excuse the mess."

Bonnie laid out her crude idea, asking for Frank to help her make a plan. It was going to be complex—port of calls, distances, coal availability, coal quality BTU equivalent. That was just the travel; food and other passenger requirements would have to be planned.

Frank, "This is a challenging endeavor. If we can pull this off and I am the First Mate, I will be able to write my own ticket."

Bonnie explained, "We have to come up with a workable plan in a couple days. In several weeks, this ship is to sail."

Frank said, "We have a couple of weeks."

Bonnie further explained, "In a few days, we have to have a schedule ready for publication, so we can start selling tickets. It is not about sailing around-the-world, it is about carrying satisfied passengers around-the-world. They pay for everything, including our wages and the coal we will burn."

That evening, Bonnie was going through a stack of papers, looking concerned. She had been given a job that she did not know if she could succeed at. Bonnie realized she had done it again; she had to learn to keep her mouth shut.

Joseph told her, "You do not have to do this. You do realize that if you succeed, Dad will expect more. Dad likes to push people, test their limits, getting the most from them."

Bonnie answered, "As I have gotten older, I realize that I cannot resist a challenge. Why else would I travel halfway across the county in railroad freight cars following a dream, looking for my long-lost grandfather? Looking back, I now realize it was as much the challenge as following a dream. I read too many adventure novels. I was and still am gullible when challenged."

"Bonnie, you are a special lady, one I love and will always love. I know better than to tell you what to do." Joseph smiled and said, "Just ask me and I will help in any way I can."

"I love you dearly. When will this ship be ready to sail?"

"Four weeks from today."

Bonnie said, "I will hold you to that."

* * * * *

Bonnie was given a list by two of her carpenters. It was of women willing to go to sea and work. They were looking for an opportunity. The list included talents, skills, and education.

In two days, early morning, Bonnie went to see Harvey Smithfield, President of Smithfield Steamship Lines and President of Smithfield Shipyards. She did not have an appointment. His secretary had been to her wedding, requested to attend filling the cathedral. Bonnie was admitted quickly to see the President.

Bonnie said, "Mr. Smithfield, I believe I have a plan that will meet the requirements for an around-the-world cruise. It still needs a lot of work, especially in passenger services, but it is a basic plan."

Dad told Bonnie, "Bonnie, will you please call me something other than Mr. Smithfield. Harvey, Father, or Dad will do. You are one of the family. Now show me what you have."

Bonnie handed her father-in-law a stack of papers, "Here is the proposed route with stops. We are still working on getting some of the necessary clearances. It appears that most destinations are eager to have the *Bonnie Duffy* stop at their port. Good-quality, high-BTU coal will be a problem in some areas, but we believe we can have a coal ship meet us at two critical points. As a backup, we can burn low-quality coal. This will be at a loss in speed, but it is a viable backup. Provisions of food and other supplies are still being worked out. We do not see any major problems, though. The chefs might have to get creative with local fare, for example, a Polynesian luau with authentic local fare." Dad, held his hand up and paused Bonnie.

He said, "Time for people to earn their pay."

Dad went to his secretary and told her to have Miss Gibbs come to the large conference room. Dad escorted Bonnie to a large room with a large table and told her, "Remember, it is your plan. You are the boss. Now for the little details."

There was a knock on the door. Dad invited in a tall and slender woman in her mid-thirties. "This is Miss Charlotte Gibbs. Charlotte, this is Mrs. Bonnie Smithfield. Bonnie is the manager of the ship named after her. Bonnie, if acceptable to you, Charlotte will help you with the little details. Charlotte is very knowledgeable in the operation of a passenger-carrying steamship. Charlotte is hardworking and trustworthy. Bonnie, welcome to the world of business. Good luck, you will need it." Then Dad left.

Charlotte asked, "What can I do for you?"

Bonnie said, "Mr. Smithfield asked me for a plan for an around-the-world cruise. I have spent two long and hard days coming up with a plan of dubious value. He hardly looked at my plan and escorted me here and introduced us. What next?"

"Ma'am, Mr. Smithfield made you manager. He obviously has a lot of confidence in you. Now we will have to get approval from the legal, advertisement, sales, logistics, budgeting, financial, international affairs, navigation, and safety departments. They all have to be coordinated, working together."

Bonnie said, "I just heard Mr. Smithfield say you were knowledgeable, hardworking, and trustworthy. Please help! I do not know where to start."

Charlotte smiled. "I hope you are tough. You are going to need it."

Charlotte left for a few minutes, saying, "I will get the crew moving."

People entered and left, returned, and left again. Some were introduced. In short order, Bonnie's neat stack was strewed all over the large table. Bonnie received a continuous barrage of questions. To some, she had answers; some she did not. She was asked to make choices, and on numerous occasions, Bonnie asked for more information to make a proper choice.

Eventually, Bonnie stood up and asked for quiet. "Please, the *Bonnie Duffy* is a new class of ship. We refer to it as a Luxury Liner. I would like it to not be referred to as a steamship or ship or passenger ship. Mr. Smithfield wants the *Bonnie Duffy* to set a new standard of luxury. The name *Smithfield Steamship* will stand out."

With all the traffic, the door was left open. Bonnie had not realized it, but her father-in-law was just outside the door. He had not totally deserted Bonnie; he often walked by and observed. He tried not to interfere. His management style was to put good people in charge, motivate them, and then monitor and observe. That is what he had done with his son, and now it was Bonnie's turn.

Mr. Smithfield stepped into the crowded room. "I like that—the Smithfield name will stand out. Keep up the good work. Mrs. Smithfield, how about lunch in half an hour?"

"Yes, thank you, Mr. Smithfield."

The procedure was that people would first talk to Charlotte, then if they were directed, they would talk to Bonnie. Bonnie sat, while Charlotte stood, moving about the room. Somehow, she kept track of all the papers Bonnie had brought and the mass of paperwork that was accumulating. Charlotte directed people as to whom they needed to talk or what papers they needed. Bonnie was getting an education that could not be learned in a normal classroom. Legal disclaimers, maritime law, legal responsibilities, the art of advertising, organization, planning, coordination, and things that Bonnie had never heard or thought of. There was even a plan for freshwater with a backup plan. Freshwater consumption had to be calculated, with a reserve.

Dad put his hand on Bonnie's shoulder, announcing, "Lunch time."

It was a short carriage ride to a private club for lunch. Bonnie was unaware of all the things going through her mind at the same time.

Dad asked, "Feel a little frazzled? How are you holding up?"

Bonnie responded, "That is the exact right word, *frazzled*."

Dad, "If things get too bad, you can just walk out, calling a break. They will wait for you and possibly work around you. This is your project. I have confidence in you. If you need me, I will be nearby for you. I really think that you do not need my help, and my interference will not be appreciated and counterproductive. I will observe and watch over you and our employees."

Bonnie said, "You said *our* employees."

"You are a Smithfield. It is a family business, and you are a manager. I heard a rumor about you putting the First Mate in his place. Just remember, at sea, the Captain's rule is absolute."

The break was needed, Bonnie returned composed and ready to face the problems. The afternoon seemed less hectic, as things were coming together. The documents to be signed were reviewed by Charlotte, and she would initial them. Bonnie would read, ask questions, and then sign. They would actually go around-the-world twice! If a passenger boarded in Rio De Janeiro with the proper ticket, they could disembark in Rio De Janeiro, completing a circumnavigation of the world, on the SS *Bonnie Duffy's* second trip around. A passenger could buy a ticket for any leg of the trip. Cost would be by class and segments traveled. For multiple segments, there would be discounts. First-class circumnavigation was a special rate and a special ticket giving special privileges. The scheduling and rate charts were the most complex ever attempted. There would be twenty-two ports of call on every continent except Antarctica, subject to changes required by weather and political issues. Five of the Earth's seven oceans would be crossed as well as many seas. A lot of the work was not completed, but they could start advertisement and begin selling tickets.

Mr. Smithfield was briefed and gave his approval. Tomorrow, Bonnie would return in the afternoon. She had some business to attend to aboard the *Bonnie Duffy*. She would have to get the ship's crew as well as construction up to date. Now Frank would not dare chase her out of the boiler room. In reality, Bonnie and Frank had come to a mutual understanding and had a good working relationship. Without Frank's help, she could not have completed her plan. Being late fall, it was past dark when Bonnie returned to the ship.

At dinner, Joseph asked her, "How was your day? Besides being long."

Bonnie answered, "Your dad did not fire me. He actually made me the manager of the SS *Bonnie Duffy*. Does that make me your boss? Are you ready to put on a dress? Thought that I forgot about that, did you? Are you going to renege on your bet?"

"This ship is still under construction. Until Dad takes possession, I am still the boss."

"I can't wait until I see you in a dress."

"We are going to have to move in a week or so. Where are we going to live?"

Bonnie said, "That is a problem. Please do not get too mad. I think I will need to stay here. I love you. I am sorry."

"I was afraid of that. With my mother, Dad, and the business, our lives are not our own. All the people who work for us, count on us. Their lives are dependent on the business. I guess we are all slaves to the family business."

Bonnie said, "If we go and mine gold, we will then be servants of the mine."

"I am going to stay with you until the last minute. As a child, I dreamed of sailing around-the-world, and now you are going to fulfill my dream. Can we renegotiate the dress thing, though?"

"I think you will look cute in a dress. Let us go to our room. Maybe we can discuss the dress. I wonder if one of my old dresses can be let out to fit you? What do you think, frills and lace, or plain and practical?"

Late morning the next day, Bonnie arrived at the Smithfield Steamship office and went right to Dad's office.

Dad said, "Excellent timing. Let's have lunch."

Bonnie informed him that she thought she should go on the cruise. Dad questioned if everything was good with her and Joseph. Bonnie made it clear that neither liked the idea of being apart, but they both agreed it would be good for the business, and she wanted to see the project through. They could endure the temporary separation.

Dad stated, "Bonnie, people are buying tickets with little advertisement. Newspapers worldwide are printing articles of the new class of ship, the Luxury Liner and an around-the-world cruise. Keeping the *Bonnie* lit up at night with electric illumination is worth hundreds in advertising. I even got a telegram from Mr. Thomas Edison asking when it would be on the East Coast so he can see!"

Bonnie asked, "Can I keep Charlotte, or do I have to give her back?"

"I think she is single. Ask her if she wants to cruise around the world. She sure would be an asset aboard the ship. It will be hard replacing her here at the office. You will need to give her an appropriate title."

Charlotte had a stack of paperwork for Bonnie to go through. Bonnie was amazed at how organized and efficient Charlotte was. They went through the paperwork together. Charlotte did not only organize but she also informed and educated.

Bonnie asked, "Did Mr. Smithfield look at any of this?"

Charlotte answered, "Every paper and note. We were both up late. People think that Mr. Smithfield is lackadaisical running the business. I do not think that anything in his businesses happens that he is not aware of. Mr. Smithfield watches over everyone and everything. He only interferes when he sees a problem—that is his way."

"Charlotte, thank you for the insight, I was getting worried. That fact relives a lot of my concerns. I really appreciate all your help. You are a very accomplished and knowledgeable business woman. I intend to stay on the *Bonnie*, hopefully to complete this project. Mr. Smithfield has granted me permission to ask you if you would like to continue your work aboard the *Bonnie Dufy* as Passenger Service Director."

Charlotte's eyes opened wide with a sparkle. "For how long?" she asked.

"I do not know your personal situation, but hopefully, at least one time around the world."

"I am a single, childless old maid. As long as I do not have to buy my own ticket. The ticket cost would be several years' salary for me."

"All expenses paid, and I will insist that you will receive a pay increase. It should go with the title."

"When do I start?"

"Finish up affairs here, pack what you will need, and come down to the ship. I have an office that we can share. I will put your name on the crew roster. I will arrange for you to have a small private cabin in the officers' quarters, if that will be acceptable. In about thirty days, the ship will be moving to the coal dock, public dock, then a short cruise, and then back to the public dock. Any questions?"

"Will I need any new clothes, a uniform, or anything else?"

"You look appropriately dressed for business to me. As you, I like a simple business dress. Frills are saved for society. Maybe one nice dress for dinner. We both know there will be a boutique, beauty salon, general mercantile, as well as other services aboard."

Bonnie gave Charlotte the list of names, saying, "We will need many people to fill all the service needs of the ship. Finding good male help in the area is difficult at this time. This is a list of women that are looking for an opportunity and are willing to go to sea. If we can give any of them a chance, it would be appreciated. If you want to contact any of them, just ask any of the women laborers working on the ship. They will forward the message."

Before leaving Bonnie reported back to Dad.

Dad gave Bonnie an envelope. "This is the Captain's sailing orders. Read them over, if you approve give them to the Captain. I am appointing you the ship's owner operator's representative in my absence."

* * * * *

At 8:30 a.m. the next day, Bonnie went to the bridge to give the Captain his sailing orders. The watch told Bonnie to come back later.

Bonnie informed the bridge crew, "I am Bonnie Smithfield, I represent the owners, and I have the Captain's sailing orders. I am required to give the orders directly to the Captain. Please inform the Captain that I am waiting for him."

In about fifteen minutes, the Captain came to the bridge escorted by his First Mate, Frank Krupp. The Captain looked like he had not changed his clothing for days. He reeked of rum and body odor. His eyes were bloodshot and looked glazed over. The Captain, First Mate, another officer, and a sailor were with Bonnie on the bridge. Bonnie was wondering about the competence of the Captain, and she could only hope that at sea he would do his job. Bonnie decided to read the orders out loud and then present them in writing to the Captain so there would be no confusion and witnesses that he received his orders and what the orders entailed. As Bonnie read, the Captain appeared lucid. The look Bonnie got when she read the provision of her authority as representing the owner operator made Bonnie wonder if he would make her walk the plank. The Captain was obviously not impressed. Bonnie realized how devious her father-in-law could be. He could have given these orders to the Captain. Now the Captain would have to work with Bonnie.

Frank escorted Bonnie out and, in a hushed voice, said, "Please excuse the Captain. He is a fine sailor and Captain, we are lucky to have him. He has been under the weather as of late. I know that once we get under way, he will again be himself. Congratulations, it sounds like your daring plan had been accepted." Then he asked, "Are you going to be sailing with us?"

"Yes, I will. It looks like we will be going around twice."

"Ma'am, are you saying back-to-back circumnavigations?"

"Think you can handle it?"

"Sounds like a sailor's dream."

* * * * *

The next couple weeks were hectic. Charlotte moved in and was immediately put to work. Passenger Services seemed to include everything except steering the ship and shoveling the coal. The stewards, housekeeping, laundry, boutique, beauty salon, bank, mercantile, food services including their menus, medical services, onboard messenger services, entertainment, deck chairs, dining room seating, and a lot more were given to Passenger Services to administrate. Charlotte and Bonnie worked as a team, not always agreeing, able to discuss and compromise in the interest of the ship. Charlotte's knowledge gave her the lead. Bonnie respected and admired Charlotte. This was all new to Bonnie.

The scheduled departure was set for noon on December 28, 1893. It was December 10, so that left eighteen days. People needed to be hired and trained. One of Smithfield's older ships that catered to passengers made port in San Francisco; some of its crew was switched to the *Bonnie Duffy*. A manager and his wife of a respected hotel were lured with lucrative contracts. Their children were grown, and they were enchanted by the call of the sea. The woman had run the housekeeping and other guest services at the hotel. Other competent employees from the many establishments in San Francisco were lured away.

Charlotte informed Bonnie, "The ship is desperate for three oilers to work in the engine room. They needed training. This is a low-level entry job that men do not want. It is a job usually done by orphan boys."

Charlotte did not know anything about engines and did not know how to get to the engine room. Bonnie knew how to get to the engine room but did not know exactly what an oiler did. Charlotte warned Bonnie, "This is going to be a tough one." Bonnie was taken to the service entrance, where Bonnie was introduced to five girls being detained by a guard.

The guard reported, "Ma'am, this is the third time that I caught these girls trying to sneak aboard. If they would be boys, I would give them a good thrashing and send them on their way. They told me they heard women can get a job here. They said that they were to see Miss Gibbs but did not have an appointment. They want to work for food. The word is that the Chief Engineer is looking for boys as oilers. I am sorry, ma'am. I felt sorry for them, I did not know they were going to involve you. I thought that if they were given pants and their hair cut, nobody would know them from boys. I will haul them to the gate and send them on their way."

They were dressed in rags and looked malnourished, and upon questioning, it was found out they were ten to fourteen years old, one set of twins. They were sisters that were orphaned. They tried to stick together. They were moderately literate. They promised to work hard for food and shelter.

Bonnie thought she had had it hard, but nothing like this.

Bonnie talked to them for a while to get acquainted. She could not resist their sincere pleading for a job, and they convinced her that they wanted a job, not a handout. Bonnie could see some of herself in these street urchins. She dismissed the guard. She than sent

Charlotte to tell Frank, the First Mate, to meet her in the engine room in an hour. Bonnie was really busy, but she would make a little time for these five waifs. Bonnie took them to the crew's cafeteria, where they were fed; they ate hardily. Bonnie went to the engine room with the five girls in tow. The few men working in the engine room looked on, they knew of the lady's reputation and position, they went about their work.

The First Mate showed up.

Bonnie said, "I heard you need three oilers, here are five workers eager and ready. Five for the price of three."

"But they are girls," Frank protested.

"Very observant. I was told that oiling was usually done by boys. In my experience, adolescent girls are just as strong and agile as adolescent boys."

Frank stated, "The Captain will have me keelhauled if he finds out that I hired girls to work in his engine room."

"Tell him that I hired them. He would not dare have me keelhauled."

Bonnie wondered what *keelhauled* meant; it sounded nasty. She would have to look it up.

Frank pointed to one of the three enormous machines that were as high as a three-story building. "See the narrow walkways around the base and over half way up the engine? An oiler has to walk there while the engine is running and oil all the moving parts. It is very dangerous and dirty. The walkways get oily and very slippery. This is what is used to apply the oil." He held up an oil can.

Bonnie addressed the girls, "You girls heard the First Mate. Can you oil that engine?"

The five girls glared at the enormous engine with a look of total bewilderment. The sight of the engine intimidated Bonnie.

Bonnie said, "Girls, want a job? Show us what you can do."

There were only three oil cans on the bench. The five girls ascended, carefully climbing up the engine, three of them squirting oil all over the place. It was obvious that they were nervous, carefully moving about. Bonnie's only consolation was that if were not these girls, boys would be found to do the dangerous work. The girls wanted a job and were willing.

Frank stated, "They are squirting oil in all the wrong places."

Bonnie said, "Come down, girls, and put the oil cans away." She addressed Frank, "I guess that they will have to be trained just like you would boys."

Frank stated, "They will have to wear pants, boots, and short-sleeved shirts. Also, they will have to keep their hair tied up or cut. Loose items will get caught in the machinery, pulling one into the works, resulting in mutilation and death. What am I going to get out of this?"

Bonnie said, "Knowing that you gave five street urchins a chance and a future favor from me."

Frank introduced the Chief Engineer, who was standing behind them, listening, "This is Mrs. Smithfield. She is an owner and a very persuasive lady. This is Smitey, the Chief Engineer. Smitey, here are your oilers. Please do your best. Have them dress appropriately, train them, shown them where to eat, and show them the women's crew's quarters. Have them instructed on their proper place and etiquette. Tell the crew, hands off. That is an order. Will there be any problems?"

Smitey responded, "Sir, women carpenters, why not oiler girls? Do not blame me if they get ground up."

Bonnie, "Thank you Smitey, I hope they work out. Any trouble with them, tell me. I will have them disciplined harshly." Then she addressed the girls, "Hear that, girls. Want a home, behave, work hard." She again spoke to Smitey. "Get them some appropriate clothes, send the bill to passenger services, my authorization. Tell the

*Steam Engine of the
RMS Lucania 1890s*

crew, hands off, or I will have their stupid asses keelhauled." Bonnie thought, *I have to look up* keelhaul.

After Bonnie left, Smitey said, "Sir, is she as tough as she talks?"

"The Captain takes his orders from her, and she has put him and me in our place."

* * * * *

December 20, the coal bunkers were filled, and they moved to the public dock.

On December 21–22, 1893, they took a twenty-four-hour shakedown cruise to check the ship's operation. Two hundred people were given a free cruise to test the ship's operations. Most were employees and families of Smithfield Shipyard and Steamship Line. Mr. and Mrs. Smithfield, Sr. showed up with several friends. Mom wanted her cruise. Mom and friends took over first class. The rest of the passengers were sent to second class. Bonnie greeted several of the women she had hired and their families, and they all thanked Bonnie for giving them an opportunity. A few reporters, politicians, and their families that were thought to be friendly to the Smithfield family were also invited, given first-class accommodations. A real treat—most could not normally afford first-class.

During the cruise, Frank had the crew run drills for fire suppression, man overboard, and lifeboat deployment. One of the sailors got his leg crushed; he did not follow instructions deploying a lifeboat. He was placed on a stretcher and rushed to the infirmary. The onboard Doctor believed that because of quick treatment, he did not bleed to death and he would probably regain the use of his leg. It was a tragic accident that could have been worse.

While at sea, rooms were cleaned and bedding changed, laundry was done, and meals were prepared and served. The mercantile was open, and souvenir copper tokens could be bought for a penny.

They tried to test everything.

Bonnie went up to the bridge on two occasions, but her presence was not appreciated. The Captain appeared sober, alert, and in control of the ship and crew. Bonnie's fears were somewhat eased.

They were steaming three-quarters speed, and on Bonnie's request, she and Joseph went to the engine room. It was hot and smelly, and the sound was a deafening blare of noise. Bonnie looked at one of the enormous engines, its huge parts thrashing about so fast they looked like a blur. Next to the second engine were two small people carrying oil cans. They disappeared, moving around the engine. Bonnie looked up, and there was a small person reaching into the mechanism, timing their squirts of oil as the large component flew up and down. The components were larger than the person. The person moved from one component to the next. The sight horrified Bonnie, so she left with Joseph.

She asked, "Is that the normal way to oil an engine?"

Joseph answered, "That is the only way to do it. The boys that do it are experts. They are like acrobats and trapeze artists, all in one. They are amazing! You would not get me that close to those moving parts."

"That was not a boy, it was a girl, and that is my doing."

Joseph said, "Maybe a girl can do everything a boy can. Some oilers become engineers. Who knows?"

Bonnie trying to get her mind off the girls. "Then boys can also wear dresses."

Joseph replied, "You get ahold of something you cannot let go."

There were mistakes made; efficiency needed improvement, and more training was needed. Most passengers were having a wonderful time. One sailor would need recovery time. There were several cases of seasickness. Even at a penny, few of the souvenir tokens were sold. Bonnie purchased a handful, handing them out to the children. One success was the casino's gaming tables. They were opened up, kernels of corn were bet, and winners were paid in corn. It was just for fun and kept some of their passengers busy and entertained, and the employees were trained as well. Eventually the casino was to be self-supporting.

After they docked and their guests had disembarked, Charlotte had a meeting in the crew's cafeteria with all the staff. Charlotte demanded Bonnie did the speaking. Several ship's officers attended, including Frank the First Mate; the Captain declined. The staff did get a few complaints: it was not long enough, the beds were too comfortable, and the food was too good. Everyone had an opportunity to express their concerns and comments. Several had suggestions to alleviate some problems. Housekeeping carts in the passage ways were a problem, blocking access, and that would have to be resolved. Many possible problems were identified, and solutions were already implemented.

Bonnie summed up the cruise, "I want to thank everyone for their help in having a successful shakedown cruise. In the weeks to come, we are all going to become part of the history of transportation, the first 'Luxury Liner.' Nobody before has traveled the seas in a safer or more comfortable ship. We should all give each one another a hand. Let us serve one another a delicious meal prepared by our chefs. Everybody take a break. Tomorrow we will clean up and prepare for sea."

Bonnie had noticed five girls in plain dresses seated together, and she went and sit next to them.

The oldest girl said, "Mrs. Smithfield, thank you. You are wonderful! We get all the good food we can eat."

Another girl said, "We all have our own comfortable bed and look at our new dresses. We got pants and shirts and underpants and socks too, all brand-new."

"We all got new boots," the youngest girl exclaimed. "Look at how nice they are!" The girl pulled up her dress to show her new boots, which were already oil-stained.

One of the twins said, "I saw you today in the engine room. I was oiling the connecting rod wrist pins. It is scary, and you have to be careful."

The other twin added, "Smitey told us that we will get paid and we can use the money for anything we want. Is that true?"

Bonnie answered, "Yes, you will all get paid, and the money will be yours to spend on what you want. You are earning it fair and legal. You should save some of your money in the bank. I think all of you should have schooling—reading, writing, and arithmetic."

One of the twin girl said, "Smitey is making us learn to read all the labels on the machinery. He says we will have to learn to read the engineering books. He says all oilers have to learn to be engineers."

The oldest girl added, "Thank you, we promise to work hard and not cause any trouble. You do not need to worry about us. The women in our cabin are looking out for us and teaching us to be ladies. A lot of people are helping us."

The next day, December 23, Bonnie went to a bookstore and bought a copy of *Moby Dick* by Melville. At a secondhand store, she bought a dress that was way too big for her. At the jeweler's, she bought two diamond stick pins, a special brooch, and a lady's pin-on watch. She had the jewelry and dress wrapped for Christmas.

In a few days, they would sail off, and it appeared that they were going to have a successful cruise. Things started to look good. Bonnie gave Charlotte the lady's watch for Christmas.

Bonnie told Charlotte, "Open your gift on Christmas morning. Tomorrow, I will be unavailable. Have a wonderful holiday."

Bonnie went to bed early with her book. Tomorrow would be the eighth anniversary when she started to read this book. In several days, she would be headed to sea on a long voyage, facing unforeseen challenges. Captain Ahab had haunted her for eight years, and now it was time to put Captain Ahab's ghost to rest. The electric light above her berth was bright enough to read by. It had been so long she decided to read the book from the beginning.

Joseph was concerned, seeing his wife in bed so early.

He asked, "Are you feeling poorly?"

"Not at all. Things are looking good for the cruise."

"What are you reading?"

"*Moby Dick.*"

"Is that the kind of book to read before a long cruise?"

"It is a ghost I need to put to rest."

"Can we talk about it?"

"Maybe, after I finish the book."

Bonnie put her book down and told her husband, "There is a package over there for you. Open it and see if the contents fits. An early Christmas gift."

Joseph unwrapped the package, held up the contents, and promptly threw it on the floor, saying, "No."

Trying hard to not laugh, Bonnie said, "I want to be made love to by a man with a dress on."

"Absolutely not!"

"I want to see how you look in a dress before I take you out in public in a dress."

"Bonnie, no, no, no."

"Guess I will go back to my book. What do they call a man who does not pay his gambling debts?"

Bonnie went back to reading. She was determined to finish this book but wanted some distractions along the way. Joseph disrobed, crawled in bed, and tried to tease his wife with touches, but she just tucked the bedding about her.

Joseph protested, "You are not playing fair."

"Fair. Pay your gambling debt. Where is your dress? That is fair."

Now Joseph's mind was on his wife. As she read, he tried to come up with alternative approaches. Joseph knew his wife was head strong. He tried to squeeze his head between the book and Bonnie's face, trying for a kiss, but that did not work.

Joseph had watched several women put on dresses, and he had watched his wife quickly don a dress numerous times. It was not as easy as it looked. Joseph thought, *At least she did not buy me a corset to go with the dress.*

Bonnie watched her husband, with a big grin on her face. It was a little snug, but it fit. He had unbuttoned a few dresses, but he found it was a different matter buttoning the many buttons. The dress had to be slid around and adjusted to hang right. Bonnie was watching with her hand clasped over her mouth, hiding her grin, resisting laughter. Joseph looked at himself in their tall mirror and curtsied. Bonnie lost it. It was contagious, and they both broke out in uncontrollable laughter. Bonnie got out of bed and insisted that Joseph stand still as she unbuttoned each button one at a time. Each button was accompanied with a kiss to his neck, chest, gradually descending to his belly. Bonnie then grabbed the long sleeve's ends.

On at a time, from one to the other, she pulled them over his hands. At last, she slid the dress over his hips to the floor. Bonnie led Joseph by the hand to their bed. She lay down and pulled him on top of her. Bonnie thought of how deeply she loved this man. He was so masculine that even wearing a dress did not threaten his masculinity. There was nothing he would not do for her. She was a lucky woman.

Joseph thought how much he loved his wife. She was so beautiful, charming, sensual, intelligent, hardworking, creative, caring, strong, and yet playful and fun. She made him feel so alive. He knew he was a very lucky man. It was one of those loving, tender, deeply passionate, satisfying moments.

As they lay in each other's arms waiting for sleep to come, Bonnie whispered, "Promise me that you will never wear a dress for anyone but me."

Joseph emphatically declared, "I have paid my gambling debt in full. I have learned my lesson. I will never bet with you again."

"Want to bet?"

Sleep soon came to them.

In the morning, Bonnie said, "Thank you for being you. I love you. Please be patient with me. Today I need to purge Captain Ahab's ghost from my mind."

Joseph knew that Christmas Eve was the anniversary of Bonnie's parents and grandfather's deaths. He knew that Bonnie had some unfinished business with Moby Dick and Captain Ahab. He was astute enough to give her the space she needed. He went to get coffee and breakfast, which he served Bonnie in bed. Joseph had to finish his Christmas shopping too.

Joseph knew that his wife, on the cruise, would be dining with the rich and powerful. The Smithfields were well-to-do, and he wanted his wife to feel like she fit in and was part of society. Several weeks before, he had ordered her a special Christmas gift. It was more appropriate now than when he had ordered it. Today, he would pick it up. First, he was shown the bracelet diamonds and blue sapphires. It was everything that the jeweler promised. Every stone had fire in it. It was an eye-catcher. Next was the necklace. The jeweler was dramatic. He held his hand over the center stones; it was exquisite diamonds and blue sapphires—every stone had fire. Finally, the five-karat tear-drop blue sapphire flanked by two-, three-karat tear-drop white diamonds. Jewels fit for a princess. He knew Bonnie would not accept such a gift graciously, but that would be part of the fun. She would be embarrassed. He could watch her squirm. The bigger the audience, the better.

It was early evening when Joseph returned to the ship. Bonnie had finished reading *Moby Dick*. She was still in her nightwear. She asked if they could dine in. She wanted to be just held until Christmas.

Bonnie told Joseph, "I am sorry, Christmas Eve is a dark day to me. Captain Ahab is dead, killed by the great white whale. Christmas Eve is a day of loss and remembrance to me. The world will start anew tomorrow."

Joseph went to get dinner.

They dined in.

Joseph held Bonnie.

Tomorrow came.

CHAPTER 9

Christmas

Joseph was awakened when Bonnie brought in coffee and breakfast. He had breakfast in bed. A first since he had been sick as a child. They were not expected at the mansion until one in the afternoon. Later, there was to be a party with close friends and associates. Tomorrow, they would have to move out. Bonnie would take a room in the officer's quarters. It was a double room three decks up. It had portholes, which the room they were in now did not have. The room was an equal to the Captain's quarters. It suited her position as the owner's representative. They did a little packing and ended up back in bed. It was decided Joseph would go on the first leg, cruising to San Diego, where he would take a train back to San Francisco. They started to call it their honeymoon. The things that they had stored were moved to Mom's mansion. They had almost finished packing when it was time to leave. Joseph was insistent that Bonnie wear a low-cut evening dress in a warm blue. He said it was his favorite.

Bonnie asked, "Joseph, would you like to wear the dress for me?"

Joseph smiled. "It is too small for me. I need an extra large with small bosoms."

With laughter, she said, "One of the many reasons I love you, you make me laugh!"

Joseph replied, "You are the humorous jester. Do not blame me."

Bonnie quipped, "Want to bet on that?"

They arrived at one. It would give them time to exchange presents among the family before the dinner guests arrived. Bonnie felt she had done good. Mom said that she loved the brooch. Both dad and Joseph said that the diamond stick pin was special. Joseph and his mom and dad had gone together and gotten Bonnie a beautiful set of blue sapphire tear-drop earrings accented with teardrop diamonds.

Bonnie said, "This is much more than I deserve! They have to be worth a fortune. I'm afraid I will lose them. I love all of you. They are so beautiful." They all got a hug and a kiss from Bonnie. "This is the best Christmas ever! The best Christmas present I ever got before this was a Winchester repeating rifle."

That got a laugh from all the family.

Bonnie pinned her hair back behind her ears so her earrings could be easily seen. Now she knew why Joseph had her wear the blue dress; it matched her earrings and her wedding ring, which was a blue sapphire and two diamonds. Joseph was so considerate. She loved him so much.

There must have been thirty guests at a superb Christmas dinner. For an after-dinner story, Joseph embarrassed Bonnie by telling them that before today, Bonnie's best Christmas present was a Winchester repeating rifle.

Bonnie replied, "Then I lived in the woods in the Black Hills. There a good rifle is a prized possession. You often need to shoot your dinner. But now I do not need to shoot dinner."

Bonnie helped set herself up. Joseph had moved behind her, telling her to be still. He reached over her, held the necklace in front of Bonnie so she could see it, and then placed it around her neck. There were several wows and ooohs. Bonnie did not say a word; she just breathed heavily, her chest moved up and down the gems moving with her breaths. Bonnie was sitting with her hands on her lap. Joseph picked up her right hand and fastened the bracelet about her wrist. Bonnie had a broad grin with a few large tears running down both of her cheeks. She looked at the bracelet and she did not say a word.

Joseph looked at his mother, and she too had a couple of tears running down her cheeks.

Someone offered a toast, "To the Luxury Liner, the SS *Bonnie Duffy*."

Bonnie managed to raise her glass and say with everybody else, "To the Luxury Liner, the SS *Bonnie Duffy*."

After an extended pause, Dad came to the rescue, "I have been taking with the Union Pacific people, and they tell me that they are planning an express passenger train from Chicago to here and return, a day and a half either way. They say with interconnections, that's three and a half days from here to New York or Washington. That is unbelievable. The world is getting smaller."

One of the guests asked, "Bonnie, how long will it take for your around-the-world cruise?"

Bonnie replied, "A little over five months. We are not going a direct route. We will make many stops and do a lot of sightseeing. We will stop on six continents and cross five oceans and many seas."

"What if you took a direct route and made only necessary stops?"

Bonnie answered, "I guess about fifty to sixty days. We have not plotted that course."

A guest said, "It took Magellan's ships three years. And he died along the way."

Another guest asked, "Mr. Smithfield, how big a ship can you build?"

It was Joseph who answered, "We think it is feasible to build a ship one thousand feet long."

That got a few wows.

After the party, on their carriage ride to the ship, Bonnie was quiet.

Joseph inquired, "Are you all right? You are really quiet."

"I am confused. I am happy and mad at you at the same time."

"You are confusing me."

Bonnie sighed, "You have given me these beautiful jewels, but I do not deserve them. I am not a princess."

Joseph positively stated "I think you deserve them. To me you are a princess."

"I know. That is why I cannot be mad at you. But I am mad at you. You made me cry again and I do not cry. You promised no more surprises."

"I ordered the necklace and bracelet before I made the promise."

Joseph got a similar reaction minus the tears from Bonnie when the ship was named after her. She got over that. Maybe it was a woman thing.

They returned to their cabin with hardly a word said. Joseph was tired; it had been a long day. Bonnie was taking off her dress slowly. Joseph just got undressed and crawled into bed. He watches his wife as she removed all her clothing, leaving only her jewelry on. She admired the gems in the mirror. Joseph admired his wife, wearing only jewelry. Eventually she slowly took her jewelry off one piece at a time, laying them carefully on the dressing table in the precise location it was worn. Bonnie walked to their berth and crawled in, and rolled Joseph onto his back and crawled on top of him without a word, and slowly, meticulously made love to him.

Joseph woke in the middle of the night. There was a light on. Bonnie was by the dressing table, putting on her new jewelry. Joseph quietly observed. After admiring the jewelry, she took them off, neatly laying them down on the dressing table. Then she returned to bed and snuggled close to Joseph. Joseph concluded that he did not understand his wife, but he did love her. At least she liked her Christmas presents, even if she would not admit it.

In the morning, Bonnie resisted letting Joseph up. It seemed Bonnie could not get enough of her husband. Joseph was not complaining; he was getting worn-out though. Finally getting dressed for the day, Bonnie wanted the boxes for her jewelry, but Joseph had left them at the mansion.

Bonnie asked, "What do you mean you left them at Mom's? How could you have forgotten them? They are important."

Joseph responded, "I will send a messenger to pick them up. Will that be acceptable?"

"Where will I put them until I get the boxes? They are so beautiful. I love you so much. Why did you buy them for me? I do not deserve them."

Joseph put his arms around Bonnie and tightly hugged her.

She said softly, "I am not a good wife for you. You deserve a wife who is beautiful and glamorous, not a hobo gold miner."

Joseph replied, "You are not only beautiful and glamorous but you also have character, strength, and courage. You are a very special lady that cannot be replaced. You are the woman I've always dreamed of. You make me the luckiest man in the world."

Bonnie snuggled close to her husband as she said, "I am the luckiest woman in the world."

Bonnie finally carefully wrapped up her jewels in a couple of handkerchiefs and Joseph put them in his coat pocket. As they left for breakfast, Bonnie latched onto Joseph's arm on the side the jewels were on. Joseph wondered if she had her compact revolver on her. He knew she had one, but he pretended he did not know, and she did not tell him. A little secret. After all she had been through, he understood. Joseph mused, "My wife is my private bodyguard."

* * * * *

At breakfast, they sat with Charlotte.

Charlotte said, "Here is your cabin key. It probably still smells of shellac. It was just finished, one of the last cabins finished. And here is your private safe key and its combination." She then handed Bonnie a sealed envelope.

As they ate, Bonnie would occasionally reach over and feel Joseph's coat pocket for her jewelry.

In two days, they would be sailing. Charlotte was very confident in her job. She reported to Bonnie that everything was almost ready. Some of their passengers were to arriving by train. But there were no arrangements made to transfer luggage from the train station to the ship. Some of their passengers with special-tickets would be arriving tomorrow, a day before their scheduled departure. The special tickets gave the holder full use of the ship's first-class accommodations for six months starting on December 27, 1993, or the date specified on the ticket. There had been thirty-six special-tickets sold; that alone paid for the operation of the ship for three weeks. There were another 480 tickets sold for varying passages. Another 259 tickets were sold for their special inaugural cruise to San Diego. The inaugural cruise tickets were sold at a special discount price to try and fill the ship on its maiden voyage for advertisement purposes. A fully booked ship looked good on the front page of a newspaper. Steerage passengers were not counted as regular passengers. At departure, if necessary, some of the steerage passengers might be upgraded to second-class and second-class upgraded to first-class, to fill the cabins, making a fully booked ship.

Listening to the ladies made Joseph realize that building a ship was only part of the business.

After breakfast, they went to Bonnie's new cabin. On her door was a bronze sign, "Mrs. Joseph Smithfield, Owner's Representative. There were two rooms, one a comfortable day room with a substantial desk, chairs, and a couch. The second room had a double berth with built-in cabinets, a closet, and drawer space. It was small but adequate for a compatible couple. With the day room, it was spacious. Charlotte was right; it smelled of shellac. There was one port hole in the bedroom and two in the day room. They were opened, letting in fresh air.

Finding the safe was a challenge that Joseph took on with a passion. He was a little embarrassed that he did not know where the safe was on the ship he had been the construction superintendent.

This was not overlooked by Bonnie, who proceeded with making a point of his lack of knowledge. Bonnie was still Bonnie, and life was not boring with her. He loved her so, but until he found the safe, he would not speak of love and Bonnie would not let him be.

It was behind the desk, behind a hidden panel. The carpenters had done a superb job fitting the panel so it was almost invisible.

Joseph said, "Let me have the key and combination, and I will open it up for you."

"Look out of my way, it is my safe."

"You do not trust me?"

"I trust you completely, but it is my safe."

Bonnie was having difficulty with the combination opening her safe.

Joseph interrupted, "Better let me open it. You seem to be having problems."

Bonnie stated, "You are full of shit."

"What are you going to put in it?"

"My jewels and other things."

"What other things?"

Bonnie answered, "The jewels are beautiful. Thank you. I love you!"

Bonnie got the safe opened.

Joseph handed the jewels to Bonnie, and she examined them carefully and placed them in their boxes that had arrived, then into her safe. Joseph was looking the other way, but out of the corner of his eye, he saw Bonnie take something from under her dress and place it in the safe. It looked like a compact revolver. Joseph thought, *Lord help the person trying to rob her.*

Bonnie rechecked that the safe was locked at least three times before they left.

All the luggage carts as well as the housekeeping carts were recut to be narrower and equipped with straps that could be easily attached to the hand rails. Joseph thought that maybe the passages should be made wider on the next ship; it was still early enough in construction that the change could be easily made.

Joseph said, "Bonnie, if you see anything that should be changed on the next ship, please tell me."

"I will definitely tell you, be assured. I will make a list."

It did not take long till they had made the move. Some things Joseph would take back to the mansion, where he would live while Bonnie was gone, providing his mother did not drive him crazy. It took most of the rest of the day for Joseph and Bonnie to tour most of the ship. There were a few minor things they wanted resolved. First-class was like an abandoned hotel. Charlotte and housekeeping had done a final inspection. Second-class was receiving its final cleaning and polishing, as well as the dining rooms, casino, and smoking lounge. The deck railings were being polished, as well as all the ship's fittings and hardware. The entire engine room staff, including the oiler girls, were wiping everything down. The engine room deck was given a final swabbing. In the boiler room, they ran into the First Mate, Frank Krupp. Bonnie introduced Joseph and Frank, for they had never met before. Frank was also on an inspection. Frank gave orders that the air intakes needed a thorough cleaning.

Frank said, "Mrs. Smithfield, because of the importance of the air intakes and possible hazard of them taking on water in case of an emergency, I have initiated strict procedures as to their inspection and operation."

Joseph replied, "That is something that should be addressed in the design. With electricity, we could possibly have status light here and in the bridge."

Frank said, "In the interest of safety, maybe all critical hatches should have status indicators, if that is possible."

Bonnie had some issues she wanted to attend to, so she excused herself. Joseph and Frank would not miss her; they had some important issues to discuss and resolve.

* * * * *

Harvey Smithfield had a family business meeting before the *Bonnie Duffy* departed.

Joseph gave his report. "We have signed a contract to design and possibly build a heavy cruiser for the United States Navy for use in the Pacific Ocean. We will have to submit a design that will need to be approved by the Navy, built to their specifications."

"The second ship of the Bonnie class is under construction. The keel is laid, and the hull framing has started to take shape. There is going to be an engine and boiler upgrade that will improve efficiency, the electrical system is a part of the design. The accommodations are part of the original design. The design process had become more difficult, but the build will go smoother with less changes and work arounds. Although there is a lot of tension, Connie and Rachel are an asset to the firm, they make the male architects work harder. Connie and Rachel are not afraid to confront the male workers, women on the work site is a regular thing. Men that do not want to work next to women need not apply. A lot of the interior wood work will be prebuilt and will only need to be installed. This will decrease the time from keel laying and launch. Increasing the productivity of the shipyard. Adjoining property has been purchased to add another two slips. Three ships can be built at the same time. Shop space is being increased including a new plate rolling mill. Dad has talked of a thousand-foot dry dock in the future as funds become available."

Bonnie reported, "The SS *Bonnie Duffy* will be ready to sail on schedule. Ticket sales are exceeding what was forecast, and if things continued, the ship should be very profitable. There are still a few concerns that Miss Charlotte Gibbs seemed to be resolving in her usual confident way. There are still a few upgrades to the ship's systems that are being addressed. Joseph will sail on the Bonnie to San Diego to overseeing some final improvements, including some innovative safety devices. The morale of the officers and crew is high, we are ready."

Mom, "The department store is having the best year in our history, both revenues and profits are up." Then she held up the current issue of *Harper's Weekly*.

"We did not make the front page but page 3. The article is by Billy Frisco. He covered the Civil War, now he covers the Wild West thing. Why he is the reporter does not make sense to me. It is not his kind of story. It looks like the SS *Bonnie Duffy* is not a big story to them. The article says nothing derogatory but says that they will cover the new ship's progress. They say that they have concerns whether the new ship can live up to all the claims. To compete with the long established British maritime companies is definitely risky. He closes his article by wishing the SS *Bonnie Duffy* good sailing and luck."

"Even if Mr. Frisco is not that impressed, all that went on our little cruise are giving rave reviews. Some have bought tickets. Joseph and Bonnie, I am impressed and proud of both of you. The SS *Bonnie*

Duffy exceeds all my expectations. I need to find a good manager for the department store so I can go on a long cruise."

Dad said, "The shipping business is going through changes. We are contracting with other shipping companies and some independent ships to meet our obligations. The entire business is growing at a pace that makes for some real challenges. I need more ships to keep up with the demand."

Dad, in his usual way, complimented everyone on their good work and sent all on their way.

On the ride, back to the ship, Joseph told Bonnie, "My mother is very stingy with complements, her words give me some reservations, I wonder if she is up to something,"

Dinner on the *Bonnie* was the last time for a while that the crew could meet together, for tomorrow they would have passengers. There seemed to be a lot of enthusiasm of their voyage among the crew. Joseph and Frank were still making plans for ship upgrades. The Captain was a no-show.

Bonnie addressed the assembled crew, "I want to thank all of you on a job well done. I am proud to be part of this crew." Bonnie got a round of applause, which appeared to embarrass her.

The First Mate said, "Everyone here should be proud to serve on the finest ship on the seas." Again, a round of applause.

That evening, Joseph informed Bonnie that he would be gone in the morning. He had to arrange for materials and workmen to complete some of the improvements that were going to be made as the ship started its cruise. Bonnie wanted Joseph to join her in their brand-new berth, but he was busy at her desk with pencil and paper making plans. Eventual, Bonnie's patience ran out. She closed the portholes and assured their curtains were closed and checked the door, making sure it was locked. Bonnie removed her nightwear and crawled upon and across her desk and onto Joseph's lap. He got the message without Bonnie saying a word.

The next day, Joseph left early. Bonnie joined Charlotte for breakfast. They were ready for the first-class passengers, though there was still some work to be done in the second-class cabins and dining rooms. Bonnie would greet the passengers as they arrived while

Charlotte would try to complete their preparations. The First Mate joined them, asking if they needed anything. He complemented them, telling them he had never seen a ship so shipshape. Bonnie told him Miss Gibbs deserved all the credit.

The first passengers to arrive were Mr. and Mrs. Franklin. She was the sister of Mr. George Hurst. She said she had heard many good things about Bonnie and hoped they could talk later. The way they were dressed and the jewelry she had on said they were very wealthy. Next were Mrs. Green and her teenage daughter from Denver. The daughter's tutor would be traveling second-class. Mrs. Green had so much jewelry on that Bonnie thought it gaudy. She told Bonnie to call her Megan and her daughter Peggy. Megan seemed to know all about Bonnie, telling her that she was also a miner and had helped her husband when he first started mining, and the deeper they dug, the wider the silver vein was. Bonnie arranged that the tutor could come aboard a day early and get a cabin in the second-class. Next, a railroad baron's son and his bride on their honeymoon, around-the-world. An hour after, the inbound Union Pacific passenger train arrived. Bonnie was overwhelmed by arrivals and sent for a hostess to help. The sales department had not kept them informed of the last-minute ticket purchases. More passengers would be arriving tomorrow morning. By late afternoon, Bonnie felt frazzled. So many people, and she thought she was responsible to remember all the names and faces. The first-class boarding gangway would remain open all night with a hostess and deck officer in attendance.

Bonnie had to get ready for dinner, and Joseph just made it in time to dress. It was a formal dinner, and they had over fifty guests. At first, Bonnie was not going to wear her jewels, but Joseph insisted. He threatened to take them back if she did not wear them.

Dinner was a grand event. There was a small orchestra playing music in the background. Men in tuxedos and women in formal gowns. Bonnie was glad Joseph had insisted she wear her jewels, all the women had jewelry on, and Bonnie got several compliments on her jewelry. She realized she would need more formal gowns. The Captain did not show up; instead, he sent the First Mate. Dinner was a success, service excellent, food delicious with appropriate presentation.

The First Mate said, "On behalf of the Captain, I welcome all aboard. A toast to the lovely lady for whom this ship is named. I give you Bonnie Duffy, now Mrs. Smithfield. Please stand, Bonnie."

Bonnie stood and graciously smiled. She wanted to crawl under the table and hide as people raised their glasses to her.

Back in their room, Bonnie got into Joseph's face.

"You enjoy embarrassing me, don't you? I know you put Frank up to that! Why do you do that to me?"

Joseph calmly responded, "You are lovely even when you are angry. I love you even when you are mad at me, and I did not put the First Mate up to anything. It is tradition that a toast be made, especially in reference to the ship."

"You are lucky I love you. Otherwise, I would want to hurt you."

"Yes, you are right. I am lucky, especially to have a wonderful wife like you."

"Sometimes you make me so mad. Stop sweet-talking me. You are full of shit!"

"You like embarrassing me too. We do have fun, do we not?"

Bonnie, responded, "I love you. You make life interesting. And you are still full of shit."

Chapter 10

Departure

Joseph again left early in the morning, unfinished business. Bonnie was having breakfast in the dining room with many guests sitting at many tables. Breakfast and lunch were served like in regular restaurants. Dinner last night was special; all first-class passengers were invited to the Captain's table.

Charlotte came and sat with Bonnie. She reported that except for a few minor incidents, all was going well. They were ready; all their scheduled ports of call were informed of the tentative arrival dates and necessary clearance arranged. They would keep the home offices informed of their progress and needs by telegraph. The home office would try to arrange for their necessary provisions and supplies at each port. They had a large supply of canned goods and other nonperishable supplies, they would not go hungry, though, it might not the finest cuisine that they would endeavor to provide to their passengers. Charlotte and Bonnie agreed that they were enthused and yet apprehensive. They would be responsible for hundreds of well-to-do and influential people and for their needs. These people expected luxury and comfort for months on a daring and unprecedented voyage. Charlotte and Bonnie agreed that they would endeavor to meet their responsibilities and face all the challenges ahead.

Passengers were already boarding in all classes, and it looked like they were going to have a fully booked ship. Bonnie would again try to greet the first-class passengers. It was not necessary, but a nice touch.

A page hurriedly came up to their table. "Mrs. Smithfield."

"That is I."

"Ma'am, your presence is immediately requested on the bridge."

"What is it?"

"Ma'am, you are needed on the bridge. I do not know why."

Charlotte said, "Better go. Keep me informed if you need anything."

Arriving on the bridge, Bonnie was met by Frank and three other ship officers and the ship's Physician.

The First Mate, Frank, said, "Ma'am, we have a problem. The Captain was found in his berth dead."

The Physician took over. "Ma'am, it appears he had a heart attack in his sleep. There is nothing that suggests foul play. I am ruling it death by natural causes. That can be overruled if there is an inquest. The local authorities have been notified and should be arriving shortly. My sincere condolences, ma'am."

Bonnie looked at Frank. "We are to sail in a little over six hours. What does this mean?"

The First Mate said, "Ma'am, we cannot sail without a Captain."

"As First Mate, do you not automatically take command?"

"At sea, I would take command. We at port, our home port, and we have to have a Captain to sail."

Bonnie asked, "What are the qualifications for Captain?"

"Ma'am, Master's papers and appointment by the operator and or owner."

Bonnie asked, "Do you have Master's papers?"

Frank responded, "Yes, ma'am, but I have only recently received my master's papers. A ship like this is given to an experienced and proven Captain."

Dad arrived. "I am Harvey Smithfield, President of Smithfield Steamship Lines."

Bonnie said, "Mr. Smithfield, we have lost our Captain."

"So I have been informed."

Bonnie, "Sir, we are scheduled to leave in six hours."

Mr. Smithfield stated, "Your departure will have to be postponed. I do not have an experienced Captain available. One will have to be found."

Bonnie felt panicked; she had worked so hard for this, and so many people were depending on this ship sailing. So many people had made arrangement and schedules had been made, promises given.

Bonnie asked Dad, "Mr. Smithfield, can I see you in private in my office?"

His reply was, "Certainly."

Bonnie led him to her cabin.

When Bonnie left her cabin, in fifteen minutes, she witnessed the Captain's body being removed on a stretcher. All the crew present saluted as his body passed by.

Bonnie then confronted the First Mate. "Sir, can I see your Master's papers?"

The First Mate retrieved an oil-skin envelope for his jacket vest pocket and opened it, then he presented his papers to Bonnie.

Bonnie asked, "Can I take these with me? I promise to return them."

"Yes, ma'am."

In another fifteen minutes, Bonnie returned to the bridge with Mr. Smithfield. Bonnie returned Frank's papers to him.

Mr. Smithfield approached the First Mate. "Mr. Frank Krupp, you have been highly and persuasively recommended. Congratulations, Captain. The SS *Bonnie Duffy* is yours. Take good care of her. Here are your sailing orders." Handing a letter to Frank, "In my absence, you will receive your orders from Mrs. Bonnie Smithfield, my representative, whom I believe you know. In accordance with maritime law, at sea, you will be in command with the authority and responsibility for the safe operation of this ship and the safety of the passengers and crew. I would like to see this ship depart on schedule. Good sailing."

The new Captain replied, "Yes sir. Orders understood. Thank you, sir."

As Dad walked out, he said to Bonnie, "Good job, Bonnie. It appears you are unstoppable."

There was quiet for a moment. Then the new Captain read his orders out loud for all present to hear.

The Captain then gave orders to the officers present, "Inform the crew of the loss of our Captain and inform them of the change of command. Let us prepare this ship for sea."

All the officers left, following their orders. The new Captain and two seamen that were assigned to the bridge remained.

The Captain looked at Bonnie. "Thank you, ma'am, for your confidence in me. Now I have a problem. At thirty-six, people will question that I am the Captain of this ship."

Bonnie replied, "Congratulations, Captain! I do have confidence in you. Excuse me, I have passengers to greet."

The last few passengers boarded. Then just as the boarding gangways were being raised, Joseph arrived, almost having been left behind. His excuse was he heard the Captain had died and he did not think a replacement was available.

Joseph asked, "Have you met the new Captain?"

Bonnie replied, "Yes."

"What is he like?"

"He is all right."

"Do you think he will work with me on the improvements?"

"I do not know, you will have to ask him."

"Is Frank still the First Mate?"

"No, he has been replaced."

"Who is the new First Mate?"

"I do not know; I have not been introduced yet."

Joseph stated, "I have brought material and workers, and I will have to work with a new Captain and First Mate. Can you introduce me to the new Captain?"

Bonnie said, "I think he is busy now. Wait till we get to sea."

"Are you still the owner's representative?"

"Yes."

"Can you talk with the Captain and explain the importance of the upgrades?"

"Maybe. Promise to not embarrass me anymore."

"Bonnie, you are a pain in the you-know-what."

With a smirk, Bonnie replied, "That is part of my job being a wife."

Joseph said, "Let us go up to the observation deck and watch the land disappear off into the horizon. We are supposed to be on our honeymoon."

They held hands on the observation deck, and Bonnie said, "We are invited to the Captain's table this evening. Dinner's at six."

Joseph asked, "Who decides who is invited to the Captain's table?"

"I do. Excuse me I need to get to work."

Bonnie met up with Charlotte in their office.

Charlotte asked, "The rumor is that you hired our new Captain."

"Mr. Smithfield hired him."

Charlotte asked, "Did the Captain thank you for your confidence in him?"

Bonnie asked, "What is our passenger count?"

"We are full. Some wanting first-class are sailing second-class, some wanting second-class are sailing steerage. Mr. Smithfield had to step in and close ticket sale. Sales wanted to sell tickets that we did not have a berth for."

"How are sales at other ports?"

"Good," Charlotte said. "And did the Captain thank you?"

Bonnie replied, "I recommended him as a possibility."

"I heard that Mr. Smithfield said nothing stops you."

Bonnie responded, "Charlotte, you should not listen to rumors. How are we set for stores with so many bookings?"

Charlotte responded, "You like to change the subject, do you not? All right. We need to have a meeting tomorrow with all the group heads. May I suggest ten o'clock a.m.? We are operating at capacity. We did not anticipate this demand."

Bonnie assured her, "I have confidence in you. You make the calls."

Charlotte replied, "This is my second time at sea. The first was last week. I have always worked at the business from an office. I am getting a little nervous. It is quite different when you see the people and not just numbers and names on paper."

Bonnie stated, "We are on a good ship with good people. We will make it work, one way or another. And this is also my second time at sea."

* * * * *

Bonnie prodded Joseph to be a little early for dinner. She had specified some of the seating: the Captain at the head of the table, on the port side, next were Joseph, herself, Megan and Peggy Green; and after that, it was random from the first-class passengers. Bonnie wanted to get to know Megan Green. She sounded like she was interesting, definitely outgoing. Bonnie had a message sent to the Captain: "Arrive a little late."

Bonnie was ready. As Frank approached, she rose. "A toast to Captain Frank Krupp, the Master and Commander of the SS *Bonnie Duffy*."

All rose and toasted the Captain as he stood at the head of the table. Bonnie got from Joseph the dirty look she had hoped for. Bonnie inquired as to the First Mate.

The Captain informed her, "Mrs. Smithfield, the First Mate appointment is traditionally made with the advice and consent of the owner-operator, and at this time, that would be you."

Bonnie got another look from Joseph; this time, though, it was a smirk with a little nod. Bonnie could almost hear him say, "You got me back. You just wait, now it is my turn." Bonnie has a list of the guests. She had already introduced the Captain, and next she introduced herself and her husband.

Bonnie started to introduce Megan when Megan stood up. "I am Megan Green, and this is my daughter Peggy. Please, everybody just call me Megan. If you cannot remember Megan, just call me anything you want. I am hungry! Let us get the introductions over with, and dig in."

Everybody followed suit. First names seemed to be the preference.

Over dinner conversation, Megan and Bonnie became friends quickly. Megan told a story of lighting the wrong end of the fuse on dynamite and waiting two hours with her hands over her ears, in anticipation of the blast, while burning up a whole roll of fuse that was not connected to anything. Megan told the story with her hands and sometimes her whole body in animation, and she had everybody laughing. Her daughter Peggy, though, looked embarrassed.

Bonnie was goaded into telling a story, she felt obligated. "At about thirteen, while mining, I slipped and fell into the creek. I came up with a minnow in my blouse. Not knowing what it was, I pulled my blouse off in front of my grandfather. My grandfather said, "Until you grow some bosoms, you are just minnow bait." It was not as funny as Megan's story, but people politely laughed.

A lot of the guests ended up telling stories. The Captain's table got a reputation of being rowdy and fun. They would try to randomly rotate the guests at the Captain's table every evening, with appropriate exceptions. A tradition was started. At the Captain's table, everyone introduced themselves and first names were acceptable. If someone did not want to be rowdy, they could decline the invitation.

After dinner, Bonnie and Joseph went for a walk on the deck. The moon was out, near full. Joseph told Bonnie that he went over every one of his questions and Bonnie's answers, as to the new Captain, he found no lies, but, a lot of deception. Bonnie replied that Joseph had not asked the right questions and asked if he still wanted her to talk to the Captain for him. Joseph did not reply, but asked Bonnie why she did not tell the story working as a mule skinner, saying how she could honestly embellish it with some colorful language. They ended up at the bow. Joseph's ship was cutting through the waves and water in beautiful form.

Joseph said, "We are running at three-quarters speed. The engines have to be broken in before full speed is attempted. Three more days cursing, and they will be broken in."

Bonnie put a finger on Joseph's lips, looked him in the eyes. They embraced in the moonlight with the sound of the ship parting the ocean. They kissed.

Bonnie whispered, "Let us start our honeymoon."

Turning they stopped. There, illuminated by the moon above and hundreds of small lights was the Bonnie Duffy looming over them. The moonlight was dancing on the wave tops, flanking the enormous unreal image, the nippy ocean air stirring their hair. The smell of the sea, the feel and muffled sound of the throbbing engines, the feel and warmth of each other's presence. All their senses were stimulated.

Bonnie asked, "Is this a dream?"

Joseph answered, "Yes, it is a dream we are sharing."

They stood side by side, arms around each other, letting themselves be overwhelmed by their senses.

The trance was broken by a seaman making his rounds. "Are you all right. It is nippy out here."

Joseph responded, "We were just admiring the ship."

The sailor turned and looked, "She is a proud ship, sir."

They retired to their room.

Early the next morning, Joseph was off working with his crew installing the hatch status indicator system. Charlotte and Bonnie were discussing some passenger concerns and trying to prevent future passenger concerns. One lady complained to Bonnie that the Captain's table was disruptive to their dining experience. Bonnie suggested they either dine earlier before the Captain's table was seated or accept an invitation to the Captain's table and set a good example. The lady accepted the invitation to the Captain's table, for herself and her husband. Bonnie decided to seat them between Megan and the young newlyweds from Pittsburg. They were young and seemed to be on the rebellious side, their family name represented wealth.

Bonnie then went to the bridge. With the deceased Captain, Bonnie felt unwelcome and barely tolerated. Now she was welcomed and offered a Captain's chair to sit in. Bonnie was told she was always welcome, except in an emergency situation. She asked how the speed was set and determined. They were presently at three-quarters speed. She was shown and explained the operation of the engine room telegraphs. There were three telegraph mechanisms, one for each engine. Via a mechanical mechanism, orders could be given and acknowledged from the bridge to the engine room. The engine room could also signal that they had a problem and the bridge could acknowledge receipt of the information. Bonnie was shown an instrument, a knot meter, also called a log, that indicated they were traveling at seventeen knots. Bonnie was fascinated and wanted to learn more, but she had other duties that needed to be attended to.

Bonnie inquired, "Captain, do you have someone in mind for First Mate?"

Bonnie was introduced to the Second Mate, Adam Fitzpatrick. He looked to be the same age as the Captain.

The Captain said, "Ma'am, Mr. Fitzpatrick is an excellent seaman and understands the operation of a large steamship. He is respected by his fellow officers and his subordinates. I believe you will find him very personable, though he has limited experience dealing with passengers."

Bonnie asked, "Do you recommend and want Mr. Fitzpatrick as your First Mate?"

The Captain responded, "Yes, ma'am."

Bonnie offered her hand to Adam, saying, "Congratulations, First Mate. Do I need to sign anything?"

The Captain said, "No, ma'am, nothing to sign. Thank you, ma'am."

Adam said, "Thank you, ma'am."

Bonnie responded, "I want to get out of here before I hear one more *ma'am*. It makes me feel old."

Bonnie stepped out on the bridge-deck and paused around the corner and listened.

She heard Adam's distinctive Irish accent, "Now that is a lady."

The Captain agreed, "Yes, she is a lady. Warning, she is one tough lady who will not hesitate putting you in your place. She deserves respect."

As Bonnie headed for her meeting, she wondered, Was she really that bad?

Charlotte had everything organized. They were to arrive in San Diego at dawn the next day. Six teams of crew members would go ashore with six shopping lists. There were concerns that their next stops, Acapulco, Mexico, and Valparaiso, Chile, would not have all they needed. They had a lot of passengers disembarking, especially second-class, but they had reservations for additional passengers, some with special tickets. Charlotte believed more reservations were being taken while they were at sea. There was no way to communicate. They would get their messages sent by telegraph to San Diego. They would depart San Diego at dusk. Bonnie signed vouchers for cash at the ship's bank. Some vendors did not extend a line of credit to Smithfield Steamship Lines, especially for fresh produce, so cash would be needed.

That afternoon, Joseph found Bonnie in her office that she shared with Charlotte, doing paperwork. He insisted that she accompany him to the bridge. He showed Bonnie a panel that had red buttons on it. Joseph asked that Bonnie watch the panel. The ship's small signal whistle was blown. One at a time, ten of the red buttons lit up. Joseph was excited; he explained that the ten red lights indicated that ten hatches were closed. Bonnie did not understand the significance. Joseph explained that if there was an emergency, for example, a storm or a collision, the officer on duty could look and see if the necessary hatches were closed. If one or more hatches were open that should be closed, he could order crewmen to go and close the hatch.

Reading the names of the hatches on the panel, Bonnie said, "I see. If these four lights are on, the air intakes are all closed and the boilers would downdraft!"

"Yes, you got the idea. I plan to patent the idea. What do you think?"

"I think my husband is brilliant!"

Bonnie than looked at the First Mate, who was on duty, and said, "What do you think?"

First Mate answered, "Ma'am, I think your husband is brilliant."

Bonnie stated, "I was referring to the light panel."

First Mate answered, "Ma'am, it is valuable to the bridge crew in determining hatch status without having to send a crewman to investigate. As long as it works properly, ma'am."

Bonnie quipped, "I think the panel should be checked daily to ensure its reliability." Bonnie then said to Joseph, "Now let us get out of here before I hear one more *ma'am*."

On their way to their cabin to dress for dinner, Joseph said, "You were sure hard on the new First Mate."

"The Captain warned him."

"Sometimes I just do not understand you."

Bonnie replied, "Just understand that I love you, and everything will be all right."

That evening, Joseph and Bonnie dined together. This would be their last dinner together for some time. Bonnie wore her blue dress and all her jewels. As they were leaving the dining room, it was obvious to Bonnie that the people at the Captain's table were enjoying themselves. The lady who had complained to Bonnie earlier had a very loud and distinctive laugh.

They went for a walk on the deck. They noticed they were passing near an island that was visible in the moonlight. On the end of the island was a navigation light. Its light was reflected in the waves. They sat in deck chairs holding hands, watching the island pass by.

* * * * *

They retired early that night, for they both had a full day tomorrow that would start early. Neither of them slept a lot; they both wanted to savor every minute with each other.

Joseph informed Bonnie he was leaving the two women carpenters and a machinist onboard with instructions to complete a few projects and aid in the ship's operations. They would be part of the crew. Bonnie informed him that the two women carpenters were already part of the ship's crew and worked for her.

The *Bonnie Duffy* was greeted by the whistles of the other ships in the harbor. They docked in a very seaman-like manner, with four tugboats helping nudge them up to the dock. Even though it was early, there were a lot of spectators wanting a look at this new ship. Nothing like it had ever cruised the Pacific Coast before.

Joseph had midmorning reservations on the *Southern Pacific* that would take him and his crew back to San Francisco. Bonnie wanted to go see him off, but Joseph said he did not want a long goodbye; it was already hard enough. Bonnie watched him go down the gangway. Her eyes moistening as he turned and waved goodbye.

It was going to be a busy day, and Bonnie had duties that called.

Charlotte was going to tend to supplies and prepare for their new guests. Bonnie would thank their departing first-class passengers, wish them well, and greet the new arrivals. Many of their passengers that were continuing wanted to spend the day ashore, shopping and sightseeing in San Diego. It was not long, and Western Union delivered a stack of telegrams. One was from company sales, informing them they were booked up clear to Buenos Aires, Argentina. There was a long list of passenger names. There were another twenty-two special-ticket passengers boarding in San Diego. If things went as planned, these passengers would disembark here in June after completing a world circumnavigation. This gave Bonnie an idea, a special medallion for all that completed their circumnavigation, "Smithfield around-the-world traveler." They would not be needed until they returned to San Francisco.

It was not long, and Bonnie had arrivals and departures at the same time. Cabins were not ready for some of the arrivals. Bonnie was surprised that they were understanding, realizing that they arrived early and appreciative that they were permitted onboard. Cabin preparations for these early arrivals would be given first priority. Bonnie was proud of herself; she was managing a lot of things all at once and felt she was doing a good job.

About noon, all the departing passengers were gone and half the arrivals had boarded. Most all the cabins were cleaned and ready, and the few remaining cabins had double staff working on them. In an hour, all the cabins would be ready.

The Captain came to Bonnie, "Ma'am, may I see you for a moment?"

Bonnie asked one of the hostesses to take over for her.

The Captain said, "Ma'am, the local police want to see us."

At the service ramp were two police officers. They showed the Captain a couple of papers, and Frank handed them to Bonnie. One was on Smithfield stationery; it was their shopping list for produce. The other was a carbon copy of a receipt for a cash withdrawal of two hundred dollars from the onboard bank. It was signed by Bonnie.

The police officer reported, "These papers were found on a man with his head bashed in. Witnesses had seen the attack by two men. Later, two men fitting the description were seen buying train tickets to Los Angeles. After a chase, they were arrested."

Bonnie had a page go get Kirk, the Food Services Manager. Bonnie told the Captain she would attend to the problem and asked him to make sure the ship was ready to sail on time. The Captain knew Bonnie could handle the situation but wondered if the policemen could handle Bonnie.

Bonnie and Kirk were taken to the morgue. The victim was their head chef. The police had in custody two of the ship's cooks that were to help the chef in getting fresh produce. Bonnie and Kirk signed a complaint, and each of them signed an affidavit as to the facts as they knew them.

The Police Captain told Bonnie that with the witnesses and evidence, the two suspects would probably be hanged for murder and robbery. Bonnie asked if she could have the shopping list, but she was informed that it was evidence. So instead, Kirk copied the list onto another piece of paper. Bonnie asked if she could see the prisoners.

Bonnie told them, "You two are stupid! I regret that I cannot stay and watch you be hanged for a hundred dollars each, that you did not even have time to spend." Bonnie thought of the two murdering crooks she had shot, an incident she did not want to be reminded of. The Irish Redhead ire would come out.

Bonnie signed a receipt and was returned 196 dollars; they had managed to spend four dollars of their ill-gotten gains. Bonnie and Kirk then went to the farmer's market and filled the shopping list. They hired a teamster and his wagon, and they managed to return to the ship and get the produce aboard. People watched as a lady in a fine dress handled bags of potatoes, onions, and baskets of fruit and vegetables like a man. Bonnie was angry at the idiots and was working off her ire.

They departed on schedule, with four tugboats helping pull them into the main channel. It was dark as they cleared the outer harbor markers. The residents of San Diego got to see a ship lit up with electric illumination.

Aboard the ship, Charlotte and Bonnie dined together. So far, they had managed to keep things on track. In three days, they would be docking in Acapulco, their first foreign port of call. They were short a chef and two cooks, but they could manage for now, although eventually, they would have to be replaced. A chef was promoted to head chef by the Kirk. Shopping money would have to be handled differently. Possibly, the Captain could suggest something.

As they were ready to leave, the Captain approached their table.

"Ladies, it is a pleasure seeing both of you."

Charlotte acknowledged, "The pleasure is ours. Would you like to join us?"

"Sorry, your companion has me assigned to the big table over there. Miss Gibbs, how about lunch tomorrow?"

Charlotte said with a subtle smile, "About twelve, would that do?"

"Miss Gibbs, I will see you about twelve tomorrow." Then he addressed Bonnie, "Mrs. Smithfield, you farther-in-law seems to know you well. I did hear him say *unstoppable*. Impressive, the way you handled the situation today. Thank you for dealing with it so well."

Bonnie asked, "Would I be an inconvenience if we went up the bridge for a little while? I would like to see it when it is dark out."

"You are always welcome on the bridge. That is standing orders, except in an emergency. Excuse me, I am late to my table. I have my orders."

Charlotte and Bonnie went to the bridge.

On the way, Bonnie asked, "Lunch with the Captain, need a chaperone?"

With a look of "none of your business," Charlotte said, "No, thank you."

The First Mate welcomed them to the bridge, and introductions were given. The moon was nearly full, and the First Mate pointed out an island to starboard, telling them it was South Coronado Island, Mexican territory. They were invited to sit down. Now there were two Captain's chairs with a railing for the feet. From these chairs, one could look out the windows and see the horizon. A crewman was out on the deck, looking into an instrument; they were told it was a sextant that measured the angle from the horizon to a star, or in this case, the moon, to determine their position on the sea. They would take a reading on several heavenly bodies and look in a book the Nautical Almanac and, with a little mathematics, pinpoint their position on a chart. Bonnie wanted to know more but decided to not overstay her welcome, though she did ask how the hatch indicator panel was working. The First Mate informed her that they check it daily and it was working properly. Charlotte asked what she was talking about. Bonnie informed her that it was one of Joseph's inventions.

They then begged their leave and departed.

Bonnie found her bed big, cold, and lonely. She would have to get used to it.

Tomorrow would be New Year's Eve.

CHAPTER 11

Eastern Pacific

In the morning, Bonnie was walking through the passageway to breakfast when she was stopped by a woman in her fifties that Bonnie recognized as having boarded in San Francisco with a special ticket. She whispered to Bonnie, "I do not like to complain or cause trouble, but there is something wrong with the casino. I really like this ship, but I do not like what I hear of the casino. They wanted money for some friends and I to sit to a table for a friendly game of cards." She winked as she continued her stroll, saying, "Thank you for the information."

Bonnie thought, *What a nice lady*. She did not want anybody to know that she had a complaint, or gave a warning. She did not want to make a scene; she wanted to be discreet.

Bonnie met up with Charlotte for breakfast. Bonnie asked Charlotte what she knew about the casino. Bonnie was informed it was managed by a Bernard Hobart. He seemed secretive and kept to himself. Charlotte said she had heard a few curious comments from some of her staff, but nothing specific. The casino is not taking in a lot of money; their bank deposits are small. The casino was to be self-supporting, but the ship was having to supplement their payroll. Charlotte also told Bonnie there were several poker games going on around the ship other than in the casino. She thought the casino was to be a fun game room, not just for gambling. That was what Bonnie believed the casino was supposed to be.

Bonnie then wished Charlotte good luck at lunch and told her to wear something really pretty, something that would show off her nice figure. Charlotte, in her own discreet and subtle way, told Bonnie where she could put it.

Bonnie had never gambled, except some friendly bets with her grandfather and her husband. These bets had never been for financial gain buy for fun. Bonnie thought she should at least go and have a look. It was mid-morning; there was very few people in the casino, and there appeared to be more employees than passengers. There were three men playing what Bonnie believed to be roulette. She did not recognize the men and thought they were probably second class. First and second class had access to the casino. The casino was clean and neat; the employees were dressed appropriately, although some of the women were dressed like saloon women.

Bonnie was approached by a man that had the demeanor and dress of a maître d'.

"Ma'am, may I be of service? Possibly some refreshment? Or maybe you would like to try your luck at a game of chance?"

Bonnie said, "No, thank you. I am on my mooring stroll, just passing through."

Next Bonnie was approached by a young lady. She was obviously a waitress. Her dress was cut low, and her corset fit to lift her breasts. Bonnie knew it was an eye-catcher for men.

"Would ma'am like something to drink or eat?"

"No, thank you."

Bonnie walked slowly and easily, a woman on a leisure stroll.

She noticed two men that gave her pause. They looked like and had the demeanor of Pinkertons. They were against the wall near the roulette table watching the three men gambling. There were raised voices. The three men gambling were not happy. The two Pinkerton-types moved close, and one said something to the three gamblers. The three gamblers headed for the door followed by the tough guys. Bonnie thought, this was not what she envisioned as healthy entertainment.

There was one man sitting alone in the corner. He was dressed like a real dandy. Bonnie had seen him before, though she had not been introduced. She believed he was Bernard Hobart. Bonnie wanted to confront Mr. Hobart and find out what was happening, but instead, she just stared at him for a moment, getting his attention. Bonnie was hoping he got the message: the casino was not his and she was watching him.

Bonnie continued her stroll. She went to the bow to feel the wind in her face and hair. It awakened her senses and brought visions of her Joseph. As she turned to go back into the ship, she saw the two Pinkerton-type men from the casino. Were they following her? Bonnie strolled down the deck toward the stern, greeting people as she went. There was Megan at the rail, looking out to sea.

Bonnie greeted her, "Megan, how are you this fine morning?"

"Soaking up the scent and view of the sea. Woo, somebody is in trouble."

"Am I missing something?"

Megan said, "The casino goons are watching somebody."

Bonnie responded, "Probably me, should I be scared?"

"They do not scare me. Though, I heard they roughed up a couple of second-class young men that got a little rowdy."

Bonnie asked, "Do you think they serve a function?"

Megan replied, "They are the casino complaint department."

Bonnie said, "I think I need to inform them that there is no casino complaint department."

"Honey, please be careful. If I were you, I would get yourself a little army."

Bonnie asked, "What is the gossip of the casino?" Her curiosity had been piqued now.

Megan answered, "Now I do not know it as a fact, but the games are fixed, and if someone wants a friendly game, the casino boss want a cut. The casino wanted money from the girls and I to have a friendly game of bridge at one of their tables."

Bonnie asked Megan, "Can you gather me a little audience, right here, in about ten minutes?"

"You got it."

Bonnie continued her stroll down the deck, making it easy to be followed.

Megan shouted, "Everybody! Everybody! We have a situation that needs everybody's attention."

Bonnie turned and strode up the two casino goons.

"I am Mrs. Smithfield, I represent the owner of this ship. Do you two work for Bernard Hobart?"

"Yes, ma'am, we do."

Bonnie informed them, "My condolences, you are unemployed as of immediately. You will be put ashore in Acapulco. Questions?"

"We work for Mr. Hobart."

"He does not have a job either. You two behave and go to steerage, or if you prefer, I believe our brig is vacant."

Two tough guys were surrounded by about twenty people applauding a young lady that had just humiliated them. Being that they were aboard a ship, there was nowhere for them to go. They knew who the young lady was, but they believed young ladies were supposed to be easily intimidated. They had their own concerns of their boss's behavior and his orders; they knew he was pushing his luck.

Bonnie had momentum and was not going to slow down. Her blood was up; the Irish Redhead was in command. Word spread fast, and as Bonnie entered the casino there were several passengers and some of the crew who wanted to witness the expulsion of Mr. Hobart, a man who had made enemies and few friends.

Bernard Hobart was sitting in the corner, shuffling a deck of cards.

"I am Bonnie Duffy Smithfield," she said. "And you are fired! Get your ass to steerage, where it belongs."

Hobart said in an authoritative and demanding way, "This is my casino! I have a contract. These people work for me."

The Captain showed up.

Bonnie told him, "Captain, this man, Bernard Hobart, was employed to manage the casino, I believe he has mismanaged the casino and has used intimidation, including attempting to intimidate me, for his own gains. I would like him confined to a cabin in steerage pending an investigation."

The Captain said, "I have received several written complaints against Mr. Hobart and his associates varying from extortion to intimidation. Mr. Hobart, you will go with these sailors to the brig, where you will remain pending an investigation." Mr. Hobart had a revolver removed that was hidden under his coat.

Hobart exclaimed, "This is bullshit! You will get yours. You cannot prove anything."

Bonnie added, "Want your dismissal in writing?"

The Captain said to her, "Mrs. Smithfield, may I talk to you in private?"

In private, the Captain said, "I made a big mistake, you made a big mistake. We both were aware of a problem, but we did not communicate. You reacted first. You involved the passengers. I was trying to not involve the passengers. It is okay to be unstoppable, but can you just slow down a little bit?"

Bonnie replied, "I am sorry, he just angered me. He sent his goons to try to intimidate me. I did not want to bother you with a little employee problem."

Captain explained, "It is more than an employee problem. I planned on explaining it to Charlotte at lunch. Can you let Charlotte and me investigate this matter? We will keep you fully informed. Now what are you going to do with the casino?"

Bonnie thought a moment. "Can you suggest someone to run the casino?"

The Captain replied, "You."

Bonnie thought to herself, *He sounds like my father-in-law. Now what am I going to do?*

Bonnie realized she had done it again, gotten herself into a situation where she did not know what she was doing. She would do the best she could; there was no other choice. She went to the casino and had a "Temporarily Closed" sign put up. Then she gathered the staff together.

"When we went on our little shakedown cruise, I saw many people here in the casino having fun, gambling for kernels of corn.

This casino does not have to make money, but it does have to be fun. It is for the pleasure of our passenger. As usual, I do not know what I am doing. All of you know what you are doing. I am going to get out of your way and turn this place over to you. It is New Year's Eve. Have a party tonight, celebrate."

Bonnie decided to use her father-in-law's business plan, to let good people do their jobs. She would observe and give these people an opportunity. Besides, she did not have any other ideas. Hopefully things would work out for the better in spite of her ineptitude.

Bonnie continued her walk. She realized she had reacted with emotions; she did not think out what she was going to do. She involved the passengers. At sea, this ship belonged to the Captain, and she had violated his authority. She did not know the outcome of her actions that was to come. Bonnie concluded she would have to change her ways; she would have to learn to control her temper. Her decisions affected many people. She had to be responsible, would have to accept the consequences of her decisions. She had to learn to use her authority wisely. There were nine hundred passengers and about six hundred crew and servants aboard, along with about four hundred in steerage.

Bonnie went back to her cabin and wrote an apology to the Captain. She had overstepped her authority and abilities. She would endeavor to consult him in all matters affecting his ship. She would let Charlotte handle the problems. She would accept the responsibility and consequences of her actions. Bonnie sealed the letter in an envelope and sent it to the Captain by a page.

She went to the office she shared with Charlotte. She had decided to move her things to her day room desk, letting Charlotte run Passenger Services. Charlotte came in and closed the door.

Bonnie asked, "How was your lunch with the Captain?"

Charlotte said, "Very good, we mainly talked ship business."

Bonnie admitted, "I really made a mess of things this morning. I have decided to let you run this office before I really make a mess of things."

Charlotte stated, "No, you better not abandon me. I need you. I am a paper person. You are a people person. People look up to you."

Bonnie replied, "I never quit on anything. I just have to learn patience, perception, understanding, and my limitations. I have to grow up."

Bonnie and Charlotte went over all the things they thought were needed. A couple of chefs several cooks, a few more maids, more help in the laundry, and an assistant for each of them. They had not planned for or envisioned that they would be fully booked. They original optimistic forecast was to have an 80 percent occupancy, not 100 percent. The financial people determined that the breakeven point would be an occupancy of 60 percent. If their high occupancy continued, the *Bonnie Duffy* would pay for itself in less than two years. They would try to fulfill their needs in Acapulco, but the language would be a problem. Cash for shopping would still be a problem.

Late afternoon, Bonnie went to the casino. It had many passengers seeming to enjoy themselves. Megan was playing bridge with three other ladies.

As Bonnie walked by, Megan stopped her. "Honey, this casino is wonderful. Thanks to you."

The sound and feel of the ship changed, a lower pitch to the ever-present throbbing of the engines. Bonnie had been thinking of her oilers, and she felt guilty putting girls to work at such a horrible job. She felt that she had little choices, as the alternative was to send them back to the streets. The only consolation was they would be given an opportunity, regular meals, and a warm, comfortable place to sleep.

Descending into the engine room, Bonnie saw Smitey looking at a bank of gauges. Smitey looked up and made a gesture with his left hand. Bonnie looked up, and there on the narrow catwalk at the top front of each engine was a small human form. The one on the port side that Smitey appeared to be looking at and motioning to was turning a large valve. The three telegraphs were pointing at one-half speed. They had slowed the ship down. Bonnie watched, intently observing; these huge engines were terrifying and fascinating all at the same time. Smitey waved both of his hands over his head. Two of the people headed down narrow ladder to the engine room deck, while the third picked up an oil can next to her and headed to the top of the starboard engine.

Smitey, seeing Bonnie, came over to her and said, "They are learning, ma'am."

Bonnie asked, "The girls are doing a good job?"

"Ma'am, most of the boys I have trained over the years have been a little addled. That is probably why I got them. These girls are smart. They learn fast. See how quickly we synced the engines? If they were boys, I could easily make engineers out of them."

"Why did we slow down, and why does being a girl makes any difference?"

"Ma'am, you will have to ask the bridge about the speed. Your second question—they will not let a woman be an engineer. It is unheard of!"

Bonnie went up to the oldest girl, who had just come down off the engine. "How are you young ladies doing? Anything you need?"

"Ma'am, we are doing really good. We love our jobs! We are important to the ship."

Bonnie watched as the other girl and a man that looked like an engineer recorded something in a journal. Upon Bonnie's inquiry, she was told, "We have to keep records, ma'am."

Bonnie concluded that Smitey and the engineers were making the girls feel at home, at least useful.

Up on deck, Bonnie looked, and again, she had gotten oil splatters on her dress. A hazard of going into the engine room. Bonnie went and changed, immediately putting soap on the stains, hoping the stains would come out. Laundry had given her some special liquid soap with instructions. Laundry was getting tired of trying to clean the stains from her dresses. It seemed to work.

On the bridge, it was explained that they wanted to arrive at Acapulco at dawn. The harbor is not well marked, and a daylight entrance would be the safe way. Slowing down would give them the proper arrival time. The log read that they were traveling at thirteen knots. The Navigator took the time to show Bonnie the chart in the pilothouse. He explained dead reckoning and told Bonnie if she waited fifteen minutes, the sun would set and she could see how they got a celestial fix at dusk. The Navigator and the officer on the bridge went out on the bridge-deck with sextants, pencil, paper, and a pocket watch. Bonnie followed. The Navigator explained how he used the sextant to accurately measure the angle from the horizon to a star. He took three measurements to three different stars. With each measurement, he recorded the time to the second with a rail-road watch he carried. Each of the stars he used had a name, and he explained that only certain stars were used. They were called navigation stars.

In the pilothouse, both the Navigators used a book called the Nautical Almanac to look up the stars' position in the celestial sphere and the celestial sphere's position to Earth at that particular date and Greenwich Mean Time. They amazed Bonnie with their mathematics. They both put three lines on the chart using some instruments. All six line crossed at the same point. Bonnie was told that was their fix, their position on the ocean. Their dead reckoning position was within a fraction of a nautical mile to their fix. They would be arriving at Acapulco at dawn in a day and a half.

Bonnie met up with Charlotte for dinner. Tomorrow, they would meet with the Captain, getting his input on handling the ship's money on shore. It had been a long day, and they decided to celebrate with their passengers and bring in the New Year. The New Year's celebration spilled over into the dining rooms and onto the decks. They had gone south enough that it was a mild evening. The party was a success.

The next day was uneventful. The Captain agreed to send a ship's officer and a couple crew members with the shoppers. He also agreed to try to hire some local law enforcement for additional security.

Bonnie ask the Captain, "Why cannot the oiler girls be trained as engineers?" The Captain got his ship's crew roster. "I have five oilers listed. All are listed with only initials and the last name of Adams. They all have legally signed on as crew with an initial and last name, their mark as required. As an oiler of this crew, they are eligible for training, appropriate for their jobs, if sponsored by the Chief Engineer and it does not interfere with their duties."

Bonnie said, "It sounds like you have that memorized."

"As Captain, I must abide by all rules, laws, and regulations. There is nothing in the regulations requiring me to ascertain gender. There are requirements of being able-bodied. I believe the oilers are all able-bodied to fulfil their responsibility as oilers."

Bonnie said, "Captain, you are a good man."

The Captain had the First Mate and Charlotte investigate Mr. Bernard Hobart. He was not as smart as he thought he was; he had a second set of books that proved he was embezzling money. They could not find anything on the two goons, so they would be put ashore with enough money to get a low-cost train ticket back to San Francisco. Mr. Hobart's stash of cash was confiscated, and he would be turned over to the Mexican authorities, with sworn statements of his crimes. He would be their problem. It was said that with the Mexicans, Mr. Hobart would have a real problem. He would be probably placed in hard labor to earn his keep.

Acapulco was also known on the charts as Guerrero. It was conquered by Cortez in the 1500s and established as a shipbuilding center and trade center to the Orient for the Spanish.

Bonnie woke up early. It was a couple of hours before sunrise. The sound of the ship seemed to be the same as when she went to sleep. They were still cruising along steadily. The operation of the ship and navigation yesterday had stimulated Bonnie's curiosity. She decided to get dressed and test the invite to the bridge.

The bridge was busy. The Captain was on the bridge.

"Good morning, ma'am."

"Good morning, Captain."

"We are nearing port. You are welcome to stay if you keep out of the way and quiet."

"Yes, sir."

The Captain, Second Navigator, one bridge officers, one helmsmen, one crewman, and four lookouts out on the bridge-deck and two lookouts in the crow's nest were on duty on the bridge.

Bonnie stretched to see—south, thirteen-knots. Stepping into the pilothouse that was lit with red lights to help in night vision, she looked at the chart with the current DR position and she concluded that soon they had to turn east. A steward in ship crew's uniform asked, "Would ma'am like coffee?" Bonnie did not know the bridge crew had their own steward. "Two lumps, please."

Shortly, Bonne got a cup of coffee that she enjoyed as she sat in one of the Captain's chairs.

The Captain ordered, "Rudder two points port, to east by south."

The order was repeated by the helmsman as he turned the ship's wheel. Bonnie felt nothing, curiosity got to her, and she bent over, craning her neck to look at the compass. The ship was very slowly turning toward the east. The moon was waning; it was half-full over the east horizon. In the distance to the east appeared to be mountains dimly lit by the moon. Bonnie realized that they were relying on their charts and instruments for their destination was not visible, they were headed to what looked to be a wall of mountains. This was almost as exciting as running alongside a freight car preparing to hop, just not as physically exerting. The engines were doing the work with the oiler girl help.

There was a dull whistle; the bridge officer held a horn, on a flexible tube to his ear, and he said, "Crow's nest reports a light three points off bow to port."

From the pilothouse, the Navigator said, "Acapulco light, twenty-seven-second period, one point off course to port."

If Bonnie had not been warned and looking in the right direction, she would have missed it, a quick flash of light. The Captain and the bridge officer held up their watches and watched in the direction of the light flash. There was another flash of light. The Captain said, "Twenty-seven-second period, Acapulco light."

The Second Navigator explained, "A period is the time the lighthouse light takes to revolve once. Each light had a different period so they can be easily identified from sea by the time it takes from flash to flash."

A lookout on the bridge-deck was using an instrument mounted to the rail. "Acapulco light thirteen degrees to port."

The Navigator confirmed, "Bearing verifies plotted position."

The helmsman announced, "Course, east by south," returning the wheel to its center position.

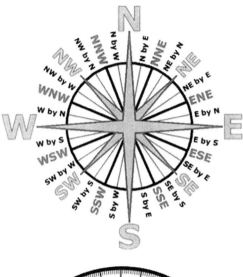

The Navigator confirmed, "Course, east by south."

The Captain turned to Bonnie. "Ma'am, Acapulco dead ahead."

"Thank you, Captain."

Bonnie felt like she understood most of what had just happened—so professional, so exacting, so scientific, making one turn heading to port and verifying their plotted position. She was hooked and wanted to know more.

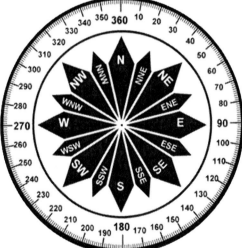

The Second Navigator seen Bonnie's curiosity and explained, "The old tradition used compass points. There are thirty-two compass points, starting at north, then north by east, north-northeast, northeast by north, northeast, northeast by east, east-northeast, east by north, east, east by south, this pattern continues all the way around the compass till north is again reached. The newer system uses degrees. There are 360 degrees in a full circle. North is 0; east, 90; south, 180; west, 270. Each compass point is equal to 11.25 degrees." We sometimes call a half point, like one half point north of northeast, which would be between northeast and northeast by north, which would be about thirty-nine degrees.

Bonnie thought she would understand with practice.

Gradually the mountains neared, the light flashed every twenty-seven seconds and the day started to break. A few lights started to be seen ahead as the eastern sky started to turn from black to purple and the stars started to fade. Upon orders, a crewman pulled the lanyard, ship's large deep whistle sounded one long blast, probably waking up many on the ship as well as many in Acapulco. The city, harbor and shoreline started to become visible. Bearings were continually taken on landmarks such as mountain tops, an ancient fortification, the harbor light, as well as a church spire. These were called out to the Navigator in degrees and plotted. The Captain ordered the engines slowed to one-quarter speed.

The Captain ordered, "Steer four points to port to north-northeast," meaning how much the rudder was turned, and the next course. "Port engine full stop, starboard engine half-speed ahead."

This could be felt as the ship resisted the force of the engines and rudder to turn the immense hull. The ship slowly came about.

The Captain ordered, "All engines, one-quarter ahead."

Helmsman announced, "Course, north-northeast."

The Captain often checked on the plot on the detailed harbor chart that was now being used.

They were headed directly toward the city.

Bonnie started to be concerned. Were they going to stop, turn, or end up on the beach ahead?

The Captain ordered, "Mid-ship engine dead stop, rudder hard to port, port engine half astern."

The vibrations of the engines working could be felt and heard as the ship was turning.

As they turned, they slowed and appeared to be moving slightly sideways toward the approaching dock.

The Captain ordered, "Prepare all lines, to starboard."

The bridge officer went to the bridge-deck and shouted over the starboard side, "Prepare all lines to starboard."

As they crept forward, nearing parallel to the dock, the Captain ordered, "Starboard engine dead stop, mid-ship engine one-quarter ahead, port engine one-quarter astern."

Bonnie slipped out the door to starboard and watched from the bridge-deck as the ship slowly moved to the dock.

The Captain ordered, "All engines dead stop."

Under the directions of the bridge officer, lines were thrown that were used to pull large hawsers that were put around the mooring bollards. The hawsers were pulled by the ship's steam-driven windlasses pulling the ship up to the dock. The sun rose over the mountains just as the spring lines were set and tightened and the gangways were extended to the dock.

The Captain came next to Bonnie, saying, "The wind and tides were right. Tugboats were not needed."

Bonnie expressed, "Amazing, totally amazing! Thank you, Captain."

The Captain escorted Bonnie into the bridge, pointing to the main whistle lanyard, and said, "One long blast please, wake them up. The SS *Bonnie Duffy* is in port."

As Bonnie pulled the lanyard, she realized that she could not cover both ears as she blew the whistle.

* * * * *

Today was going to be a big day. They were to depart late afternoon. Bonnie was almost finished with breakfast when Charlotte showed up.

Charlotte said, "You are up early. I assume we are safely in port? Big day today."

Bonnie, "I wish I did not have to conduct business. This port looks enchanting, a sightseer's paradise."

A page showed up with three stacks of telegrams addressed to passenger's service, Bonnie, and Charlotte. As another page went through the dining room announcing the names of people who had telegrams. They quickly went through the telegrams; they were booked up to Rio de Janeiro, with only several openings on to

Havana. Most of the telegrams were of general business concerns. Bonnie got two personal telegrams, one from Joseph telling how much she was missed and one from her father-in-law, telling her she was doing a good job.

Charlotte prepared a telegram to the main office requesting some additional supplies be arranged for in Valparaiso and they were on schedule.

Bonnie prepared a telegram to Joseph. "MISS YOU MUCH STOP BEAUTIFUL LARGE SIZE DRESSES HERE."

One telegram she prepared for her father-in-law. "FIRED HOBART CASINO CROOK STOP REPLACEMENT WORKING OUT."

As planned, Bonnie and the Captain would take care of official business with customs, Mexican authorities, and the local bank. Charlotte would try to hire more help and coordinate the ship's shopping. Charlotte was to be accompanied by three of the ship's crew and one ship's officer, she laughed as she joked, "my own little army." The local bank's security would handle all cash transactions between the ship's bank and the bank on shore; it was mainly to exchange foreign currencies.

Exiting the ship, Bonnie and the Captain were approached by a man that said he represented the New York Times here in Mexico, wanting an interview. "Yes, the ship was on schedule without incident. No, we had not broken any records. Yes, we have all cabins filled, no berths available. Can you please excuse us? We have business to attend too?"

Everything went smoothly. Their US dollars were appreciated. The Mayor presented Bonnie with a tintype photograph of the SS *Bonnie Duffy* nearing the dock.

The Mayor said, "This it was a historic moment! The *Bonnie Duffy* is the largest ship to ever visit Acapulco and the only major passenger liner to visit."

Bonnie politely smiled, "As beautiful and friendly as your historic city is, I am sure more people will come to visit."

Bonnie manage to do a little shopping. Acapulco was known for its silversmiths, so she bought herself an exquisite, finely worked silver bracelet and her mother-in-law a gorgeous silver tea service. Keeping mother-in-law happy helps keep husband happy.

As Bonnie returned to the ship, she as surrounded by four happy girls skipping on their way, dressed in matching plain dresses and work boots. Upon inquiry, she was told their sister stayed onboard to keep the generators and other equipment oiled. They each had bought a small bag of candy, and they were taking their sister a bag. Smitey had given them an advance on their pay. They were on their way back to the ship for they had chores to do before departure. Two of them had to get some sleep; they had the first half of the night watch. Bonnie admired these young ladies. They were determined and had good attitudes. She promised herself to support them but give them their own space to grow and develop.

They reminded her of herself.

Charlotte had been successful. She had vegetables and fruit, some that Bonnie had never seen before. Charlotte said she had done some sampling and the passengers were in for some new delightful tastes. She had two cases of a local alcohol to sample called tequilas, saying it was inexpensive. There were also chickens, ducks, and pheasants in cages, sides of beef and swine, crates of eggs, cans of fresh milk and cream. Everything, not in stores, to feed almost two thousand people for over a week.

Bonnie watched as Charlotte gave an orientation through a translator to twenty new employees, the majority of them women. Later Charlotte told Bonnie that five of her new hires spoke English as well as Spanish. Charlotte had a plan: some of the present employees would be promoted letting the new hires fill in the open positions. That way, they would have more supervision by experienced people. They would be working bosses, making a couple more pennies an hour.

The coal bunkers were filled to capacity.

Midafternoon, the ship's whistle blew, warning all of their impending departure. Time to hurry back to the ship or be left behind.

Bonnie excused herself; she wanted to be on the bridge. Again, she was in awe. The hawsers were removed, they nudged forward with the midship engine, rudder hard to starboard, against a spring line running from the ship's bow to a bollard on the dock behind the ship pushing the stern away from the dock. Then they reversed, rudder hard to port, against a spring line running from the ship's stern to a bollard at front of the ship pushing the bow and stern further away from the dock. The lines were thrown free, and slowly they reversed away from the dock. All this required exact engine and rudder control. Eventually, the ship seemed to pivot about, the ship pointing toward sea.

As they exited the harbor, a three-mast sailing ship was coming into the harbor. The wind was light, and they had all their sails set coming into the large harbor. Many people lined the rails to see the sailing ship. The sun was setting, and for a brief moment, the sailing ship's sails all turned bright red, creating something magical, one view Bonnie would never forget.

By dusk, they were to sea headed south.

Bonnie was about to head for the dining room when the Captain ordered all engines full speed ahead. Bonnie felt like she should hold her breath as the throbbing of the great engines accelerated. Many aboard sensed the change in the rhythm of the engines and wondered what speed this new ship could obtain. The engine room and boiler room were forewarned and ready. The boilers had been stoked ready for the demand for steam, and the engines were given extra attention in being oiled. A small group on the bridge as well as a small group in the engine room watched their logs knot meters, as the speed slowly rose. It took a while for the gauge to creep up to 22.4 knots.

The First Mate exuberantly shouted, "Yes, if we can maintain that speed, we can set records."

The Captain responded, "We will give her one hour and then back off a little. I want a full evaluation before we push our ship too hard. If we can maintain twenty-knots across the Atlantic, we will have bragging rights. Mr. Fitzpatrick, you have the bridge. I am going to the engine room and boiler-room to check on their status."

Bonnie asked, "Captain, may I accompany you?"

"If you promise to stay out of the way."

In the engine room, the air was filled with a mist of oil. It was difficult to see across the room. The noise was deafening. Another dress stained. The crankshafts were spinning so fast they were a blur. The connecting rods were a blur going up and down and around. At the middle engine was

Boiler Room of a Large Steamship 1890s

a small figure that was squirting oil on the crankshaft journals. Bonnie thought, next to the engine. the girl looked like an ant busy at work, ready to be crushed.

Smitey approached, "Captain, they look solid and sound happy."

The Captain said, "The ventilation is bad."

Smitey replied, "Yes, sir, several ventilators are positioned wrong. We are correcting the problem. We also over-oiled, a precaution. We are still breaking the engines in."

The Captain gave his orders, "In an hour, ease off a bit to twenty knots. After, I want a written report of all pertinent factors and your professional assessment. I would like a full report of pressures, steam temperatures, coal consumption, and engine-bearing temperatures, along with a written assessment of sustaining this speed. Also, I have looked in the regulations and see nothing about gender to become an engineer. They probably overlooked it, thinking it would never be an issue. Woman engineer, ridiculous. Keep up the good work."

Smitey said, "Thank you, sir."

The boiler room was filled with activity, men wheeling wheelbarrows with coal, other men shoveling coal into the boilers. There was a wind blowing from the air intakes to the boilers. The heat from the boilers was so intense that Bonnie had to step back and keep turning to keep from being overcooked on one side. Gazing into the firebox of the nearest boiler, she saw a blinding bright blue-white glow that made her think of hell. Bonnie followed the Captain to the other side of the boilers; there was again men feeding the boilers. The boilers were stoked from both sides.

They were approached by a man with no shirt on. "Captain, sir."

The Captain asked, "Can you maintain this pressure and temperature?"

"Yes, sir, to keep it up for days will require more hands. Men can only work so long and hard, then they start to fall over."

The Captain inquired, "Overall opinion of the boiler room?"

"Good ventilation. Better than most ships I have sailed on. Boilers solid and well built, access to coal bunkers good, and stoking acceptable. Most men can throw the coal to the center of the fire box."

The Captain said, "Keep up the good work. I will see if I can get you more help."

"Thank you, Captain. And thank you, ma'am. First time I have been visited at full steam by a lovely lady."

They went up a ventilator shaft. The down draft was quite noticeable.

Bonnie tried to return to her room without being noticed to change out of her oil-stained dress, but she was stopped twice. People wanted to know their speed.

Bonnie made it to dinner just in time before the kitchen closed. Charlotte was hosting the Captain's table. The people wanted to know how fast were they going. The engines had slowed some. The hour had passed.

Bonnie announced, "Out top speed was 22.4 knots, now 20 knots for evaluation."

It appeared that everyone on the ship knew what was going on. Most of the men acknowledged their approval as well as several of the ladies. Bonnie thought, *Most Luxurious, Safest, and if we can add Fastest, Smithfield will be the number one name in steamships.*

As Bonnie went to sleep, she was thinking about what she had overheard in the bridge. Seven days to Valparaiso at twenty knots; that would be a record.

At breakfast, Megan asked to talk to Bonnie. "I heard a rumor that some of the maids, and pray tell, some ladies in the engine room are illiterate. I have talked to my daughter's tutor. She is willing to help them. With your permission, she will hold classes in the crew's cafeteria."

Bonnie replied, "Bless you, I will help pay her salary. What time will she be available?"

"Let us let them work that out. They all have their work schedules. Peggy, my daughter, wants to help as well. I think it will be good for Peggy. She is a little bored."

Charlotte arrived for breakfast.

Bonnie told her, "School in the crew's cafeteria, any problem?"

"Wonderful!" she exclaimed. "You got a teacher?"

"Yes, Mrs. Green's daughter's tutor."

Megan stated, "Willa is a college-educated lady, and my daughter Peggy will also help. Maybe it will keep Peggy out of trouble. You know, that idle mind thing."

Charlotte enthusiastically said, "I will be glad to arrange it."

A few of the steerage passengers were signed on as crew to help man the boilers.

Late afternoon on the second day, they passed west of the Galapagos Islands. Besides being the fabled islands of Charles Darwin, this marked passing over the equator. The whistle was blown, and King Neptune with his court paraded around the deck. All choosing to participate who did not bow to His Majesty got doused with water by his siren Consorts. Some of the passengers had come prepared with costumes, other did some creative work. That morning when Bonnie went to the bridge to check on their progress she overheard the bridge crew talking. They were discussing crossed the equator and the traditional ceremonies. At first, when Bonnie questioned the crew, they were reluctant in telling her; they actually discreetly laughed at her being naive. Bonnie did not take offence. Instead she went along with the tease, and after some pleading, she was told of the traditional celebration. With the help of one of the seamen, she managed to get a pair of raggedy pants, worn-out shirt, oversize boots, a large red bandanna, and with her beat-up cup-bowl, she had a costume. With the red bandana tied about her head, with her hair tucked in, some soot smeared on her cheeks and forehead, nobody recognized her. Several people put some change in her cup-bowl, and Bonnie quickly reverted to being Bennie B, a role she knew well. She had about two dollars in change in her cup-bowl before Megan figured out who she was. People wanted to know if a teenage boy had sneaked up from steerage. Megan was the siren queen in charge of water dousing. Even though Bonnie had deeply bowed to King Neptune, when her identity was discovered, she got doused with several buckets of cold water.

After the ceremonies, everyone got ready for dinner and the costume party to follow. Bonnie went to the boiler-room, and in the heat, her costume quickly dried. She went through the crew's mess and saw about twenty young women and some boys at a corner table. Peggy and her tutor, Willa, were conducting a class on English. Bonnie noticed some adults at the back of the class intently listening. They had a blackboard installed on the wall, where they were writing the lesson. Bonnie was stopped returning to the first-class decks, she was told to return to steerage, where she belonged. It took some explaining, and one of the junior officers finely recognized her and let her pass. Bonnie mused, "Eight years previously, steerage would be where she belonged, though she could not have afforded passage in steerage." She believed she could still fit into the steerage culture.

At dinner, several people wanted to examine Bonnie's cup-bowl. They concluded that it had been made from a peach can. When asked where she had procured it, Bonnie told the truth. That got a lot of laughter. Bonnie was complimented on how well she played her part. She was almost credible, though she could never pass as a real bum. Bonnie wanted to explain the difference between bum and hobo and tell them that she was a hobo. Bonnie did not know rather to take it as a compliment or insult. She concluded that it was meant as a compliment since they did not know the truth. Next time, she would go as a mule skinner; after all, she knew the language. She would need a costume. Bonnie received the award of having the most creative costume, which entailed a photograph taken of her with King Neptune and his court. The ship's photographer offered copies for thirty cents.

Later, Megan asked Bonnie, "Is the story of your cup true?"

"Sometimes the truth is less believable than fantasy."

Megan replied, "It is fun to deceive people with the truth."

The next five days were taxing on the crew. All of the crew and passengers knew what the goal was, and all were rooting for success. It was the pride in being a part in achieve a goal: 3,382 nautical miles in 169 hours, one hour over seven days. They were running short of fresh vegetables, fruits, eggs, milk, and most all perishables. They had underestimated their needs. Complaints were few, though most inquiries were as to their progress. The progress was posted as plus or minus in minutes on every watch change by the ship's Navigators.

On the seventh day, Charlotte said, "Nobody but us aboard this ship knows of our great goal."

Bonnie responded, "The last I looked, we were plus seven minutes. Win or lose, accolades or boos are immaterial. It is the quest that matters. The important thing is we complete the journey."

The coal bunkers were emptying. It would be near dark when they entered the harbor. The plan was to anchor out until daylight once they made the large harbor. The anchors had never been used before. If the anchors failed, they could slowly steam out to deep water and await daylight. Many cases of champagne were found, and win or lose, the bottles would be open and shared upon reaching harbor.

As they neared, Bonnie went to the bridge. Bonnie was learning quickly, a look at the chart and she knew barring some mishap they were going to make it. Charlotte joined the bridge crew, Bonnie suspected that she and the Captain were discreetly spending time together. As they neared the port there seemed to be an extra effort. They had been cruising at 20 knots; now they increased to 22 knots. Shore was visible; bearings were coming in and plotted.

As they were nearing the port, the Captain said, "Mrs. Smithfield prepare to blow the whistle, one long blast please."

Bonnie responded, "It is Miss Gibbs's turn to blow the whistle."

Charlotte protested, "No, it is not my place."

Bonnie grabbed Charlotte's hand, putting it on the whistle lanyard, saying, "This is an order. Pull long and hard."

As Charlotte was prepared to pull, she was interrupted by several loud booms, from the cannons in the sixteenth-century fortress. Also, heard were other steam whistles. They were being greeted and saluted. Did they know?

The Captain ordered, "Miss Gibbs, blow long and hard. We have a lot of steam."

They made it, with twenty-two minutes to spare.

They successfully anchored for a well-deserved rest. Rest would have to wait, though as everybody wanted to celebrate. The people in Valparaiso lined the docks, marveling at the great steamship lit up with Edison's illumination.

Come morning, there was still enough fire in the boilers, and with two tugs, they lay alongside the dock of Valparaiso Chili. They were greeted by many people on the pier.

At breakfast, flapjacks with syrup or preserves, Bonnie and Charlotte discussed where to send telegrams to announce the record-breaking voyage. A messenger brought them a large stack of telegrams. Most were giving congratulations on their speed, distance, and endurance record. One was from President Grover Cleveland. After Bonnie had read the one from Mr. Harvey Smithfield, it was apparent that the Captain had telegrammed the boss just before leaving Acapulco, telling him of his plan. Mr. Smithfield and his staff could not resist using it for publicity. It was also great publicity for Acapulco and Valparaiso. They were given a special edition of the local newspaper that had an illustration of the Bonnie Duffy. They could not read the article, though it being in Spanish. Charlotte would have to get one of her translators to read and translate it for them. The one benefit, involving the two governments made it undisputable.

Later, the Captain joined them, apologizing, he did not think that they would take the risk of embarrassment if they failed. Charlotte explained that publicity was all good. Even if they failed, the fact that they made the attempt would be a publicity success.

The Captain and Bonnie were welcomed by many government officials, and all their paperwork went without any problems. They were given a certificate stating their exact arrival time at port, signed by the provincial Governor and Mayor. Smithfield Steamship Lines had established a line of credit with the Bank of Chile, making paying for coal and most other supplies easy. They were given checks that could be easily used and would be easily verified and cashed at the local bank.

They were two days ahead of schedule. That meant three days in port to leave on schedule. They met up with Charlotte and two chefs, with escort. The Captain volunteered to go with her on her ship's shopping mission. Today they would only purchase enough perishables for two days since they were staying three days. They were informed that there was a coal shortage; there was labor problems in the US coal mines. They would have to pay a premium, and even so, there might not be enough top-quality coal available to fill their bunkers.

Bonnie went for a walk along the huge harbor. There were a variety of ships and boats. Everything was painted colorful. The brighter the paint and the greater the contrast, the better. Bonnie found a chandler, and she could not resist. Quickly, she realized she did not have enough money on her and went back to the ship and made a withdrawal from the ship's bank. On her walk, she saw a silversmith. A leisurely walk turned out being two missions. At the silversmith's, Bonnie inquired about making medallions commemorating their record-breaking cruise. When Bonnie told the silversmith, she wanted fifteen-hundred he got excited. The language barrier became a problem, and Bonnie needed an interpreter.

The man at the chandler spoke a little English. Bonnie spent her salary for who knows how long, because she had never talked to her father-in-law about salary. One quality sextant, one Nautical Almanac for the current year, one book on celestial navigation, and several books varying from seamanship, tidal charts, to navigation lights and aids to navigation. Bonnie knew that these purchases were impulsive, but her curiosity was unstoppable. Her time on the bridge had been a tease and challenge to her.

As Bonnie arrived at the ship, struggling, carrying a bundle of books and a mahogany box with polished brass hardware, she was met by Charlotte and the Captain.

The Captain offered to help Bonnie with her load, relieving her of the mahogany box.

He noticed the label. "I am impressed—a gift for someone, or do you want to be a Navigator?"

Bonnie explained, "I thought I might learn a little about the ship's operation."

Captain asked, "Working your way up to take my job."

Bonnie quipped, "Do not be ridiculous." Then she asked, "Charlotte, after I put these things away can I borrow one of your ladies that speaks Spanish that can translate for me."

Charlotte responded, "Sure, let us put your things away first."

Charlotte, Bonnie and Candida, their interpreter, went to the Silversmith. Charlotte thought it a great advertising promotion to have a commemorative coin minted of their record-breaking cruise. She did question giving them away. Perhaps, she suggested, they should have them for sale? Bonnie knew that she would be testing her authority. What would her father-in-law do? Fire her. Working with the silversmith, he would make dies to restrike a Chilean two-reals silver coins. It would be a little larger than a US quarter and contain two-tenths of a troy ounce in silver. On one side would be the image of a steamship with four funnels surrounded by the words "SS *Bonnie Buffy*, Smithfield Steamship." On the tail side would be the outline of Southwestern North America and South America with a line from the position of Acapulco to Valparaiso, surrounded by words and numerals, "3382 N-Miles Avg. 20 Knots Jan. 1894." The silversmith drew what the coin would look like. It would be oval, and a hole was to be added to make it distinguishable from currency and make it easily attachable to a chain or added to a watch fob. Bonnie gave the silversmith twenty-five pesos as deposit for a sample to be ready the next afternoon. With approval, upon inspection, fifteen hundred medallion coins would be struck for the sum of 450 pesos, about 430 US dollars. Candida was told to keep the coins a secret.

The next day, the ship was moved to the coal dock. The bunkers were filled. Half of the coal was bituminous and ignite coal, lower quality than the hard anthracite coal that was preferred. All the Anthracite coal that was available was purchased at a premium cost. Smitey said they would manage with the lower-quality coal, but they would not have the power for full speed. He would use the lower-quality coal first, saving the hard anthracite for when it was needed.

The handful of medallion coins that exceeded Bonnie's expectations were delivered. They were shiny works of art. Bonnie gave the silversmith another one-hundred pesos, and the final payment would be upon delivery of the balance of the fifteen hundred medallions, promised the following afternoon. Bonnie sent her father-in-law a telegram telling him of her purchase of commutative medallions.

While they were at the coal dock, most of the passengers enjoyed the day ashore. Valparaiso was a colorful, friendly, and interesting place to visit. The locals treated the passengers as honored guests. Many souvenirs were purchased from the local artisans and craftsmen, and many sampled the local culinary fare.

Their last day in port was hectic.

Valparaiso was a good port to replenish supplies. Around noon, the silversmith delivered the medallion coins. The medallions were taken to the ship's bank where they were weighed, counted, and inspected. The silversmith received payment in full along with a fifty-peso deposit to remake the tail die with the outline of the world surrounded by the words "World Circumnavigator 1894."

Before departure, Bonnie received a telegram from Dad: "Save me a medallion."

Valparaiso was a wonderful port of call, and everyone enjoyed their stay. All the crew had shore leave. The oiler girls had received their first pay, and they each bought a bag of candy and they pooled their money to buy a couple books to read.

Finally, resupplied and rested at sunset, they headed for sea. The funnels were blowing heavy black smoke burning the lower-grade coal. Although it was plotted as a seven- to eight-day trip, 3,030-nautical miles to Buenos Aires, they were planning for ten. Around the Cape of Horn could be challenging.

CHAPTER 12

Cape Horn

Shortly after departure, Bonnie gave a medallion to a few special people. Putting on a stained dress, Bonnie made a special trip to the engine room and gave five medallions to the two girls on duty, with instructions to share with their sisters. The two girls were elated to receive the medallions. Smitey got medallions for himself and the others engineers and his crew.

At dinner, it was announced that all passengers and crew who sailed from Acapulco to Valparaiso could get a complementary commemorative silver medallion from the bank. This was announced in first-class, second-class, and the crew's cafeteria, as well as posted on the bulletin boards. Distribution would by the honor system. Bonnie had a bag of a hundred medallions to give out.

As the city disappeared over the horizon, they headed south-southwest. At dusk, Bonnie was on the bridge, handing out medallions and, with her new sextant, trying to get a sighting on Sirius, one of the fifty-seven navigational stars. The First Mate, Mr. Fitzpatrick, who was on duty, took pity on Bonnie and helped her. Studying the book and actually doing it were different things. Bonnie only got one-star sight before the horizon blended into the night sky. With Mr. Fitzpatrick's help with the math and charting, one line of position was plotted.

Mr. Fitzpatrick, "Not bad for a first try. Only twenty-seven nautical miles off. It takes practice."

Bonnie realized it was a lot more difficult than the Navigators made it look.

Bonnie asked about two graphs on the pilothouse wall.

Mr. Fitzpatrick explained, "We are trying to establish a coal consumption speed relationship and distance traveled. We burnt 1,430 tons of our 1,500 tons of coal on our voyage from Acapulco to Valparaiso. That was 8.6 ton an hour at 20 knots. We have recorded our coal consumptions at 12, 14, 16, and 20 knots, and the distance traveled per ton. The graph clearly shows that on long voyaged we cannot travel at a full speed without exhausting our coal. If we had traveled at 22 knots on our last voyage, we would have not made port. Other factors will have to be considered including the sea conditions, wind, coal quality, and our cargo load."

It was mid-winter in the north, mid-summer in the Southern Hemisphere. The days were getting shorter the farther south they traveled. After dinner, Bonnie went to her cabin to study her books. She remembered looking at the charts in the pilothouse. Bonnie had noticed that their projected course would take then to fifty-eight degrees south latitude. Reading about rounding Cape Horn and sailing in the south fifties and sixties latitude started to scare Bonnie. The only thing good was that they would be traveling west to east with the prevailing westerly winds. Bonnie read where Captain Bligh spent thirty-one days trying to round the horn and gave up after traveling only eighty-five miles, he tried to go east to west.

That night, Captain Ahab visited Bonnie's dreams. They were locked in a battle to follow Moby Dick around the horn in seas that were as high as their main mast. Bonnie woke up with all her bedding in a ball that she had her arms and legs wrapped about. She had been hugging the mast in her dream to keep from being washed overboard.

Looking at grandfather's watch, it would be breaking daylight soon, Bonnie got dressed and headed for the bridge with her sextant, Nautical Almanac, celestial navigation book, and her grandfather's railroad watch. She went up the stairs from the officers' quarters, all inside the ship, to the pilothouse. She looked out the bridge windows; it was raining hard. It was raining so hard the foredeck could not be seen. The telegraph was set at full speed ahead on all three engines; the log, knot meter, said they were traveling at seventeen knots. The lower-quality coal was dropping five knots off their maximum speed. The Captain was on the bridge, and Bonnie asked permission to leave her sextant in the pilothouse, saying it could be used by others. The Captain gave permission, stating that he would have her name engraved on the plate that was provided for the owner's name. The Captain warned that the barometer was falling quickly and they might be in for some heavy weather.

Bonnie took her books to study and went to breakfast. Charlotte arrived as Bonnie was finishing her breakfast. They soon concluded that everything was going smoothly. The casino was popular and operating as planned. Neither had any issues that needed addressed. Bonnie did warn Charlotte of bad weather. Charlotte congratulated Bonnie on her commemorative medallion, saying that people want to buy any extras. They discussed having more struck and both agreed that if they had more struck, the value would decrease. For now, they were special. The medallions were meant as a keepsake for those who were part of the endeavor.

Charlotte was planning on spending the day getting her bookwork up to date; she still had to enter some of their Valparaiso transactions in the books. Bonnie was going to spend some time studying celestial navigation.

By midday, the ship was rolling back and forth, and Bonnie was starting to feel nauseous. Bonnie decided to get out of her berth and go to the bridge to check on their progress. It soon became apparent why Joseph had insisted on hand rails everywhere. Bonnie had difficulty walking, and the hand rails were necessary to keep from being thrown onto the deck. Going to the dining room to get something to drink, she passed many who were definitely seasick; the ship had the smell of vomit. The odor added to Bonnie's queasiness, and she headed for the rail. She went to starboard, the wrong side of the ship, and was immediately pelted with wind and driven rain. Her dress was blown up over her head. With difficulty, she managed to reenter the ship. She barely made it to the leeward rail to find that she was joining others losing their breakfast. It was easy to find water running with the torrential rain for Bonnie to wash off her mouth and chin. Bonnie breathed deeply and willed herself to overcome the seasickness and returned to her cabin to put on dry clothes.

With willpower, Bonnie made it to her room and then the bridge. The higher she went, the more violent the rolling motion was. The only thing that could be seen from the windows was the lookouts on the bridge-deck in their foul-weather gear. Bonnie checked the chart; they did not have a fix since the last evening's sights. They were using dead reckoning, calculating course and speed, putting in factors for currents that were estimated on the charts and drift caused by the wind. The Captain was in the pilothouse. Bonnie listened in while he and two of his officers discussed their options. The decision was the Captain's, though he wanted his officer's opinions to weigh the options. The Captain ordered the ship to half-speed and to a new course of west-southwest. They were to go in the wrong direction, into the wind and waves. After they were on their new course, the Captain acknowledged Bonnie, who was trying to be inconspicuous so she would not be asked to leave. She was curious.

The Captain said, "You look fit. I thought you would be under the weather by now. If it were not for the passengers, I would have held course and speed. Slowing and heading into the wind will lessen the ship's motion and ease the passengers discomfort. It will add more time to our passage. We will be gaining on our southerly course A compromise. Do you agree?"

Bonnie replied, "Captain, I have full confidence in your decisions. Besides, I do not have the knowledge or experience to even guess at what course of action would be appropriate."

The Captain said, "When the rain clears, you might want to come here and go out on the bridge-deck and see what a well-found ship can do. I think the rain will clear by late afternoon. A little advice—you are better to stand and move about than sit or lie to avoid seasickness. The aft of the ship and closer to the keel has less motion in a seaway."

Bonnie said, "Thank you, Captain, for the advice. I did lose my breakfast."

The Captain stated, "You are welcome on my bridge any time. Be careful, I might put you to work."

Still feeling queasy, Bonnie was keeping her composure by sure will. She slowly headed down and toward the stern. Arriving in the engine room, she stood in front of the mid-ship engine. Soon Bonnie was feeling better and was flanked by the twins. They both thanked Bonnie as they showed the medallions they had strung on a piece of twine about their necks. They told Bonnie they had to keep them tucked into their shirts when working for safety.

Bonnie asked, "Have you been going to school?"

The twins said almost in perfect sync, "Yes!"

One added, "We are learning to be good readers and writers. If we study hard, someday we can become engineers."

Bonnie asked, "Is there anything you need or want?"

One of the twins said, "More books to read."

"Anything else?" Bonnie asked.

The other twin said, "No, everything is wonderful."

Bonnie headed back to the dining room; she was hungry.

Although it was early for dinner, there were a few other diners. All were sharing one table.

Charlotte showed up. "I am all caught up on my paperwork. Why is the ship bouncing around so much?"

Bonnie asked, "Have you stepped out on the deck today?"

Charlotte said, "No. Why?"

Everyone at the table had a little laugh.

Bonnie replied, "We are in a violent storm."

Charlotte replied, "I thought that the ship was rolling around a lot. Now it seems to be going up and down a lot."

More laughter seemed to embarrass Charlotte.

After a light late lunch, Bonnie was in a hurry to get to the bridge before twilight, hoping it had stopped raining. Charlotte went along with her. Upon their reaching the bridge, they saw the rain had stopped. The sky was covered with thick gray clouds. Charlotte and Bonnie looked out the window. The bow of the *Bonnie Duffy* was diving into huge waves and then coming up to the top to dive into another. The top of each wave was washing over the decks of the *Bonnie Duffy*.

Charlotte exclaimed, "Oh my God, I think I am going to be sick! The waves are huge. Are we going to sink?"

The Captain tried to reassure Charlotte, "No. We are in a good ship that can handle a lot worse than this. Soon we will come about and run with the waves and wind. That will be a difficult maneuver."

The motion did not seem to affect Charlotte, but the visual certainly did. She excused herself. Bonnie started out onto the bridge-deck and was warned by the Captain, "The wind out there is wicked. Hang on real tight."

Bonnie checked the engine room telegraphs, three-quarters forward on all three engines. Speed, eleven knots. The engines were working hard against the wind and waves.

The Captain said, "We are burning the good coal to try to keep our power and speed without stressing our engines. Soon we need to turn."

As soon as Bonnie stepped out the door, she felt like she was going to be blown away. Holding tight with her hands, the skin on her face was being pulled back tight, and looking into the wind was painful on her eyes and skin. She had to squint. Then her dress blew up and over her face. Bonnie felt strong arms about her as she was pulled back into the bridge. Bonnie got her dress back where it was supposed to be and looked at the men on the bridge. They were all looking forward, with no expressions on their faces.

Bonnie said, "At least I should get a smirk out of that."

That brought some subdued laughter from all five men on the bridge, including the Captain.

Bonnie then added, "That is better. Dumb things happen to all of us. Think of the story you can now tell, and I will not be able to deny it. That wind is really strong."

The Captain explained, "Wind is over sixty knots from the west by south. Add the ship's speed of eleven knots, that makes over seventy knots apparent wind velocity."

The Captain then issued orders to one of his officers. "Go close both port boiler-room air intakes and the hatched in the bulkheads. Tell the boiler room I want full steam available. Tell the engine room to prepare for fast maneuvering up to full power. Then I want you to get six husky sailors, three to stand by each open air intake hatches, and stand by ready to close the hatches if we breach. When you are in position, send a messenger to inform the bridge. Orders understood?"

"Yes, sir, orders understood."

The Captain addressed Bonnie, "Mrs. Smithfield, we are going to make a port turn to the east. In these winds and waves, that can be difficult even in a large ship. As we head down one wave, we will commence our turn and try to complete our turn on smaller waves. We will try to pick a series of waves that are smaller with a long spacing between them. The danger is that a wave hitting on our quarter will tend to roll the ship. If the bow is in a wave, it will tend to make the ship trip or a wave can break over the ship being a breach, or the ship can roll on its side. If you wish to stay on the bridge, please stay clear and keep quiet."

Bonnie acknowledged, "Yes, sir, I understand your orders."

In about fifteen minutes, a messenger came to the bridge saying all was ready, repeating what was ordered.

Captain Krupp checked the hatch status indicator panel and said, "The hatch status panel indicates all critical hatches are closed."

First Mate went up into the crow's nest.

The Captain gave everybody detailed instructions. "When the whistle blows, be prepared—two on the wheel, one on each side."

The wait seemed to be forever, the suspense was near unbearable for Bonnie. The First Mate was the spotter. He would pull the whistle lanyard that ran up next to the crow's nest. They wanted to complete the turn while it was still light out. Two large waves passed, and the whistle blew. The third wave was huge.

The Captain ordered, "All ahead full."

The ship neared the top of the wave.

The Captain shouted orders, "Rudder hard to port, port engine full astern, starboard engine full ahead, mid-ship engine full ahead!"

The ship started to turn on the down slope of the wave. All the forces could be felt; the ship groaned as the hull plates were moving against each other. The forces started to list the ship to starboard.

Bonnie heard the Captain holler, "Turn, turn, turn."

As the ship reached the bottom of the wave, the bow pierced the oncoming wave forcing the ship's bow to port listing the ship to port. As the shop rose to the next wave, the ship continued to moan and groan as the bow rose. The ship continued to turn. As they reached the wave crest the ship was aligned with the wave. As the wave crest passed the stern started to feel like it was sliding down the back side of the wave, listing the sip to starboard. At the bottom, between the waves, for a moment, it felt like the ship was caught between the two waves on an angle. Slowly, the stern came around as it rose in the next wave, the ship listing to port. On the back side of the wave, the ship completed the turn.

The Captain ordered, "Rudder amidships, all engines ahead one-half. New course east by south."

The Captain turned to Bonnie. "Mrs. Smithfield, your husband builds good ships. She came about smartly, not a hint of a broach. That big wave was about one hundred feet high."

Bonnie felt herself slightly quivering as she checked the knot meter, thirteen knots. The waves were moving faster than the ship. The waves were coming onto the ship's starboard stern. The helmsman steered to port, anticipating the wave lifting the stern trying to push it to port. Then rudder to starboard as the wave passed. His timing kept the ship on a steady course. The ship's motion was much slower and gentler. The clouds remained thick gray and ominous, so a navigational sighting was impossible.

Bonnie said, "Thank you, Captain. You and your crew totally amaze me. That was thrilling. I see that the hatch indicator lights are working properly," pointing to the panel showing two of the air intake hatches closed as well as most all other hatches.

Bonnie mumbled to herself, "That was better than hopping a freight car."

She must have been louder than she intended. The Captain gave her a very inquisitive look.

The Captain sent a messenger to tell the engine room and boiler room to resume normal operations and they could open the air intakes and other hatches as appropriate. The First Mate came down from the crow's nest.

Bonnie slowly and cautiously stepped out on the bridge-deck. With the wind coming from the stern made it manageable, although it was cold. The six sailors on watch, four on the bridge-deck and two in the crow's nest, were in heavy wool coats. Returning to the pilot-house, Bonnie checked the chart. Their plot showed they had moved west and south of Valparaiso, it is still a long way to Cape Horn. A massage came over the horn from the crow's nest.

The officer listening repeated the message, "Ship sighted, two points off port bow."

After a wait, there was another message: "Steamship, two points off port bow heading west."

Bonnie peered out the window. By the conversation she heard, others were seeing the ship; it eluded Bonnie's vision. Bonnie finally spotted it on top of a wave, then it disappeared again. In about thirty seconds, it appeared again. About every thirty seconds, it would appear on top of a wave. The distance between the waves was longer than the *Bonnie Duffy*. The six-hundred-foot-long *Bonnie Duffy* would have its bow on one wave and stern on another or be parched upon one wave. The Captain sent a messenger, ordering that they burn the low-grade coal and increase the speed to seventeen knots. Now they had the wind and waves pushing them along.

Eventually, they passed port to port with the other ship. The bridge identified it as a German freighter with two funnels and was about three hundred feet in length and displacing around eight thousand tons. Taking bearings, the Navigator said that the ship was heading west-northwest at about five to six knots. The German freighter was fighting its way west. It looked small next to the waves it was climbing up. As Bonnie checked the chart, the Captain told her they were steering further south to have sea room, avoiding land. That was a safety precaution until they got a fix. In the weather and waves, their dead reckoning position had a margin of error that had to be considered.

It was getting dark, and the clouds were not clearing. Bonnie headed for the dining room.

In the dining room, Charlotte looked a little peaked.

She told Bonnie, "It is not really bad, but one of our oilers got hurt."

Bonnie, with concern, asked, "Oh no, how bad?"

Charlotte said, "She fell and broke her arm. But the doctor said she should be okay. She is in the infirmary."

Arriving at the infirmary, the girl was propped up in a bed with her arm in a cast. She was the second oldest of the five.

Seeing Bonnie, she said, "I am sorry, Mrs. Smithfield, I slipped and fell. Now I will not be able to do my work."

Bonnie answered, "Do not worry about your work. You just get better. What is your name?"

"Ma'am, I am Betty, second born. I owe Smitey money. If I do not work, I will not be able to pay him back."

Bonnie replied, "Do not worry about your pay. You were hurt working on the job. Your pay will continue. Now, Betty, how did you get hurt?"

"Ma'am, I was taking the shortcut from the top of the starboard engine to the mid-ship engine when I slipped and fell."

"Sounds dangerous, how can we make it less dangerous?"

"Ma'am, it was my fault, I should not have taken the shortcut. Smitey told us not go that way. I should not get my pay. I disobeyed orders."

"You will still get your pay. Sometimes orders are for safety, that is why we must follow orders. Now tell me, what are your sisters' names?"

"Ma'am, Annie, I am Betty, then there's Cathy, Dotty, and Eavey. Our mom used to call us her Alphabet Adams Girls. Thank you for letting me have my pay, you are a great lady."

"Betty, if you or your sisters need anything, send me a message. Do you need anything now? I want you to get better."

"I have all that I need. Thank you, ma'am, you are wonderful."

Bonnie went to her cabin and retrieved *Moby Dick*, the only novel she had, taking it to Betty, telling her that after she was done with it, to share it with her sisters.

Back at the dining room, Charlotte asked, "Is she going to be all right?"

Bonnie said, "I think she will be all right. That girl has spunk."

The ship's motion was easier since their daring course change. Some of the passengers made it to dinner. Both Charlotte and Bonnie hosted the Captain's table. Bonnie told the guests that the Captain was busy with his duties due to the weather. Several had been concerned for the ship or the weather and some for the maneuvering that they had felt and of hearing the engines working hard and the ship moans and groans.

Bonnie told them, "Today I have spent time in the engine room, bridge, and pilothouse. I can assure all that our ship is sound and seaworthy. Our crew is confident and the best of seamen. I have full confidence in them. We are in the process of rounding Cape Horn, which is known for its extreme weather. The Captain and crew have been maneuvering in an effort to lessen the ship's uncomfortable motion to make the passengers as comfortable as possible. Though out course was south, the Captain had the ship sail west-southwest to lessen the ship's rolling. This is adding distance to our trip, but the comfort of our passengers is our priority. We are now heading east by south and should round the Cape of Horn in a couple days. I apologize for any discomfort. I can assure you that in a lesser ship, in these conditions, the voyage would be much rougher."

Megan stood up. "I have been around the Cape of Horn twice before. One time it was calm, and the other time it took two weeks, and I can tell you that this ship is smooth and steady compared to that ship."

A middle-aged man stood up. "Twenty years ago, I came to San Francisco on a clipper ship. It took us three weeks to round the Horn. I was a young and healthy man at that time. We had to tie ourselves in out berths. Going on deck was near impossible. Even as a passenger, I had to help man the pumps for four two-hour shifts a day for three weeks. The seamen said that they had seen worse. I said 'never again' until I saw this ship. Now I am enjoying sailing around the Horn. In a few days, all of us will have bragging rights: 'Sailing around Cape Horn in a storm.'"

An elderly man stood. "Before I settled in San Francisco, I was a ship's officer for twenty-five years and sailed around the Horn numerous times on several ships. This is the finest ship I have ever been on."

Another middle-aged gentleman added, "Fourth time around the Horn for me. So far, this has been a great voyage."

Others stood up and gave accounts of sailing around the Horn; some had uneventful trips where others had harrowing passages.

The old salts seemed to be the ones hungry, ready for dinner.

A toast was given. "Rounding Cape Horn!"

Early in the morning, Bonnie went to the bridge. The Captain was there; he had changed the course one-point south to east-southeast.

He said, "I am concerned of northerly drift and wanted to give Patagonia plenty of room."

The First Mate arrived on the Bridge. The Captain had been up all night on watch.

First Mate announced, "Reporting for duty, sir."

Captain updated the First Mate. "I ordered a course of east-southeast to give us sea room. The wind and waves has not abated. We have not been able to get any bearings or positions. We are still on our dead reckoning plot. Mr. Fitzpatrick, you have the bridge. I will be in my cabin."

It was the change of watch. The First Mate gave orders to the new watch, "Look closely for other ships or land, stay alert."

In the pilothouse, Bonnie listened intently as the Navigator briefed his relief. They were concerned of northerly currents. In the News to Mariners, there were several reports that the currents were inappropriately reported on the charts. If there was an error, it would put them further north than they wanted to be. They had two dead reckoning plots, one using the chart currents and one with the reported currents. If they could get a sighting, even on the sun, they could better establish their position. Without land insight and the heavy cloud, they could only continue using their calculations of course, speed, time, and factors for drift. Every ten minutes, the course, speed, apparent wind direction, and apparent wind velocity would be recorded. These recordings were used for their dead-reckoning calculations.

Bonnie went to have breakfast with Charlotte. Charlotte had not slept well; she had a mild case of seasickness. Rough count, about half the passengers made it to breakfast. The breakfast menu was smaller due to the number of cooks and helpers under the weather. Service was slow even with the reduced number of diners. Charlotte reported that housekeeping, laundry, and other related services were behind schedule.

Hence, Charlotte, and Bonnie borrowed maids' uniforms and helped clean up the ship, Willa, Megan, and Peggy showed up along with a couple of other passengers, helping out. The maids seeing them helping out appeared to help moral. Later Charlotte heard that some that were staying in their births were shamed into getting up and going to work. By afternoon, the ship was mostly cleaned up and many were recovering from their seasickness. The Captain told Bonnie that most people got used to the motion in a day or two and would recover from seasickness.

By late afternoon, Bonnie changed out of her maid uniform and returned to the bridge, hoping to get in some more practice with her sextant. The Captain and First Mate were on the bridge. Bonnie noticed the engines were working harder. Bonnie looked at the knot meter, twenty-one knots. The waves and wind were the same. It was still overcast, and the sun was obscured.

Watching the log, Bonnie saw that when the ship was on the forward side of a wave, the knot meter would nudge twenty-three knots and closer to twenty when on the backside of a wave.

Bonnie looked inquisitively at the Captain. He pointed out a ship in front of them.

The Captain said, "We think it is British. Looks like a man of war. We have been gainer on her for the last three hours. We can show the Limes what the Yankees can do!"

Bonnie asked, "Can we catch them and pass them?"

The Captain said, "When we first saw them, they were going about four knots slower. When they saw us, they stoked up their boilers. So did we. Unless they can find more speed, we should be abeam them in an hour."

Bonnie exuberantly stated, "Let us show them the Stars and Stripes and the Smithfield flag."

The Captain agreed, "Yes, Mrs. Smithfield, we will do our best."

HMS Centurion 1890s

Bonnie asked, "Do I have the Captain's permission to let our passengers know."

"By all means do. We will try to pass on their starboard. They will be on our port side."

Bonnie went to the casino where there were several passengers. Bonnie asked a few there to spread the word.

"Want to see us overtake and pass a British Man of War on the high seas? Look to port in about an hour."

The word was spread to the entire ship. The steerage passengers could get a look from the fantail; that was a part of their territory.

When Bonnie returned to the bridge, it was obvious to her that they were gaining on the ship. The Captain ordered all hands on deck. "Prepare to give honors."

As they neared, a spyglass let them read the name, the HMS *Centurion*. A book was consulted. Displacement 10,500 tons, length 360 feet, four ten-inch guns, ten 4.7-inch guns, launched August 1892. It was a new British Battleships. It had a mast like sailing ship.

As they approached, the Captain gave two prolonged blasts and one short blast on the whistle. This was the signal saying that the *Bonnie Duffy* intended on overtaking the other ship on its starboard side. The HMS *Centurion* responded with prolonged, short, prolonged, short blasts on their whistle, which was an acknowledgement.

First Mate, Mr. Fitzpatrick, said, "I will bet that the skipper of that battleship is cursing right now, being overtaken on the high seas by a passenger ship, an American ship at that!"

The Captain ordered, "Give honors."

All of the available sailors on the *Bonnie Duffy* stood on the port top rail and saluted. Even in the rough seas, all the port rails on every deck of the *Bonnie* were lined, including the fantail. Everyone wanted to participate, from the passengers, cooks, maids, to the boiler crew. Seasickness seemed to disappear.

Bonnie looked and saw the *Bonnie Duffy* was displaying a large Stars and Stripes flying from the mast with the Smithfield Steamship flag under it. Because of the strong wind from the stern, the flags were flying toward the bow.

The HMS *Centurion* also gave honors. There were a lot of sailors on the British ship. They were close enough that they could almost see the crew's faces. As the bridges were abeam, the Captain stepped out onto the bridge-deck, stood at attention and saluted. A man on the other ship's bridge, assumed to be the Captain of the *Centurion*, also saluted. He had a large fancy hat on that was pointed in the front and back. His uniform had large shoulder pads that looked like scrub brushes. As the Captain of the *Centurion* saluted; a cheer came from the passengers and non-deck crew of the Bonnie Duffy.

Bonnie heard the *Bonnie's* Captain mumble, "No respect."

Bonnie asked, "Is there a problem with our passengers cheering?"

The Captain responded, "The Captain of the HMS *Centurion* will have to enter this incident in his ship log. It sounded more like jeers than cheers to me. He will have to report to the British Admiralty that his ship was overtaken at sea by an American passenger ship and was jeered by its passengers, cooks and maids. My log entry will be positive for the ship and crew. We actually have an advantage—we have a longer ship. The longer the ship, the faster the maximum hull speed."

It was getting dark, and the *Bonnie Duffy* was lit up as they cruised away from the British ship.

Bonnie concluded that she would report this to her father-in-law; maybe it would be good for his sale to the US Navy. Another conclusion was that the *Bonnie Duffy* was a beautiful ship where the HMS *Centurion* was an ugly ship.

Bonnie had a good night's sleep, and when she looked out, it was still overcast. No stars visible.

At breakfast, Charlotte reported that everything was returning to normal. Even though the seas were still high, their course held the ship's motion to a tolerable level. As predicted, people were getting used to the ship's motion.

In the pilothouse, Bonnie read the ship's log. The mast lights of the HMS *Centurion* went below the horizon at 2030 hours' local time, or 8:30 p.m. The rest of the night was uneventful. They had slowed to eighteen knots. The coal consumption report indicated that they were in good shape. If they were cruising against the wind, the situation would be different. According to the dead reckoning plot, they were nearing south of Cape Horn.

The Captain asked Bonnie, "Mrs. Smithfield, do you think it would be of any inconvenience if we will arrive a day early at Buenos Aries? We could stop at Montevideo on our way to see if they have anthracite coal."

Bonnie answered, "I think it will be all right. I will double-check with Miss Gibbs and her schedule."

Bonnie went to the infirmary to check up on Betty.

The Nurse said, "Betty has been released. She is to come back in five days for a checkup. Thank you for bringing her the book, it kept her busy. She is a very active young lady. We did have to help her out with a few words."

Bonnie looked in the woman's crew quarters, no Betty. Next, the engine room. Bonnie found Betty on a stool in a corner, reading a book that she had propped up on her cast. Asking to see the book, Bonnie was surprised by the title: *Operation, Service and Maintenance of Multi-Stage Reciprocating Steam Engines.*

Bonnie asked, "Do you understand what is in this book?"

Betty answered, "Ma'am, not all of it. That is why I am studying it."

"No working. Go see the Doctor in five days. If you have any problems, go to the infirmary. Those are your orders."

"Yes, ma'am."

"Did you like *Moby Dick*?"

"Yes ma'am, it was a little scary. We were told we might see whales. We are okay though. We are in a really big ship with big engines."

"I will let you get back to your studying. Follow your orders."

"Yes, ma'am."

Before leaving, Bonnie looked up, and there was the youngest sister, Eavey, oiling the connecting rods wrist pins of the starboard engine. Every time Bonnie saw any of the girls oiling, it gave her goosebumps.

Betty set a good example.

Bonnie then went to her room and studied celestial navigation.

Late afternoon, it was still overcast, and the wind and waves continued. There was a little snow that melted on contact. They had changed course to east. There was nothing of interest in the ship's log. The dead reckoning plot indicated they were south of Cape Horn.

Bonnie asked the Navigator, "When are we going to start on a more northerly heading?"

"That will be the Captain's decision. Maybe by morning."

The bridge crews had gotten used to Bonnie's visits and now mainly ignored her nosing around.

At dinner, Bonnie asked Charlotte about stopping in Montevideo.

Charlotte answered, "I told the Captain it would not be a problem."

Bonnie replied, "You just keep telling the Captain. Keep him on course."

This got Bonnie a none-of-your-business look from Charlotte.

Early-morning twilight brought some clearing. The Captain, First Mate, Navigator, and Bonnie struggled to get good sightings. As soon as Bonnie identified a star and tried to get it in her sextant scope, the fast-moving clouds obscured it. Eventually Bonnie identified a star; even though it was soon obscured, she remained ready.

It reappeared for a brief time; she got an angle and time. Bonnie had practiced counting seconds from the time she got her sighting until she looks at her watch. She would write down the watch time, subtract her count, then compare her watch to the ship's marine chronometer, accurate ship's clock. The *Bonnie Duffy* had four chronometers. The ship's chronometers were set to display Greenwich Mean Time. Three of the chronometers were backups. Navigation requires accurate time. Knowing the star, time of sighting, angle to the true horizon, then a factor of the height of the observer's eye above sea level, a line of position could be calculated and plotted. Bonnie needed help reducing her star sight to a line of position. They had five lines of position, including Bonnie's. All five were plotted. They had a fix. They were within twelve nautical miles of the center of their two dead reckoning plots. Bonnie was proud of her lone sight that coincided with the others. Their latitude was 61 degrees, 43 minutes, 20 seconds, south. A minute was one sixtieth of a degree and a second was one sixtieth of a minute. They were in the Southern Ocean; the boundary was 60 degrees south latitude.

Now she had to work on her calculations that used spherical trigonometry. Bonnie had never heard of spherical trigonometry until she started to read her celestial navigation books. The wind had eased, though the waves were still enormous. The Captain ordered a course change to north-northeast toward the Falkland Islands. He also ordered a speed reduction to twelve knots, considering the passengers' comfort. Now they would have a quarter following sea, which would make the ship roll.

Bonnie informed the Captain, "You have the approval of the ship's owner's representative to add Montevideo as a port of call."

With permission, Bonnie took the Navigator's pencil calculations of his two sights and Bonnie's one sight to study them to try to understand the procedure to reduce a sight to a line of position. The Captain gave Bonnie his calculations. Now to breakfast then to study.

Midday the ship was rolling, and Bonnie started to feel queasy. On the bridge, the compass indicated north. Checking the chart, their heading would take them west of the Falkland Islands. The wind had abated, but the waves had become huge ocean swells.

The Captain said, "Ship is rolling. Making it uncomfortable for the passengers."

Bonnie replied, "Captain, if we sailed the course to make the passengers comfortable, we would end up at the Cape of Good Hope. Our next destination is Montevideo, Uruguay."

The Captain said, "You just might have what it takes to be a sailor. You are just in time for local noon sun sight. We will show you how to take a noon sun sight. It is a valuable tool in navigation.

Bonnie got readings that were consistent with the others taking a sight. The math of reducing this sight was different and easier.

Getting up and moving around settled Bonnie's stomach. She then checked with Charlotte. Charlotte reported that except for some seasickness, things were going smoothly.

At twilight, Bonnie got two sights. With help, she reduced them to lines of position. One had an unacceptable error; the other coincided with the Navigator's sights. If they kept their course and speed at morning twilight, the Falkland Islands should be visible to their starboard.

In the morning as daylight started to break, land could be seen off the starboard bow. First, they took several celestial sights and plotted them. Then the Navigator instructed Bonnie on taking bearings on the identifiable land-marks on the Falkland Islands. The bearings were taken with an instrument mounted to the deck railing, called a pelorus. With the celestial sights and bearings, they were able to establish their position within yards. In three days at 14.5 knots on a course of north by east, 1040 nautical miles, they would be at Montevideo. The wind was light from the southwest and the waves were abating, the skies clear. It was beautiful sailing weather.

Over the next few days, Bonnie honed her celestial navigation skills. The noon sun sights were interesting. According to one's preference, the observer would sight on the top or bottom of the Sun, called the upper limb or lower limb sight. The procedure would be to catch the exact time and angle of the Sun's zenith, top of its arcing path. The time would be the celestial local noon. With an accurate chronograph, longitude could be accurately calculated and latitude could be reasonably determined, depending on the clarity of the horizon's view.

At early morning twilight on the third day, land was sighted to the north. To the north by west, a light could be seen with a period of thirty-one seconds. It was the Montevideo harbor light. No morning celestial sights were taken; they were not needed. In two hours, they entered the harbor. A little over 3,220 nautical miles, their course further west increased their distance traveled. They had sailed around Cape Horn in eight and half days, 203.5 hours, averaging 15.82 knots around the Horn.

Charlotte had joined them on the bridge, and she was given the honor of waking up the city.

The coal dock was near the business district. They docked at the coal dock. Two large piles of coal could be seen; the Captain said that one looked to be black anthracite coal. They managed to dock at the coal dock without the aid of tugs. They had not made prearrangements, so Bonnie and the Captain needed to report to the harbor customs, to clear quarantine, customs, and pay the necessary fees. With the prospect of economic gains from sales, they were welcomed. The *Bonnie Duffy* was a ship the likes never seen in Uruguay. Upon their return to the ship, the gangways were extended to shore. The passenger poured out with cash in hand to explore this bonus port of call. After rounding the Horn, all wanted shore time.

Midafternoon, they would leave for the short cruise to Buenos Aries. The Captain, Charlotte, and Bonnie went to the coal yard office.

The coal yard owner told them, "I am sorry, all the anthracite coal has been assigned to the British Navy."

Bonnie said, "We are willing to pay market price, and I can have funds wired to you today."

The coal yard owner responded, "We are expecting a British man-of-war in the next few days. I received a wire from the British Admiralty requesting all our Anthracite coal."

The Captain said, "That will probably be the HMS *Centurion*."

The coal yard owner asked, "How would you know that?"

The Captain answered, "We overtook and passed them several days ago."

The coal yard owner loudly laughed. "You overtook and passed the arrogant English Navy's new battleship? My congratulations."

Charlotte asked, "Do you have a contract to sell the British the coal or just a request?"

The coal yard owner thought for a minute, then he responded, "The British take at least two months to pay me every time I sell them coal. Every time, they inspect the coal, looking for one leaf or a bird dropping to downgrade my coal, asking for a discount. Then being the mighty British Navy, they expect a discount from market costs. You say you can have my bank wired certified funds today."

Bonnie said, "Write it up, and I will go to the telegraph office. I will give you today's market price."

The coal yard owner again laughed. "I will enjoy telling the arrogant British Captain that the American steamship that passed them got all my good coal, that they were too slow. They will probably have to buy my pile of bituminous coal. When I heard your deep and loud whistle, I thought that today might be a good day."

Bonnie did not see much of Montevideo. She was escorted by the First Mate to the bank telegraph office then back to bank, and finally, to the coal dock. While at the telegraph office, Bonnie telegrammed her father-in-law telling him of the *Bonnie Duffy* embarrassing a new British battleship while rounding the Horn and of their need to stop at Montevideo for coal.

Fresh produce and other perishables were in limited supply; Montevideo had not been informed. Charlotte only purchased a small amount, knowing that Buenos Aries knew of their pending arrival.

They had burnt all the low-quality coal. The *Bonnie*'s coal bunkers had been nearly empty. Montevideo had a well-equipped coal yard with a steam shovel; many wagons and men were employed. Now three quarters of their coal bunkers were filled with high-quality coal. When the British arrived, they would not find any quality coal awaiting them.

As they were ready to leave, the ship was sold a bundle of a special edition of their local newspaper. Translated, its basic theme was of how Montevideo was becoming a world recognized port of call by the visit of the Grand American Luxury Liner, the SS *Bonnie Duffy*. There was also an article that detailed, with time and location in longitude and latitude, of the powerful and modern Luxury Liner, the SS *Bonnie Duffy*, overtaking and passing the mighty British Battleship the HMS *Centurion*, in heavy seas and wind. The paper said they got their information from a reliable anemones source.

As they pulled away from the dock, they could see the coal dock owner putting a copy of the special edition on the door of the coal dock office.

They would be arriving at Buenos Aries in a few hours, so Bonnie and Charlotte decided to eat early, knowing they would be busy in Buenos Aries.

Bonnie said, "I think we have been a little hard on British pride. I wonder who told of the incident with the *Centurion*. It had to be someone on our ship with navigation knowledge giving the longitude and latitude details."

Charlotte said, "I will never tell. You have to admit, though, it is good publicity at the British's expense."

"Who told."

"There are numerous people on the bridge that like to talk."

Buenos Aries was expecting them; the good people of Montevideo had telegraphed ahead. They were greeted with ship whistles and a cannon salute from an ancient fortress protecting the harbor. The harbor was narrow, so it took several tugboats to turn them around and nudge them to the pier. The mayor greeted the Captain, Bonnie, and Charlotte and escorted them to the customs house that stayed open for them. The Captain was asked if it was true that they overtook and passed a British man-of-war and took all the coal that the British thought was theirs in Montevideo? The Captain did not acknowledge it, but Charlotte acknowledged it was all true.

They were told how the British, eighty years previously, had occupied their wonderful city and stolen the treasures, food, and anything of value, leaving them to starve. It was a story passed down from generation to generation and was taught in their schools as part of their history of a horrible time. In their main square, they had a monument to the many that suffered and died. They had only hatred for the English. Allegedly, half of the population of Buenos Aries had died from malnutrition and disease because of the incident. The United States and Argentina had good relations, for the United States quickly recognized Argentina as a nation when they won their independence from the Spanish. The two nations had good trade relations.

Many of the passengers went ashore to enjoy the vibrant night life of the vibrant city. Bonnie and Charlotte spent most of the evening ashore and even attempted to dance the tango; it was a very new experience for them. Both the ladies found it sultry and intriguing, something they would not dare do in public at home. They both thought they were being naughty. It was fun. And they were not alone; many of the passengers enjoyed the night life. Megan showed that she was not the least inhibited; she was, as usual, the life of the party.

Many slept in the next day, including Bonnie. They were scheduled to leave that evening, but by popular demand, their departure was postponed till the next morning. That would give them more time to resupply in this friendly port. Most wanted another night in Buenos Aries.

Their coal bunkers were filled with good-quality anthracite coal. They left some for the British, though there was a question as to how desperate the British would be for coal. The Argentineans would require cash from the British and top price.

Bonnie wished she had not slept in; she had little time for sightseeing and personal shopping with all the shopping for the ship. Bonnie and Charlotte did steal away from ship business long enough to buy a couple of Latin-style dresses with all the appropriate accessories, including shoes. They giggled; they were going to be sultry in Buenos Arties. It was the style here, so they would not stand out; they would just fit in.

They were not alone. Leaving the ship for the evening life, most of the ladies were dressed in Latin-style attire. Their extra night's stay was a boost to the Argentinean fashion industry.

Late evening, returning to the ship, Bonnie had one regret, that Joseph had not been here to enjoy the party. She really missed her husband and realized she would have to keep busy to occupy herself. Bonnie bought an assortment of books that were in English. Bonnie's reading choices had changed from what she liked as a girl to books about cultures, travel, history, geography, and the sciences. The adventure novels no longer interested her. She believed that Twain and the likes would be boring compared to what she had and was still living.

CHAPTER 13

Western Atlantic

Three days, 1,140 nautical miles to Rio de Janeiro. The ship got into a routine, as well as Bonnie. Bonnie was up before dawn, dressed, and had coffee on the bridge. When weather permitted, she practiced her navigation. She was becoming proficient in taking her sights and reducing them to lines of position. Along with the Navigator's sights, they become part of the ship's plot. Then Bonnie would review the ship's log before meeting Charlotte for breakfast, where they would discuss ship's business. Charlotte and Bonnie would then tour the ship, often taking different paths and looking at different things. They often walked through the casino; it was very popular with the passengers and there were no complaints. On a special occasion, Bonnie had managed to get Charlotte to even go with her into the engine and boiler rooms. The oiler girls were always eager and met them with enthusiasm. The sight of the huge mechanical beasts thrashing their huge components about then the sight of one of the girls reaching into the blur of iron components squirting oil horrified Charlotte. Charlotte refused to continue the tour to the boiler room.

In the crew's mess, there was the start of a library. Charlotte and Bonnie agreed the ship should have a library available to all: passengers, crew, and steerage. Bonnie would do her noon sun sight, then it was study time. Evening sights, then dinner. Afterword some reading before bed.

The passage to Rio de Janeiro was uneventful except for outrunning a German gun ship. They had been cruising at seventeen knots and were overtaking the German ship. That was about the maximum speed of large naval ships. They were shorter and broader with a similar displacement, and they had thick steel armor plating, greatly adding to their weight for their length.

The Germans fired up their boilers, not wanting to be overtaken. The First Mate was on duty, and not wanting to wake the Captain, ordered full speed. They were running at twenty-two knots, gaining on the Germans, then the Germans changed course, going further out to sea. The bridge crew congratulated themselves, saying the Germans gave up when they knew they were going to lose. When the Captain read the log entry the next day, he said nothing. He knew that he had a good crew that was proud of their ship.

They had decided to try to arrive at port in the morning and leave the next morning, giving their passengers a day and night in port. As planned, they arrived early morning in Rio de Janeiro. Customs in Rio seemed to be interested in collecting a multitude of fees to every branch of their government. But a bribe to a high official, as was advised, seemed to expedite all the paperwork. All of the fees and the bribe together were not unreasonable. Charlotte had learned whom she could trust and delegated a lot of the shopping to. Charlotte and Bonnie had a little time to explore. Bonnie and several passengers bought books; many were eventually donated to the ship's library. The outfits they bought in Buenos Aries would be appropriate here. They were told of a respectable dance hall where they could experience Rio's evening social culture. The people of Rio enjoyed dancing; they had a spacious dance hall.

They invited all the passengers; many went out to sample Rio de Janeiro's culture. They thought the tango was sultry, but the samba was sensuous. They all heard the Latins were warm blooded. To the American sensibility, this was a cultural shock, totally unacceptable and a lot of fun. The locals were helpful and eager to help these Yankees learn to do the Samba. The Brazilians were as much a curiosity to the Americans as the Americans were to the Brazilians.

Again, Bonnie wished Joseph was here to share the adventure.

Morning came early, and Bonnie did not have sights to take, being in port. Most of the passengers were asleep when they departed. They had filled their coal bunkers. A reserve of coal was stored in their mostly empty cargo holds. Next stop was Havana, Cuba, at 4540 nautical miles, at fifteen knots, thirteen days. They would have to keep their coal consumption under six tons an hour. This would be their longest passage yet. Fifteen knots seemed to be an economical and comfortable speed. With good coal, it was not a strain on the engines or boilers. They had to sail east to get around the eastern horn of South America and then north followed by a northwest path. They would have to maneuver around Puerto Rico, the Dominican Republic, and a score of other islands, then across the north coast of Cuba to Havana.

The ship settled into a routine as did most passengers and crew. On the fourth day, they again crossed the equator. Again, King Neptune made an appearance with his court of sirens. Five of his sirens were young ladies dressed in fancy dresses from Rio de Janeiro doing a rendition of the samba. Two orphan boys had stowed away in Buenos Aries. Smitey volunteered to put them to work so they could earn their keep. Now the ship had five oilers; the two oldest sisters were promoted to motormen, third grade.

Megan and Charlotte had conspired to douse Bonnie. Bonnie was careful and thought she had gotten away without being drenched in water. But she was ambushed by five beautiful young sirens each with a bucket of cold water. The way Betty handled a bucket, no one would know she recently had a cast removed from a broken arm.

Afterward, the six of them sit on the deck laughing. Then they conspired, with Willa and Peggy's help, Charlotte and Megan were paid back. The ten of then started to form a good relationship.

Except for some isolates squalls they had good sailing. Bonnie had a lot of practice on celestial navigation and passing through the Caribbean Islands, a lot of practice taking bearings on landmarks.

Havana was a lot different from the other ports that they had visited. The Spanish still ruled Cuba and the relations between the Americans and Spanish were turning bad. The Spanish were also hated by most Cubans. They should have chosen a different port in the Caribbean. The Spanish restricted when and where the passengers could go. Some locals lobbied for the United States to aid in their plan to rebel against the Spanish. After loading some needed supplies and a partial load of coal, they departed for New York. The way the Spanish administrators of Cuba treated the crew and passengers, there was a lot of animosity. Even though the home office knew their destination was Havana, they received no telegrams. Bonnie sent a couple of telegrams through the Western Union office. In Havana, they had been forced to pay for everything in cash. The cost of coal was inflated. The ship's bank funds were being depleted. Their next stop was New York, where their funds could be replenished.

New York, that was where Bonnie had started her journey eight years previously.

She thought of her parents—were they given a grave? The friends she played with on the street, her schoolmates, her parents' possessions, her mother's coffee pot. Mrs. O'Neal's appearance of caring, then her betrayal, her thievery, and sending her away. The mean people that owned the mercantile who used her as a slave. Bonnie realized that those people were what made her what she was. Had the people whom she thought had treated her unjustly really done her a favor, forcing her to be determined and strong? They had not managed to break Bonnie's spirit.

Across to Florida and up the eastern seaboard, it was congested with ships of all sizes and typed. Many fishing boats had to be avoided. The three-day trip ended up being three and a half days. When Bonnie left New York, there were raising money to build a platform for the Statue of Liberty. Now Miss Liberty was standing proudly, welcoming all to the great harbor of New York.

First stop was Ellis Island for customs and immigration. All steerage passengers had to disembark and go through immigration and health inspection. Prior to making port, the Captain and Bonnie, the owner's representative, had to sign papers for all crew members.

Annie and Betty Adams, the two oldest oiler girls, were made motor-men third grade, a non-licensed position above an oiler. The first-class and second-class passengers went through customs aboard the ship. The ship's crew were interviewed and were required to show their papers. Being a US-registered ship made the procedures easier. The ship was responsible for the crew. All crew was to depart with the ship. Any crew jumping ship had to be reported to immigration. The exception were US citizens that had documents showing their citizenship. Smithfield Shipping Lines had arranged that they dock at Pier 39. They did not dock until the next morning. The residents of New York and New Jersey were able to admire the SS *Bonnie Duffy* anchored on the Hudson River, electrically illuminated. Over half of the passengers were to disembark. They had not received a telegram since Rio de Janeiro, so they did not know what to expect. The last they heard they were half-booked to Liverpool England.

Bonnie would see all their departing passengers off, thanking them for sailing on Smithfield Lines. It being early morning when the gangway was extended to the dock, only a few passengers were ready to disembark.

Bonnie looked up, and there was Joseph coming up the gang-way. Bonnie ran down the gangway; enthusiastically, she charged her husband. She was so excited that they almost went over the rail into the Hudson River.

Bonnie exclaimed, "How did you get here?"

"I hopped a couple of freight cars."

"Yeah, you jumped into a Pullman Sleeper."

"I am not as tough as you."

Bonnie smiled broadly. "I have missed you so much!"

"I really have missed my hobo."

"I have missed my strong, handsome man."

Joseph asked, "What happened in Havana?"

Bonnie answered, "We were not welcome. It was not the Cubans but the Spanish administrators. I did not tell others. I was told in confidence that the Spanish had seized all telegrams to the ship. The telegraph office manager asked that I not tell others or he and his family would be thrown in prison. He was genuinely afraid that if I made a fuss, it would cause him and his family problems. Did you get my two telegrams?"

Joseph said, "Yes. The way you worded your telegrams told me you had concern and you planned to leave expediently. We should have some code words so we communicate discreetly. Telegrams are not very private, especially to governments."

Bonnie said in exuberance, "You make me happy. It is so good to see you."

Joseph replied, "Four days to get here felt like forever, but your kiss and hug made it well worth it. You are the most beautiful woman in the world."

This got Joseph a big kiss and hug. As well as a "You are full of shit."

He kissed and hugged back.

Bonnie said, "I love you and your lies. Come, let me show you off."

Bonnie introduced Joseph to everyone she could find. "This is my husband, who built the ship we are on."

With each introduction, Joseph would say, "I did not build this ship. I am just a manager of the company that built this ship. A lot of talented, hardworking people built this ship."

They eventually went to Bonnie's cabin, where they both lost control of their suppressed emotions and they passionately attacked each other.

They both still had a busy day, so they saved some of their passionate aggression for later. Joseph had company coming at noon to look at the ship's electrical system, including his hatch status indicator panel, which he was patenting and hoped to market.

Bonnie could not resist. "In Buenos Aries, I bought a new dress just for you."

"I have not lost any more bets. I am not going to wear any more dresses!"

"It is too small for you, it fits me just right. Wait till you see it. It is a Tango or Samba dress. You are going to have to learn how to dance Latin-style."

"I have trouble dancing American-style. Let us talk of ship building instead."

Bonnie asked, "All right, how are you doing on the SS *Rebecca Smithfield?*"

Joseph responded, "Now you are going to name the new ships."

"I think it would be a good idea. It would make your mommy happy."

"You are a pain."

"I know, in the ass. That is part of my job as your wife."

"I have missed you too, Bonnie. Life has been boring and bland without you."

Bonnie asked, "Do you have the hull ready?"

"Another week and we will start on the decking."

They continued to banter as they walked and greeted people.

At noon, Joseph went ashore and escorted a middle-aged man aboard for a tour.

Joseph said, "Mr. Edison, I would like to introduce my wife, Bonnie Smithfield, Bonnie this the Mr. Thomas A. Edison."

Bonnie said, "Mr. Edison, welcome aboard, it is the greatest of pleasures to meet you."

Mr. Edison, "The pleasure is all mine."

Joseph said, "Mr. Edison wants to look at our electrical system. He also has some ideas of a ship powered by steam turbines and electric motors."

Mr. Edison commented, "Beautiful ship. I have read a lot about your ship, "The most Luxurious, Safest, and Fastest ship on the seas. This ship is a wonder of science and engineering."

Joseph asked, "Mr. Edison, would you mind if my wife accompanies us on our tour? She knows this ship better than I."

"I will not complain of the company of a beautiful lady."

Bonnie resisted telling Mr. Edison he was full of it; compliments made her uncomfortable. Mr. Edison's prestige required Bonnie to be on her best behavior.

They started in the engine room. They were met by five girls and two boys swabbing the engine room deck. Mr. Edison wanted to see everything.

Bonnie said, "This is Mr. Edison, he wants to look at the engines."

Annie started to give an in-depth explanation of their engines.

Bonnie admonished her, "Shush now, if Mr. Edison needs to know anything, he will ask."

Mr. Edison said, "Let her talk. She seems very knowledgeable of your engines."

He then intently listened, getting a description of the specifications and operation of the engines.

Mr. Edison finally asked, "Who oils the engines?"

Annie answered, "We do. We are the oiler girls. We have two boys in training."

Mr. Edison suggested, "You should think of installing automatic oilers."

Bonnie could see that the girls knew who Mr. Edison was and had many questions. "Girls, leave Mr. Edison alone. He has work to do."

Mr. Edison said, "Thank you, young ladies, it has been informative."

Bonnie intently listened. Mr. Edison asked many questions of the design, mechanics, electricity, organization, and operation of the ship. Most of his questions were quickly answered by a sister or Joseph. By his questions, it quickly became apparent to Joseph and Bonnie they were having the privilege of witnessing a great mind at work. Joseph was filling his notebook with notes. He tried to write everything down; he would sort through the ideas later.

Some of the ideas were for future ships. Mr. Edison proposed making a ship with steam turbine generators and electric drive motors. The engines would not need to be stopped and reversed. The driving electric motors would be stopped and reversed. With turbines, there would be few moving parts. Instead of four large boilers, banks of Scotch Boilers with forced draft would be more efficient and easier to service. A conveyor system from the coal bunkers to the boilers and powered stokers to the boilers. The coal conveyers could be reversed for loading the coal bunkers, and this would eliminate some hard labor, making the job safer, more efficient, and faster. A telephone communication system thought out the ship. Every cabin would have its own telephone. In critical areas, the telephone ringers could also have a flashing light indicating an incoming call. Mr. Edison's company, General Electric, manufactured telephone switch-boards that would meet the requirements. Water tightly hatches could be remotely controlled with electric motors. The anchor release could be powered remotely from the bridge. Remotely controlled fire suppression systems could be installed in critical areas. Power lifts between decks could make the moving of materials and people more efficient and safer.

Everything that Mr. Edison looked at, he saw what could be.

Some of Mr. Edison's ideas could be fitted to the *Bonnie*. A telephone system between critical areas would be installed. Instead of sending a messenger or shouting into a tube a telephone would make communication between the bridge, the engine room, the boiler room, the crow's nest, and the forecastle where the anchor was released, more efficient.

After the tour, Mr. Edison was taken to the dining room for a late lunch. They were joined by the Captain and Charlotte. Mr. Edison captivated all with his prediction of the future. Machines that could travel on roads at the speed of trains. Machines that people could get into that would fly like birds, changing transportation for-ever. Boxes that could be talked into communicating with people anywhere in the world without wires. Machines that would do the most complex mathematics at great speed. Mr. Edison told Bonnie of his Kinetoscope, where a person could see photographs in motion like real life.

Joseph gave Mr. Edison a letter of intent to cooperate with General Electric in the development and sales of new marine innovations.

After Mr. Edison departed, all agreed that Mr. Edison's visions of the future were valid and insightful but would be the world of their great-great-great grandchildren.

Joseph was determined to research all of Mr. Edison's ideas. The *Bonnie Duffy* would have telephone communication between important areas in the interest of efficiency and safety. Automatic oilers on the engines. Joseph was not worried about the oiler girls' jobs; his wife would find them a better job. It was obvious to Joseph that his wife had taken an interest in the sisters. The five young ladies had impressed him.

Even though the coal miners were on strike, creating coal shortages, Joseph's father had arranged for a special train carrying premium Pennsylvania blue anthracite coal. The train was to deliver sixteen hundred tons of coal to New Jersey. The train was to have Pinkerton guards aboard, preventing delays by the striking miners.

The next morning, the *Bonnie Duffy* was to sail to a New Jersey coal yard to accept the coal.

* * * * *

Bonnie wanted to find out if her parents had a grave and visit her old neighborhood. Joseph insisted on escorting his wife. They left early. After being sent to several different buildings and departments, they finally found the officials who had access to the burial records. They paid a small fee for research and several bribes to expedite the research. Bonnie was promised that if she returned the following morning, they would have the information of her parent's bodies disposition. Bonnie was told the archived records would have to be researched.

Bonnie and Joseph took a carriage over the Brooklyn Bridge and rode past the site of the garment factory where her parents had worked. A new six-story building was on the site, another garment factory. On their way, Bonnie bought a newspaper, and on the front page was an illustration with the headlines "New American Luxury Liner, SS *Bonnie Duffy*, Docks in New York." Next, they went to the tenement where Bonnie and her parents had lived. The building looked as if it needed repair; it looked neglected. Bonnie asked Joseph to let her handle her own ghosts.

Joseph stood back by the street as Bonnie knocked on the door. The door was answered by Mrs. O'Neal. She looked as if time had not been good to her.

"I am Bonnie Smithfield. My maiden name was Bonnie Duffy. A little over eight years ago, I lived in 3B with my parents. They were killed in a fire at the garment factory. You stole everything that was my parents', including the money that they had saved. And you drugged me with tea then sold me to a policeman into child labor. Do you remember me?"

Mrs. O'Neal nervously said, "Oh, sweetie, I wondered what happened to you! I did what I had to do. I thought the police would find you a good home. By the way you are dressed, I can tell you have done well for yourself."

Bonnie was trying hard to keep the Irish Redhead at bay. "Mrs. O'Neal, I am not your sweetie. I want my mother's coffeepot, the money you stole from me, and the hair combs that are in your hair that were my mother's. I know that my parents did not owe you any rent. If necessary, I will hire an attorney, bring the police, make a scene in front of all your neighbors, and send you to jail."

"Honey, the law is on my side. I am a landlord."

She held up the newspaper. "See the ship on the front of this newspaper? That ship is named after me. I do not think you want a war with me. I do not need the money. I will give it to charity. This is a matter of principle—drug then steal from a naïve, vulnerable, twelve-year-old orphan girl then sell her into slavery and then have the audacity to wear her mother's special hair combs."

Mrs. O'Neal said, "I am sorry. We are all just poor Irish. I will get your coffeepot and your money."

Mrs. O'Neal went into her flat and returned with the coffee pot and a handful of money. She took the two combs from her hair and handed all to Bonnie.

Bonnie descended the stoop to the sidewalk. A small group had gathered to witness the confrontation; Bonnie had tried to speak loud enough to get some attention.

Looking at the money, Bonnie said in a loud voice, "So this is what thirty pieces of silver looks like." She looked back at Mrs. O'Neal as she threw the money into the air.

The gathered crowd scrambled to retrieve the money blowing in the wind down the street.

In the carriage, Bonnie looked at Joseph and said, "That was not as satisfying as I thought it would be. Vengeance yields hollow rewards."

Next, they stopped at the mercantile where Bonnie had worked. Joseph insisted on going in with his wife. The merchandise had changed. It was more of a neighborhood store, with fewer high-end goods. A young lady came up to Bonnie and Joseph, asking if she could help them find something.

Bonnie asked, "Should you not be in school?"

"I went to school this morning. School is out now. It is after four o'clock."

"I worked in this store for a while when I was your age."

"That was probably when the old owners were here. My parents now own this store. I work a couple of hours each day, helping out."

"Do you have rain slickers?"

"Yes. We have two kinds in several sizes."

Bonnie selected two slickers, one for herself and one for Joseph. The young lady asked, "Cash or credit?"

Bonnie responded, "Cash."

A woman in her middle thirties came and said, "Brittany, good, you made a sale. Can you manage?"

"Yes, Mother. They are three dollars each, so that will be six dollars for two."

Bonnie said, "Ma'am, I am Bonnie Smithfield. When I was twelve, I worked in this store as a foster child for the previous owners. I slept in the basement, and one day, I ran away. I hid a few things in the basement. Would it be possible if I could look? I will pay you a reasonable amount for what I find."

"I am Caroline O'Donnell. It is dirty down there, mainly old junk and a coal furnace. You are welcome to look if you like."

Caroline escorted them into the basement. It was as Bonnie remembered; the cot was gone. None of her clothes that were hung on nails on the wall were still there. Her girl shoes were not where she had left them. Bonnie checked in the coal furnace; it was stoked with hot coal. The draft was set right.

Bonnie said, "Part of my job was to tend to this furnace."

Bonnie removed a couple of bricks that were lose alongside the double wall brick coal bin. She pulled out a couple of hair ribbons, an old hairbrush, an old magazine opened to an illustration of Theodore Roosevelt, and a lady's handkerchief that was wrapped around a small Silver Celtic Cross on a delicate chain. Bonnie fought back the tears; the cross had been her grandmother's, mother's, then hers. Bonnie had forgot about the necklace. The loss of leaving it was so great that she had purposefully erased it from her memory. Bonnie had Joseph fasten it around her neck. Now Bonnie understood *serendipity*, having found something lost that she did not know was lost.

Caroline, the store owner, refused to accept anything for Bonnie's recovered treasures.

Bonnie, in sincerity, said, "Thank you, thank you. The time I spent here was a difficult time in my life. Coming back here makes me reflect on how fortunate I am. God bless you and your family."

Back at the sales counter, Bonnie gave Brittany a Double Eagle, telling her to keep the change.

* * * * *

As Bonnie and Joseph returned to the pier, the SS *Bonnie Duffy* was being tied up. All their coal bunkers were overfull. In two days, they would leave for England. Bonnie went looking for Charlotte. Since Joseph had arrived, Bonnie had ignored the ship's business, letting Charlotte do all the work.

Bonnie and Joseph found Charlotte in their office. It was a first. Charlotte appeared to be in a state of disorganized panic. It looked like she was searching through a disorganized a mess of papers on her desk.

Bonnie inquired, "What is wrong? How can I help you? I am sorry, I've been ignoring my duties."

Charlotte responded, "Please do not do anything. I have to work my way through this."

Bonnie replied, "What is wrong? Talk to me."

Charlotte was obviously suffering from frustration. "Please sit down."

Charlotte explained, "Of all the ports we have visited, New York is the most corrupt. Everything is about money. I have spent more on bribes to police than for food. They do not sell protection.

With them, it is more blatant—pay or go to jail and get beaten up on the way. The police charge us for every wagon we unload into the ship. They say it is for protection. I bought produce in New Jersey, and an assistant police commissioner tried to charge us two hundred dollars for import fees under the threat that they would board the ship throwing all contraband overboard. Brooklyn is a separate borough. Buy something in Brooklyn and they want a bribe, then the New York police want a bribe for paying the Brooklyn police a bribe. I telegraphed the boss, and now we have twenty Pinkertons following us around. The local police are afraid of them. The Pinkertons came with the coal. Since we have the Pinkertons as guards, I have not heard from the assistant police commissioner."

Bonnie asked, "What can I do to help?"

Charlotte responded, "Do not say anything. The Governor and others in state government are investigating, including the federal government. I have been warned, do not get in the middle of anything. One more day, and we will be at sea. People who file complaints are often found dead. The Pinkertons have connections across all jurisdictions, making them a formable force, and their reputation of having a high standard of conduct scares local police. I was told that the police know that they are being investigated and do not want the Pinkertons involved. Without the Pinkertons' good reputation, great companies would not retain them. I have always covered bribes in the books as administration fees. This is way too much for me to cover in the books."

Joseph responded, "Write it up as bribes to corrupt government officials. I will explain it to my father. We have had similar problems in the past. Mr. Harvey Smithfield knows how to handle this type of problem. Just go about your duties and ignore the problem."

Bonnie added, "I will sign for the unnecessary expenses."

Charlotte said, "Thank you. Now get out of my way, and I will straighten out this mess. Please go and finish your honeymoon."

Bonnie knew when Charlotte needed space.

That evening, they had a special dinner, afterward, a tango and samba party. All the ladies got dressed up and showed off their Latin dance steps and attire. Tomorrow would be the day for most new passengers to arrive. Latin-style dancing in 1894 America was not socially acceptable, but the few new passengers were soon convinced by Megan it was the Latin American dance craze and it was fun. Even the most prudish joined in. At first, Joseph was shocked. With a lot of prodding, Bonnie was able to teach him a few dance steps. He soon became quite the dancer.

When they returned to Bonnie's cabin, Joseph molested Bonnie, dress and all. The dress was well worth the investment.

The next day, Bonnie and Joseph went to the city's registrar of graves. Bonnie received the information that she requested. All the unclaimed bodies from the garment factory fire were buried in a mass grave on Hart Island. Bonnie stopped and bought a wreath of flowers. It took them all morning to get to Hart Island. They hired a private boat to take them. The ferry went two days a week, and one of the days was not today. An older man who was a convict in chains that was working as a grave digger agreed to take Bonnie to the grave site for a dollar and three dollars to the prison guard. Landscaping was a herd of goats that grazed along with several head of cattle. The old man paced off from a tree, south then east. The old man, on his hands and knees, looked in the high-dried grass, finding an old wooden stake. Wrong grave. Moving over, he found the gravesite. Numbers were branded onto the stakes. He exposed four stakes. It was the size of four standard-size graves. He told Bonnie, ten wide and two deep was what the city requires in Potter's Field. The document said there were twenty bodies, eleven with names and nine unknowns. The list had a Mr. and Mrs. Duffy, but no first names. The old man, along with Bonnie and Joseph, cleared some of the heavier grass off the gravesite by hand on their hands and knees as the prison guard watched. As Bonnie placed the wreath, it started to snow.

Bonnie quietly told her parents, "I am well, have prospered, and I am happy."

Bonnie introduced her husband, saying, "This is Joseph, my husband. I am a very lucky woman with Joseph as my husband." Bonnie held up her left hand, showing them her wedding ring.

Then Bonnie said the Lord's Prayer. Joseph, the guard, and the old man folded their hands and bowed their heads in respect. Bonnie had noticed an occasional bouquet of dried-up old flowers and a few widely spread grave marker.

As the snow continued and started to cover the ground, Bonnie told Joseph, "What a cold and lonely place. At least they have each other. The one thing I remember mostly of my parents was the love for each other. Their love overflowed onto me."

Bonnie asked the old man, "What about a grave marker?"

The old man said, "There are no provisions for grave markers. The city has ordered us to remove them in the past, especially over the mass graves. Some people have their loved one's bodies exhumed and reburied in another graveyard. That is expensive."

Bonnie asked, "My parents died in a fire eight year ago. How would you know which bodies were theirs?"

"Ma'am, with all due respect, after eight years, to be honest, we would guess. I have a life sentence and have worked here for over fifteen years. I believe 'ashes to ashes, dust to dust.' The souls of all here are in the Lord's hands."

Bonnie said, "Thank you for your words of wisdom. I know my parents are together with Jesus, still sharing their love."

Bonnie tried to hand the convict a ten-dollar gold piece, but he refused, saying, "That will just get me beaten up. God bless you."

After their boat ride, on their carriage ride back to the ship, Bonnie told Joseph.

"I left New York a scared, naive girl who had a lot of anger that fueled my determination. Thank you for standing by me as I buried my childhood ghosts. My grandfather told me my anger, passion, and determination were hereditary. They came with the Irish Blood and Red Hair. Thank you for putting up with me."

"Putting up with you makes life good."

Bonnie replied, "Those are two of the many reasons I love you, your understanding and patience. Even if you are sometimes full of shit."

Passing a book store, Bonnie had them stop where she bought several books.

Joseph looked at her selection, which included European History, European Cultures, Fundamentals of Electricity, The Great Trade Routes of the World, and a few other intellectual selections.

Joseph said, "You totally amaze me."

Bonnie replied, "A little reading help me keep my mind occupied, so I do not miss you so much."

Joseph quipped, "Now who is full of shit?"

Bonnie answered, "That is not shit."

That evening, Joseph took Bonnie to the Bijou Theater on Broadway to see *Miss Dynamite*. Bonnie wore her blue sapphire and diamond jewelry with an exquisite dress, while Joseph wore a tuxedo. They were escorted by two Pinkertons. The play was not a hit; only half the seats were filled. Joseph said that the play's name reminded him of his wife. They had reservations at Delmonico's, and they were seated at a table reserved for their best guests. It soon became apparent that the staff had told people who the young couple was, for people were eager to introduce themselves.

"Are you the Smithfields of the steamship lines? We are the . . . one of New York's first families."

"Yes, I am Joseph Smithfield, and this is my wife, Bonnie."

"The lady the ship is named after."

It was obvious that most were looking for an invitation to sit down with the Smithfields. An opportunity to promote their own social standing. The SS *Bonnie Duffy* was big news in New York. They had a lot of good publicity. An American steamship that was challenging the Europeans. New York was big business and finance. Who you knew was important in establishing social standing and possible promotions in business.

* * * * *

Back at the ship, a few crew members had jumped ship and they were replaced. A few extra fireman, maids, and seamen were hired. The stores were full. All passengers were aboard. first and second-lass was fully booked.

At daybreak, Joseph went down the gangway just as it was pulled up. He had some extra luggage, a tea service for mom, as well as a few medallions for dad.

Bonnie already missed Joseph as his feet left the gangway.

CHAPTER 14

Across the Big Pond

The lines were cast off. For several hours, the boilers had been stoked and the hot coal banked, ready for work, steam pressure was up. The large steam whistle was blown as the *Bonnie Duffy* was eased away from the dock with the help of three large tugs. As the bow was pointed south to exit the upper harbor, the lines to the tugs were cast off. The three propellers churned the water as the boiler air drafts were opened full and the hot coal spread. As they passed Ellis Island, then the Statue of Liberty, they picked up speed. They reached the lower harbor and turned east. Although it had not been posted or publicly announced, most knew that they were going for the record.

Two weeks earlier, a new westbound record was established by the RMS *Lucania*, a new steamship operated by the Cunard Steamship Lines. The *Lucania* averaged 20.9 knots over a distance of 2,911 nautical miles. Compared to the *Bonnie*, the *Lucania* was a little longer at

RMS Lucania 1890s

622 feet with an advertised maximum speed of 23.5 knots. Captain Krupp thought his ship could maintain a faster speed over a distance. It was a challenge.

As the *Bonnie* passed north of Sandy Hook, New Jersey, the starting line, Bonnie looked at the knot meter: 21.8 knots. The vibration from the engines could be felt all over the ship as they strained to push the ship forward. The *Bonnie Duffy* was sitting low in the water from an over load of coal, and they were sailing against a moderate wind. The iceberg season would not start for a couple of months, lessening the North Atlantic sailing hazard. The question was, Could they keep up this speed for six days?

The Navigator took bearings, establishing their course base. The whistle was blown, and they were off. As land disappeared over their stern, Bonnie went to breakfast. In the dining room, many wanted to know their speed.

Bonnie pointed her two thumbs up and said, "We are cruising at 21.8 knots against a moderate head wind."

Charlotte asked, "Can we keep this speed for six days? The engines are shaking the whole ship."

Bonnie asked, "Is the vibration bothering our passengers?"

Charlotte replied, "Some of our passengers bought passage hoping to be part of a record. They want to be part of history. Many are looking at this voyage like a great sporting event, America challenging the mighty British at what they claim to be the undisputed best. All dining rooms and cafeterias have chalkboards where our speed is to be posted at the change of every watch. There are several gambling pools as to our success. The big pool is the time we finish abeam of Fort Perch Rock Light, marking the entrance to Liverpool in Greenwich Time. Guesses are to two seconds, one dollar a guess. The pool is over a thousand dollars and growing."

Bonnie asked, "What is your guess?"

"I cannot participate. The rules say no ship's officers. The ship's officers have their own pool at five dollars a chance. I have not put in my guess yet. I am hoping you will help me."

"I thought you and the Captain were close?"

"Where did you hear that?"

"The harder you try to be discrete the more obvious it becomes. A bit of advice, do not win the pool, or there will be talk."

Charlotte asked, "Just hypothetically, would an indiscretion jeopardize my job?"

Bonnie answered, "You are an attractive woman, and the Captain a handsome man, both single. With a moderate amount of discretion, it is nobody's business."

Charlotte stated, "I love my job. I do not want to jeopardize it."

"Do not worry about it. You are too valuable for an indiscretion to disrupt your career. A little gossip would only make you more interesting. Like what you say about advertisement."

Charlotte, responded, "Thank you for the advice. I do not like the advertisement reference, though."

Bonnie then changed the subject. "How is everything going? What do you need me to help you with?"

Charlotte said, "It is almost scary. Everything is going smoothly. The casino is very popular. They are not making money, but they are keeping people busy and entertained. They now have a piano and pianist that are working out, along with the guitarist. People love good music. The casino is run by a committee of three that are elected by the employees. I asked them if they were making a profit. They said no, by your orders. They are self-supporting. Any excess money is given to employees as bonuses. After the incident with the crook Hobart, they are endeavoring to run honest games. They fully disclosed all to me, showing me their books. There bonuses are reasonable. The bonuses are making for some very motivated people wanting satisfied customers. Do you want to do anything?"

"I did say something like that. That was not exactly what I meant, but if it is not broken, do not fix it. I have asked and not heard anything derogatory about the casino. What do you think?"

Charlotte sighed, "No loss, no crime. Everyone says the games are honest."

Bonnie went to change into an oil-stained work dress and headed for the engine room. Smitey pointed to the engine room knot meter, 21.9 knots.

Bonnie said, "Good speed."

Smitey answered, "The best coal—hard, dense, high BTU, low ash, low moisture content, low Sulphur—burns very hot with a blue flame. Northeast Pennsylvania blue anthracite, best steam coal in the world. At 195 PSI steam with all three engines wide open, turning sixty-five RPM. We are getting a little propeller cavitation. That is the excess vibration you feel. The engines are solid. I foresee no problems. Let us check out what your new motormen are doing."

On top of the midship engine were Annie, Betty, and the Second Assistant Engineer, installing what looked like tubing. The engine was running at full speed, and the moving parts appeared to be a blur to the eyes.

Smitey said, "They are installing automatic oilers. The oilers will only have to fill the oil reservoirs once a day and oil some small parts. It will make it safer and improve efficiency." He then adamantly stated his position, "My oilers will not be available for other work. I need them. They will be the next generation of engineers. They are working as apprentice engineers improving the engines. What will I have to do to get them acknowledged as motormen and apprentice engineers."

Bonnie said, "According to the official ship's roster, two are already motormen. I will take care of it if you continue watching over them. With five apprentice engineers, this engine room should be a showcase. What if all of them do not want to be engineers?"

Smitey stated, "It better be something good for my girls."

Bonnie went into the boiler room. The boilers were so hot it felt like Bonnie's dress was going to burn, like she had done to her socks long ago. The air coming in the air intakes was cold; it was very uncomfortable. Roast on one side, freeze on the other. Bonnie concluded that the men working here were working with one foot in hell and the other in the arctic.

There was coal piled all about, leaving little room to walk.

Bonnie asked, "What if one of those coal piles catch on fire?"

The Chief Fireman answered, "We shovel it into a boiler. At this speed, we shovel about twelve tons of coal an hour."

After that, Bonnie went to her cabin to study. She wanted to understand great circle courses. The shortest distance to England was to sail northeast along Nova Scotia then Newfoundland. Bonnie absconded a ball from the exercises room and drew lines on it representing longitude and latitude. Then with a string stretched, it became obvious.

At twilight, she was on the bridge. The southern part of Nova Scotia could be seen on the horizon. Bonnie took three star sights. With practice, she felt she was becoming confident in taking astronomical sights. Her math to reduce a sight to a line of position was getting better. A bearing on Nova Scotia gave Bonnie four lines of position. Bonnie's practice coincided with the Navigator's official position. The knot meter read 21.9 knots; they were traveling in the Golf Stream, adding to their speed that the knot meter did not show.

Megan, Peggy, and Willa joined Bonnie and Charlotte for dinner.

Willa asked, "Mrs. Smithfield, I asked the Navigator if he could explain navigation to the students. He recommended you, saying he made things sound complicated and you would be a better teacher. Will you help out for a couple of hours tomorrow morning? It would help explain the uses and need for mathematics."

Bonnie answered, "I would love to help out. What time?"

After, Bonnie took her morning sights and a bearing on St. Johns, Newfoundland. She got a porter to help her and headed for the crew's cafeteria for school. Bonnie was excited, she always liked school, except for the bullies. Bonnie was going prepared—sextant, books, ball, adjustable parallels, protractor, dividers, pencils, and charts. Bonnie suddenly realized she was going as a teacher, not a student. She was prepared to learn, but Bonnie admitted to herself she did not know anything about teaching. She had done it again, getting herself in a situation she was not prepared for.

Bonnie asked, "Willa, what do I do? How do I start? There is so much!"

Willa smiled. "I see you brought lots of things. Show the students what you brought and let them ask questions. What is in the wooden box?"

"That is my sextant. It is used to take sights on celestial objects."

Willa responded, "That sounds like a good start to me."

Bonnie put all her things on a table, and as the students arrived, they all looked, but none touched.

Willa pointed to the sextant. "What is that fancy-looking thing?"

Bonnie answered, "This is a sextant. With it, I can take an accurate measurement of the angle between a heavenly body and the horizon. With that measurement and knowing the time and information from a Nautical Almanac, I can determine a line of position. With three lines of position, I can determine where I am on Earth. Sounds real complicated, I know. It really is not all that complicated. It is really a series of simple steps that must be learned and done in the right order." Bonnie then showed on the blackboard what she meant by angle from celestial object and horizon.

Bonnie then laid out the chart that she had plotted her fix that morning. She explained that at 6:42 that morning, they were at the fixed position she had plotted, just off the coast of Newfoundland.

One student asked, "Where are we at now?"

Bonnie looked at her grandfather's watch, and went to the blackboard, wrote down the formula, TxS=D, elapsed time, multiplied by the speed, equals distance traveled. It was a lesson in math. Speed 22.0 knots, time one hour, fifty minutes equals 1.833 hours, equals 40.33 nautical miles. Then back to the chart. With the compass rose printed on the chart, a line at the proper course was drawn, and the distance was marked off using dividers, determining their present dead reckoning position. Bonnie tried to do everything slowly, explaining what and why she did the things she did.

At first the questions came from Willa, then the student's curiosity overruled their shyness. Then Bonnie got a question that she did not want to answer.

A student asked, "At what time are we going to be at the Fort Perch Rock Light?"

Bonnie answered, "That is the thousand-dollar question. If all goes right, in a little less than five days from now."

Willa said, "Can we as a class calculate an estimated time of arrival? We will do the work, just tell us what to do."

Bonnie instructed them how to lay out a great circle course on a large-scale chart of the North Atlantic. She was not proficient and had to refer to her books. All the students wanted to be part of the exercise, including reading the books. Bonnie struggled to keep her hands off and let the students do the work. The marked-up ball, representing Earth, and a string stretched made it clear to all what a great circle course was. It was also a lesson on longitude and latitude. They measured off the distance, with 22.5 knots selected as the average speed. A factor was added for the Gulf Stream current that was marked on the chart. The Gulf Stream current speed decreased as they neared the north of their course. A couple of the older students worked to average the Gulf Stream factor. Distance and time left to travel were calculated. Another lesson on time zones and Greenwich Mean Time was given by Willa. Some of the students thought they would go faster, some slower. Each student picked out their time. If they bought a lottery ticket, they would have to select from the times still available. Out of the eighteen students, Bonnie thought all but two could afford a one-dollar lottery ticket.

Peggy said, "Anybody need a dollar for their bet, see me. The deal will be, if you win, you will give me one hundred dollars out of your winnings. Last I heard, the pool was nearing seventeen hundred dollars."

After class, Willa told Bonnie, "Thank you, Mrs. Smithfield. Mathematics now means something important to all the students. Everyone including myself learned many things. You are an excellent teacher." Bonnie wanted to tell Willa that she was full of it, but she held her tongue.

The oiler twins, Cathy and Dotty, wanted to borrow one of Bonnie's books to study navigation. Bonnie lent the girls two books and told them she would help them when she could if they so wished. The twins were enthusiastic; they wanted to learn navigation.

At evening twilight, Bonnie took her sights. Bonnie was gaining confidence in her navigation skills. She reduced her three sights to lines of position. Two gave the same fix that the Navigator derived, one had a small error. Bonnie was slower than the Navigator, but with practice, she hoped to gain speed. Bonnie had been told that accuracy was more important than speed in navigation. A mistake in navigation could land a ship upon rocks.

Bonnie asked, "Captain, can I have your permission to bring two young ladies to the bridge and pilothouse for a tour?"

"When?" the Captain asked.

"Tomorrow morning at twilight."

"Permission granted."

Bonnie went to the engine room.

"Smitey, where is Cathy or Dotty?"

Smitey pointed up. "She will be down in a couple of minutes."

There on the catwalk, around the top of the starboard engine, was one of the twins.

The twin came down, and Bonnie waved, getting the girl's attention.

"Hi, Mrs. Smithfield. I am Dotty. Want your books back?"

"No. I do not need my books now. I would like to know if you and Cathy would like to come with me to see the bridge tomorrow morning at the break of day? I can show you how navigation on the ship is done. If it is all right with Smitey."

Smitey looked at his roster schedule. "I can spare them until noon."

Dotty said, "Yes, ma'am. Can we wear our fancy Rio de Janeiro samba dresses?"

"All right, fancy dresses but no dancing. I will meet you in the crew cafeteria at five in the morning. Can you get up that early?"

"Yes, ma'am, we will be there. We will bring your books."

Bonnie said, "See you in the morning."

At dinner, Charlotte asked, "Bonnie, what are you up to now?"

"What are you talking about?"

"Two young ladies to the bridge at daylight."

"You know I helped Willa at school. Two girls are interested in navigation. So I thought I could show them how it is really done. Who have you been talking to? As if I did not know."

Charlotte bantered back, "From oiler to Navigator?"

Bonnie quipped back, "I think you need a young helper, an apprentice. So you can pass on your great knowledge."

"If I need a helper, I will select my own. Are you ready to pay for me to have an assistant?"

Bonnie said, "If you need an assistant, hire one."

Charlotte asked, "Am I right about the oiler girls?"

"Yes, you are right. I have a soft spot for them. If I remember correctly, you introduced them to me. So it is your fault."

"I was proud of that until I saw them at work."

Bonnie said, "We? If I remember correctly, you gave the problem to me and left. You were busy."

Charlotte replied, "Yes, we. I knew you would take care of them. After seeing them at work, I question my involvement. Seeing them at work has given me nightmares. Here they at least have a chance, if they do not get mutilated. At least they get good food and a berth to sleep in. I will blame you if one of them gets ground up."

Bonnie said, "They scare me too."

* * * * *

The next day, Bonnie arrived early to find the twins eager and ready. They did look cute in their samba dresses.

Bonnie said, "We are going to the bridge and pilothouse. The men there are operating the ship. We must keep quiet and stay out of the way. If they tell us to leave, we must leave immediately. Can both of you follow those rules?"

Bonnie received two "Yes, ma'am."

The twins followed Bonnie through the ship. They went up the inside stairs to the pilothouse.

The Navigator greeted them. "Who are these beautiful young ladies?"

Bonnie replied, "These are Cathy and Dotty. Which one is which is your guess? Girls, this is the Second Navigator."

The twins did not make a sound; they just nodded.

Bonnie chuckled. "I did not mean that you had to be that quiet. Say hi and tell the Navigator your names."

"Sir, hi, I am Cathy Adams."

"Sir, hi, I am Dotty Adams."

With a smile, the Navigator shook each of their hands saying, "Welcome to the pilothouse! This is where we do all the ship's navigation. Do you know what navigation is?"

After a brief silence, Bonnie said, "It is all right, tell him what you know. It is okay to answer questions."

Cathy responded, "Sir, Mrs. Smithfield showed us a little. We plotted a course to Liverpool and calculated the distance and our guess for our arrival time. We are in the pool now."

Dotty added, "Sir, if we win, it will be thousands of dollars."

Bonnie said, "These are two of our oilers. They want to study navigation."

With a smile, the Navigator said, "Now I am going to do a DR plot, DR stands for dead reckoning. If you want to watch, I will try to explain what I am doing. When daylight starts to break so we can clearly see the horizon, then I will take some sightings on the stars and planets so we can get an accurate fix. If you have any questions, please ask. Just keep your voices low so we do not disturb the men on the bridge."

The Navigator showed the girls the compass for their heading, writing it down. Then he showed them the ship's log, knot meter for speed 22.3 knots, writing it down. The twins watched and listened intently as the Navigator took the recordings for the last hour and weightily averaged them. He then did his calculations, adding for the Gulf Stream's effect and wind, then he drew a pencil line of their course. Then with dividers, he marked off the distance, placing a X, writing down the time, and initialing his work. The Navigator patiently explained his every step.

The Navigator asked, "What do you ladies think? Any questions?"

Dotty asked, "Sir, we did our calculations, figuring 22.5 knots. Our guesses will be wrong."

The Navigator replied, "We will increase speed as we burn coal and get lighter. Now we have a head wind. I think that will change, which will help our speed, so 22.5 knots sound good to me, at this time."

The Navigator and Bonnie went out to the bridge-deck with their sextants, the twins following. The air was nippy.

The Captain was on the bridge-deck. "Good morning, ladies. It looks like it will be a nice day, a little cool though."

Bonnie said, "Good morning, Captain. These are Cathy and Dotty. Do we have permission to stand on the bridge-deck, sir?"

"Permission granted, do not get in the way."

Cathy said, "Yes, sir, Captain."

Dotty echoed, "Yes, sir, Captain."

They had a few minutes until the horizon became clear and distinct.

The Captain pointed to the sky. "That star is Bellatrix, over there Betelgeuse, there Adhere, and there Pollux. They will be good navigation stars to get a celestial fix this morning."

As dawn broke, the Navigator had to accomplish his task while the light was correct and the horizon clearly visible. Bonnie handed her sextant to one of the twins, explaining how to twist the knob and look through the lens and adjust till the horizon and star lined up. "Let us sight on that star over there, Pollux. When the star and horizon line up, say 'Mark,' and I will read the time. Do not turn the knob anymore. We will read the angle from the curved bar and knob."

The Captain shocked Bonnie when he addressed the other twin. "Which one are you? You both look alike."

"I am Dotty, Captain, sir."

"Dotty, let us see if we can get a sighting on Betelgeuse." He handed Dotty his sextant.

It took several tries. The Captain told Dotty, "It takes a lot of practice to learn to get accurate readings from a sextant."

The horizon started to blur as the Sun started to rise, but each girl had a sight. It felt good to return to the pilothouse out of the cold air. Bonnie helped Cathy as the Captain helped Dotty, reducing their sights to a line of position. It was confusing to the twins; it had been very confusing to Bonnie the first time. The twin's sights were within ten nautical miles from the Navigator's fix. This was sort of a test for the twins. If they persevered to learn how to reduce a sight, then they had what it took to be a Navigator. Bonnie would lend them her book on celestial navigation.

As they were leaving, the Captain again astonished Bonnie.

The Captain said, "Here is my old sextant. It still works good. You can borrow it to practice if you promise to take good care of it."

Dotty exclaimed, "Thank you, Captain, sir. We will guard it with our lives."

Cathy said, "Yes, sir, thank you, Captain."

Bonnie was proud of her samba girls; they looked so cute in their dresses and had been so polite. She than took them to the first-class dining room for breakfast.

Charlotte joined them, "How did you do on your navigation lesson?"

Cathy answered, "Not very good. It is hard."

Bonnie added, "Yes, it is very hard. It took me a lot of practice to learn how. I still need more practice. If it was easy, being a Navigator would not be an important job. It takes a special person to be a good Navigator and a lot of study and practice."

Charlotte said, "All ships need a good Navigator. I see you have your own sextant."

Dotty explained, "It is the Captain's. He lent it to us. The Captain is a real nice man."

Cathy added, "The Captain is not scary after you get to know him."

After breakfast, Bonnie escorted the twins to the crew's cafeteria. Bonnie was rewarded with two big sincere hugs. Bonnie thought, *I gave them the opportunity, now it is up to them.*

* * * * *

The fourth morning, it had become cloudy; they had a fresh west wind. The plot showed that they were about halfway. The speed was a phenomenal 22.8 knots. They no longer would get an assist from the Gulf Stream. That speed meant little if they could not sustain it over a distance.

First Mate said, "The North Atlantic High-Pressure Center is south of us and should push us all the way to Liverpool. As long as our coal holds out, we are looking at a record. We are burning about twelve tons an hour."

Bonnie did the math in her head. *Six days is 144 hours. At twelve tons an hour, that is over their sixteen hundred tons of coal, the question is, what is about twelve tons an hour?* They had some coal aboard before taking on the sixteen hundred tons. There was some coal in their cargo holds.

At breakfast, the Captain joined Bonnie and Charlotte. The way the Captain and Charlotte looked at each other, the stare, then the purposeful look away, it was obvious to Bonnie there was a close connection there.

The Captain said, "Mrs. Smithfield, I was informed that you are aware of our coal situation. We need to make a decision that I think should include the owner. Should we play it safe or go for the record?"

Bonnie informed Charlotte that at full speed, the coal might run out before they make Liverpool.

Charlotte stated, "We have to go for the record. The prestige will insure the Smithfield Steamship name. How bad is it?"

Bonnie said, "Captain, I will defer to your judgment. I want a record, but the safety of the ship, crew, and passengers must come first."

The Captain said, "If we run short of coal, we can easily make Belfast, adding a port of call. Would that be acceptable?"

Bonnie looked at Charlotte and got a nod of approval.

Bonnie said, "Belfast would be acceptable if appropriate."

The Captain stated, "Thank you. Full speed, Belfast will be an alternate destination."

After a pause, the Captain continued, "For the safe and efficient operation of this ship, I have made two ship's crew reassignments. Effective immediately, C. Adams and D. Adams are reassigned from oilers to bridge crew assistants. They are being informed of their reassignment by the Chief Engineer. The bridge crew can use the extra help, and it is the responsibility of the ship's officers to train the next generation. As bridge crew, they will have to dress appropriately as seamen. While on duty, dresses will not be permitted.

As Charlotte smirked at Bonnie, Bonnie said, "Yes, sir."

After eating, the Captain excused himself and left. Bonnie perceived it was uncomfortable for the Captain and Charlotte to sit together and act like they were just acquaintances. It made Bonnie yearn for her Joseph.

After the Captain left, Bonnie told Charlotte, "Good move, Charlotte."

"What are you talking about, Bonnie?"

"Go ahead and play innocent and naive if you like. You don't fool me."

"I think that the Captain made an appropriate decision. Between you and me, for the Captain to acknowledge gender may be a political problem. For the time being, they are Seaman C. Adams and D. Adams, as they are listed on the ship's roster."

Bonnie said, "I do not like it, but I understand."

Bonnie's curiosity got the better of her. Midmorning, she went to the bridge. It took a lot of restraint for her to not break out in laughter. There was one of the twins in a sailor's uniform that was hastily taken in. Whoever had done the tailoring must have had no experience or wanted to make a crude statement. The pant legs had been rolled up and crudely tacked. The waist had a large pleat sticking out the back. Her shirt was likewise tacked to make it smaller. She had her hair stuffed up into a sailor's hat that was too large, which covered her ears. On her feet were her oil-stained work boots, which looked like someone had hastily tried to polish them. If she did a little dance and sang, it would make a memorable vaudeville comedy act.

Bonnie observed that the twin had a notebook and pencil and was watching the chronograph. When Bonnie looked over her shoulder, it was obvious that she was recording the ship's course, speed, apparent wind speed, and apparent wind direction every ten minutes. Speed was 22.7 knots.

After the twin had finished recording her readings, Bonnie asked, "Which twin are you, and do you like your new assignment?"

"Ma'am, I am Seaman D. Adams and I like my new job. It is an important job. It is cloudy, so we cannot get a fix here on the high seas. My readings are necessary for our dead reckoning, which is crucial. Mrs. Smithfield, thank you. If I were not on duty, I would give you a big hug."

Bonnie chuckled, "Might I suggest that you have a uniform fitted for you? The ship provides uniforms. See the ship's tailor."

"Ma'am, I am sorry I did not have time. I borrowed this uniform from a sailor and tried to make it fit without ruining it. Tomorrow, I will have a new uniform."

Dotty whispered in Bonnie's ear, "The Captain laughed at my uniform and ordered me to get a uniform that fit before I report for my next duty. Do you think I look funny?"

Bonnie said, "A cute kind of funny. If you need anything, see Miss Charlotte or me."

A look at the chart showed that they were making good progress. The ship's log showed that two other ships had been sighted, both westbound. Bonnie decided to go to her lonely and cold berth to read.

* * * * *

Morning, day six. Today would be the day. By late evening, they would be heading toward Belfast or continue to Liverpool. Bonnie went to the bridge early. There was a twin in a uniform that fit appropriately, busily recording the compass course and the speed that was now 22.8. Now they had been running at full speed for 120 hours. As scheduled, in twelve hours, they would be near Belfast or, in twenty hours approaching Liverpool, pending no mishaps. The clouds were clearing, so a star sight might be possible. During the night, they sighted a westbound ship, and the mast light of a ship could be seen ahead, eastbound. They had gained four hours in local time. On schedule, Liverpool would be at dawn.

At twilight, Bonnie managed to get one sight and the Navigator two, between the clouds. They had their fix, and now they had to make a small course correction.

At breakfast, everyone wanted to know their progress and coal status. Bonnie told people that it looked promising.

Charlotte asked, "Honestly, how does it look?"

"This evening, the Captain will make the decision, Belfast or Liverpool. Either way, it will be a record at our present speed."

Charlotte asked, "How are our new Navigators?"

"Busy, a long way from being Navigators. They are conscientious and determined with good attitudes."

Bonnie's next stop was the engine room.

Smitey greeted her, "You stole two of my girls. I forgive you, you gave then good jobs. All five of them have become the daughters I never had."

Bonnie replied, "You have remarkable daughters that you have a right to be proud of. And for the record, I did not steal then, the Captain needed them."

"Thank you," he said. "Now as for what you came here for, our coal stores will be close at this speed. I have no answer for you, sorry."

Bonnie started to wonder if Smitey ever slept; he seemed to be always on duty.

In the boiler room, there was a cold draft on one side and a roasting on the other. Bonnie walked along the coal bunkers. Many were empty and their floors swept clean. The floor sweepings were dangerous; fine coal dust could be explosive. The bunkers would be swept with water, the sweepings caked and dried before burning. Five days ago, all the bunkers were full and coal was piled in every available spot. Coal was being brought from the ship's holds. Bonnie did some quick math in her head—sixteen hundred tons plus the one hundred forty tons they had would be 3,480,000 pounds. They had taken on water into their ballast tanks to hold the ship on its lines. It was going to be a long day.

Bonnie went back to the bridge. The clouds made a noon-sun sight difficult, and the First Navigator got an upper-limb sun sight that he was not totally confident in. Charting it did give a little confidence in their DR plot. They were gaining on the ship in front of them. It was a fast ship. Plotting indicated that at their current speed and the estimated speed of the ship in front of them, they would overtake the ship in a couple of hours. It would be several hours before the evening sights, landfall, and the point where the Captain would have to make a decision. Bonnie checked their speed, 22.9 knots, and went and took a nap.

Bonnie did get a little rest and felt like she was ready for the upcoming event. The sky had cleared, and at twilight, they got a good fix. They were right on course and steaming at 22.8 knots. The ship that was ahead had taken a more southerly course and was out of sight, it was probably headed for the west coast of Ireland. Seven hours to Belfast or twelve to Fort Perch Rock, the entrance to Liverpool. Everyone had to wait for the decision of the Captain.

Bonnie's heart ached for the Captain. She knew the decision he would make had long-term consequences for the ship and for him. Play it safe and dock in Belfast; it would be the smart thing to do. The Captain would get praise and would set a record. His ship, passengers, and crew arrived safely without any incident, although he stopped short of Liverpool, the advertised destination. The risk, run out of coal and having to get a tow to port, or maybe get lucky and limp in. That would be a career destroyer for a Captain and negative for the ship. Slow down and arrive at the destination safely, the smart thing to do. No record. The record would also establish the reliability of the ship and crew. Risk all, and if successful, the headlines could read, "SS *Bonnie Duffy* Sets Transatlantic Record. Wins Blue Riband. The Skipper, the young Captain Krupp on his First Command, Goes into the Record Book."

The First Mate was in command of the bridge. Bonnie assumed that the Captain was resting. It would be a long night for their Captain. Bonnie went to the engine room. There she was met by Annie, the oldest of the five girls. Bonnie got a big hug and a thank-you, also another soiled dress. Annie was now a motorman and helped run the engine room.

Bonnie asked, "Annie, how are things going?" Bonnie got a tour.

"Mrs. Smithfield, everything is wide open. All three of our babies are happily purring. Just listen to them." To Bonnie, the sound was a deafening cacophony.

"Ma'am, steam almost 200 PSI, 210 PSI, and the relief valves will blow. Port and starboard engines turning 68 RPM, amidships 66 RPM. The amidships propeller has to deal with the resistance of the keel and rudder apertures. The auto oilers really help. Over five days wide open, and they are still solid and happy. And thank you for helping, Cathy and Dotty. They are really happy. Eavey wants to be a motorman than an engineer. She is studying hard, she is studying electricity. Smitey says that electricity will be an important part of engineering in the future. Anything else you want to see? The Captain and Smitey are in the boiler room checking on the coal."

Bonnie, "Thank you for the tour and your good work."

In the boiler room, Bonnie found the Captain and Smitey looking at the coal bunkers, each with pencil and paper.

The Captain said, "I suppose you want to know our next port?"

Bonnie replied, "Captain, that is your decision when you decide to make it. I have confidence in you. I will support you whatever your decision and the outcome."

The Captain said, "I appreciate your vote of confidence. Please do not tell people yet. No matter how we calculate it, we are there. Anything—a small steam leak, a little head wind, another ship we have to steer around, a few shovels of bad coal, anything and we will be embarrassed. Mrs. Smithfield, what do you think?"

Bonnie said, "I am glad that I do not have to make the decision. No matter what happens, I—and I am sure, Charlotte—will support you. I also believe that the crew and passengers will support you. You are a good man who is respected by all."

"Thanks for your support. What I really need are a few more tons of coal as insurance. A couple hundred pounds would make me feel better."

Bonnie asked, "Captain, is it all right if I wait on the bridge?"

"Yes, I might need some moral support."

It was a few minutes before 10:00 p.m. when Captain stepped on the bridge and asked for a report on the situation from the First Mate.

The First Mate reported, "Sir, we have started a gradual turn to starboard, one rudder point, heading for the Irish Sea, to a course of south-southeast passing the Isle of Man to our port, or we can divert to Belfast. Speed is 22.8 knots. We have a fifteen-knot wind from the northwest. We have plotted a couple of bearings from land navigation lights, giving us a good position. Lookouts report one ship that should pass to our starboard and a fishing boat to our port. We are shipshape, and moral is high, waiting for your orders, sir."

After what seemed to be an uncomfortable pause, the Captain said, "Best course to Liverpool, full speed."

Bonnie was sure she heard a silent cheer. She did hear a muffled "yes" from Cathy.

Bonnie silently said a little prayer for the Captain and the ship, knowing the consequences.

Charlotte showed up.

Bonnie said, "Charlotte, hold off any announcement. Plans might change, Liverpool."

Charlotte shouted, "Yahoo!" which got her a disapproving look from the Captain and Bonnie.

Bonnie said, "Charlotte, restraint please. One little thing going wrong could abort our run."

Charlotte said, "I am sorry, it is just so exciting."

Looking at Charlotte, the Captain said, "In three hours, there will be no turning back, we will be committed."

Bonnie excused herself and went to the engine room. The entire engineering crew was on duty.

Bonnie asked, "Smitey, what is going on? All the people."

Smitey said, "All hands at their duty stations."

"I did not hear that order."

Smitey nodded, "No order needs to be given for the ship."

In the boiler room, which was a hellhole, there were more people than what was needed. All the coal had been removed from the cargo holds. Bonnie watched as men used wheelbarrows brought coal from the bunkers to the boilers as other men shoveled the coal into the boilers. Most all the coal bunkers were empty. They were scraping the floors.

Bonnie returned to the engine room. "Smitey, are they shoveling coal too fast?"

Smitey pointed to a gauge. "Unless I get orders from the bridge, 190 to 200 PSI steam, full speed ahead."

Bonnie asked, "There seems to be more people working than is needed."

Smitey said, "Pride in their ship, all hands at their duty stations."

Bonnie returned to the bridge. There was no unnecessary talk; everyone seemed intent to their jobs. There were six men on the bridge-deck as lookouts and two in the crow's nest.

At three in the morning, the Captain spoke. "Miss Gibbs, if you wish, you can announce that we will make Liverpool in four hours, if all goes well."

Charlotte acknowledged, "Thank you, Captain."

Dotty showed up and was pressing herself into the corner of the pilothouse, technically not on duty, trying to be inconspicuous.

It was a long and suspenseful night. There was no unnecessary conversation. The tension could be felt by all.

At a little before seven, local time, they were nearing the channel marked by Fort Perch Rock Light. All knew the coal was gone. The vibration of the engines was abating, and the speed had fallen to 18.2 knots.

The Captain ordered, "Seaman C. Adams and Seaman D. Adams, prepare to sound the main whistle."

The Second Navigator, who was taking a bearing to the Fort Perch Rock Light, signaled.

The Captain ordered, "Blow long and hard."

The twins obliged with a long whistle blow on the main whistle. Several checked, including the First Navigator, the ship's chronometer marking down the time to the second.

Charlotte lost control of herself and threw her arms around the Captain's neck and tried to give him a kiss.

The Captain reeled back and said, "Miss Gibbs, please control yourself!"

The Captain ordered, "All engines one-quarter ahead."

The engine room was signaled, and the signal was acknowledged.

They made it—3,100 nautical miles in 5 days, 17 hours, 45 minutes, average speed 22.5 knots with two minutes, twelve seconds to spare. A new record.

Bonnie realized the real record did not belong to the ship but the Captain and the crew. The ship was just a machine. People brought it to life, gave it a heart and soul.

It was only four miles to the dock. They had enough steam as the remnants of the coal in the boilers burnt to make it to the pier and keep the generators turning for several hours.

Bonnie stepped out onto the bridge-deck. The rails were lined with passengers and crew. The celebration had started. The most Luxurious, Safest, and Fastest ship, flying the Stars and Stripes, proudly sailed into the great British port.

The Captain and Bonnie went ashore to clear with costume and the port authority. They were overwhelmed with paperwork and treated with extreme British snobbery. They had been forewarned that bribery would land a foreigner in prison in England. Working their way up the chain of command, they were finally told.

"Britain rules the seas. You upstarts must learn your place. Throughout the world, the British Admiralty has priority for all resources, including coal that they reserved in out-of-the way places. The Blue Riband is a British Trophy."

Bonnie just smiled at the government official, wanting to say, "You are sore losers."

They were also informed that all anthracite coal in Britain was assigned to the Admiralty and was not available to foreign ships. Bonnie just smiled, knowing that they were winners.

After several hours, they had cleared the ship, and now each passenger or crew member would have to go through customs to go ashore. They arranged for several wagonloads of bituminous coal to be delivered to the ship.

The ship was met by several reporters from several countries, including a reporter from the *New York Times*, not one reporter from Britain. It was obvious that the SS *Bonnie Duffy* was being ostracized by the British.

Communications by telegraph was amazing. The transatlantic cable was busy. By noon, the congratulatory telegrams started to come in. Some of which were of note: President Grover Cleveland, Andrew Carnegie, John D. Rockefeller, Thomas A. Edison, California Governor Henry Markham, George Hearst, and many others who were shaping American's industry, economy, and politics. From the telegrams, it became apparent it was a matter of American Pride. America was no longer just a bunch of rebellious colonies.

There were also requests. One from the US Secretary of the Navy, Hilary Herbert, through the US Embassy in London. He requested that a US Naval Attaché from London sail aboard the SS *Bonnie Duffy* and be given access to the ship where appropriate. A similar request came from Kaiser Wilhelm II of Germany through his Admiralty; his attaché would board in France.

The Captain explained to Charlotte and Bonnie, "The Blue Riband had two separate listings, one for west-bound and one for east-bound. After verification, the SS Bonnie Duffy will hold the record for east-bound. The Luciana will still hold the west-bound record. West-bound is considered more difficult, fighting the prevailing west winds and against the *Gulf Stream*. We broke the record by a substantial amount. Everybody will be trying to catch up. To catch up will mean new ships. The passengers are also giving rave reviews of the experience. Everyone wants faster reliable ships, and all want more luxury. The Germans want to be a major naval power and want to be a major force in the passenger liner market. They all want to look and see our new ship."

Bonnie telegraphed Dad for his advice.

Bonnie got a telegram form her mother-in-law: "CONGRATULATIONS STOP TEA SERVICE EXQUISITE STOP LOVE MOTHER."

Charlotte and Bonnie found a silversmith who agreed to make silver commemorative medallions for their record-breaking transatlantic voyage. They would have the head side match their other medallion with the ship's image and name, on the opposite side would be an image of northeast America and the British Isles, with an arc joining them, inscribed with the words "February 1894, 3100 NM, 22.5 Knots Avg."

The city's merchants were friendly and courteous, wanting to sell to the ship and its people. The British economy showed signs that their depression was ending, and the merchants were grateful for any business. They managed to fill the coal bunkers with a coal mix that was mainly anthracite with some bitumen's mixed in. The coal did not meet the British Admiralty's high-standard. Smitey was told the coal was purposefully accidentally mixed for sales to foreign ships.

The $2,332 pool was won by an elderly widow traveling back to England her home. Her American husband had died. The ship's officer's pool was won by a junior deck officer. They both said that they listened to other people and just made guesses. The guesses that most of the students made were within minutes.

* * * * *

Bonnie went into the passenger service office looking for Charlotte and found a young Hispanic woman sitting at Charlotte's desk going through paperwork.

Bonnie asked, "Excuse me, who are you? And what are you doing?"

"Mrs. Smithfield, I am Candida Diaz, Miss Gibbs's assistant. I met you at the Silversmith in Valparaiso. Can I be of assistance to you?"

"Ah. Yes, I remember you now. Where is Charlotte?"

"She should be back in a few minutes. She went to the galley to check provisions."

Bonnie asked, "Mind if I sat and wait for her?"

"I was told that was your desk over there and no one was to touch anything on or in it, except you."

Bonnie sat to her desk and waited.

Charlette showed up in a while. "I see that you met my assistant, Candida. I instructed her that she is to assist you whenever you ask for help."

Bonnie said, "You need anything?"

"No. Everything is good. Got any good advice dealing with these Limeys?"

Bonnie answered, "Yes. Do not call them Limeys to their face."

Charlette sarcastically responded, "Thanks for the advice."

Bonnie suggested, "Candida can use my desk. I hardly ever use it, and I have nothing personal in it. Most of what I need is in my office. She can clean it out, and if she finds anything personal of mine, just save it for me."

Charlotte stated, "I got first claim to your desk. You took the biggest and best, originally. I got what was left."

"Originally, there was only one desk in here. Another large one would not fit. You were lucky to get a desk at all."

Charlotte said, "Love you too."

Candida then said, "Mrs. Smithfield, if you need anything, just ask."

Bonnie said, "Charlotte, see you at lunch."

"Lunch."

At lunch, Charlotte agreed to share Candida as long as Bonnie did not give her too much work. Candida was one of the bilingual women that Charlotte had hired in Acapulco.

* * * * *

Eavey had taken an interest in a small softbound reference book given to her by Mr. Edison on electrical wiring. Smitey caught her installing a light over his small desk without permission. Upon interrogation, she admitted that she and her sisters believed his eyes were going bad and he needed more light. Examining her work, Eavey was reassigned to work on the ships electrical systems. Part of her job was to replace burnt-out electric light bulbs, of which there were many, and inspect electrical connections and string new wire where necessary. The insulation on some of the wire that they originally used was defective and did not last for long. In New York, Mr. Edison arranged that new improved wire be delivered to the ship, along with telephone equipment and other supplies, purchased by Joseph.

Eavey inadvertently became part of a new trade, recently given the name *electrician*. Mr. Edison had sold an in-depth book on electricity to the ship, which Eavey has been enthusiastically digesting. Her sisters had all been busy and did not paying much attention to her. Smitey had noticed her studying the book and thought it a good use of her time. The boys took care of most of the oiling. All the electrical work had been done by the engineers. None of the engineers liked the work; they did not understand it. To them, it was not real engineer's work. It was soon apparent that Eavey knew more about electricity than anyone else aboard. Which was really not saying a lot. Only scientists had some understanding of electricity, even they were still trying to understand it with experiments and theories. By the time they reached Liverpool, Eavey had a reputation of being a wizard when it came to electricity. She even earned the nickname Little Edison. None of the engineers complained. They had more work than they could handle, and electrical work was not considered real engineering work. Upon Smitey's request, Eavey was promoted to Electrician Mate with a small raise in wages. As far as anyone knew, E. Adams was the First Electrician Mate. No standards or requirements had been written yet for Electrician Mate.

While they were in port, three of the boilers were allowed to cool so they could be cleaned inside and out. The three engines were wiped down and inspected, with adjustments made where appropriate. The connecting rod and main crankshaft journals were tightened.

The ship's carpenters had built and installed bookshelves in the crew's cafeteria with railings to hold the books in place in a seaway. At each stop, their library was getting larger. In Liverpool, Megan and Bonnie bought a large quantity of books from a bookstore that was closing, and they donated the books to the ship's library. It was not uncommon to see a first-class passenger in the crew's cafeteria borrowing a book. Bonnie wired Joseph telling him to include a library on the next ship's design, so it would be available to all aboard.

Bonnies father-in-law telegrammed her, "YOUR DECISION STOP ADVERTISEMENT STOP NEW FRIENDS STOP GOOD JOB"

Bonnie sent telegraphs to London and Berlin accepting naval representatives.

On their third and last day in port, the crew that had not had liberty was given a day's liberty. People did not pay attention as the five sisters left the ship wearing their samba dresses. It was not long, and the bobbies had them in jail. If they had been dressed in rags falling off them, it would have been acceptable. No matter how beautiful, short hip-hugging dresses with low-cut tops and slits up the sides revealing their lower thigh were not sociably acceptable in stiff-upper-lipped England, even when worn by adolescent girls. They had shown the police their ship's papers and were being held for providing false identification. The Captain, Charlotte, and Bonnie went to the rescue. The police said they thought it ridiculous, but they had had a complaint from an upstanding citizen. The Police Inspector told them they should give the girls papers that said they were domestic servants, as that would be believable. The sergeant asked what an Electrician Mate was. Bonnie had to shush Eavey as she tried to give a detailed explanation; Eavey was proud of her new job.

Later, in more appropriate dresses, the sisters still had several hours shopping and sightseeing, each buying a bag of candy. Mysteriously, two used, serviceable sextants appeared in the pilot-house. They were identified on new brass plates, C. Adams and D. Adams. Included in each box was a brass-cased pocket watch.

Late afternoon, a US Naval Commander arrived with his wife and three boys. In his full dress uniform, he certainly stood out. He had a voucher for second-class accommodations to be billed to the US Department of the Navy. Bonnie had planned to put the US Naval Officer in the officer's quarters not thinking he had a family with him. Bonnie thought they had no accommodations available. Charlotte told Bonnie, the Smithfield Steamship lines would upgrade a US Naval Commander to first-class accommodations at no additional cost and made the arrangements.

Commander Roberts and his wife were invited to dine at the Captain's table.

The Commander was given a two-year duty assignment as Naval Attaché with the US Embassy in London. He did not expect sea duty with his family. He was obviously an officer with a promising career. He said the *Bonnie Duffy* was quite different from the frigate he had served on. The Captain invite him to the bridge after they were to sea.

The commemorative medallions arrived before their departure and were handed out. The first- and second-class passengers that had disembarked were mailed their medallions to the addresses they gave. Candida took over managing the medallions, except a bag that Bonnie would give out.

Bonnie said, "Now that Candida will do your paperwork, you will have a lot of spare time. Please do not distract the Captain from his duties."

Charlotte tersely told Bonnie, "Go study your navigation and hand out your medallions."

CHAPTER 15

East Atlantic

They hired a local pilot to help them navigate through the treacherous waters of the Irish Sea and St. Georges Channel. The pilot would travel with the ship to La Rochelle, France, and return by ferry to England. The light early-morning fog made navigation hazardous.

The boilers were all fired and the hot coal in them was banked, ready for the drafts to be opened and the coal spread, quickly giving the required heat. As soon as there was enough light to see, two tugs helped nudge the Bonnie toward sea. Bonnie was told they would cruise at twelve knots arriving at La Rochelle at dawn in two days. Going faster would be of no benefit.

Bonnie noticed the USN Commander standing at the bow with a boy about ten.

She went to the bow to talk to the Commander. She was the person who invited him, so she felt responsible. The Commander introduced his son, Bobby. It was not long, and they cleared the harbor, heading west to clear Wales before turning south. It was a little nippy, and a light fog blurred the view. Bonnie invited them on a tour. When they arrived in the engine room, the Commander looked astonished when they were greeted by Betty.

Bonnie said, "Commander Roberts, this is Motorman B. Adams. I am sure she can answer any questions you have."

The Commander asked, "Are you in charge here in the engine room?"

Betty replied, "Sir, Chief Engineer Smitey is in charge. He will be right back. I think he is relieving himself."

"Can you brief me on the engine's present operation?"

Betty answered, "Sir, we are running at twelve knots, 160 pounds of steam, all engines turning thirty-five RPM. At port, we tightened up all the engine journals. Running slower will give them an opportunity to run in."

The Commander asked, "How old are you, miss, and how long have you been a motorman?"

Smitey arrived, stood back, and listened to his trainee.

Betty said, "Sir, I am thirteen and was recently promoted from oiler after we installed auto-oilers."

The Commander asked, "What are the specifications of these engines?"

"Sir, they are triple-expansion six-cylinder reciprocating steam engines each capable of producing nine-thousands shaft rated horsepower at 195 PSI steam turning sixty-five RPM. They each turn a twelve-foot diameter four-flute propeller."

"Thank you," the Commander said. "You are remarkable. It is obvious that you are an asset to this ship."

The Commander's son, Bobby, said, "Dad, she is just a girl."

"Yes," he agreed. "A very smart girl."

Bonnie introduced Smite, the Commander, and his son, Bobby.

The Commander saluted Betty and Smitey, saying, "I am impressed."

As they walked away, Bonnie said, "Betty and her four sisters are orphans. Two months ago, they were dressed in rags, hungry, sleeping under porches. They asked for a job, willing to working for food. At that time, we needed engine oilers, usually a job given to orphaned boys. All five of the sisters arc assets to this ship."

Next, they went into the boiler room.

Bobby complained, "This is hot and dirty."

The Commander explained to his son, "It is a hot and dirty job. Burning the coal makes the steam that makes the engines go." He then asked Bonnie, "At full speed, what is your coal consumption?"

"When we were running at full speed across the Atlantic, we burnt about twelve tons an hour of top-grade Pennsylvania blue anthracite coal."

As they went through the crew's cafeteria, school was starting.

Bobby asked, "Is that school?"

Bonnie replied, "Yes, you and your brothers can go if you want, it is free."

The Commander asked, "What do I have to do to enroll them?"

"Have them show up. The teacher is college educated. She teaches a variety of subjects. It is not a publicly organized school but a service provided to passengers and crew."

* * * * *

Twilight found the bridge crowded. They were approaching Ynys Dewi, an island off Wales. There were many islands to be avoided in the Irish Sea. The Commander was coaching Dotty, trying to get a sight on Betelgeuse. Bonnie got a sight. They were also able to get a couple of bearings on Wales.

The Commander said, "That girl is not much older than my son, and I do not let him touch my sextant. I should be teaching him."

Bonnie explained, "Dotty is called D. Adams on the ship's roster for political reasons. There is nothing in the merchant maritime regulations about gender, but we do not want any trouble."

"I will keep that in mind while I write my report," he said. "Thank you for the tour this morning. It was very informative, and my sons are going to your school. Their mom is going to help out. Your young motorman gave my son a real eye-opening education. He sees girls differently now."

During the night, they sailed out into the Celtic Sea, past Land's End in Cornwall, getting several other bearings.

By the next evening, they were sailing past Brest, France, and into the Bay of Biscay. Many ships from many nations had been sighted. Mostly commercial cargo ships. Several ships of war were spotted, from Britain, France, Germany, and the Netherlands. That evening, after dinner, Commander Roberts wanted to hear of the Bonnie's encounter with the British battleship the HMS *Centurion*. Charlotte volunteered to tell the story as the Captain listened. The Commander said the incident had alarmed the British Admiralty and they were lobbying their Parliament for funds to design and build a new class of battleships. He said he heard it was to be called the Dreadnought class. He wanted to know if it was true that in heavy seas and gale winds, the passengers lined the rails and taunted the British seamen as they overtook the *Centurion*.

Charlotte said, "We certainly did. We were getting bored and needed something to do."

The Commander replied, "That is part of their problem. Most of the British sailors were seasick, and they were passed by a bunch of civilians acting like they were out on a yacht in light seas, having a party. The Admiralty has a team of naval architects studying a ship's motion. A healthy sailor is better than a seasick one. They know they have the best sailors on earth. It must be the shape and size of the ship. While you were at Liverpool, the *Bonnie Duffy* was being closely studied.

"I was briefed that Smithfield Steamship Company has a tentative contract to build a heavy cruiser for the Navy. The keel has not yet been laid, and the Navy is considering an upgrade to a battleship, built on the lines of the Bonnie Duffy. I am sort of a spy. That is why I am here."

Bonnie said, "Oops, I invited a German Naval Attaché. If the British wanted a look, I would have gladly given them a tour."

The Commander replied, "Knowing the British, their egos would not let them ask for a tour. As for interested people, you might have French, Italian, and even Japanese as guests before you are done. Do not worry about it, it is expected. This ship is setting a new standard."

The following dawn was beautiful as they arrived at La Rochelle. The harbor was small. The size of the *Bonnie* required they dock in the outer harbor, giving them over a mile walk to the shopping district. It was one of the most beautiful harbors they had visited. It had historic stone fortifications guarding the inner harbor and the spires of a grand cathedral could be seen. They were enthusiastically welcomed. The Mayor and a few other dignitaries met the ship upon docking, giving Bonnie a symbolic key to the city.

School was held touring the city, a history lesson—it was Willa's idea to try and make education interesting. "Since the American Revolutionary War, the French and Americans have had a special relationship. A great American ship visiting their city is special to the residents of La Rochelle. This is an ancient city predating the Romans." Bonnie and other adults accompanied the students. "For over two millennia, people have fought over the control of this beautiful harbor. The Romans established trade in this small harbor. Several French factions warred over its control. The English, Spanish, and Portuguese have fought for control of this strategically located harbor. It played an important role in the expansion of Christianity across Europe. At one time, it was a stronghold of the Knight Templar. Historically, it is known as the Rebel City for its sense of independence and early democratic ideals."

The five sisters were also able to attend the tour. The girls wore their conservative dresses. With the French sense of fashion, they could have worn their samba dresses, only raising a few eyebrows.

That afternoon, Captain Fritz Vanderhaven, a German Naval Officer, arrived with a young woman. He had first-class reservation. Bonnie greeted the German Captain. He was a second cousin of the Kaiser, and the lady with him was his mistress. He spoke impeccable English; his mistress spoke only German. Next of note was a French Captain, Amole Bateau, with family, announcing he was with the French Admiralty with first-class bookings. He graciously requested an audience with the ship's owner's representative.

Bonnie said, "I am Mrs. Smithfield, the owner's representative. What is your request?"

"I was hoping to be given permission to tour your marvelous ship."

"After breakfast, tomorrow, I will gladly give you a tour."

As the gangway was about to be raised, a carriage arrived. Another unexpected passenger. A distinguished man in his forties who introduced himself as Commodore Vladimir Petrovitch. He was accompanied by his wife and two children. He was a cousin to Tsar Alexander III. The Commodore's English was marginal, but his wife and eldest daughter spoke fluent English.

Bonnie was glad when the gangway was raised; she did not want any more foreign Naval Officers.

Bonnie went to her Captain, asking for advice as to what to do with four Naval Officers of different countries. The Captain was busy and told Bonnie it was her problem and he would not be available for the Captain's table.

Charlotte suggested two Captain's tables, one for the navies of the world and one for the normal passengers. Charlotte volunteered to host the regular passengers table. Bonnie told Charlotte she would be better with Naval Officers. She had personal experience dealing with Captains.

Charlotte refused, saying, "I am passenger services, you represent the owner. International affairs are your responsibility."

Bonnie realized again she was in a situation where she did not know what she was doing.

A little before sunset, they departed for Lisbon, Portugal, a 680-nautical-mile cruise. At twelve-knots, they would arrive in two and a half days, in the morning. Because the coal had a small percentage bituminous coal in it, the stacks smoked heavier than usual. After clearing the harbor, they headed southwest-by-west across the Bay of Biscay.

The conversation at the Naval Captain's table was interesting. Fritz was eager to share what the Germans were doing. They were building a large, heavy, and fast battleship, that would set a new standard in naval power. He bragged that the keel was laid for the SS *Kaiser Wilhelm der Grosse*, a Luxury Liner that would be larger and faster than the *Bonnie Duffy*. The *Kaiser* would be sailing the North Atlantic in two years.

Bonnie remembered Joseph telling her that the Germans were building a large ocean liner. Bonnie wondered how big and fast it would be, so she asked.

Captain Fritz answered, "Six hundred sixty feet long, displacing twenty eight thousand ton."

Bonnie said, "Yes, that will be bigger than the Bonnie."

The French were building a series of medium-sized battle cruisers that would be maneuverable. They would fire torpedoes and smaller-shelled artillery, making their guns' rapid fire. Their tactic would use overwhelming numbers, which would decimate their opposition.

The French Captain said, "A hundred bees can make the bravest of men run away."

The French were presently building two heavy battleships for the Russians.

The Russian Commodore, with the help of his wife's English, warned of the Japanese building fleets of gun ships and their aggression toward Asia. Currently, the Japanese were threatening the Korean Peninsula and Manchuria. China was willing to work with the Russians to protect their borders.

The USN Commander respectively listened.

Wanting to participate in the conversation. Bonnie said, "My father-in-law is planning to building a thousand-foot dry dock. He thinks that will be the future of steamships"

That ended the conversation of steamship size. Bonnie invited all to a tour of the ship in the morning, after breakfast.

Later, in private, Commander Roberts asked Bonnie, "Is it true that your family is planning for a thousand-foot ship?"

Bonnie said, "That is what my father-in-law believes will be the future of ships."

The Commander nodded. "His company built a six-hundred-footer, so why not a thousand-footer? This ship, along with other things, is changing the minds of many Europeans. In the near future,

America will be a power to be reckoned with. Better a friend than a foe."

The tour the following morning was interesting. The Russian Commodore had a request that got some unusual looks from the others. "Can my daughter, Margarita, accompany me as an interpreter?"

Bonnie said, "Ladies are always welcome. Follow me, gentlemen."

Mrs. Smithfield, a woman, giving the tour was completely unexpected.

In the engine room, there were introductions to Smitey, the Chief Engineer.

Smitey said, "This is Motorman A. Adams. She is an apprentice engineer. Part of her training is to answer questions about the engines and their operation. Would you please indulge her?"

Annie was well prepared. The first question came from Margarita. They being approximately the same age, it was a personal question. Basically, it was why a girl would be working in the engine room.

Annie replied, "I was given an opportunity, and this is good, honest work. I like working on machines."

The men soon followed with many questions. Some of the questions and answers were not understood by Bonnie. Some of the questions were about pressures, ratios, and bore sizes. It was apparent that the men were impressed with Annie. She explained the gauges, logging their operations, and explained their procedures in the operation, care, and maintenance. The real shock was when Eavey, Electrician's Mate, showed up and explained their electrical system.

Bonnie looked at Smitey. He was grinning like a proud father. Bonnie knew Smitey had arranged the show, he seemed to enjoy seeing men's reactions when his girls did the talking and they were intelligent and well-informed.

In the boiler room, they were met by Motorman B. Adams, an apprentice engineer. Betty explained the firing of the boilers, logging of pressures, and coal consumption. The French Captain wanted to know what their coal consumption was at full speed.

Betty said, "Across the North Atlantic, burning premium Pennsylvania blue anthracite coal, we burnt about twelve tons an hour and maintained 22.7 knots for three days in a light following wind and seas."

The tour was a success, and after it, the Naval Officers decided to go to the casino and discuss their observations over a card game and drinks.

Midday, they were avoiding the many small islands off the northwest coast of Galicia a northwest independent province of Spain. The weather turned warmer, and many passengers were enjoying the weather on the decks. Bonnie saw the Commander with one of the twins, and Bobby, the Commander's son, each with a sextant taking a noon-sun sight. The Commander was patient, explaining that they needed the sun's zenith's angle, which would give them a close latitude, and accurate time would give them an accurate longitude.

The Russian Commodore and Margarita came from behind, startling Bonnie.

It was awkward talking through Margarita; she was a good interpreter talking as her father.

"Do you think that your father will build me a thousand-foot battleship? A real intimidating ship."

Bonnie answered, "You will have to ask him and the United States Government."

The Commodore asked, "Are those children the Commanders?"

Bonnie replied, "The boy is. The girl is a Navigator trainee assigned to the bridge."

The Commodore said, "I have trouble getting good, loyal sailors that stay sober. Maybe I should start recruiting girls."

Margarita said, "I asked my father if I can I learn to be a Navigator."

Bonnie said, "If you would like, come to the bridge at dusk. Bring your father if he would like."

Margarita replied, "Thank you, Mrs. Smithfield."

Late afternoon, on the bridge, Bonnie got a disapproving look when she introduced the Commodore, until Margarita was introduced and curtsied, saying, "Thank you, Captain. You have a beautiful ship with a remarkable crew. Now I am going to ask my father to take me on some of his cruises. Is it acceptable if I watch your Navigators? I promise to stay out of the way."

The Captain said, with what looked to be a hint of a smile, "You are quite welcome. If you like, we can find you a sextant so you can try to get a celestial sight. Why not a Russian woman Navigator."

Margarita smiled, "I think my great-great-grandmother Sophia would approve."

Bonnie was gullible, "Sophia? That is a beautiful name."

Margarita said, "That was her name in the family. Others call her Catherine the Great."

Bonnie wished she had not asked; she concluded she had to learn to keep her mouth shut.

Bonnie watched as the Commodore instructed his daughter. Nobody on the bridge understood their conversation. Some technical words of navigation were in common in English and Russian.

Bonnie fantasized of having her own children and passing her knowledge to them. She knew that would not happen with her husband on the other side of the world. Bonnie knew she was young and there would be time.

* * * * *

At the break of day, the *Bonnie Duffy* neared the Port of Lisbon. The bridge-deck was crowded. There were Cathy, Dotty, Bobby, Margarita, and another boy she recognized as son of the French Captain. All had a sextant and no adult interference.

Bonnie said, "Captain, I will clear the children off your bridge."

He responded, "They are not in the way. Please give them room. They are learning."

Bonnie felt a little snubbed; the children were welcome, and she was told to not get in their way.

Bonnie thought, *What an unlikely group of children, varying in age from about nine to thirteen. They are working together, helping each-other, getting along. There are two orphan girls from San Francisco, a USN Commander's son, the son of a French Captain representing the French Admiralty, and a young lady that is part of the Russian Tsar's family. Maybe the next generation can learn to cooperate and not go to war.*

Bobby and Margarita were given the honors of blowing the whistle, waking everyone up.

The Captain politely dismissed the children.

Lisbon had a large harbor that was well protected from the sea.

Willa again lead an educational tour of the city. Her tours became as popular with the adult passengers as it was with the children.

"Lisbon has a long history of trading. The Ancient Greeks and Phoenicians traded here. At one time, Portugal had a lot of colonies spread across the globe. In recent years, many of their colonies have become independent. Portugal still has colonies in East Africa. At one time, Lisbon was a center of the African slave trade. Lisbon is still a hub of trading. They are on the crossroads of many of the great trade routes."

Midday, a heavy rain started. All the shore activities were canceled.

The next day, in heavy rain, they departed early morning for Monrovia, Liberia. They headed toward deep-water, sailing southwest. At eighteen knots, it would take a little over five days.

The Naval Officers and their families were behaving like they were on vacation. It looked like they were settling in for the long haul. Bonnie would have to check with Charlotte on their bookings.

Besides cards, the Naval Officers all seemed to take an interest in training the children in the art of navigation and seamanship; they were all fathers. The German Captain said that he regretted not bringing his son along. Most of the children on the ship could be seen with a length of rope practicing their knots as they walked around. Bonnie wondered if it was some sort of competition. Who was best at marlinspike seamanship, the art of working with ropes? All the children were bonding together in their own group. Bonnie could not resist helping with the navigation and was learning the art of working with ropes. Bonnie added to her list for Joseph a larger bridge-deck or possibly one for passenger observation and training.

The fourth day, they were sailing off the coast of the French Colony of Senegal. Lookouts spotted a small sailboat awash, near sinking. People were reported hanging on; some appeared to be children. It took close to an hour to slow down from their eighteen knots, turn around, and come alongside the sinking boat. They stopped alongside toward windward. A cargo net was lowered on a davit to the sinking boat, where two men, two women, three children, and a few of their meager possessions were loaded. Their boat was old, rotten, and falling apart.

It became immediately apparent that there would be a communications problem. They were Negroes and did not speak English. The ship's Doctor quickly checked them and reported no apparent signs of the plague or other infectious diseases. The rescued were suffering from exposure and dehydration. The Doctor ordered that they be taken to a cabin, in the crew's quarters, for quarantine, and be given food and water. The Doctor said he would check on them later and ordered the quarantine to protect all the crew and passengers. As the *Bonnie* pulled away, the small boat rolled over and quickly sank.

It was determined that the rescued people spoke a West African dialect of French. With difficulty, one of the maids helped interpret. She had lived in Louisiana and was fluent in Creole French, a mixture of French, Native American, and African languages. They were runaway slaves from a sugar plantation up the Saloum River. They had come down the river on a raft then stolen the boat. They knew nothing of boats, they just wanted to find a place they could live free. They begged to not be returned to their masters.

At breakfast the next morning, Bonnie met with Charlotte and Captain Krupp. What should they do with the seven rescued people? The ship was legally responsible to take them to their next port of call or transfer them to another rescue vessel. If they turn them over to the Liberian authority, they could be send back to the country of origin. At Monrovia, the ship would be required to report them to customs. They would not make port until late afternoon, so they postponed their decision until lunch, wanting for the Doctor's report.

The Doctor joined them for lunch.

The Doctor reported, "I find our seven guests in good health and physically fit. There is some signs of malnutrition, especially with the children. They are quickly recovering from their ordeal.

All, including the children, have permanent scars from numerous harsh floggings. As a Physician and Christian, I strongly protest any attempt to send them back to their life of slavery. The three children appear to all be about ten to twelve, two males and one female. I cannot verify who is related to whom, though I believe there are two bonded adult couples. I believe the two women are too young to be the mothers of ten-year-old children."

Bonnie asked, "What do you suggest we do?"

"Give them jobs, put them to work as free people. Give them the opportunity to be free productive members of humanity."

Bonnie looked at Charlotte with a questioning look.

Charlotte said, "I can put the women and children to work in the kitchen, laundry, and, housekeeping."

The Captain said, "There is precedent where rescued shipwreck survivors join the crew of their rescuers. Smitey can use two more strong men. I will need their mark, willingly signing on as crew. Can you ladies handle the details? Smitey oversees the hiring of the boiler room crew."

The Doctor said, "Thank you. I will sleep better tonight."

Bonnie, Charlotte, and their interpreter headed for the crew's quarters.

On their way, Bonnie said, "Charlotte, you handle it. You will be their big boss."

Charlotte retorted, "You just do not want any more people calling you a great lady."

Bonnie replied, "Charlotte, you are full of shit."

When they approached the door, they heard singing from within. It was a unique rhythm and quite beautiful. Though not fast, it sounded happy. As soon as Charlotte knocked, the singing stopped. Promptly the door was opened, and all but the man opening the door were sitting in a circle on the floor. As soon as they saw Charlotte, the hurriedly lined up.

Charlotte said, "At ease." That seemed to make them stand stiffer.

Charlotte asked the interpreter to tell them to relax. They relaxed a little. Charlotte then asked through the interpreter if they wanted to stay on the ship and work for the ship. This brought excited confusion. The seven guests were talking rapidly at the same time in a language unknown to Charlotte or Bonnie. Bonnie and Charlotte just looked at each other in confusion. Was something misinterpreted or misunderstood? Eventually, one of the men shouted what must have meant, "Shut up."

The first question was, were they slaves aboard the ship? The second question was, what was work? They had been slaves for generations, and the concept of being free people was not completely understood. They were full of suspicions and concerns. When it was made apparent to them that they could stay together in the room they were presently in and would be fed and could leave when they wanted, they relaxed a little. Charlotte, Bonnie, and the interpreter took them on a tour of the part of the ship they had free access to. A stop at the crew's cafeteria where they selected for several dishes what they wanted to eat seemed to soothe some of their apprehensions. With difficulty, the interpreter explained that this is where they ate when they were hungry. The crew's cafeteria was open all hours and was next to the galley. Some of the fare was what was overprepared from the dining rooms. Bonnie and Charlotte agreed to save explaining freedom till later; for now, their guests seemed to relax. The issue that was divisive was when they were given shoes or boots to wear. Trying them on was an unpleasant situation. The uniforms were no problem. A compromise was made that they would wear footwear while working. They were handed off to others to be mentored. Some of the mentors gave up keeping footwear on them. The two men working in the boiler room soon wore their boots without complaint. The entire ship was aware of the rescues and most had sympathy for the new crew members. There was some racism that was dealt with. Since they all held low-level positions, it was sociably acceptable. It was agreed that it would take time for them to acclimate; if they were treated fairly, they would adjust.

They arrived at Monrovia early evening. It was a small harbor with limited facilities. After five and a half days at sea, they had to replenish their produce and other perishables. In Monrovia, feelings toward Americans were mixed. Libera had basically become an

American colony. Many spoke English. Many ex-American slaves had immigrated here after the Civil War. Some willingly and some by coercion. Many of the repatriated slaves had been made promises that America did not honor. Unbelievably, slavery was still practiced on plantations in Liberia. Slavery was not publicly acknowledged but was blatantly evident. Slaves shackled together around their necks were used to make deliveries to the ship. Few of the passengers or crew went ashore; instead, they watched from the decks.

Bonnie and Charlotte believed they had been deceived when they inquired about Monrovia. It was obvious that a lot of misrepresentation of Liberia were presented to the American people; a good view was presented. With their American connection, they thought it would be a good port of call. There was plenty of fresh fruits, vegetables, and other perishables, except the available milk was goat milk. Those not wanting goat milk would have to get by with condensed canned milk. There was an abundance of fresh meat, most wild game. Several species of antelope as well as wild hog would be on the menu. A lot of the meat selections were passed on like monkeys and gorillas. Poultry and swine were available. The produce was picked while they waited. Although the coal was costly, all local products were inexpensive. In reality, there was no immigration; a port fee of twenty dollars US was paid. The twenty-dollar bill went into the pocket of the administrator. A small detachment of colorfully dressed troops guarded the ship. Nobody knew if they were to protect Monrovia or the ship. Their rifles were antiques, and some wondered if they would fire. If it had not been for the obvious poverty and seeing men, women, and children in shackles, it would have been a good port of call. They loaded on a cargo of ivory destined for San Francisco, their first cargo of any size. The ivory was paid for out of ship's funds. They had all the proper documentations, including a purchase order from Smithfield Steamship Lines. Charlotte was aware of the cargo and procured a bill of sale.

While they were in port, the small telephone switchboard was installed in the pilothouse by the electrical crew. The crew had run near a mile of telephone wire over the last few weeks. Eavey did the final hookup, it being a small space and her being Little Miss Edison.

The bridge officers, including the Captain, watched as Eavey connected the batteries, plugged in the connection, cranked the crank, and called her sister Annie, who was waiting for the call in the engine room.

"Engine room, Motorman A. Adams."

"Bridge, Electrician Mate E. Adams."

There was a pause; neither knew what to say next.

"Bridge, can you hear me?"

"Yes, I can hear you. Can you hear me?"

"Yes, I can hear you, the telephone works."

"Telephone works."

Another pause. Both were uncomfortable with people observing them and the experience of hearing a voice from an earpiece. Neither knew how to hold a conversation with someone they could not see. The small lights on the switchboard went out as they both hung up.

The Captain said, "I want to talk to the Chief Engineer."

Eavey handed the earpiece and mouthpiece to the Captain. She said, "Captain, sir, you have the mouthpiece and earpiece mixed up."

The Captain looked a little embarrassed as he switched the pieces.

Eavey made the connection and cranked the ringer.

"Engine room, Motorman A. Adams."

"Let me talk to . . . aah, the Chief Engineer."

"Who wants to talk to him?"

"This is the Captain."

"Yes, sir. I will get him for you, sir."

The Captain said to all listening, "I do not think this is going to work."

"Yes, sir."

"Who is this? I am the Captain."

"Chief Engineer Smitey, sir."

"I will want full steam for maneuvering in four hours. This is the Captain."

"This is the Chief Engineer. Full steam in four hours for maneuvering. Captain, sir."

The Captain then asked Eavey, "What do I do now?"

Eavey replied, "Hang the earpiece and mouthpiece up here, sir."

The Captain gave orders. "Mr. Fitzpatrick, figure this contrivance out. Electrician Mate E. Adams, train your sisters how to work this thing. That is an order."

Eavey said, "Yes, sir, train all the Adams crew members, sir."

"Mr. Fitzpatrick, you have the bridge. I will be in my quarters. They hung one of these telephone things on the wall in my quarters. Does it work?"

Eavey responded, "Sir, when you are ready, I will connect and test it for you, sir."

The Captain said, "Let us get it over with."

The Captain led Eavey to his quarters, opened up the door, and told her, "Do not make a mess," as he left.

With Eavey being the head lightbulb changer, there was not much of the ship she had not seen. She had been in some similar rooms but never the Captain's quarters. The engineers had installed the phone. It was actually two rooms, a day room and a bedroom. The door to the bedroom was left open. The deck, desk, and even the chairs had stacks of books, charts, clothes, and other things. The telephone was installed on the wall behind the desk next to the bedroom door. The wires had been strung in the ductwork that went along the edge of the wall and ceiling. Eavey saw something that caused her to stop and look; her curiosity prompted her to go and look closely. It was a woman's nightgown draped over the side of the double berth.

Eavey went to work and was standing on a chair on the desk. She was trying to fish the wire out of the ductwork and down the wall. The cabin door was not fully closed, and in came Charlotte. This startled Eavey; she slipped and hung by her hands from the duct opening. Charlotte quickly rescued Eavey, throwing her arms around her, lowering her to the desk.

Charlotte said, "The Captain told me that you were installing a telephone in his quarters. I thought maybe I could help you."

"Thank you! You scared me and I almost fell. Is the nightgown on the Captain's berth yours? It is really pretty."

Charlotte closed the door tight, checked that the portholes were closed, and said, "Can we have a girl-to-girl talk?"

"All right, I have to get the Captain's telephone hooked up. I am under orders from the Captain."

Charlotte went and put her nightgown in a closet and said, "Eavey, I know that you really like the Captain and I know that the captain really likes you."

As Eavey worked back up on the chair and Charlotte stood by close to catch her if she fell again, Eavey said, "The Captain is a great man. He is a nice man. He is a man who is respected."

Charlotte said, "I know that you would not want to hurt the Captain, make him feel bad, would you?"

"Nobody can hurt the Captain. He is too important."

"Can you keep a secret? Never telling anyone for me and the Captain?"

Eavey replied, "For the Captain, I would do anything. I love him."

Charlotte thought to herself, *You are not the only one.* She said, "Can you keep it a secret that you saw my nightgown in the Captain's quarters and we talked about the Captain? Keep it a secret."

Eavey promised, "Yes, a secret. Can you pull slowly on that wire hanging down, please? I will not tell anyone that you are sleeping with the Captain."

As Charlotte pulled on the wire, she said, "Eavey, it is really important to keep it a secret, a secret between us girls."

"Miss Charlotte, I will keep it a secret. I am happy that you and the Captain like each other. I will keep it a secret. Pull a little more . . . that is good, thank you."

Charlotte watched as this ten-year-old girl took tools from her bag and wired the telephone and wired the batteries. This telephone had a mouthpiece sticking out from the oak box and a handheld earpiece hanging on a hook on the side. Eavey cranked the telephone several times as she listened. Finally, she said, "Nobody knows how to answer the switchboard. I will go to the bridge. Miss Charlotte, can you please stay here and answer the telephone so I can test it?"

Charlotte asked, "How do I work it?"

Eavey explained how to answer the telephone and call her back. Eavey then left for the bridge.

Shortly the telephone rang. Charlotte lifted the earpiece from its hook and listened and heard, "Miss Charlotte, can you hear me?"

"I can hear you. Can you hear me?"

Eavey said, "Yes, I can hear you. Can you call me back to test it both ways?"

Charette called back.

"Bridge, Electrician's Mate E. Adams."

"This is Miss Charlotte. Can you hear me?"

"Yes, I can hear you. Want to talk to the Captain?"

Charlotte, with hesitation, said, "Yes, I guess it is all right."

Eavey handed the handpieces to the Captain, who had returned to the bridge, and said, "Miss Charlotte wants to talk to you, Captain."

The Captain asked, "Where is she at?"

Eavey said, "Your cabin. She is helping me test the telephone. Is that all right?"

"Miss Gibbs, this is Captain Krupp. Can you hear me."

"Yes, I can hear you, Captain Krupp."

After a long and what was probably embarrassing moment for both of them, the Captain said, "Nice talking to you, Miss Gibbs."

Charlotte replied, "Nice talking to you, Captain." She then hung up the telephone.

Eavey took the handpieces from the Captain and said, "Captain, sir, the telephone in your cabin works."

Charlotte had some produce to check up on, and on her way, she saw Bonnie.

Charlotte said, "I talked to the Captain."

"What did he say?"

"Nice talking to you."

"And . . . ?"

"We talked on the telephone."

Bonnie asked, "The telephones work?"

Charlotte replied, "Yes they work. I do not think I will use it much. I do not like it. It is uncomfortable talking to someone in a box on the wall."

They left midmorning the following day. The one tug available was small and would give only a little assist. The Captain, engine room, and crew amazed the naval guests with their seamanship. Clearing the harbor, fighting a wind and an opposing tide. The Captain gave credit to the ship's design. Three powerful engines, one propeller in the rudder-keel aperture, giving the stern side thrust. He also said, the telephone helped in communication with the engine room. Seaman D. Adams manned the telephone on the bridge while motorman A. Adams manned the telephone in the engine room. They relayed the messages. The engine room telegraph was still used, but with the telegraph, the commands could not be specific like "Give me just a few turns, port engine, reverse, really easy, a little more please."

At sea, they headed south-southeast, destination, Cape Town. It would be a seven-day cruise.

As they passed the equator again, King Neptune made an appearance. Bonnie stayed in her room, studying, and on the bridge, she was avoiding a dousing. On her way to the dining room for dinner, however, she was surrounded by women and girls that forced to the deck, where she received a good water dousing. It was her punishment for her failure to show King Neptune his due respect. Bonnie concluded there was no way to avoid King Neptune. She also concluded that she had friends who loved her.

In the next three days, the main areas of the SS *Bonnie Duffy* were connected by telephones. Everyone that used the telephones had to learn to operate it and to talk into the machines. A procedure was established that the caller would tell the switchboard operator where they wanted to be connected to. A person answering the phone would give their name or title. The caller would then give their name and state their business. It sounded complicated, but soon it became second nature.

Bonnie called Charlotte to test the system.

Ring. "Switchboard."

"Passenger services please."

"One moment, ma'am."

Ring. "Passenger services, Miss Gibbs speaking."

"Bonnie, ready for some lunch."

"See you in the dining room in a few minutes"

"Bye."

"Bye."

The telephone etiquette was easy and prevented a lot of "Who is this?" "What do you want?" "Is anybody listening?" and "Do you hear me?" New inventions require new ways to make them work correctly.

At lunch, Bonnie and Charlotte were joined by the Captain. The discussion centered on the telephones and how they could be used to improve life and safety aboard the ship. It was decided a few more telephones would be installed—one in the infirmary, one in the Doctor's quarters, one in the galley, as well as others.

Charlotte said, "If all of Mr. Edison's predictions come true, life will change in many ways."

Bonnie agreed, "Yes, I think Mr. Edison has a vivid imagination. Flying in machines sounds like a Jules Verne novel. I will stick to trains, wagons, horses, and ships."

* * * * *

Africa was in turmoil. The great European Nations had divided Africa up among themselves in the Berlin Conference of 1884–1885. Some of the indigenous people had their own states and agreements with European powers. Large areas were changing hands from one European power to another. Imperialism was at its height, and the European powers were determined to control their areas. Conflicts still existed between European nations. South Africa was a British colony, but the Boers, early Dutch settlers, had established their own country. The Boers were trying to overthrow the British. In areas, slavery was still practiced and slaves were still being shipped from East African ports to the East Indies and the Mideast. Many indigenous people were rising up to shed the yoke of the imperialistic rule and its injustices. In some cases, the European settlers were in rebellion. From the advice of the American Embassy in Lisbon, only two ports of call would be made in Africa. Their stop in Madagascar was canceled. There were no boardings or disembarkations scheduled for Madagascar. The French and German Captains were to disembark in Cape Town and return to Europe by other passenger ships. The American Commander and family would continue to San Francisco, and the Russian Commodore and family would continue on to China. He was to negotiate an easement for the completion of the Trans-Siberian Railway that would run through part of Manchuria, Chinese territory.

Except for a few squalls, the passage to Cape Town was pleasurable. Their schedule was to arrive at daybreak and leave the following evening. After they had arrived, sporadic cannon fire could be heard. The Boers had mounted an attack against the British on the city's outskirts. The coal yard was run by an American company. They had an ample supply of Pennsylvania blue anthracite, and they were glad to sell it for fear it would be confiscated by the Boers. The coal bunkers were overfilled, and some coal had to be placed in the cargo holds as a reserve. Since they canceled the Madagascar stop, they would have a 4,600 nautical-mile cruise to Bombay India, and they would have to cruise at a coal-conserving speed. They would have to keep their coal consumption to less than six tons an hour. At midday the next day, the cannon fire seemed closer and more intense. The larders were full, and by unanimous consent they departed. All first-class and second-class accommodations were full. There were a lot of people wanting to flee the threatening war, making steerage over capacity. Many steerage passengers were from India, wanting to return home and avoid the conflict.

CHAPTER 16

The Indian Ocean

Bombay, India, would be a thirteen-day cruise at the economical speed of fourteen to fifteen knots. The SS *Bonnie Duffy* was sitting low in the water with nineteen hundred tons of coal aboard. Many were making plans to keep busy and entertained. Megan had written a play of her early days in the mining fields of Colorado, and she had persuaded enough people to play the parts. They were rehearsing for a performance. The Captain had planned lifeboat drills, man overboard drills, fire drills, and training. With the help of the USN Commander, the Russian Commodore, and other crew members, the ship was going to have training in seamanship and navigation. The classes were to be held on the aft deck, weather permitting. The training would be available to all, including steerage.

Bonnie and Charlotte had talked and agreed that steerage did not have to be a dismal experience; if Smithfield Steamships could establish a reputation for providing a good cruising experience for steerage, it would be beneficial for the company. From the first, they had tried to provide good nutritious food for steerage. Although the berths were four high, small bunks, they were planned to be comfortable and deck space adequate for daily life. The personal hygiene facilities, although shared, were adequate and healthy. Neither Bonnie nor Charlotte had received many complaints and had been given a few compliments and several thank-yous. Bonnie hoped to get a better idea of sailing steerage. All of her grandparents had come to America as steerage trying to escape starvation during the Great Irish Potato Famine, looking for a better life. Bonnie understood she was lucky; now she lived a life of privilege.

With the consent of the Captain, hours were established when the steerage could have access to the library in the crew's cafeteria and could borrow books. One of the maids that were bilingual and educated was promoted to teacher to teach classes in the steerage cafeteria. To start with, English, Spanish, and mathematics would be taught.

For the passengers, the cruise to India was a time to enjoy life and relax. When they passed near Madagascar, the Captain posted extra watches and was prepared to go to full speed in a moment's notice. They had heard reports of piracy that made the Captain and the officers apprehensive. The Captain believed the SS *Bonnie Duffy* could outrun any pirate ships if they had sea room. But they had concerns of cannon fire. As a preventive measure, all ships would be given a wide berth. When another ship was sighted, a course would be established to maintain a large distance between them, giving the *Bonnie* sea room.

The seamanship and navigation classes were a success, but the large attendance made it a challenge. The help of many made it was doable and rewarding. Megan's play was a success as well. It had love, romance, and adventure with a healthy amount of humor. They did four performances, one in the first-class dining room, one in the second-class dining room, and one in the crew's cafeteria. Megan insisted on doing a performance for steerage in their cafeteria; her early years were of meager means. Megan had no qualms letting people know it was about her, and she also had no problem letting people know how inept she could be. Most of the humor was at her expense.

The lifeboat drills, fire drills, and man-overboard drills were run without incident. Some of the passengers voluntarily participated in the lifeboat drills. Captain Krupp wrote a report suggesting all passenger ships regularly conduct such drills. He would submit the report to International and US maritime authorities in the interest of adverting a catastrophe. The Captain, officially, in writing, informed the ship's owner's representative that there were not enough lifeboats or life preservers for all souls aboard.

This report upset Bonnie. Five hundred people would not have a lifeboat or a life preserver in case of an emergency. The stress of the negative report, all the stress-organizing training, classes, and the Naval Officers were affecting Bonnie. Bonnie had not been sleeping well. She missed Joseph and the political issues along with the safety issues deeply concerned her. Bonnie attributed the fact of the stress as the reason she missed her monthly curse.

Bonnie was in bed missing Joseph, thinking of all the politics and safety issues, when she got a craving for dill pickles. No matter how hard she tried to think of something else, she wanted a dill pickle.

Bonnie got dressed and went to the galley. In the galley, they were in the process of preparing the pastries and baking the bread for the next day. The head baker, seeing Bonnie, asked if he could be of assistance. Bonnie asked if they had dill pickles. Bonnie was escorted to a cooler and shown a twenty-gallon earthen crock full of dill pickles. Bonnie thanked the baker, and he excused himself, needing to get back to work. Bonnie proceeded to set on some crates next the earthen crock and devour dill pickles. When Bonnie had her fill, she went back to bed and slept soundly.

In the morning, Bonnie awoke feeling a little nauseous. She attributed it to her late-night snack. As she got dressed, she noticed that her corset was tight around her bosoms. Maybe just swelling before her time with Mother Nature. Bonnie want to the bridge and took her dawn sights, getting her wakeup coffee. There was nothing of note on the ship's log. A couple of ships were spotted overnight and avoided. As she went to the dining room, the smell of food again made Bonnie nauseous. She passed on breakfast. Bonnie got busy with her classes on the aft deck. Bonnie had trouble concentrating on the subjects and found her mind thinking of Joseph. She desperately missed him.

Bonnie skipped lunch and made up for it at dinner. She ordered a large rare steak and devoured it, not leaving a scrap. People noticed her attacking the steak with fork and knife, stuffing it in her mouth, and they politely ignored the spectacle.

As they passed the equator, Bonnie tried to prepare, but she was denied playing the role of King Neptune. So much for her authority. Bonnie was allowed to be the first assistant to the head siren, Megan. It was more fun than just being doused, although she got just as wet doing the dousing.

They were nearing Bombay, and Bonnie had tried to ignore the morning nausea, food aversions, moodiness, weight gain, and her breasts swelling, becoming tender. Bonnie's corset was not fitting appropriately. She looked at herself in the mirror. She was wondering what was wrong with her, and she suddenly realized she might be pregnant. She had not had a bout with Mother Nature since before New York. The timing was right. Bonnie had adamantly denied herself the privilege of crying. Only Joseph had made her cry, tears of joy. Bonnie gave in to her desire and went back to bed and had a good cry. She did not know why she was crying. Was it happiness or something else? She just wanted to cry.

Bonnie went to seen the ship's Doctor. He pronounces that in his professional opinion, Bonnie was probably pregnant. The Doctor warned her to not overeat, get plenty of rest, avoid strenuous activities. Gentle sex was permissible. He also congratulated her.

Bonnie said, "Gentle sex? My husband is on the other side of the world! That will be a great feat. How do I word the telegram informing him he is going to be a father?"

"Ma'am, I am a Doctor, not a poet or magician. I would like to see you in two weeks. Take care of yourself."

Bonnie met with Charlotte.

Bonnie said, "We have a problem."

"What is wrong?"

"I am pregnant."

After a pause, she said, "What? I am so happy for you. Is that a problem?"

"I am happy that I am going to have a baby, but what will Joseph think? And how will that affect the ship?"

"I am sure Joseph will be happy and the ship will be good."

"Are you saying the ship does not need me?"

"Bonnie, the ship needs you. I need you. Get control of your emotions. I am jealous."

"I am sorry. One moment I am happy, the next I am worried, then I want to cry. I feel all confused and mixed up."

"I have heard that pregnancy does strange things to women until their bodies adjust. Boy babies are worse, making a woman crazy. Girl babies make a woman cry a lot."

"Who told you that, is that some of your shit?"

Charlotte, "Yes, that is some of my shit."

They both had a good, hearty laugh.

"My mom said she cried all the time when she was pregnant with me and beat up Dad, the ice man, and their dog several times when she was pregnant with my brother."

"I have not felt like beating anyone up yet and have cried. Does that mean it is a girl?"

"I do not know. It is just a guess. It is human nature to guess. What is your guess?"

"Twin boys."

"Twin boys. Somebody is going to get beaten up. Maybe I should stay away from you."

That brought about another good laugh.

It was good to talk with Charlotte, sharing her news and talking a little nonsense.

* * * * *

Bombay was a city of contrast. Opulence and grandeur next to poverty and squalor. The government and the social structure were complicated, interwoven. Many entities and people shared in the power—East India Company, British Raj, the Punjab, the Bombay Presidency, the Royal India Army, as well as others. There was great wealth here. Social position seemed to be based on birthright more than wealth. For an Indian, on their caste. A well-to-do merchant could be considered socially undesirable, a low-class person not to be associated with, a low caste. Almost all Indian women of every caste wore jewelry. Legally, a woman could only own what they wore. Some women wore gold and gems on every part of their body. Women did not worry that someone would steal their jewelry. Culturally, that was totally taboo.

The British nor Indians seemed to not know what to make of the Americans. The SS *Bonnie Duffy* was the largest ship to ever arrive at Bombay, so they could not be dismissed. There were a few larger ships, but they stayed in the North Atlantic.

Megan seemed to have contacts wherever they went. She invited Bonnie to accompany her to an afternoon tea, telling her to put on her finest and to wear her jewels. At first, Bonnie declined, telling Megan she would not fit in high society, having afternoon tea.

Megan said, "Honey, with all the publicity of the Smithfield Steamship Line and their great ship named after you and your last name Smithfield, you are American royalty to them. Do not disappoint them. They want to meet you."

Bonnie said, "Royalty my ass! I am the daughter of poor Irish immigrants."

Megan replied, "That is what makes America great. That is what fascinates these people. They can never be more than what they were born into, maybe up one notch with the right marriage. You represent all the possibilities that they long for. To them you are Cinderella, Annie Oakley, and Calamity Jane all in one."

Bonnie could not say no to Megan; she was a special lady and a good friend.

On their way, Megan told Bonnie, "Do not try to be them with their snobbery. They will think you are mocking them. Be that free-spirited American girl who mines gold and shoots dinner. These people are fascinated by Buffalo Bill Cody and Annie Oakley. Be yourself. They will love you for who you are."

They went in a carriage that was fit for a queen. Arriving at a grand palace, they were met by male attendants dressed in uniforms that were colorful and fancier than any dress Bonnie had ever owned. It was so grand it would not have been a surprise for Bonnie to see the Queen of Great Britain, being also the Empress of India, Victoria herself. Bonnie thought, *Mother-in-law would be envious.* Inside was as grand as the outside. Bonnie did not know what to expect.

They were escorted into an ostentatious setting room where about a dozen women were setting about, being served tea by two fancily dressed Indian boys. When Bonnie was introduced to a Countess, she followed Megan's lead and did not curtsy but shook hands. Bonnie felt uncomfortable.

Megan said, "I would like to introduce Mrs. Joseph Smithfield. Before marriage she was Bonnie Duffy, a gold miner from the Dakota Territories, Black Hills."

The Countess said, "How exciting! The Dakota Territory! I have read books of the Wild West . . . so many brave and exciting people."

Another lady said, "The stories in the books, are they true?"

Bonnie smiled, "Some of them have some truth, they are romanticized to sell books. Most of the people are hardworking Christians trying to make a better life for themselves and their children."

The Countess said, "Come and sit, have some tea, and we will talk."

"Thank you," Bonnie responded. "I must tell you that this is the grandest place I have ever seen. It takes my breath away."

The Countess replied, "Do not let all this impress you. Tell me about gold mining."

Bonnie told how she and her grandfather worked in the creek shoveling sand and gravel into a saucebox then removing the gold from the captured enriched gravel using a pan. Bonnie told how they were lucky in having a good claim. All the ladies gathered about to hear the many questions and Bonnie's answers. Answering one question, Bonnie said that she knew Sheriff Seth Bullock, which prompted many more questions. Bonnie tried to be truthful in answered the many questions for an audience that seemed to want to hear every word. She realized it was not her but the life she had lived and where she had lived it. The western novelists had done a good job romanticizing the American West. Bonnie knew all too well her imagination had been captured by the written page as a girl. She decided to let these ladies have their fantasies; they had to face their own realities as she had to face hers.

Bonnie was finally asked the one question she did not want to hear: "Have you ever seen a man shot or hanged?"

"I have never seen a man hanged, but I have seen men shot. It was a horrible thing that I chose to not relive."

That ended the questions. Teatime was over. All the ladies thanked Bonnie for sharing with them some of her grand life of adventure. The Countess sincerely thanked Bonnie, telling her it was one of the best teas they had ever had.

On their carriage ride back to the ship, Megan said, "Bonnie, you should write a book of your adventures."

Bonnie answered, "I cannot write a book glorifying my life. The men I said I saw shot, I did the shooting. I still have nightmares over it."

Megan said, "I have, like, two closets in my head—one for the good times and one for the bad times. I try to keep everything in its place. My first husband was shot for our silver mine, then I married the meanest son of a bitch I could find, to keep the mine and for revenge. A few years later, he was hung for murder. He killed a man over a prostitute."

Bonnie said, "You do not tell the tea ladies that story, do you?"

"My daughter does not know that story. She thinks her father was killed in a mining accident."

"Let us keep our ghosts where they belong, buried."

Bonnie also talked to Megan about her pregnancy, looking for advice.

Megan said, "Honey, do not fret about it, it is a natural thing. Knowing you, you will be a great mother. I am happy for you. Even though it is hard, it is a great experience, one that men cannot enjoy or appreciate."

* * * * *

Bombay had been an introduction to Asian cultures, India was a country of great contrast and inequities. They had a large turnover of passengers. Bombay was a destination for many, and many wanted to go to Singapore. As was the case in Cape Town, they were turning passengers away. Bonnie and Charlotte had established a maximum steerage count of four hundred. Many who wanted passage in steerage were turned away.

Their coal bunkers were full of good-quality anthracite coal from India. Here, the British Admiralty did not have as much authority as they thought they should have. In six days, they should be in Singapore.

After they were at sea, Bonnie went to the bridge. In frustration, the Captain had ordered the twins to have their initial and last name on their uniforms, he got tired of asking, "Which one are you?" The entire crew liked the idea, and all but the Captain had their names embroidered on their uniforms. There was no mistaking the Captain with the four gold stripes on his sleeves and on his shoulder boards.

Bonnie asked Dotty their course and where it would it take them.

Dotty was quick to show Bonnie on a chart, telling her, *We will sail south around India, then south of Sri Lanka, north of Sumatra, and southeast through the Malacca Straights. Bonnie pondered, Several months ago, this girl was dressed in rags and her main concern was her empty stomach. Now she is dressed in a clean, tailored uniform with her name embroidered on it, explaining our course across the Indian Ocean.*

The Captain said, "Seaman D. Adams, what is our true plotted course?"

"South, sir,"

"What is our plotted magnetic course?"

Dotty stood on a stool, leaned over the chart table, examined the compass rose on the chart, and announced, "Variation 2 degrees east, magnetic plotted course is 178 degrees, sir."

"What should our compass steered course be?"

Dotty looked at a chart on the pilothouse wall. "Compass deviation at 180 degrees is 4 degrees east, compass course steered should be 174 degrees for a true course of south, sir."

The Captain asked, "Helmsman, what is our present compass steered course?"

The helmsman replied, "One half point east of south, sir."

Bonnie turned to Dotty. "Dotty, very impressive."

The Captain said, "Seaman D. Adams is learning. Seaman D. Adams needs to work on her multiplication and division."

Dotty said, "Yes, sir."

Dotty got out a math book, pencil, and paper. She opened her book to a page and appeared to stare at the page, pencil and paper in hand. Bonnie looked over her shoulder. It was long division problems.

Bonnie proceeded to help Dotty with the problems, not doing them for her but guiding her along step by step. Bonnie looked up and caught the Captain with a smirk on his face. She realized the whole thing about the course was for her benefit and the statement about math was to get Bonnie to take more of an interest in the girls. Bonnie felt sorry for the Captain; he had to appear, at all times, in command and control, and fraternizing even with a personable twelve-year-old girl would have to be held to a bare minimum. No favoritism could be shown. Emotionally, he had to be like a rock, strong and unwavering, showing no emotions. He was the Master and Commander of the ship.

Bonnie checked the schedule and would return when Cathy was on duty to help her with her math.

She returned to the bridge for the late-afternoon watch. Cathy was on duty.

Seeing Bonnie, the Captain asked, "Seaman C. Adams, what is our true plotted course?"

Cathy said, "South by east, sir."

"What would that make our true course be in degrees?"

"169 degrees true, sir."

"What would that make our magnetic steered course in compass points?"

Cathy took a pencil and paper and wrote down "169" then "-4" from the compass rose variation then "-4" for deviation from the wall chart, coming up with "161 degrees." Cathy reported, "161 degrees compass, that would be close to south-southeast, sir."

The Captain looked at the plot. "New course, south-southeast true. Seaman, what will be our compass course?"

Cathy quickly did her calculations. "Captain, southeast by south, sir."

The Captain ordered, "Helmsman, southeast by south."

The helmsman responded, "Southeast by south, sir."

The Captain ordered, "Seaman C. Adams, enter the course change and DR plot on the chart and enter it in the ship log."

Cathy responded, "Yes, sir. Enter the course change on the dead-reckoning plot on the chart and ship's log."

Under the watchful eye of the Navigator on duty, Cathy made the calculations of the distance they had traveled on the previous course, marked off the distance on the chart. Then she drew a light pencil line of the new course. Cathy then circled the spot on the chart of their position when the course was changed, writing down the time and initialing her entry. The Navigator added his initials, verifying her work. Then Cathy entered in neat print the information in the ship's log, initialing her work. This was also verified by the Navigator. Procedures required all navigation and entries into the log to be verified by a ship's officer.

Cathy then took her position on the bridge, scanning the sea. All crew stationed on the bridge that were not doing other duties were required take their duty station and be a lookout.

Bonnie was impressed. The Captain took the training of the twins seriously.

Cathy reported, "Ship, two points starboard on horizon."

Crow's nest reported, "Verified ship on horizon, two points starboard of bow."

The Captain looked through his spy glass and said, "Seaman C. Adams, let us see what you have learned. Course, speed, and identity of ship off starboard bow."

Cathy replied, "Yes, sir."

She went to the bridge-deck pencil and paper in hand and took a bearing on the ship with the ship's pelorus, an instrument mounted to the bridge railing for taking bearings. Bonnie noticed Cathy counting seconds as she checked the ship's chronographer. Bonnie tried to lend Cathy her grandfather's railroad pocket watch.

Cathy said, "What a beautiful watch! Thank you. But I have to practice counting seconds. When it is dark out, you cannot see a watch. I do have my own watch." She pulled a brass-cased timepiece from her pocket. "It is a good watch. It loses about a minute a day. It is easy to figure the time. I set it every day at noon from the ship's chronograph."

In the next fifteen minutes, Cathy took numerous bearings, recording the angle to the ship and time. The Navigator helped Cathy. The problem was not an easy one. They knew their ship's course and speed. They had a series of angles from their ship's course and the time the readings were taken. They plotted the information; then it was the math. Cathy and Bonnie watched as the Navigator worked through the problem, explaining each step he took. Bonnie realized she needed to work on her math as well as Cathy. Then it was a spyglass to ascertain the ship's identity as they were abeam.

Cathy reported, "Captain, sir, the Navigator did most of the work. The ship is an Italian three-mast merchant ship, the *Sophie Lauren*, about three hundred feet long on a reciprocal course to our course and traveling at an estimated five knots, sir."

The Captain said, "Thank you, Seaman C. Adams. As you were."

Bonnie asked, "Captain, permission to work with Seaman C. Adams on mathematics."

The Captain said, with a slight smile and a nod, "Permission granted."

Bonnie and Cathy went over the Navigator's math. After a couple of hours' study with a navigation book and hints from the Navigator, they thought they understood what the Navigator did. With practice, they thought they could do the work.

Cathy showed Bonnie on a large-scale chart how they were going to sail south of their rhumb line to the equator so they would pass through, longitude 90 degrees east, latitude zero, the equator. West of South America, their course passed through, longitude 90 degrees west, latitude zero, the equator. "These are two opposite points on Earth. When we return to San Francisco, passing through two opposite global points will technically make it a circumnavigation of the globe."

The ship went into its routine. Accommodations were made so all the crew members wanting to go to school could, on their own time. With help, they had evening school. Many subjects were covered, and at many ports of call, there was a lesson on the history and the culture of the locales. Some of the lessons were part of a tour where circumstances permitted. Annie and Betty did a class on steam engines along with a tour of the ship's engine room. Even Eavey had her turn, giving a short lecture on electricity and a demonstration on how a telephone worked, with spare telephone parts. Cathy and Dotty participated and helped in the navigation classes.

The three children that were rescued from the west coast of Africa were learning English and learning to read and write. They were teaching the adult emancipated slaves. In Bombay, the seven rescues disembarked for a few hours, with a lot of apprehension, walked as free people. They did not venture out of sight of the Bonnie, their new home. Although they had received a small pay, they did not spend a penny. It would take time for them to accept and be acclimated to their freedom. The rescued were hard workers and an asset to the ship and were accepted by most of the other crew members. There was some prejudice.

They crossed over the equator on April 1, 1894. They actually went a couple of minutes south of the equator and then crossed back into the Northern Hemisphere, making it their fifth and sixth time crossing the equator. King Neptune was in his glory, demanding adoration, ensuring a safe passage.

Bonnie was using her determination and willpower to fight off the morning sickness, food aversion, and mood swings. So far, it was a standoff. In Bombay, she procrastinated sending a telegram to Joseph announcing her condition; instead, she told him how much she missed him and that the next ship needed more lifeboats and life preservers as well as more room on the bridge-deck. Bonnie consoled herself on her procrastination with what Joseph did not know would not distract him from his work. Even Bonnie thought it a lame excuse.

* * * * *

Singapore was a bustling British colony. It was a trade center for Asia, Africa, Australia, New Zealand, and all the Americas. Ships were constantly coming and going. The SS *Bonnie Duffy* was an oddity amongst all the cargo ships. Many, including sailors, came to the dock to look upon this huge seagoing vessel that was alleged the future in sea travel. The Russian Commodore and American Commander, in an onshore officer's club, seemed to stir the interest of many Captains from many countries. Many Captains were given tours, and Bonnie and Charlotte thought it good advertisement and publicity. Megan purchased back issues of *Harper's Weekly*. Three issues, one to two months old, were of great interest to Bonnie and Charlotte. One issue, on page 3, had a raving review of the Bonnie's voyage from San Francisco to Acapulco. Another issue had a front-page illustration of the SS *Bonnie Duffy* at dock in San Francisco, with the headline "American Steamship Sets Record." The third newspaper had the headline "American Ocean Liner Outsails British Man of War. At sea, the SS *Bonnie Duffy* overtakes the new British Battleship, the HMS *Centurion*, rounding the horn in heavy seas." Charlotte and Bonnie now understood why the British welcome to them was not friendly. The articles were written by Billy Frisco. Billy was a popular contributor that was famous for his Wild West stories of famous Western characters.

Now they had a mystery. The reports were factual, only moderately exaggerated and romanticized. Someone had to be feeding information to the Billy Frisco.

Charlotte said, "I love it. Best advertisement we can get."

Bonnie quipped, "Do not try to bullshit me, Charlotte. Sounds like one of your tricks."

Charlotte replied, "I wish I could take credit for this one."

For a dollar a day, a rickshaw could be rented. There were rickshaws in San Francisco but not for a dollar a day. They went shopping. Bonnie bought a couple of exquisite Chinese vases that were allegedly from the Song Dynasty. Bonnie did not care how old they were; they were beautiful and would hopefully please mother-in-law.

While at port, a freighter arrived, flying the Stars and Stripes with the Smithfield flag. It was the Sacramento. The officers of the Sacramento were invited to dine aboard the *Bonnie*, and four of their officers showed up, including their Captain. Bonnie and Charlotte listened to old sea stories most of the evening. The guests wanted to hear the story of the British Man-of-War, the *Centurion*. Mr. Fitzpatrick was glad to tell the story. Of course, he added a little Irish blarney. He had to keep the blarney to a minimum because many at the table had been there. The Russian Commodore wanted to know what they knew or saw of the Japanese naval buildup. The officers from the Sacramento said they had saw two large battleships with large guns on their stop last February at Shizuoka, where they delivered a load of scrap metal. The *Sacramento* stopped here in Singapore for coal and then was off to Bombay to deliver a cargo of Singer sewing machines. In Bombay, they were to pick up a load of Persian rugs and brass goods along with some china place settings for the American market and whatever other cargo they could find for America. The *Bonnie* took on thirty-two Singer sewing machines, twelve for Perth and twenty for Sidney, from the Sacramento. Father-in-law was it the shipping business.

The SS *Bonnie Duffy* was off to Perth, Australia, which meant crossing the equator again. Australia would be their sixth continent visited. The voyage should take six days. The first and second classes were almost booked up, but they only had half of the steerage passengers that they could accommodate.

Not far south of Singapore, they again crossed the equator. The SS *Bonnie Duffy* was keeping King Neptune busy. The passengers looked forward to any excuse to have a party, act like children having water fights, dress up in costumes, and be silly. Bonnie had managed to get what she needed; she showed up in buckskins, ten-gallon hat, and work boots with a bull whip.

Megan asked, "Who do you think you are?"

"I am Bennie, a tough-ass mule skinner hauling heavy freight from Cheyenne to the Home Stake Gold Mine in Lead, Dakota Territory."

Megan, "What do you think you are going to do with that whip?"

Bonnie tossed the business end of her whip out across the deck, holding the handle. "Get your stupid asses out of my way before you feel the sting of the devil on your mangy hide."

Megan, "Stand back, everyone, stand back."

Bonnie cracked the whip three times. "Pull you sons of a bitches, pull."

Most of the onlooker backed up a few steps, some with concerned looks on their faces. Bonnie coiled her whip back up, looked at the assembled people, and bowed. Bonnie got a round of applause.

The Commander said, "You could be in Buffalo Bill's Wild West Show. Where did you learn to use a whip?"

"Driving mules, hauling freight in the Black Hills."

The commander just shook his head and walked away.

Walking around in her costume, carrying her whip, Bonnie finally managed to not get doused with water. Though later, she got some comments from the people that knew her well.

Captain said, "If I need to give someone a flogging, I know who to get."

Megan said, "The rumor is that you really were a mule skinner. I told them that I did not think so," winking at Bonnie.

Charlotte said, "You better give me your whip for the safety of the passengers and crew in case it is a boy and you want to hurt someone."

For the second time, Bonnie got the award for Best Costume.

Bonnie thought, *The tea ladies have made me feel more comfortable with my past. It is part of who I am.*

* * * * *

In the straits between Sumatra and West Java they were unexpectedly hit by a Tsunami in waters that were 20 fathoms deep (120 feet). The bow dove into the wave, washing one of the passengers overboard. It was actually a series of three waves. Another passenger, seeing the man go overboard, threw a life-ring, but the rope was too short as the ship proceeded forward, so he released the rope, hoping the man could swim to the life ring. The First Mate was on duty on the bridge. The First Mate, seeing the incident, ordered the ship to slow to a speed where he could keep steerage to manage the next two waves while he ordered two lifeboats manned ready to be lowered when the waves had passed. As soon as the third wave passed and it was safe, the *Bonnie* stopped and two lifeboats were lowered. The crews of the lifeboats rowed back, looking for the passenger. After a half hour, a white signal flare was fired from one of the lifeboats, signaling that the passenger was found. An hour and a half later, the passenger was back aboard, and they were again underway as the lifeboats were chocked and secured. The man was a second-class passenger with a ticket around the world. Few around-the-world tickets were issued to second class. The ship's Doctor declared the passenger had no serious injuries, only some bruises, and was very lucky.

Bonnie shook the man's hand and said, "Now you have a real interesting story to tell, but will people believe it?"

The passenger replied, "Ma'am, I am Willian Johnson and write for *Harper's Weekly* under the name Billy Frisco. Believe me, this story will be told in print, with your permission. I was sent by *Harper's Weekly* to report on this great ship. My editor wanted me to not reveal that I was a journalist to get an honest story. This ship got a lot of publicity before sailing, and my editor wanted fact, not publicity. Now I can honestly report that the SS *Bonnie Duffy* is the Most Luxurious, Fastest, and Safest Ship with the best crew on the high seas."

Bonnie said, "You will have to thank our Captain for that. He is the one that insists on the crew having safety training. The Captain is adamant about safety."

"When I surfaced and saw the *Bonnie* stern and the size of the waves, I was sure I was a goner. I made my peace with the Lord, asking him for forgiveness for my many sins. As I was taking store of my sins, I realized I have been a very bad boy. I will try to change my ways. I will endeavor to immortalize the Captain and this ship. George Armstrong Custer and William Cody were nobodies until I started writing about them."

Bonnie replied, "Please write about our ship and Smithfield Steamship Line. You may want to ask the Captain if he wants to be immortalized. Personally, I do not want any publicity. Will you come to the Captain's table in the first-class dining room tonight at 6:00 p.m.?"

The Captain was not interested in being immortalized, and Charlotte volunteered to help Billy immortalize the SS *Bonnie Duffy* and Smithfield Steamships.

Bonnie was a little concerned putting Charlotte and Billy Frisco together. Charlotte had a lot of enthusiasm with publicity for the ship. Would Bonnie get some of the publicity, which she did not want? People from her past might come forward with embarrassing stories.

CHAPTER 17

Down Under

P erth was about twelve miles up the Swan River, which was navigable by only shallow draft boats. Fremantle was the harbor town at the mouth of the Swan River. Fremantle harbor was known as a difficult harbor to dock at with little protection from the sea. Their government was in the process of improving the site. There was an inner and outer harbor. The inner harbor was too shallow and small for the Bonnie. The outer harbor was nothing more than a long jetty extending out into the sea. Western Australia did not have any good harbors for ships of the Bonnie class.

Midmorning Bonnie was on the bridge. She could not resist being part of the ship's operation. The crew was forewarned to be ready for a difficult docking, all-hands-on deck. A few miles at sea, they took on a local pilot.

Upon the pilot reaching the bridge, he reported to the Captain, "Sir, this is the largest ship to ever arrive at this port. Cross winds and tides can make docking difficult. Luckily, today, there is only a gentle breeze and the tide is right. This ship, the SS *Bonnie Buffy*, and you, sir, have a reputation of being the finest on the seas. I believe we should have you safely docked in a few hours. It will require the aide of several tugs. With respect, sir, there is another issue that I should make you aware of. Last evening, another ship made port. I believe you know of the HMS *Centurion*. She is taking on coal, and some of her crew has liberty ashore."

The Captain asked, "Mr. Fitzpatrick, are we ready?"

"Yes sir, all lines and the crew is ready."

The Captain ordered, "Seaman D. Adams, connect to the engine room by the telephone and stand by for orders."

The Captain and pilot discussed the task at hand. Fortunately, they spoke the same language, that of master seamen. The Bonnie had a large audience with people on the jetty as well as many of the crew of the British Man-of-War were on their decks, watching. With the Bonnie's engines, the tugs, and finally, the steam windlasses, they had turned around, bow pointing seaward and were safely alongside the jetty, just to seaward of the HMS *Centurion*. Again, Bonnie and other were amazed at the professionalism and skill to maneuver such a large and heavy vessel up next to the dock.

The Pilot said, "That telephone connecting you to the engine room is bloody marvelous."

R. J. Jellico R.N. Captain of the Centurion 1890s Obtained Rank of Admiral of the Fleet, British Royal Navy Distinguished Naval Service, 1872 to 1919

The Captain and Bonnie went to reported to customs, as was required by international law before anyone else could disembark. By international law, the SS *Bonnie Duffy* was under quarantine until cleared by customs. Not strictly enforced at some ports. Only the Captain and a representative were permitted to disembark until they were cleared. Bonnie was concerned getting through customs and immigration after what they went through in Liverpool, especially with the *Centurion* in port. Bonnie was hoping that the officers and crew of the *Centurion* did not hold too much of a grudge against the *Bonnie*.

Upon entering the customs office, they were met by a British Naval Officer in dress uniform. "I am Captain J. R. Jellicoe, Captain of the HMS *Centurion*."

"Frank Krupp, Captain of the SS *Bonnie Duffy*, and this is Mrs. Joseph Smithfield, representative of the Smithfield Steamship Line. It is a pleasure to meet you, sir,"

As they shook hands.

Captain Jellicoe nodded. As he offered Bonnie his hand, he said, "It is a great pleasure to meet you, ma'am."

Bonnie said, "The pleasure is mine, Captain."

Captain Jellicoe looked at Captain Krupp and added, "I want to compliment you, on your ship, your crew, and your seamanship. Your docking was exemplary."

Although Bonnie was not averse to conflict, she thought it was a good time to offer an olive branch.

"Captain Jellicoe, would you and your officers do us the honors and dine with us this evening aboard the *Bonnie Duffy*?"

"Yes, that would be our pleasure. What time would be appropriate?"

Bonnie said; "Would six p.m. be acceptable?"

Captain Krupp added, "Perhaps they would like to come earlier for a tour of our ship."

Captain Jellicoe said, "That would be appreciated. The SS *Bonnie Duffy* has quite the reputation."

Captain Krupp asked, "Would four p.m. be acceptable?"

"That would be quite acceptable. With your permission, I will bring two of my officers."

Bonnie said, "See you and your officers at four p.m., Captain."

Bonnie's fears were not justifiable; they went through customs expediently and were treated with respect. There were no hints wanting a bribe.

It would take over a day to have coal delivered by wagon and loaded into the bunkers. They were forced into accepting a coal mix, 90 percent anthracite and 10 percent bituminous. They were told the coal was inadvertently mixed by a careless worker and the coal was no longer acceptable by the British Admiralty. They were offered a small discount for accepting the coal mix.

Some of the passengers took carriages and went to Perth; others spent the afternoon in the port town of Fremantle. Charlotte and her crew went to Perth to buy supplies. Now with Candida in the office, passenger services were available even when Charlotte and Bonnie were busy. Candida was very confident and a great addition to passenger services. She understood discretion, a necessity in her position.

Bonnie and the Captain agreed they would offer their guests a tour of the engine room if they so wished. None of the crew was given liberty at that time, as all available hands were to help clean and polish the ship. It needed a good cleaning and polishing.

Promptly at 4:00 p.m., the Captain and two officers from the *Centurion* showed up, asking for permission to come aboard. Captain Krupp and Bonnie greeted them. They were introduced to two British Royal Naval Commanders, one the Executive Officer, and the other the Chief Engineer.

Bonnie said, "Captain Jellicoe, would you like to tour our engine room? The crew informed me that they have been working to get it ready for inspection."

Captain Jellicoe replied, "Yes, we would like to see the engines that can push this remarkable ship for six days at a remarkable speed across the North Atlantic."

As Bonnie was leading the way, Captain Jellicoe said, "Mrs. Smithfield, I do not expect you to accompany us into the engine room."

Bonnie replied, "I enjoy going to the engine room. To me, it is the heart of the ship. When underway, we all feel its pulse."

"Yes, ma'am, lead the way."

As they entering the engine room, there was a line of eight, the officers and the crew, standing at attention, all dressed in dark-blue uniforms that looked clean and pressed.

Smitey, at the head of the line, said, "Captain, we are ready for inspection."

Captain Krupp said, "This is Smitey, our Chief Engineer, and his officers and the engine room crew. This is Captain Jellicoe, Captain of the HMS *Centurion*, and his Executive Officer and Chief Engineer. Smitey, what is the engine room status?"

"On standby, awaiting your orders, sir."

Captain Krupp then asked their guests if they had any questions.

The Centurion Chief Engineer asked, "What are the specifications of these impressive engines?"

Smitey responded, "Who would like to answer that question?"

The entire line took one step forward and said, "Sir."

Smitey said, "Take your pick, Commander. Ask any one of them any question you wish."

Smitey liked to show off his crew; he was proud of them.

The Commander said, "Your choice, Chief Engineer."

"Motorman B. Adams, would you like to answer the Commander's question?"

Betty took another step forward and began as Smitey stood with a grin on his face.

Betty went through the specifications she had memorized.

The Centurion Commander went in front of Betty and asked, "Motorman, how old are you?"

"I just turned fourteen, sir."

The Commander asked, "What are the status of your boilers?"

Betty looked at the steam gauge on the wall and said, "We now have 155 PSI steam, enough to run our generators and auxiliary equipment, sir."

The Commander asked, "How long would it take to come to full steam and full speed ahead for an extended time?"

Betty answered, "An hour and a half to two hours. The boilers would have to be stoked, sir. We could be underway in fifteen minutes, sir."

The Commander replied, "Very good, Motorman. Very enlightening."

Smitey said, "Look around and ask any question, and we will endeavor to answer."

The guests walked about, examining the machinery, and asked several questions. They asked about the electrical generation, and Electrician Mate E. Adams showed them the generators and gave them a brief explanation of the system. They closely scrutinized the electrical system. They were interested in the automatic oiler system. The telephone on the wall was of great interest as well, and it was explained that it provided fast communication to all important areas of the ship.

Before the tour continued, the Centurion Chief Engineer said, "Chief Engineer Smitey, you have a remarkable crew and engines. The heart of a steamship is truly the engines and the crew that maintains and operates them. You have demonstrated excellence in their operation, power, and reliability in a variety of conditions."

Smitey replied, "Thank you, sir. All the credit belongs to my crew."

"Indeed, you have a remarkable crew—not typical but definitely remarkable."

In the boiler room, coal was still being transferred into the bunkers. One man was pouring water from a bucket, while another man was pushing a broom, cleaning up the deck. Upon inquiry, it was explained, "Coal dust is known to be explosive. The floor is often wet-swept, keeping the dust down, the sweeping caked and dried, to be later burnt. This also helped eliminate the problem of coal dust that causes lung problems to men. The deck has to be dry before coal is added. Wet coal can spontaneously combust."

Captain Jellicoe said, "A simple solution to a dangerous problem. We need to adopt similar procedures. Besides, it makes for a clean deck and less coal dust in the air."

They went through the casino on their way to the dining room, and it was commented that they had no casino aboard their ship.

Dinner was interesting, to say the least. Introductions were made of the other Naval Officers, and Billy Frisco who seemed to want to be part of everything. Billy believed he had access to all the ship. Nobody questioned him. All wanted to see their name in print, but not in a derogatory way.

The Russian Commodore's English had improved significantly. At first, the discussion was about ships and the men that sailed them, then world naval powers. Both the Russians and British were concerned with the Japanese military ambitions. The British Captain stated that the HMS *Centurion* was on its way to the British colonies in Asia to help support their militaries there. The British were concerned the Japanese had desires on Southeast Asia and China. The

Russian Commodore was going to China to discuss with them the Japanese threat to Korea and Mongolia, along with the completion of the Trans-Siberian Railroad. They agreed the British and Russian might become allies in the future; they had similar concerns. USN Commander Roberts stated that his country's policy was to remain neutral.

Bonnie listened and learned. She had no important input.

The discussion then went to the role of women in the future. Captain Jellicoe commented on the three young ladies in the engine room and their obvious contributions. He was informed that there were two young ladies who were training to be Navigators who served on the bridge and that Mrs. Smithfield was becoming a good Navigator herself. Commander Roberts stated that he thought women would get the right to vote in America.

Captain Jellicoe asked, "Mrs. Smithfield, what do you think the role of women will be in the future?"

Bonnie replied, "The same as men. Modern machines make men and women more equal. A woman can shoot a gun and kill just as easy as a man, operate a steam engine, or design a ship."

The Russian Commodore stated, "My great-grandmother, Catherine the Great, ruled all of Russia and was loved by her friends and feared by her enemies. Great Britain is ruled by a strong woman, Victoria. Russian woman fought alongside Russian men driving Napoleon from Russia. If necessary, I would not hesitate manning my ships with women. My own daughter is practicing with a sextant and talks of serving aboard a ship."

Commander Roberts added, "It is sort of ironic a man will take orders from a queen but he does not want to work alongside a woman."

Captain Krupp said, "I have accepted women on my bridge, and I find them conscientious and disciplined."

Captain Jellicoe seemed to agree. "Englishwomen are demanding more authority and independence. We men are going to have to live with it. This will require a lot of adjustment, but in the long run, I think it will be good."

Bonnie said, "I think this discussion will continue for many generations. I know men and women need each other. When men and women work together, great things can be accomplished."

The Russian Commodore replied, "I will drink to that."

It was the toast that ended the dinner discussion. Bonnie felt some satisfaction. She got the last word in. She was sure her mother-in-law would be proud of her.

The officers of the *Bonnie Duffy* and their families were invited to a tour and lunch aboard the *Centurion* at ten the next morning. The *Centurion* was leaving the next afternoon for Singapore and then onto the China Station to be the flagship of that fleet.

* * * * *

Bonnie telegrammed Joseph, telling him how much she missed him but, again, procrastinated telling him of her condition. Bonnie's excuse was that she did not want to worry him. Because of the routing and the many times, the telegram would have to be relayed; it would take two to three days for Joseph to get the telegram.

Western Australia was gold-mining country, which interested Bonnie and Megan. Recently opals were found in Australia. Many from the ship purchased gems to be taken home for setting. Opal was considered a rare gem, and miners were finding many fine examples of the gem. The miners needed cash to continue mining, and the competition was making the prices reasonable. Markets for export had not yet been established. Bonnie and Megan both invested several hundred dollars in opals to take back home as an investment. Bonnie still did not know if her father-in-law was going to pay her; she wanted her own money, and she did not want to give Joseph the satisfaction of her asking him for money. She was not ready to go back and mine gold; besides, she was pregnant. At least the morning sickness was not as bad.

Bonnie really missed Joseph. She needed a hug, along with some verbal and physical sparring.

Bonnie was not going to be the only woman going to the HMS *Centurion* tour. The Commodore's wife and daughter, Commander

Robert's wife with their son Billy, and Charlotte would be there as well. Billy Frisco managed to also get an invite. The *Centurion* was not the *Bonnie Duffy*. Accommodations were Spartan. The wood-work was simple and roughly finished, the bare minimum. They were not taken to the engine room. The attention was on the arma-ment. Their look matched their function—cold, hard, and without any compassion. In their design and construction, there was no con-sideration for aesthetic appeal. The *Centurion* was armed with four ten-inch guns with six-inch guns as secondary, along with smaller guns and torpedo tubes. Bonnie remembered the architects Connie and Rachel telling her, "Form for function." The *Centurion* design fit that definition in that its function was death, destruction, and intim-idation. Most all were made of cold, hard, thick steel, painted gray. The *Centurion*, although looking cold, was spotlessly clean. Every piece of bronze and brass was polished to the point of being spotless. The accompaniment was 620 souls. Many slept in hammocks that could be quickly removed, clearing areas for combat and military needs. Bonnie wondered if Smithfield built military ships, would they be like this? If so, Connie and Rachel would have to adapt.

All the sailors stood at attention as the tour passed by. Commander Roberts pointed out that every seam had three or more rows of rivets. The hull from below and above the waterline was rein-forced with what was called a belt. It was nine- to twelve-inch-thick steel with an upper belt of four-inch-thick steel, the bulkheads were eight-inch-thick steel. The *Centurion* was designed to hurl five-hun-dred-pound projectiles over ten miles and withstand the return fire.

The crew's mess showed signs they tried to make it comfort-able and homey. There were comfortable chairs and tables. Murals were painted on the bulkheads, mostly of home and country and a portrait of Queen Victoria. On one bulkhead was a mural of mer-maids on a tropical island. It appeared the artist had taken some liberty and included large breasts and a voluptuous derriere on the mermaids before they started their fish tail. Out of the corner of her eye, Bonnie saw one sailor pat one mermaid on her rear as he left. Bonnie thought, *Typical male behavior,* making her think of Joseph. She really missed her husband. Right now, a pat on her behind by

Joseph would be appreciated, although Bonnie would strongly protest unless it was in private.

The officers dining room was comfortable. Here again the steel bulkheads had murals painted on them. One long wall had an extensive scene of Nelson's Victory at Trafalgar. Two other walls had similar scenes of great moment in the history of the British Royal Navy. The fourth wall had a portrait of Queen Victoria with the words "Service for Queen and Country."

Lunch was delicious, served by Negro stewards in a very polite British way. There was little discussion at the table; the Centurion had to get ready for sea.

The time spent with the HMS *Centurion* officers was educational to Bonnie. There was a comradery of respect among seamen, merchant marine, or military navy, no matter what country.

Bonnie, as well as a lot of the *Bonnie's* crew and passengers, watched as the *Centurion* headed for sea. The crew of the *Centurion* lined their deck and gave honors. It was quite impressive. The *Bonnie* passengers waved farewell as the *Bonnie* whistled the *Centurion*, farewell.

Bonnie was approached by the reporter Billy. "How am I going to write this up? It appeared the *Bonnie's* officers and the *Centurion's* officers made friends with each other."

Bonnie said, "Yes, they all have a lot of things in common. Ships, the men who sail them, and the sea."

Billy replied, "Mrs. Smithfield, may I quote you? Great storyline, an age-old story, but still true. Men and the sea."

Bonnie said, "If you let me read it before you submit it."

"You got a deal, Mrs. Smithfield."

Electrician Mate E. Adams and the electrical crew strung temporary electric lights over the dock, next to the ship, so that coal loading could continue during the night, it being a new moon. A small crowd gathered to see the late-night show. All agreed it was better than working with lanterns. To most people, electric illumination was a strange curiosity.

First light, the coal bunkers full, the larders full, the tide right, the SS *Bonnie Duffy* headed to sea. The next port was Sydney,

Australia. Their course was to take them south then across the Great Australian Bight, 2,140 nautical miles, six days to Sidney.

It was early fall in the Southern Hemisphere, and the weather was good. The ship returned to a routine at sea. Bonnie got proficient at identifying the navigation stars in the southern sky. The Southern Cross became as familiar to Bonnie as the Big Dipper in the north.

As they passed between the continent of Australia and Tasmania into the Tasman Sea, a large pod of whales accompanied them. Everyone aboard got to admire the huge beasts. The ship's photographer took photographs. Billy, the reporter from the *Harper's Weekly*, gave Bonnie a copy of two reports he was going to file in Sidney. He asked Bonnie if she would review them for accuracy.

The first report was of their recent encounter with the HMS *Centurion*. The report was true to Billy Frisco's reputation. He had interviews with many involved, the Captain of the *Centurion*, the Russian Commodore, the USN Commander, their own First Mate, Mr. Fitzpatrick, Smitey, the Chief Engineer of the *Centurion*, and a short quote from Bonnie. The report praised both ships as being great ships, the best on the high seas, each with a very different purpose. Next, he praised the men who commanded the great ships, including the visiting naval leaders. The report stressed the similarities and camaraderie of great men of the sea. It was a raving review of the officers who served on the great ships. Although he did not have an interview with Captain Krupp, Billy honored him by saying, "Captain Frank Krupp, the Master of the SS *Bonnie Duffy*, has the respect and admiration of all who know him and served under him." The report concluded with, "No matter how well-designed, built, or how powerful, ships are only as good as the men who serve on them."

The second report was of the SS *Bonnie Duffy*. Billy told that the ship was everything advertised, "Most Luxurious, Safest, and Fastest." Billy then told of the crew. Of the men and women who operated the ship, ensuring that it made it safely and smoothly from port to port. He told of five exceptional young siblings that helped operate and maintained the ship. These siblings served in the engine room and on the bridge and changed the lightbulbs as well as installed and maintained the ship's small telephone system. Billy said this was just one example of the contribution made by the men and women of the sea. Next, he extoled the work of the people that kept the ship clean and the beds made with clean sheets. He included the many people that prepared and served the exceptional cuisine. Billy also told of the teachers that offered an exceptional educational experience to both the passengers and crew. He did not forget the people that entertained, playing music, and the blackjack dealers. His summation: "Two women, Mrs. Joseph Smithfield (Bonnie) and Miss Charlotte Gibbs, the Passenger Services Directors, dedicate themselves, making the experience exceptional."

Bonnie returned the reports to Billy. "I find these reports to be truthful and honest, though with some exaggeration. If I were you, I would not fall overboard again. After Captain Krupp reads this, he will probably not try to rescue you. Also, you must remove my name."

Billy said, "Mrs. Smithfield, I will endeavor to not go overboard again. I thought my reference to you was complementary. As far as your name and position are concerned, they are a matter of public record. Sorry, you are fair game as long as I do not slander you. Incidentally, my editor suggested a story of an interesting young lady who had collected bounties on murderers and train robbers. That might make an interesting story to investigate—it would fit in with my stories of Western heroes. What do you think?"

"It would not surprise me that a lady that collected bounties knows how to use guns."

"You are a truly amazing lady. I am glad that we are friends and not enemies."

Bonnie replied, "It is always better to make a friend than an enemy."

* * * * *

Sydney was a large and well-sheltered harbor. It was a large city that had anything anyone wanted, except a good bank. Except for a few small privately owned banks, all the banks had gone bankrupt. Seven years of depression had taken its toll. The banking system was in such disarray that Smithfield Steamship Lines had problems establishing a line of credit. A large money transfer was arranged with one of the remaining banks, for a fee. Armed guards transferred the money to the *Bonnie Duffy*'s onboard bank. With cash, gold preferred, everything was at a discount price. Checks were not accepted. Nobody trusted any bank.

The First Mate, Adam Fitzpatrick, found five hundred new quality life preservers for sale. In addition, sixteen lifeboats that nested in one another were purchased. The ship carpenters were given the job to make racks for life preserver storage where they would be readily available in case of an emergency. But the carpenters did not have enough lumber for the job. A large quantity of first-quality Australian white cypress lumber was offered for sale at a deep discount prices. This wood was considered premium for ship's interiors. It was a strong and rot-resistant wood that had beautiful grain that exhibited a variety of subtle colors. The wood was all air-dried, originally intended for yacht construction and quality furniture. There was no market for yachts. And quality furniture was not in demand, with the Depression. Bonnie bought the lumber. If her husband did not want it for his next ship, it would be a good investment. The *Bonnie*'s cargo holds were nearly empty, and lumber was a reasonably light cargo. The sale was made, saving one lumber company from bankruptcy, and getting excellent wood for the next ship at a low cost. It took two days to load the lumber. All the cargo holds were filled from deck to ceiling and bulkhead to bulkhead. After the calculations were made, they would be at their maximum weight with a full load of coal. The ivory was repositioned on top of the lumber. Now her father-in-law could not say they did not haul cargo.

They were originally scheduled for two days, three nights in port, but now it was stretched out to four days, five nights. They had scheduled extra days in case of weather or other delays. None of the passengers complained; it was a beautiful port with many things to do and see. Discounts were offered on almost everything. There were some excellent buys in consignment stores. Bonnie bought a silver service for twenty-four, for a little over the value of the silver. Bonnie also purchased a large-scale detailed model of Sir Francis Drake's ship the *Golden Hind*, the ship he completed his historic circumnavigation on. Bonnie told herself the ship model was for Joseph, for his office. For now, it would sit on Bonnie's desk in her office. Bonnie telegrammed Joseph, telling him of the lumber and that she missed him. Again, Bonnie procrastinated, telling him of her condition. She knew she was shameful. Joseph would get the telegram after they departed. Charlotte telegrammed the home office of their change in plans and giving them an update of their status.

CHAPTER 18

The South Pacific

The Philippines was under Spanish control. They were originally scheduled to dock in Manila, Philippines, but upon checking with the US Consulate, Australian officials and their treatment in Havana, plans were changed. They made the decision to go to Port Moresby, Papua New Guinea, instead. The Australian government telegraphed ahead for them, they would be welcome and expected. A few years previously, Papua New Guinea went from German control to British control; at least they knew they had a few British friends with some really big guns.

In five days, they were to arrive at Port Moresby, sailing into the Coral Sea. The ship, setting low in the water and traveling at an efficient sixteen knots made for a smooth voyage.

Now at two and a half months, the morning sickness had subsided, to be replaced with the desire to hurt someone. Bonnie was not concerned; she could handle her temper. She had a lot of practice and was getting better. It came with the Irish Blood and Red Hair. The Doctor told Bonnie that everything looked good and gave her a date of mid-November. He also scolded Bonnie for playing with a bull whip. His main concern was that she would give someone a heart attack.

The carpenters were busy making the racks for the life preservers. Most of the new life preservers would go into the areas used by steerage. Room was found on the aft deck for the new lifeboats. Now they had a life preserver and lifeboat room for every soul aboard, passengers, crew, and steerage at full capacity. The lifeboats would have to be filled to their capacity to accommodate all aboard. The capacities of the lifeboats were stenciled on all lifeboats. The crew had additional training for the new lifeboats. Bonnie thought, *The safest just became safer.* Inspecting the carpenter's work, Bonnie realized she had bought some beautiful wood. The carpenters said it was a pleasure working with the wood.

The five sisters were doing so good Bonnie no longer was concerned for their well-being. Bonnie's interest was now on the two boys from Brazil and the three rescued slave children. After several trips to the engine room, Bonnie realized the two Brazilian boys were in good hands. Now, oiling was easier and less dangerous. It now appeared that Smitey had five daughters and two sons. He was a good father. He forced his children to do their best and be proud and responsible. He set an exceptional example.

The three children from Senegal were working in the galley and laundry. They had separated from the four adults they came with. Their English had improved so they could tell their story in English. They were not related; they formed an alliance and escaped together. There were actually forty to fifty slaves that tried to escaped all at once. They each took their chances with their own plans. A few were killed, and others were assumed to be recaptured; possibly others had escaped to their freedom. Four children tried to swim away; three were picked up by the four adults that found the raft that was used to haul supplies across the river. There was another girl, the sister of girl who escaped. She drowned in the river. The girl moved into the ladies' quarters, and the two boys moved into the men's quarters. The two boys were assistant cooks and considered as good workers, and the Chief Chef said they were an asset to the galley. The girl worked in the laundry, and when Charlotte tried to transfer her to housekeeping, Charlotte was blocked by the lady that ran the laundry and offered another girl. The four adults from Senegal were respected by their supervisors, and their supervisors said that they were good workers. Bonnie wished she had not asked; she was given the names of several people that were not wanted. The recommendation was to dismiss them after they made home port, if they could not be disposed of earlier.

After leaving Sydney, Bonnie received a package wrapped in plain brown paper. It was dropped off at the mail, message room with no sender information. It was addressed to Mrs. Smithfield. It was a baby book that said it was the definitive source of information from conception to adolescence. The first chapter gave advice on improving the chances for conception and told that some positions improved the odds as to the babe's gender. Bonnie reflected on how her and Joseph had done it in New York. That was counterproductive, for it made her want Joseph more. Bonnie really missed him. She was starting to feel real guilty that she had not told Joseph, though it would not be long and she would be home. It was just on the other side of the ocean they were on, about a third of the way around the world. The Pacific Ocean was big.

* * * * *

Port Moresby was a beautiful tropical port that was well protected from the sea. The upper part of the harbor had grass huts on posts. The city was mainly grass huts with a few government and commercial buildings. Before they had their lines secured to the dock, they were surrounded by canoes, with people selling everything imaginable; even children were offered for sale. The problem was that the hull of the *Bonnie* was so high no sales could be made. The men and women were all dressed alike, with loin cloths. None of the women made any attempt to cover their breasts. Most of the children had no clothing. Bonnie mused, "Let us see if Megan follows their example and goes native."

Local soldiers with British officers guarded the dock, keeping the locals away from the ship.

As soon as the gangway was down the Captain, Charlotte and Bonnie disembarked and went to the customs office. The paperwork was all prepared, and Bonnie wrote a bank draft for the fees, which was accepted. The necessary papers were signed, and then they received a warning.

"Some of the indigenous people still practice headhunting and cannibalism. Please do not wander too far without armed guards and stay in groups. We do not have enough soldiers to protect all of you, and some of our soldiers have dual loyalties, first to their tribal family and then to us for their pay. Unless you want to be dinner for the locals, be careful, and warn your passengers, please."

On their way back to the ship, Charlotte told Bonnie, "When you offered me a position sailing with you, I thought of the adventure. It never occurred to me that might entail avoiding cannibals."

"You are the one that suggested Port Moresby in lieu of Manilla."

Captain said, "You two are both full of shit!"

Bonnie laughed, "All three of us are full of shit!"

Charlotte then got serious. "What do we tell the passengers?"

Bonnie said, "Be careful or you might be on the menus."

Bonnie got a nasty look from her companions.

Returning to the ship, Bonnie and Charlotte went to Charlotte's office and debated what they were going to do. While Candida listened in wondering what she had got into and the sanity of her bosses. In the heat of the debate, a knock came on the door. It was a messenger. The message was from the Captain. It was in the form of an informational letter to be posted.

> Notice:
> There are rumors of possible civil unrest at this port. For the safety of all passengers and crew, I am asking that all leaving the ship be in an organized group that will be escorted by the local military. My responsibility is to the safety of the passengers and crew. I am asking all to help ensure a safe and pleasurable voyage.
>
> Respectfully,
> Captain Frank Krupp

Bonnie said, "Charlotte, we do not have any problem. Your Captain has everything in control."

"Frank is our Captain, a good Captain."

"Yes, he is an excellent Captain. Whisper in his ear I have full confidence in him."

Candida did not say a word; she just listened and learned. She understood discretion.

Charlotte then said, "Be nice, or I will telegram Joseph, telling him all the news."

The Captain's letter was copied and posted. The Captain was respected by all. He said very little, though, and to most, he was a little of a mystery. When he posted a letter, all read and believed. His words were not questioned or challenged, for he was the Captain.

Bonnie went shopping, in a large group, with Annie, Betty, Cathy, Dotty, Eavey, Megan, Candida, and others. Charlotte declined and manned Passenger Services. A girls' shopping trip. They were surrounded by may wanting to sell them something, trying to get their attention.

Betty said, "They are acting like I am an important person."

Bonnie replied, "You are someone important, especially to these people. You are a member of the crew of a great ship. Do not let it go to your head. It is all a matter of perspective. On the ship, you and your sisters have important jobs—as Motorman, Bridge Assistant, Electrician's Mate—but here you are someone that has money, someone that is from a far-off land, a land that they do not understand, sailing on a great ship."

Annie said, "Mrs. Smithfield, you are so wise and smart."

"I want all of you to listen to me. I am not that smart. I still have a lot to learn. I am just ahead of you. You will catch up. My life has been a journey. I am still on my way. I realize I do not know what my final destination is. All five of you are an important part of my journey. Each of you are on your own journeys."

They were interrupted by an old woman with only a few teeth, tattoos all over, and breasts that were drooping to her waist; she wanted to sell them some small heads. The heads were very unique, very detailed.

The guide told them the heads were real people's heads that were shrunk. The skulls and brains were removed a piece at a time, then the skin was shrunk by a drying process. Their shopping trip was ruined. This was the first shopping trip ashore that the girls did not buy candy.

Bonnie thought, *These five girls have their own journeys ahead of them. They certainly have an interesting start. What will their destinations be? Assuredly, all already have interesting stories to tell.*

Port Moresby, was the most unusual and challenging port they had visited.

The coal bunkers were filled with men carrying coal in bags that were supported by straps over their foreheads. The men carried the coal in long lines right to the bunkers.

Before departing, the ship was searched, six men were found hiding in the coal bunkers. They were escorted off the ship.

As they left midday, most had mixed emotions. There was the repulsion and fear of the headhunters and cannibals, yet there were the deep feelings of the plight of poverty. There were no signs of opportunity, just despair. But it was the perspective of people with a completely different culture.

Their next port was Hong Kong, a part of China that was carved out by the British. Another British colony. It would be 3,078 nautical miles, eight and half days, at fifteen knots. Dotty showed Bonnie their course, and the Navigators decided to name it the seven-seas course. They were leaving the Coral Sea, sailing across the Arafura Sea, then the Banda Sea, across the Ceram Sea, and in the Molucca Sea, they would again cross the equator, their eight time. Next would be the Celebs Sea with Borneo to their west and then into the Sulu Sea. The final sea was the South China Sea, which would lead them to Hong Kong.

Bonnie said, "I count eight seas."

Dotty said, "Ma'am, I know, but Seven Seas sounds good. Who ever heard of eight seas? Mrs. Smithfield, we have sailed in six of the Seven Oceans. Rounding the Horn, we went below the sixtieth parallel south, giving us the Southern Ocean. Can we sail north through the Bearing Sea? That will give us the Arctic Ocean, Lucky Seven Seas?"

Bonnie said, "Sounds good, but we must get home."

"Ma'am, this ship is my home."

"Yes, I feel this ship is my home. I want to go back to San Francisco and be with my husband. That is also my home."

Dotty asked, "Ma'am, when we get back to San Francisco, are we going to have to leave the ship?"

Bonnie said, "I know that you are a part of the ship's crew, and as such, you can stay with the ship if you want. I know the Captain will not want to lose you. He relies on you and all of your sisters."

* * * * *

The area that they were sailing through was so fascinating. It seemed to almost be a crime to not often stop. They were weaving their way north and a little west between thousands of islands. Some of the islands were well-known; others just outlined on charts with names. Some of the islands did not have names on the charts but were named as island groups. Thousands of people lived on these islands. They probably had names for the many islands. Many still live as their ancestors lived for a thousand years. Bonnie pondered, *What do the natives think when they see the* Bonnie Duffy *sail by?*

Many of the passengers spent a lot of time on the deck sight-seeing, especially when they passed near land. Whales were sighted as well as many other marine mammals and strange fish. Some fish could even fly. Dhow sailing vessels were seen, sailed by their crews as they did for centuries. Oriental junks sailed by Asians, sailing as they had for many generations. A catamaran canoe was passed, and it must have had forty men paddling. As the *Bonnie* passed the canoe, all the paddlers waved their paddles. The discussion was, a friendly greeting or a threat? The consensus was that they were sailing through an alien land they did not understand.

On May 4, King Neptune was again demanding adulation from his subjects as they crossed the equator. It was the last and eight time on this voyage that they would have an equatorial crossing party. The celebration was abruptly halted as a deafening boom and a concussion of air hit all. Some people were thrown onto the deck. There were shouts from the port rail. They were sailing by the Sangihe Chain of islands. Awu, a volcano, had erupted, throwing smoke high into the air. Some rocks that were spewed out landed near the ship, even though they were about eight miles away. The volcano roared so loud most covered their ears. The ship quickly went to full speed to avoid the danger. As people watched Mother Nature's spectacle, the ship rolled violently, taking all by surprise. The eruption had created a tsunami next to the ship. The sea boiled with masses of bubbles coming from below. The bubbles gave off smoke that smelled obnoxious with sulphur. The warning was the loud boom of the volcano, and all assumed the danger was coming from above. Some of the passengers and crew were thrown onto the deck and into bulkheads. Some became sick with the offensive odor. Eyes watered from the fumes. Most coughed and gagged from the fumes. A moderate northerly breeze soon cleared the air. The infirmary was very busy. Many volunteered to help; some had medical training. Three broken arms, several cracked ribs, one broken collar bone, a couple of concussions, many stitches, and a lot of bruises. They were lucky—no life-threatening or long-term debilitating injuries. The ship's photographer was already on deck photographing King Neptune. He got numerous photographs of the volcano as they sailed away with both of his cameras, as others sketched what they saw. Six hours later and a hundred nautical miles away, they could see the billowing smoke rising into the sky. After the sun set, the smoke could still be seen; it had an eerie glow.

At dinner that evening, it was suggested that another commemorative medallion be struck. Commemorating the SS *Bonnie Duffy* surviving the volcanic eruption of Awu. It was suggested that they had not given King Neptune his proper due; Awu was his warning. A retired professor on the cruise informed everyone it was Vulcan and not Neptune who should be blamed.

William, a.k.a. Billy Frisco, was already interviewing passengers and writing his report. Billy was concerned his editor would not believe the story of the volcano and not publish it. A photograph would convince his editor, but he could not telegram a photograph. Bonnie as well as others agreed to send his editor a telegram verifying his story and the event.

Little did they know the eruption was seen and felt by thousands for hundreds of miles; the news was already being spread around the world.

CHAPTER 19

The China Sea

Hong Kong was a series of islands and bays. As the SS *Bonnie Duffy* made its way toward the harbor, they picked up a pilot. They were expected, and the pilot guided them to a nice dock near the business district. About a mile away, they could see their friend the HMS *Centurion* among other warships. Bonnie and the Captain went to the customs house. Before they could introduce themselves, they were asked if they had seen Awu erupt. It was big news. When they said they were eight miles away when it blew, all stopped what they were doing, wanting to hear the story. They tried to be polite, but a small crowd grew and they wanted the story retold from the start. Bonnie was getting impatient but was endeavoring to keep her composure when Captain Jellicoe arrived in uniform.

Captain Jellicoe said, "Have you been cleared yet?"

Bonnie replied, "No. Everybody wants to hear of the volcano eruption."

Captain Jellicoe, in a strong, authoritative voice, said, "The SS *Bonnie Duffy* needs to be cleared through customs."

That started the process, and they were soon cleared through customs. Bonnie again invited Captain Jellicoe to dinner. He declined and invited Captain Krupp to the officer's club, apologizing to Bonnie, explaining that it was a men's-only club, except on special occasions. Captain Jellicoe extended the invitation to the Commodore and the Commander.

When they returned to the *Bonnie*, they were overwhelmed by reporters, scientists, and curiosity seekers. Word had spread that the passengers and crew had witnessed the Awu erupting up close. Up to now, the ship's photographer did his job and did not get a lot of attention. Now the ship's photographer was famous. On the boarding gangway, he had posted several of the photographs he had taken of Awu erupting. Police were called because of the large crowd and were guarding the photographs and gangways, keeping people away. The photographer had taken photographs with both of his cameras, his glass-plate negative camera and his new innovative foldout Kodak camera that used rolled-up film for the negatives. The scientists wanted the photographs for study. One scientist told Bonnie that the photographs were invaluable for study. Close-up photographs of a volcanic eruption were never before taken, and eyewitness accounts were unreliable. The news reporters wanted them for reproduction in newspapers and magazines. Many people were just curious.

Bonnie found Charlotte and the photographer in a heated debate. Charlotte thought the photographs belonged to the ship, and the photographer said they were artistic property. As soon as *Bonnie* arrived, they both started rapidly talking to Bonnie at the same time, both trying to persuade her of their position. Bonnie hushed them and told them to talk one at a time.

The photographer, Samuel, said, "Ma'am, I do not get paid by the ship but make a living selling photographs, manly to the passengers. I endeavor to be an asset to the ship. I often make photographs for the officers and crew, charging only enough to cover my expenses."

Charlotte said, "Samuel is part of the crew. He does not pay his way. He gets his food, boarding, and passage as a member of the crew. If he were not aboard our ship, he would not have had the opportunity to take the photographs of the eruption. The photographs are valuable assets that belong to Smithfield Steamship Line."

Bonnie wanted to get up and walk away; she did not want be in the position to make this decision. She said, "Shit, you both have valid arguments. Charlotte, are you suggesting that the Smithfield Steamship Line go into the business of selling photographs? And can you make the photographs?"

Charlotte said, "The photographs will be a valuable asset in advertising."

Bonnie asked, "Samuel, can you mark the photographs so that they will be identified as being taken on the SS *Bonnie Duffy*?"

Samuel replied, "I can write on the negatives so that all prints made from them say anything you want."

Bonnie asked, "Can you identify them with the date taken and 'Taken on SS *Bonnie Duffy*'?"

Samuel said, "Consider it done. I have already added my signature and logo."

Bonnie asked, "Charlotte, will that be acceptable to you? We do not have to do anything, and we will get the advertising you want."

Charlotte said, "Brilliant, that is why you are the boss."

Bonnie replied, "Just remember who is the boss."

Charlotte quipped back, "You know where you can shove that."

Samuel, as he shook his head and walked out, said, "Yes, ma'am, thank you. All my negatives will be so identified."

Candida kept writing, trying to look busy and minding her own business, smart girl.

Hong Kong was an exciting and vibrant city. They were scheduled to stay two days. By request, they were going to stay three days. They had a couple extra days in their schedule.

Charlotte and Bonnie had a chance to go shipping, and they hired an interpreter to go with them. First, they found a silversmith to make a special medallion of their encounter with the volcano Awu. Bonnie had saved the dies from Liverpool. The heads die would not have to be remade. With a lot of discussion, it was decided to make the tail die of an erupting volcano with billowing clouds and a few rocks flying out with the words around the edge, "Awu Eruption, May 4, 1894." The medallions would be ready the next morning. The silversmith was also a mint that made coins for several small Asian countries.

Bonnie had her mother-in-law covered, but she had nothing for father-in-law. As she walked, she was hopping to see something special. Dad's life was ships and the business of shipping. An old man had what looked like old tools and a sword for sale. Bonnie remembered several sabers on his office wall as decorations. Upon inquiry, Bonnie was told it was a Jian, a double-edged iron sword, that was very old. It looked old and well-used but intact. It was not cheap, and as she haggled over the price, the old man pulled another sword from under a blanket. Pulling it from its sheath, Bonnie saw it was special. It appeared to be bronze and old, not what would be carried by a soldier but a high-ranking leader. The old man told Bonnie it was a Dao, very old, and came from the grave of a great Mongol warlord. It looked to be a deadly single-edged sword with a shape similar to a scimitar. Both swords cost Bonnie more than she wanted to spend, but it was for Dad and they were special.

Charlotte bought a ceremonial tea service set. It was delicate and ornate, a work of art.

Samuel got some help from some other crewmen. He purchased additional photography supplies and set up a larger darkroom in an extra cabin. He set up a table in front of the ship and sold his photographs. They were again getting a lot of publicity worldwide.

They had several requests to take cargo to America, and the requests had to be declined. Their cargo holds were already full. The costs of many desirable items were low, and Bonnie realized that a fortune could be made buying here and shipping back to America.

Captain Krupp, Commander Roberts, and Commodore Vladimir Petrovitch all seemed to have disappeared. Charlotte was concerned, as was the Commodore's wife and the Commander's wife. The four ladies waited on the deck near the gangway. It was late when the three men showed up. It was obvious they had been drinking and smoking cigars. The ladies all agreed boys will be boys. They came home where they belonged. Bonnie went to her lonely berth.

The medallions were just what they asked for. Candida managed the medallions, except one bag that Bonnie wanted so she could give them out.

Bonnie got a telegram from Joseph telling her that the wood would be great and that he missed her desperately.

Bonnie returned the telegram. "LOVE U MUCH STOP MISS U MUCH STOP NEED U MUCH."

Bonnie also got a long telegram from Dad: "SPEED ENDURANCE RECORD IN THE PACIFIC STOP YOUR OWN HARPER'S WEEKLY REPORTER STOP WINNING A STEAMSHIP RACES AROUND CAPE HORN WITH A BRITISH BATTLESHIP STOP TRANS-ATLANTIC RECORD STOP VOLCANO STOP WHAT NEXT."

Bonnie returned the telegram: "DO NOT BLAME ME STOP YOUR SHIP CREW RESPONSIBLE STOP SEE YOU IN A MONTH."

It was a short way to Shanghai, about twelve hours' cruising time. They would depart Hong Kong late afternoon and arrive at Shanghai early morning. A couple of hours before departure, Captain Krupp requested a private meeting with Charlotte and Bonnie. They used Bonnie's day room. It became crowded when the Commodore and Commander also showed up. They wanted a favor. They explained they wanted to transport four people to Tokyo, Japan, with no official records. The people would travel in the officers' quarters and be inconspicuous, remaining mainly in their room. After Bonnie and Charlotte were sworn to secrecy, they explained the situation.

They believed the Japanese were preparing to launch an offensive against Korea and Manchuria to gain territory that had iron and other mineral resources, which Japan lacked. Japan had imperialistic ambitions. The Russians, Chinese, and British were concerned of the threat to their interests. America wished to maintain their neutral status but were concerned how it would affect their lucrative trade agreements and international affairs. Charlotte would not mention it in her books and endeavor to keep the crew and passengers in the dark. As a cover story, if necessary, the extra crew was to be transferred to a Smithfield cargo ship. Bonnie and Charlotte did not ask what the extra people were going to do; they did not want to know. It was a favor in international interests.

They would arrive at Shanghai in the morning and leave the following morning.

Shanghai was a curious port. There was no clear government in control, no customs to deal with. As well as the Chinese, there were compounds with detachments of British, Russian, Japanese, German, and even a detachment of American Marines. There were also armed groups of several Chinese War Lords. All wanted to maintain a presence; none were ready for an armed conflict, so there was an uneasy peace. Officially it was Chinese territory, but China was in no position to exert their authority. Anchored out in the harbor were a British Heavy Cruiser, an aging Japanese Battleship that Japan had purchased from the British, a Russian Battleship that was built by the French for them, a German Heavy Cruiser, and an American Cruiser.

Samuel again set up and sold his photographs. He and Charlotte came to an agreement: he paid a small fee for the cabin he was using to develop and store his photographs and the ship got a full set of all volcano photographs. Bonnie got an exceptional photograph of the volcanic eruption that she had framed in Australian Cyprus for Dad.

Commodore Vladimir Petrovitch and his family departed to take up residence in the Russian compound. They were taking a full set of volcano photographs. The Commodore had business with the Chinese and others. The Commodore and his family would be missed; they had become part of the ship's society. They all got hugs from Charlotte and Bonnie and sincere best wishes. The Commodore's children, the five sisters, and the Commander's children had their own farewell. Bonnie wished that Joseph could have met the Commodore and his family. They had become good friends. Commander Roberts spent most of the day aboard the American Cruiser on official Navy business.

The Adams sisters went ashore with Megan, Peggy, Willa, Candida, and some of the crew. They returned early and showed Bonnie and Charlotte kimonos they had bought, saying they did not cost very much. Bonnie and Charlotte went to buy their own kimonos. Knowing Megan and her crew, they did not want to be left out on a geisha party. So they all got China and Japan a little mixed up.

* * * * *

Tokyo would take three days, 1048 nautical miles, and they planned to arrive in the morning—stay two days and depart in the morning.

As they approached Tokyo, a Man-of-War was exiting. It was the Japanese Heavy Cruiser, the Sankhla. It was armed with one large gun with a twelve-inch bore and torpedoes. The Japanese had several large battleships built for them by a British firm. With the aid of a French naval architect, they were domestically building a large fleet of heavy cruisers. As they entered the harbor, three other heavy cruisers could be seen were under varying stages of construction. Other ships of war could be seen off in the distance. The Japanese were seriously building a fleet of warships. Samuel was busy photographing all there was to be seen. He had been commissioned by the Russians and British. By Charlotte's agreement, Smithfield Steamships would get a copy of some of his photographs. By a request of Commander Roberts, a copy of all the photographs of military interests would be turned over to the US Navy, in his care. The SS *Bonnie Duffy* was proudly a US-flagged commercial vessel. If the United States Navy wanted photographs, the Smithfield Steamship Line would gladly oblige.

The SS *Bonnie Duffy* was given a good dock near the government offices and business district. At the customs office, Captain Krupp and Bonnie were greeted with deep bows and courtesy that was almost embarrassing.

Exiting the government office, they were greeted by a Japanese Naval Officer in full dress uniform. He deeply bowed and held out an invitation to Bonnie, saying in impeccable English, "The Minister of the Imperial Japanese Navy would like the pleasure of your company this evening for dinner at the Ministry of the Imperial Japanese Navy. I have been instructed to wait for your response."

Bonnie looked at the Captain, who nodded with a shrug. Bonnie looked at the invite; it had the time and location, and it looked very formal. "Yes, it will be our pleasure to dine with the Minister." On careful reading, the invitation was for Mrs. Joseph Smithfield and Captain Frank Krupp. A carriage would pick them up.

Bonnie got dressed in her finest. She questioned her invite. Women in Japan were not normally included in business or politics. Women's role in Japan was servitude to their husbands or other male figure in their lives. Bonnie wondered to herself, *What would the Minister of the Imperial Japanese Navy want with her?*

A carriage was sent to take them to the Ministry. Accompanying the driver was a Naval Officer in dress uniform, who greeted them in English.

The Ministry Building was like a palace. Guards in dress uniforms and rifles were stationed at strategic points all about the building. Upon their arrival, soldiers in two rows lined the steps to the entrance; they all bowed as they passed. Bonnie was learning how to return their bows. The doors were opened by other soldiers, who politely bowed. They were escorted up a grand staircase to the second floor. The dining room they were escorted to was not large and had a table that might seat eight. The Japanese gentleman that greeted them was dressed in a stylish suit like would be worn by a successful American businessman.

Saigo Judo, Minister of the Imperial Japanese Navy, introduced himself in English, with a slight British accent. He was a man in his forties that looked physically fit. He pulled out a chair for Bonnie and seated her. It was not at all what Bonnie expected. They sat in chairs, and the table was set like in any Western country, not what Bonnie thought was Japanese style.

Saigo started by complimenting Bonnie and the Captain by saying, "Mrs. Smithfield, I have heard a lot about you, all good, and you are every bit as beautiful as I have been told. Captain Krupp, you have quite the reputation as a Ship's Captain—in your mid-thirties and the Captain of one of the greatest ships of our time on your first command, setting records in two oceans. I have to compliment both of you. Soon you will complete a historic circumnavigation. Not even the arrogant British have attempted carrying passengers around the world on a cruise, and doing it on a ship that is the envy of every seafaring nation. From all the reports, I have heard the *Bonnie Duffy* is everything advertised—'the Safest, Most Luxurious and Fastest Ship on the seas.' Sailing a ship around the world is a great feat then having passengers pleased of the great experience is extraordinary."

Bonnie responded, "We sort of cheated. We have an excellent ship and an exceptional crew."

Saigo said, "I have heard many rumors. Is it true that you have ladies as Navigators, engine room crew, and girls that keep all your electricals working?"

Bonnie said, "The rumors are exaggerated, but we have some young ladies that are apprenticing into positions that are traditionally held by men. Please tell us about yourself. You are a mystery to us."

They found out that Saigo had been educated at Oxford then spent two years at Harvard, getting an advanced degree in engineering. He was married, with three adolescent children. He reported directly to the Emperor.

They were served an interesting wine that they called sake.

Saigo was a very intelligent and interesting gentleman. Bonnie could see that he could be a real charmer.

The chef brought out a grill and cooked a medley of vegetables in a deep-dished pan in front of them; the vegetables were quite delicious. Then steak strips were cooked in front of them. Again, delicious. The chef put on a show, flipping his knives around. He was very entertaining. It was a unique eating experience. The way the meal was served gave time to get acquainted. Saigo asked several questions of Captain Krupp. He seemed surprised that Frank was a single man, stating he was obviously dedicated to his duties. Saigo was obviously well-informed of Bonnie and her family.

They had been complimented and served the wine and food. Now what was wanted.

Saigo Judo said, "Mrs. Smithfield, I am smart enough to know that you are a very intelligent woman who cannot be deceived or manipulated. I will endeavor to be direct and honest with you. As you Americans would say, no bullshit. The Japanese people want to take their rightful place in the world as an important nation. I am aware that you have been in contact with the Germans, French, English, and Russians. I am aware that the American government wants to remain neutral. I and some in our government are concerned that America will get involved in the present instability of China with other countries. We are aware that the United States has a small military presence in Shanghai. Japan has a good trade relationship with America and would like to maintain that relationship. We have bought ships from the British and French before, and now they are hesitant in selling to us. The Russians buy from the French. You are probably aware of all I have just said. I would like you to take a message back to your government for me. We would like to continue our good trading partnership with America. We do not question your neutrality but respect it.

"Japan is an island nation dependent upon the sea. Japan is interested in purchasing ships from America. We realize that because of America's pledge to neutrality, they are reluctant to sell weapons. We are interested in purchasing quality passenger and cargo ships. Smithfield is the most important ship builder in the Pacific. We are trying to build quality ships. I propose that we work with Smithfield Steamships to both of our benefit without violating your neutrality. Please consider my proposal."

Bonnie replied, "I do not believe I have much influence, but I will pass on your messages."

She did not want to get involved in a deep political discussion. "It is getting late. Thank you for the wonderful meal and your hospitality. You are invited to come to the *Bonnie Duffy* for a tour and dinner tomorrow, at four for a tour, and six for dinner."

Saigo said, "I will accept your hospitality. Might I bring along one of my associates?"

"Certainly, bring along several people if you like."

* * * * *

On the carriage ride, back to the ship, Bonnie said, "I am sorry, I did not let you get a word in."

The Captain replied, "Thank you. I would not have known what to say. I think I will stay out of politics and continue working with ships."

Bonnie asked, "What do you think of what the Minister said?"

"I am glad that you are handling the politics. You should have taken Charlotte with you. Speaking of Charlotte and politics, if Charlette and I got married, do you think that would present a problem?"

Bonnie answered, "The two of you are what makes the *Bonnie Duffy* so special. That would be wonderful."

Captain said, "Please do not say anything to Charlotte. It is something I have been thinking of."

Bonnie thought to herself, *What is it with people asking me for advice? What do I know. I am only twenty years old, not a bit wise. And why is the Japanese government interested in me? I am a nobody. I wonder if Dad is behind all this. Am I doing it again, getting involved in something where I do not know what I am doing?*

When they returned to the ship, it was almost dark.

Bonnie inquired of their escort, "What is going on? Why all the people?" The pier was crowded with people, many with children on their shoulders.

Their Escort answered, "They have brought their children to see your great ship with Edison Illumination. A wonder from a far-off land."

* * * * *

In the morning, Bonnie examined herself. Her belly was growing. She would have to have a couple of her dresses let out and corsets readjusted. At least the morning sickness was gone and her desires to hurt someone and cry had abated. As Bonnie rubbed her belly, she got a warm, satisfying feeling, thinking of the life growing inside her. Then Bonnie thought of Joseph. She missed him so. She needed a hug from him. How would she tell him?

Charlotte sent her shoppers out for supplies with a couple of interpreters. She and Bonnie had decided to do some shopping and exploring on their own with a guide and interpreter, courtesy of the Imperial Japanese Navy. The most notable things were the cleanliness and neatness of everything. Another noticeable thing was the politeness. There was obvious poverty, but it did not affect this society's compulsion for order and discipline. They saw some real geisha girls and realized what they bought in China was not geisha dress. From their interpreter, they learned that a geisha was not a prostitute. The prostitutes kept to their own section of town and dressed quite differently. A geisha was a highly trained and educated entertainer. They were skilled in song, music, dance, and the art of conversation. To molest a geisha was a crime that could result in beheading. Upon inquiry, they were informed there were few laws, most was governed in tradition. Bonnie and Charlotte could not buy geisha outfits, as they were special. The strict social code of the Japanese dictated what one wore, especially for women. They were dressed as Western women in a manner that was appropriate and told all their social standing. They could buy traditional kimonos for dress in private, but it would not be appropriate in public. To Bonnie and Charlotte, it was apparent the Japanese culture was quite complex and different from Western culture. It would take a lot of time to learn the basics. The cleanliness, politeness, dignity, and values of the people spoke highly of their culture.

Bonnie and Charlotte bought traditional Japanese outfits for upper-class women in public, quite beautiful, as well as simple, plain kimonos. They told the salespeople they would take the outfits back to America to show the Americans how beautiful the Japanese women dressed. The clothing was meticulously made, As was everything that they saw.

Bonnie, thinking of her father-in-law, asked about a traditional Japanese sword. Bonnie was told that a Katana was the traditional sword of a Samurai and could not be bought or sold. A Katana could be given as a gift by the Emperor, or Samurai to a worthy man. A Katana was custom-made for a Samurai by skilled artisan and were handed down from generations to generations. In the making of a

Katana, there were traditions and ceremony that must be followed. The final temper of the blade was by passing the heated blade through the heart of a virgin maiden, ensuring its power and purity.

Bonnie decided her father-in-law was not going to get a Katana.

* * * * *

Later, Bonnie consulted Charlotte and explained the situation with the Minister of the Imperial Japanese Navy and asked for her help with the tour and dinner, knowing that the Captain did not want to be involved.

Charlotte responded, "Life around you is really challenging, embarrassing the British Admiralty, avoiding cannibals, dodging flying volcanic rocks and volcanic gases, and now I am to back you up against the Imperial Japanese Navy."

"Can I count on you?"

"Yes, you can count on me. But after this is over, I am going to write a book, "The harrowing life around Bonnie." That is, if I survive. Why did you invite the Minister anyway?"

Bonnie said, "Make some new friends. That is part of this cruise. Good public relations. Besides, they have a lot of ships with big guns. I do not want them as enemies. What about the special passengers?"

Charlotte responded, "What special passengers? We did have some extra bedding to wash. Other than that, not a clue. If all of our passengers left their rooms like your special guests, we would need only half of the maids we have."

Promptly at 4:00 p.m., Saigo Judo, Minister of the Imperial Japanese Navy, and two of his associates arrived. Bonnie was introduced to the Admiral of the Northern Imperial Japanese Fleet, in full dress uniform, and the Master Architect of the Imperial Japanese Fleet. Commander Roberts volunteered to go along on the tour as a representative of the United States Navy. Introductions were given. When asked if they wished to tour the engine room, they responded in the affirmative.

The *Bonnie Duffy* had prepared for the tour. The decks were swabbed, the engines wiped down, the crew in clean, pressed uniforms. The Minister was the most powerful man to tour the ship. He was the head of a major navy. A navy that was getting a lot of attention from great naval powers.

The engineering crew was lined up, all politely bowing. The bows were returned in polite Japanese style.

Smitey reported, "Engine room ready for inspection, ma'am."

Bonnie replied, "Thank you, Chief Engineer." She then introduced Smitey and their three guests, asking Saigo for help in pronouncing his associates' names.

Saigo suggested, "In my time in America, I observed that often, first names and no titles were used to make things more comfortable at informal meetings. Being on an American ship, might I recommend we follow that American example."

There was a consensus. The Admiral was Akito and the Architect Hisato.

Hisato said in English, "May I take a close look at your engines?"

Smitey ordered, "Motorman, A. Adams, show the Master Architect anything he wants to see."

Annie replied, "Yes, sir."

Annie followed Hisato to the midship engine. Hisato went up to the engine and, in his tailored suit, climbed up onto the lower catwalk. Annie followed. It appeared they were caressing one of the lower ends of one of the enormous connection rods, having a conversation. With the noise of the generators and the other equipment running, Bonnie and the others could not hear the conversation.

The entire tour approached and listened to the conversation. To Bonnie, it sounded like they were discussing the intimate nature and personality of the engine. "The hesitation when it was rapidly reversed, the undesirable harmonic vibration at a given revolution." Bonnie realized Annie had spent so much time caring for the engines she had developed a close relationship with the mechanical beasts. It was obvious Hisato understood the relationship. Bonnie had previously heard Annie, Betty, and even Smitey referred to the engines in words that could be considered affectionate. For example, "Our babies are happy and purring." Now Hisato asked technical questions, and Annie's answers were not like Bonnie had previously heard, like being recited from a memorized book page, but with genuine meaning, like she was talking to a friend. Hisato was learning what he wanted to know by charming Annie. Annie told that when reversing the engines, it was best to feel and listen to the engine. They would tell you when they were ready to go. They knew when they were ready and wanted the steam.

Saigo said to Bonnie, "To be in harmony, a ship and crew and the seas upon which it sails must be as one. Your young motorman, the engines, and the ship all work in harmony with the sea."

Bonnie was seeing that the Japanese culture had differences from western culture. It was not only what and how they did things but also the way they thought and related to things about them. Some things seemed to be the same, like the importance in family, tradition, pride in their work, and their accomplishments. It was almost like the Japanese looked at these engines as living things, being a part of the ship that was a part of the sea, which the crew was a part of, all worked together as one.

Saigo told Bonnie they were building their own ships. They had a French Naval Architect working with them in ship design. They were developing their iron and steel industries. Other countries did not want to sell the Japanese their machines to manufacture goods but wanted to sell the finished products. The Japanese had to innovate and build their own machinery. They did not have the large precision machine tools to manufacture quality precision parts for building large steam engines. Their steam engines were mainly made by hand.

Bonnie thought that maybe Dad could sell them engines and other equipment.

Next, it was the electrical system. Eavey took over the tour. It was obvious some of what Eavey said was not understood by any that were listening to her. She was talking of voltage, amperage, and kilowatts. Eavey had warned Hisato to not touch the wires or he would get an electrical shock. Hisato insisted on thoroughly examining one of their generators and learned what an electrical shock was. Hisato then bowed to Eavey, thanking her for the demonstration. Eavey returned the bow, not totally understanding what had just happened.

By the look on Eavey's face, she was concerned she was in trouble. The *Bonnie Duffy* was one of only a few ships that had sophisticated electrical systems. Electricity was just coming to Japan and was mainly a curiosity in their universities and laboratories.

Saigo inquired, "I notice your telephone. We only have a few in some of our government buildings. We are presently manufacturing and installing more. How many telephones do you have?"

Eavey answered, "Sir, we have twelve telephones operating."

Annie called the bridge, asking for a telephone check. The bridge returned the call.

Hisato examined details, from the plate fitting and riveting to the quality of the paint finish and ladder construction. He closely examined many things.

Saigo said, "Shall we continue our tour?" He was politely telling Hisato it was time to continue the tour.

Next, the tour went into the boiler room. Only one of the four boilers were stoked and up to pressure. The other three boilers were maintained with only a small amount of hot coal, keeping them in a standby status. Most of the boiler-room crew was busy moving coal through a hatch in the side of the ship, from wagons to the coal bunkers. They were met by the Chief Boiler Operator with Betty by his side.

"Ma'am, please excuse us. We're in the process of taking on coal."

Akito and Hisato walked around, carefully examining everything. Akito rubbed the side of his shoe on the deck in several spots and examined the marks he left. Akito approached the boiler room Chief and asked, "Might I ask how you keep the boiler room deck so clean?"

The Chief answered, "We wet-mop the deck to keep down the coal dust."

As they walked through the ship, the casino seemed to be of interest. Saigo asked if they could tour the bridge. It was not part of what Bonnie had planned for the tour, but she could not refuse. Being at port, the bridge had one crewman manning the telephone switchboard and recording wind direction, wind speed, and barometric pressures. Seeing the Admiral in his fancy uniform, Dotty was taken by surprise. She dropped her pencil and paper and saluted. The salute was returned with a broad smile. Bonnie introduced Bridge Assistant D. Adams. Dotty was not prepared to explain the bridge or pilothouse operations. It was a lot of pressure for a thirteen-year-old girl who had no time to prepare. Dotty was dressed in a clean and pressed white sailor's uniform.

Bonnie asked, "Will you show us how the telephone switchboard works? Can you call the engine room and ask what is the current steam pressure?"

Dotty plugged in the connection and cranked the ringer crank. They heard.

"Bridge Assistant D. Adams, bridge requesting current steam pressure?

After a brief wait . . .

"Steam pressure currently, 155 PSI, bridge clear."

"Mrs. Smithfield, the current steam pressure is 155 PSI, ma'am."

Akito said, "Aboard one of my ships, that would take at least ten minutes to send a messenger and wait for his return."

Next, Bonnie explained the hatch statue indicator panel, which she had knowledge of, explaining it was her husband's invention. It was an opportunity to brag about her husband.

Akito said, "We must have these innovative things on our ships. If we are to have a navy that is respected, we have a lot of work to do."

Hisato added, "Mrs. Smithfield, I would like to know if it would be possible that I send a couple of my engineers with you to study at your great Ship works? I am sure we can make arrangements such that it will be beneficial to all involved. I am sure we will want to purchase many things from Smithfield Steamships, possibly engines and boilers."

Bonnie replied, "I do not have the authority to answer your request. Because of the time difference, I can telegram this evening and possibly have an answer for you in the morning."

Hisato said, "Thank you for your efforts."

Bonnie had a messenger take a telegram to the telegraph office to send to her father-in-law.

Dinner conversation centered on the SS *Bonnie Duffy*,—their incident with the HMS *Centurion*, and the volcanic eruption of Awu. The SS *Bonnie Duffy*'s voyage seemed to be public knowledge known by everyone.

After dinner, Saigo asked, "Can we try our luck at a game of chance in your Grand Casino."

Bonnie and Charlotte went with their guests to the casino. Bonnie had little knowledge of gaming, while their guests appeared to be experienced gamblers. Saigo tried to explain craps to Bonnie. Saigo seemed to make money, and Bonnie lost money. It was fun, and Bonnie learned she was not a gambler, except with her husband. That was fun, especially when she won.

* * * * *

In the morning, Bonnie got a telegram from Dad. "YOUR DECISION STOP SEE YOU SOON."

"Damn, why does Father do this shit to me?" Bonnie sent a message to the Minister of the Imperial Japanese Navy. "I have authorization for two Japanese engineers to train at the Smithfield Shipyard. It would be acceptable for them to sail on the *Bonnie Duffy*. It was signed, Mrs. Joseph Smithfield."

The *Bonnie Duffy* was to depart early afternoon for Hawaii. The larders were full, and they had their maximum load of coal. It would be a ten-day voyage at a fuel economical speed of fourteen to fifteen knots.

Late morning, Bonnie was summoned by a messenger to the boarding gangway. On the deck, at the top of the gangway, was Charlotte. She pointed to the bottom of the gangway and said, "Your presence is requested. Another chapter in my book."

There, about twenty paces off the front of the gangway, was a Samurai warrior dressed in traditional battle dress. There was a crowd of people wanting to see the obvious show that was to take place. No one stood or passed within ten paces of the warrior. For Bonnie, the Samurai was fascinating and terrifying at the same time. He stood not like a soldier at attention but like a warrior ready for action, legs moderately spread and slightly bent, ready to spring into action. Whatever this Samurai wanted, Bonnie concluded that she has a destiny with the warrior.

As Bonnie neared, she recognized the Samurai as Akito, the Admiral of the Northern Imperial Japanese Fleet. Bonnie felt intimidated, took a deep breath, walked up to Akito, and bowed in respect.

The bow was returned, then Akito held out in both hands two swords, one long and one a little shorter, saying, "A gift from the people of the Japans."

Bonnie was in shock, not knowing what to say. She just took the swords in both hands and bowed. Akito bowed and abruptly turned and walked away. Bonnie just stood there wondering what the tradition was. Should she say something or do something? The Japanese had a tradition for everything. What was the proper etiquette for this situation?

Bonnie thought, *Maybe the proper thing is to just stand looking dumbfounded. If so, I am in luck.*

As Bonnie turned, the deck was lined with passengers and crew watching. Word spread fast aboard the ship that there was a Samurai wanting to see Mrs. Smithfield. There were no cheers or congratulations as Bonnie returned to her cabin. Nobody, including Bonnie, knew what was the significance of what had just happened. The spectators were just as mystified as Bonnie.

Back in her cabin, Bonnie could not resist and pulled the longer sword, the Katana, from its scabbard. It was gorgeous, a true work of art. Bonnie then held it in both hands and tried to pose with it as she had seen in drawings, with it over her head. The tip hit the ceiling. Looking, Bonnie realized she had put a gouge in the wood ceiling paneling—oops. Then Bonnie felt the edge to feel how sharp it was. It was sharp. Bonnie drew her first blood with her sword, her own blood. Bonnie put it back in its scabbard before she had any more accidents. The conclusion was, it was a dangerous weapon, and if she were to examine it, she would have to be calm. She was still slightly quivering from the experience of receiving the swords.

Bonnie went back to the boarding deck to see if she could help.

Megan accosted her. "Wow, I never seen anything like that before! Do you know that Samurai and what did he say to you?"

"That is the Admiral of the Northern Imperial Japanese Fleet. He told me, a gift from the people of the Japans."

"You have some awfully powerful and influential friends. You are getting quite the sword collection. Are you going to learn to use them?"

Bonnie replied, "If I have to kill something, I think I will stick to guns. I know how to use them."

In Passenger Services, Charlotte said, "My next chapter will be 'Bonnie becomes Samurai.'"

Bonnie quipped, "You are full of shit!"

Charlotte said, "Your two engineers showed up. I put them in the crew quarters that were just vacated by your other special guests. I thought it poetic justice." Charlotte then gave Bonnie a fine-quality wooden rack, saying, "This was delivered for you. I think it is a holder for your new letter openers. Be careful you do not cut yourself."

Candida announced, "You are both full of shit."

Charlotte and Bonnie looked at each other; without a word, they agreed that Candida was learning.

Lines were cast off, and tugs helped ease the SS *Bonnie Duffy* away from the dock to midchannel. The Bonnie had two Japanese Heavy Cruisers escort them to sea, and the Japanese sailors lined their decks, giving honors.

Bonnie thought, *The Japanese Navy really wants help from Smithfield in building their Navy. They are really trying to impress me, hoping that I have influence with Dad and others.*

Shortly after they were clear of the port, Bonnie was greeted by the two Japanese engineers. Their names were Shuji and Hiroki. They were in their mid-twenties and had been educated at Princeton. They also bore gifts, a Shinai, a bamboo practice Katana, and a Bokken, a wooden practice Katana. Bonnie thanked them and told them how she gouged the ceiling in her cabin and cut her finger. They laughed and told Bonnie that they practiced Laido, the art of yielding a Katana. They told Bonnie they would show her the basics of balance and being one with a Katana. They were both raised to the code of the Samurai. They also wanted to know if it was possible for them to work with the ship's engineers. They would be willing to shovel coal or other labor jobs, and they did not require pay. They were paid by the Imperial Japanese Navy. They were both officers in the Japanese Navy. They also told Bonnie they would teach her to care for and respect her Katana and her Wakizashi, her shorter sword.

Bonnie thought of Charlotte's next book chapter, "Bonnie Becomes Samurai." She would show her. Besides, she had a couple of weeks before she would be home, and navigation was no longer an engrossing challenge. She needed something to keep her busy.

Bonnie took Shuji and Hiroki to the engine room and introduced them to Smitey.

She asked, "Smitey, can you use a couple of college-educated engineers?"

Smitey replied, "I can always use some extra help, even if they are handicapped with college educations."

Shuji and Hiroki both had a look of "What have we got ourselves into?" Bonnie was not concerned; she knew it was Smitey's way. She also knew that by the time they got to San Francisco, Shuji and Hiroki would be well acquainted with the SS *Bonnie Duffy*.

CHAPTER 20

Across the North Pacific

After Bonnie took her evening twilight sights, she went to her cabin and tried to get the feel of her practices swords. It did not take long, and Bonnie would need Eavey's services. The light bulb in the ceiling needed replacing; Bonnie had smashed it with her practice sword.

After the morning sights and breakfast, Bonnie went to the engine room. She was hoping to see Eavey and get a new lightbulb without a lot of explanation. Eavey was not available, so Bonnie told Smitey, hoping he was still her boss. Bonnie was wondering how long till the sisters would be running the ship.

Shuji was getting off duty, where he worked with Betty. Bonnie thought, each could learn from one another, probably Smitey's plan. Betty knew this ship and the engines, and Shuji was a college-educated engineer. Shuji asked Bonnie if she would join him on the bow for training with her Bokken, the wooden sword. Bonnie was excited at the opportunity.

On the fore deck, Shuji told Bonnie, "We will practice Laido, the art of quickly removing one's Katana from its scabbard, attacking, and returning one's Katana to its scabbard. Laido emphasized the philosophical and spiritual aspect of the use of the Katana. A swordsman must be in harmony with all about them."

Shuji showed Bonnie how to take a sash and properly secure her bokken sheaf to her waist. The next lesson was on how to stand. Bonnie wanted to get right into the sword-fighting. Hiroki showed up and bowed to Bonnie, and she returned the bow. After a brief pause and with a loud "hi," Hiroki, in one smooth and rapid motion, was in an attack position with his Bokken raised, ready to strike his target. It was total instant intimidation.

Shuji said, "A Samurai seldom has to use his Katana. The fact he has the Katana and is trained to use it is enough. We can train you to use a Katana, but you must listen and practice."

For the next several hours, Bonnie and her two trainers practice moving gracefully from one position to another. Each position had its own name. Bonnie had trouble balancing with the ship's movement, and so they had her remove her shoes. The Japanese wore soft thin-soled shoes. They moved slowly. The purpose of the exercise was to arrive at the exact desired position with the least effort, smoothly and gracefully.

Bonnie was told everything had to be in harmony, from the planking on the fore deck to the tip of the Katana and the air in which one moved. One's feet did not stand on the deck but became a living part of the deck. One did not hold the Katana, but the Katana became one with the swordsman and the swordsman became one with the Katana. All moved together in harmony as one.

At first, Bonnie was resistant to try to think and feel in harmony. It was just so many words to get Bonnie comfortable with the sword and exercises. By the end of their practice, however, Bonnie felt she could do this. She felt like she was more aware of what was around her. Concentrating on every move seemed to heighten her awareness.

As Bonnie turned to go back into the ship, it was an "Oh shit" moment; the deck rail above was lined with an audience.

At lunch, Charlotte commented, "Three months pregnant and playing with a wooden sword. I've never heard of that as part of the pregnancy craziness."

"It is keeping me busy. Would you sooner I put my nose in your business? How are you and the Captain doing?"

"Everything is going smoothly. Go play with your wooden sword. Please leave the real one in its case, or you will scare the shit out of everyone."

"It is not a case, it is a scabbard, and I am not playing, I am practicing."

Charlotte replied, "Are you still having feelings that you want to hurt someone? Must be a boy. Please stay with the wooden sword. Sometimes you really scare me."

Bonnie quipped, "Love you too, Charlotte."

Back in her room, Bonnie practiced trying to move as one with her surroundings. She tried to follow what she was taught: feel the grain of the wood beneath her feet and move with the ship as it moved through the waves. Feel the air passing over her skin as you moved slowly and deliberately. Each move was to be exact, smooth and flowing, from one position to the next, without any extra movement. It was more difficult than Bonnie imagined, and it took every bit of her concentration she had. Bonnie wanted to learn to move like Hiroki moved; it was terrifying and captivating. She could not resist a challenge to learn something new and exciting.

Bonnie got a knock on her door. It was Eavey with tool bag, a short ladder, and a new lightbulb.

"Mrs. Smithfield, Smitey told me you need a new lightbulb?"

"Yes, come in, how are you doing?"

"I am doing really good, how are you? I saw you practicing with your sword today."

"I am doing really good too."

Eavey got on her ladder and changed the lightbulb, saying, "This lightbulb looks like it was smashed." She saw Bonnie's Bokken in her hand. "Did you hit it with your sword?"

"Yes, I would appreciate it if you did not tell people of my stupidity."

"I promise I will not tell anyone. Can I practice with you with if I can get a wooden sword?"

"You will have to ask Shuji and Hiroki. They are the trainers."

"Can you flip the switch to make sure it works and you have not damaged the receptacle?"

It worked. "Thank you, Eavey."

Bonnie thought, *That girl is learning fast.*

* * * * *

The next morning found fourteen on the foredeck practicing Laido, including three of the Adams sisters. Most the younger people aboard the ship, including the two oldest sons of Commander Roberts, wanted to be Japanese swordsmen. There were also a few adults. Bonnie noticed that the Adams sisters seemed to always have the determination to persevere, and Bonnie wondered, *Is it in their blood or the fact that they have one another and had to fight hard to survive?* Where their determination came from was immaterial. Bonnie was going to have to work hard to keep up with them. The three brats showed up in kimonos. Bonnie lined up with the Adams girls and soon was so involved in trying to concentrate on her moves she stopped watching the sisters. They practiced drawing their sword and attacking a make-believe enemy. They practiced three distinct moves. There were twelve distinct moves in Laido, and the moves could be combined in many ways for a multitude of combat situations. At the end of each move, they would slide their sword back into its scabbard, wiping the imagined blood from the sword as it entered the scabbard, step back, and bow. Everything was done slowly to perfect the move. It was stressed to be one with the Katana. Hiroki and Shuji were demanding, expecting perfection in everything. True harmony could only be achieved through perfection.

Shuji told Bonnie, "You mind is fighting your inner strength coming from your heart. Close your eyes and let your inner strength and calm come through. The true strength of a Samurai comes from his heart, not his mind. Close your eyes, take three deep and slow breaths, free your mind, let your intuition lead you, and without opening your eyes, do your exercise."

Bonnie did what was requested and felt herself calm and do the exercises with ease. A confidence came over her, and she felt an inner strength.

Shuji said, "You are approaching perfection."

After their practice, Bonnie inquired as to where the bokkens came from. She was informed that the ship's carpenters had made them. Both of the carpenters were training in Laido.

On their passage to Hawaii, the ship settled into a routine. Bonnie did her morning and evening sights. She felt she was getting better and her sights had few errors.

The Laido training became more than just handling a Katana. There was a philosophy that went with the training: Meditation and reliance on one's intuition, the oneness with one's surroundings, and respect for all things natural. Tao and Zen philosophy and beliefs gave the students a broader understanding of others and oneself. Shuji and Hiroki mixed in some poetry and philosophical thoughts that made one think, making the exercises more than just physical training. To find harmony and perfection required training the mind, heart, and body. One quote that made Bonnie think was ancient Chinese: "Know therefore the sword is a cursed thing that a wise man uses only if he must" (Li Po, China, AD 701–762).

Bonnie started to use what she had learned in Laido in taking her sights, meditating, relaxing, and relying on her instincts. Bonnie felt more confident, and her results improved. It was not like a revelation or an overwhelming event but a subtle inner confidence. Bonnie noticed the twins seemed more confident as well. They seemed to be more relaxed and confident doing their work, becoming more efficient.

Bonnie told Dotty, "Your navigation has improved. You are getting really good at all your work."

Dotty said, "Thank you, Mrs. Smithfield. I try to use what I have learned in Laido. I relax, meditate, and let my inner strength guide me."

Bonnie replied, "Yes, I feel the same. You must still study and try hard though."

"Yes, Mrs. Smithfield. It helps me study. I can concentrate on what I am studying better. Thank you for letting me do Laido with you. You are wonderful."

* * * * *

Smithfield Lines had their own dock and coal supply at Honolulu. The port was a forest of masts of sailing ships from around-the-world. It was a safe harbor and a center for the whaling industries as well as a shipping center. The Captain and Bonnie went to the customs house and were well received. The Republic of Hawaii was a relatively new nation. A year previously, Queen Liliuokalani's Kingdom of Hawaii was overthrown by a group of American businessmen with the support of the United Stated military. The Queen was under house arrest in her palace. With Smithfield Steamships are a respected member of the business community, the SS *Bonnie Duffy* was welcomed and given full use of the port.

A Smithfield sailing vessel, the *Monterey*, was also at the Smithfield dock taking on a cargo of sugar, dried pineapple, coir, dried coconut meat, and whale oil. Some of the cargo had been brought to the port by other ships from all over the Pacific and stored in the Smithfield warehouse. The *Monterey* was to return to San Francisco with its cargo the next morning. The *Bonnie* had a scheduled to stay three days to take on coal and supplies and letting the passengers enjoy Hawaii.

The *Monterey*'s First Mate had died of consumption. The First Mate was an accomplished Navigator, and the Captain of the *Monterey*, Captain Smith, visited the *Bonnie*. He wanted to know if the *Bonnie Duffy* could spare a Navigator for the voyage to San Francisco. Captain Smith needed help navigating. He had a ship to run, and navigation was a full-time job, twenty-four hours a day.

Captain Krupp said, "I have two apprentice Navigators that are proficient and conscientious that I believe will fulfill your needs. That is with Mrs. Smithfield's consent."

Bonnie said, "Are you sure that it will be appropriate, Captain? Your decision."

Captain Smith said, "Sounds good. I really need the help. Good Navigators are hard to find. Can you send them to the *Monterey* with their sea bags? We should make San Francisco in nine to ten days, and you can have them back then."

Captain Krupp said, "I think there is something you need to know. They are young and need their own accommodations."

"They can move into the First Mate's cabin. It should be no problem."

Captain Krupp said, "Seaman C. Adams, would you and Seaman D. Adams accept the duties of Navigator on the sailing vessel the *Monterey* to San Francisco? They are in need of a Navigator."

Cathy replied, "Yes, sir. I believe Seaman D. Adams will agree, Captain, sir."

The expression on the face of Captain Smiths was beyond description. Finally, after a long hesitation, he said, "How old are you and the other Navigator?"

Cathy answered, "We are both thirteen. We are identical twins, Captain Smith, sir."

After a pause, Captain Smith responded, "All right, you got me good, ha ha."

A little indignantly, Captain Krupp replied, "I am not joking. They are good Navigators that fellow orders. Take them or leave them."

Bonnie added, "I am Mrs. Joseph Smithfield. Tell your crew, hands off. I know they can safely navigate you to San Francisco."

Captain Smith addressed Cathy, "Can you take star sights and sun sights and reduce them to a line of position and maintain a DR plot?"

Cathy answered, "Yes, sir, if you have the proper charts and a current Nautical Almanac. We have our own sextants, Captain, sir."

Bonnie said, "Let us check with Seaman D. Adams. She should have a say."

Captain Krupp gave an order: "Seaman C. Adams, please find Seaman D. Adams and have her report to the bridge."

Cathy said, "Yes, sir."

Captain Smith uttered, "Captain Krupp, if it were not for your reputation, I would not believe any of this. I can use any help I can get. Can you have the Navigators report to the *Monterey*, if they agree? We will sail on the morning tide."

After Captain Smith left, Bonnie said, "Captain, do you think they are ready for that much responsibility? And do you have confidence in Captain Smith?"

"I sailed with Captain Smith as a junior officer. He is a good Captain. He could have his own steamship. He says that steamships are not real ships. He loves sailing. In ten days, the Adams twins will have knowledge of clipper ships, sailing, and have the experience they need to continue their careers."

Shortly after the twins left with their gear, Charlotte showed up in a rage. "How dare you send those two girls off to work on an old sailing ship with a Captain that could be another Captain Bligh! The two of you should be tied to the mast and flogged."

Bonnie pleaded, "Charlotte, settle down. It is only for ten days."

"I do not care, you should have asked me first."

Bonnie said, "They are sailing to San Francisco tomorrow morning and Monterey needs a Navigator."

"I do not care, it is not right."

"It will be a good experience for them and will count as experience toward them getting their Navigator's paper."

Charlotte went after the Captain, in an obvious rage.

The Captain went up to the crow's nest while Bonnie escaped out onto the bridge deck and down the outer steps. Charlotte followed the Captain up to the crow's nest; she was livid. An audience watched and listened as she verbally assaulted the Captain. She made a scene, and the Captain politely took the verbal abuse. Bonnie went to hide, amongst the passengers watching the show. Eventually, Charlotte ran out of steam and calmed down. The show over, the gathered audience were ready to leave when the Captain got on one knee, which was a feat. There was just enough room for two men to stand in the crow's nest. Then in total surprise, Charlotte went to her knees and proceeded to what all thought tried to suffocate the Captain with her lips.

They remained in the crow's nest for some time, talking and on occasion sharing a kiss. Not at all appropriate public behavior. The crowd politely dispersed. Bonnie did not want to see the hugging and kissing; she really missed Joseph. It would not be long, and she would be home with Joseph. Bonnie had not determined how she was going to tell him that he was going to be a father, it had to be special, hopefully he will be pleased.

* * * * *

Before dinner that night, Charlotte came to apologize to Bonnie, "I have no excuse for my bad behavior. Will you please forgive me? I did not understand and reacted inappropriately. I totally lost my temper. Now I would like to ask you for big favor." She smiled. "Will you, at dinner, announce the Captain's and my engagement?"

Bonnie hugged Charlotte, telling her that all was forgiven and how happy she was for her and the Captain. She told Charlotte her mother-in law had said, "Romance is an excuse for exuberance. As a wedding gift, would you like an around-the-world cruise on a Luxury Liner?"

"You will probably expect us to work our way."

"What do you expect, perfection? When is the wedding?"

"At my age, as soon as possible, before he changes his mind. I am thirty-six. Can I still get pregnant?"

Bonnie said, "I have a book that tells you how. It looks intriguing and fun. It even gives you suggestions on conceiving a boy or girl. There is a chapter on what you always wanted to know and your mother did not tell you."

"Can I borrow your book?"

"Providing I get it back before you head out around-the-world again."

Charlotte stated, "Around-the-world again—that might require a promotion and a nice raise."

"Better start being nice to me. I am related to the owner and his wife."

Charlotte quipped, "Love you too."

Bonnie and Charlotte could not resist and went to the *Monterey* and asked for permission to come aboard. They were greeted and shown to the aft cabin where Cathy and Dotty were busy organizing everything, saying everything was disorganized. They showed the ladies a schedule where they would each work an eight- and a four-hour watch daily. One of them would be on watch at all times, and each would have four hours' free time and eight hours' rest. Bonnie asked if they needed anything. The twins seemed to be busy and excited, and they said the Sailing Master was going to teach them to sail a four-mast Clipper Ship. It was obvious that Charlotte and Bonnie were in the twins' way, so they asked for a hug and were on their way.

* * * * *

Charlotte said when they left, "I feel rejected, not wanted."

Bonnie answered, "Yes, it is probably like being parents when the chicks leave the nest."

Charlotte asked, "Can I call them Navigators now?"

Bonnie responded, "Yes, they are Navigators. Now how do we get the maritime board to recognize them?"

Charlotte said, "Dress them like boys when they take the test and interview."

Bonnie found Megan and asked her for a favor. "Would she arrange for an unforgettable wedding for tomorrow evening for the Captain and Charlotte? The ship would pay. We need a last hurrah party, and I cannot think of a better excuse or a better person to make it special than you."

At dinner, Bonnie announced the engagement of Captain Krupp and Miss Charlotte Gibbs. There was applause, and Bonnie knew the incident in the crow's nest would soon be forgotten or fondly remembered as a romantic moment.

Bonnie was on the bridge-deck at first light. The *Monterey* was nearing the harbor entrance and was setting sails. Bonnie said a little prayer.

Charlotte came next to her and said, "Do you think they will be able to handle the work?"

"Yes. That is the problem—they do not need us anymore. This pregnancy is making me feel motherly. When is the wedding?"

Charlotte said, "With your permission, this afternoon in the first-class dining room, if we can get a clergyman."

Bonnie asked, "Am I invited?"

"If you promise to be a good girl and behave, no swords."

Bonnie joked, "You are full of shit!"

Charlotte responded, "That is a contagious condition that I contracted from you."

"See, Megan, she handles all weddings, under my authority."

Charlotte asked, "What are you up to?"

"See, Megan . . ." was the only reply.

* * * * *

Megan took over. The wedding was to be a traditional Hawaiian wedding.

The ceremony was held on Waikiki Beach by a Priest that was a native Hawaiian. Adam Fitzpatrick was the Best Man, Willa the Maid of Honor. Captain Krupp was dressed in his best uniform, and Charlotte had a traditional Hawaiian long straight simple white dress. A line of carriages was arranged by Megan to take the guests from the ship to the wedding. All the ship's passengers and crew, except for necessary crew, were invited. Everything was decorated with flowers. Everyone received a lei. The start of the ceremony was the traditional exchange of lei by the bride and groom as the Hawaiian wedding song was played. Megan seemed to know all the right people wherever they went. Queen Liliuokalani arrived and gave her consent to the marriage before the Priest started the ceremony. It appeared that the Queen's house arrest was not strictly enforced. Social events were overlooked in the interest of cultural concerns, giving the natives some respect.

The ceremony was typical, except all the guests sat on mats on the ground. The only person with a chair was the Queen. They brought her a throne.

The Priest did say, "Under the authority given me by the Roman Catholic Church, the Republic of Hawaii, and by the consent of Queen Liliuokalani." Shortly after, the Priest pronounced them man and wife and there was the traditional kiss. A group of Hawaiian men and women led the newlyweds away to a secret location; they would be returned tomorrow.

Then the luau started. A large roast pig was placed on a table and carved. Many exotic foods were served. There was traditional Hawaiian music as well as hula dancers. Off to the side were the three remaining sisters, Peggy, and Megan doing the hula dressed in grass skirts and Hawaiian tops. Then the Hawaiian drummers along with dancers spinning and throwing flaming torches. Word was spread that all were to give the Queen acknowledgement, approach her, and give a polite bow. Beer and alcohol flowed freely along with a wonderful local spirit called Okolehao that Bonnie found tasty. It was one of the most memorable parties of the entire cruise.

The next day, Bonnie got up early and checked in on Candida. A brief discussion, and Bonnie concluded that she was not needed. Candida had everything under control.

Candida had attended the wedding. "The wedding was very romantic. It made me cry."

This was the last full day in port, and Bonnie wanted to do a little sightseeing and some shopping. Willa asked to accompany her. They got a carriage to Pali Pass. The view was spectacular. Bonnie regretted that she could not share it with Joseph. They discussed the education on the *Bonnie Duffy* and the educational tours Willa had conducted at many ports. Bonnie knew Willa had something on her mind, so she asked.

Willa told Bonnie, "Peggy will go to finishing school in the fall. There is not a lot left that I can do for her. Megan will not need me anymore, and I really enjoy working on the ship. It is very rewarding."

Bonnie interrupted Willa, "If you want a job on the *Bonnie Duffy*, consider it yours. I will not be going along on the next trip around-the-world. Charlotte will be running Passenger Services. Charlotte and I have already discussed and agreed that you are an asset that will be hard to replace. Your tours are always special. Many of our passengers say your tours are a great addition to the cruise experience."

The shopping was not good; the city had many saloons and brothels. It was a haven for the many sailors from the many ships in the harbor. Bonnie and Willa went to the Smithfield warehouse out of curiosity. When Bonnie introduced herself as Mrs. Joseph Smithfield to the clerk at the counter looked like he was going to faint, he then went running to an office, yelling, "Mrs. Smithfield is here!"

The manager came from his office, saying, "I heard that you were here with the SS *Bonnie Duffy*. It is a pleasure to have you come and tour our facility."

It was obvious he wanted to give Bonnie a grand tour, hoping she would gave her father-in-law a good report. The warehouse had products from all over the world. Singer sewing machines from America destined to ports around the Pacific. Coir and sugar destined for ports in America and Europe. Wool from Australia and New Zealand destined for mills in America. Teak and mahogany lumber from Southeast Asia. Brass goods from India. Barrels of dried fish, salted meat, and whale oil. A large verity of canned goods as well as large assortment of distilled beverages. Everything that was traded across the ocean. Bonnie learned that as many as ten ships stopped here every week to unload and load, distributing goods worldwide. The ships coming and going were from many shipping companies and countries. Bonnie realized how extensive Dad's shipping business was. He had a network of companies and their ships transporting goods around-the-world. Hawaii was on the crossroads of the shipping lanes across the Pacific.

The warehouse manager wanted to know if the *Bonnie Duffy* had room for cargo destined for San Francisco. Bonnie explained they were loaded with lumber and ivory. Bonnie learned that some ships were privately operated and would show up with a cargo and request a cargo that they would deliver where requested, for a commission. Some of these ships were small and old, eking out a living for their Captain and crew.

Scheduled to leave in the morning, Bonnie returned to the ship, wanting to make sure they were ready to sail with all the provisions that they needed.

Late afternoon, the Captain and Charlotte returned. Charlotte went to her office and found Bonnie and Candida discussing the cruise to San Francisco.

Charlotte asked, "Are we ready to depart in the morning?"

Candida nodded, "Yes, ma'am. We still have some provisions that are to be delivered. I believe we are in good shape."

Bonnie asked, "How was the honeymoon? Where did they take you?"

"It was wonderful."

"Where did you spend the night?"

"I cannot tell you."

"Why cannot you tell me?"

Charlotte replied with a broad smile, "It is an ancient secret that cannot be talked of."

Bonnie said, "That good."

Charlotte stated, "That good. Excuse me, I have to get to work. If you cannot find me, I will be in the Captain's quarters."

Bonnie replied, "I did not need to hear that."

* * * * *

Cathy and Dotty worked hard and had the aft cabin organized. There were four berths in the cabin, and with Captain Smith's permission, they would stay in the aft cabin. The aft cabin traditionally was where navigation was preformed, officers dined, and the Captain conducted business. The Monterey was short of officers and crew. At sunset, Captain Smith ordered all hands on deck. The Captain, Sailing Master, newly appointed First Mate, and the twins were on the aft deck. The assembled crew was on the main deck. The Captain addressed the assembled crew.

"This is Ensign Cathy Adams and Ensign Ditty Adams. They will be responsible for the navigation on the *Monterey*. As officers, they will be given the respect they deserve. We will sail on the morning tide for San Francisco. I suggest that all get a good night's sleep."

Dotty realized the Captain had called her Ditty. Dotty knew better than to correct the Captain, so on this cruise, she would have to be Ditty, Ensign Ditty Adams. Ditty wondered, would the crew call her *sir* or *ma'am*? Hopefully just Ditty. Both the twins looked at the crew. They were a mixed group, some white men and boys along with some Negros, Orientals, and other races of all ages. A few looked younger than they were. In all, there were about thirty crew and five officers, including Cathy and Ditty.

The Captain told the twins, "Plot a great circle course to San Francisco. That will be our rhumb line. We are a sailing ship dependent on the wind and currents. Our course will vary dependent on the wind. You will have to work with the Sailing Master on the best course to make the best time to port. I expect one of you on duty at all times. When not doing navigational chores, your duty station will be on the deck. Access to the after deck and aft cabin is restricted to necessary personnel. As officers, you will be required to enforce all rules, regulations, and maintain discipline. The safety of this ship and crew is the responsibility of all the officers. If you have any problems, concerns, or questions do not hesitate to ask me or one of the other officers. Are my orders understood?"

Cathy replied, "Yes, sir, orders understood."

Dotty replied, "Yes, sir, orders understood."

The Captain said, "Welcome aboard! If needed, there is extra foul-weather gear in the aft cabin."

Back in the aft cabin, the twins laid out the great circle course on the large-scale chart of the eastern North Pacific that they already had on the chart table. The course did not require a lot of curvature. Neither had done a great circle course before but understood the principles and had watched the *Bonnie*'s Navigators do it before. They got out their navigation books that they borrowed from Mrs. Smithfield and double-checked then triple-checked their work.

After they were both satisfied with their work, Cathy said, "This is really scary. I did not think we would be made officers."

Dotty added, "What are we going to do?"

"The only thing we can do is do our jobs and follow orders."

"Part of our jobs might be to give orders. That is the scary part."

"Okay, Ensign Ditty. You make the beds. That is an order."

Dotty uneasily laughed. "You know where you can put that Ditty garbage! And you make my bed—that is an order."

They nervously laughed at their situation and playful verbal exchange. Both of the twins were intimidated and deeply concerned about what was expected of them and their new positions. Without saying a word, they both knew they would do their best. They had been in challenging situations before.

Before daylight, the twins were on the aft deck with the Captain. The lines were cast off and the tide pulled the *Monterey* toward sea. They watched as the Sailing Master gave orders to set one sail after another. Dotty used a handheld pelorus that they had found in the aft cabin, taking bearings, recording the time and angles as Cathy recorded their compass course and time. They used their brass-cased watches they had received with their sextant. They still wondered who was their good fairy.

The *Monterey* had one chronometer that was in the aft cabin. Cathy was given the responsibility of winding the chronometer at noon each day. The procedure to wind the ship's clock had to be followed exactly every day at the exact same time to ensure accurate time.

As they sailed away from the islands and out into the trade winds, the Sailing Master said, "What is our rum line course?"

Cathy, "Northeast by east, sir."

Sailing Master ordered, "Course, east-northeast."

The helmsman acknowledged, "Course, east-northeast, sir."

The Sailing Master told Cathy, "We will sail more east staying in the strong trade winds avoiding the North Pacific High and the doldrums." The doldrums are areas in the ocean where the wind often does not blow for extended periods.

The twins started their plot and log entries. They saw that the log had not been kept to the high standard that they had been taught. They were used to an officer initialing their work.

Dotty went on deck and asked the Captain, "Captain, sir, will you verify our log entries?"

"Are you confident in your entries?"

"We are confident in log entries, sir."

"I do not need to verify your entries. I have confidence in you, Ensign."

Cathy stayed on the aft deck, recording their course, speed, relative wind direction, and relative wind speed. Every hour, they recorded the barometric pressure, taking the reading from the barometer located in the aft cabin. The twins both had performed all the duties they were now preforming, but, under supervision before. They had full sails set and were traveling at eleven knots with a strong wind from their port stern. Cathy learned that the proper terminology was a broad reach. Each sail had its own name and Cathy counted twenty-seven sails set. Cathy also learned that they were lines and not ropes. Each had its own name, named for the sail they controlled and how they controlled the sail. There were halyards, sheets, brace, downhauls, topping lifts, and other lines. This sailing ship was entirely different than a steamship; it was scary and exciting.

Dotty was leaning on a sheet that was belayed on a belaying pin.

A sailor that was a man in his thirties said, "Excuse me, Ensign, I must tend the sheet."

Dotty stepped aside and was rewarded with a "Thank you, Ensign."

CHAPTER 21

Homeward Bound

At the break of day, the whistle was blown, gangways pulled up, lines cast off, and they were on their last leg of their epic circumnavigation of the globe. Six days to San Francisco. Seventy-six people had purchased special tickets departing in San Francisco. A total of 154 passengers had special tickets for other ports, and they would continue on to complete their circumnavigation. There was a few that would continue on to Tokyo and one couple on to Hawaii. A sense of nostalgia was felt by those that would disembark in San Francisco, including Bonnie. Other passengers still had more ports to visit and adventure ahead.

Charlotte spent two days straightening out the Captain's quarters. He had not been well organized. All the drawers and cabinets were empty. Everything was in plain sight. Now Charlotte had him organized and she had room to move in. Willa and Candida would share Charlotte's old cabin, moving into the officer's quarters.

Bonnie was spending her time trying to keep busy. She resumed her Laido training. A few had graduated and spent some of their training time using Shinai, bamboo swords, in sparring. They all put on hats with padding stuffed in and padding under their kimono's shoulders. The hard part was to pull the strike, avoiding hurting your opponent. Bonnie got a few bruises, as did her worthy opponents.

Bonnie whacked Hiroki on the top of his head. Bonnie bowed, apologizing.

Hiroki said, "You are learning. I should have blocked your blow. You are becoming proficient and in harmony. You are becoming a worthy opponent."

On the fourth day, Shuji told Bonnie to bring her Katana and Wakizashi, the shorter sword. He examined Bonnie's Katana and Wakizashi, telling her they were made by one of Japan's best Swordsmiths. Bonnie asked if it was true that the swords were tempered in a virgin's heart. Shuji assured Bonnie that it was a legend of the old swordsmiths; now the final quench and temper was done in animal's blood, usually from a bull. Bonnie was instructed on the care of her blades, polishing, sharpening, oiling and storage. Even though they had been instructed to always handle their Bokken, wooden swords, like they were deadly sharp, practicing for the real things, Bonnie was instructed on the safe handling of her swords. Bonnie was told that if she dropped it on her foot, she would be lucky if she only lost a few toes. Bonnie reflected on the gouge on her cabins ceiling and her cut finger.

On the fifth day, Bonnie was given her own area to practice in and let practice her Laido moves with her Katana. Eventually, paper targets were set up on thin wooden stands. It amazed Bonnie how clean she could cut the rolled-up paper targets. A whole pineapple was set up, and Bonnie was asked to cut it in half. It would take a sidewise strike. Bonnie set her sword in front of her and meditated for a moment and then bowed, doing the ceremony she was taught, becoming one with her Katana. She placed her Katana in its sheath in her sash and secured it. Again she bowed and took her stance ready for attack. In one smooth and graceful motion, she withdrew her Katana, swiped at the pineapple, and replaced her Katana in its scabbard. At first, Bonnie thought she had missed; the pineapple was as it was. But as she wiped off the blade, she noticed it had a wet, sticky spot. Bonnie had not thought about what she did; she had let her instincts and training rule. Hiroki picked up the top of the pineapple. Bonnie had cut the pineapple neatly in half. Bonnie received a round of applause from the audience that were gathered at the rail on the deck above. She received a bow from both Hiroki and Shuji, and she returned the bows.

Bonnie thought, *If it had been a man, he would have been beheaded.* She had not even felt the cut. This thought gave Bonnie a shiver up her spine and goosebumps. She realized she could draw and strike with her Katana faster than she could draw and cock a gun. Bonnie had not considered all the consequences of learning Laido. She reflected, "Know therefore the sword is a cursed thing that a wise man uses only when he must" (Li Po).

* * * * *

Bonnie started to get packed. She had accumulated a lot of things, and she would wait until her last sight to retrieve her sextant from the pilothouse. Bonnie decided that Charlotte needed to be promoted to the position of owner's representative. She was not going to ask Dad but tell him. Charlotte knew this ship and its crew better than he did. Charlotte was confident, reliable, and loyal. Other staff changes would need to be made as well. Most would be Charlotte's decisions. Bonnie decided to follow Dad's example and manage by putting good people in the right positions, then observe, monitor, and try to not interfere. Bonnie realized that this part of her life was coming to an end. Bonnie decided that she would try to be a good wife and, with luck, a good mother. Bonnie also realized that she had become part of the ship and crew; it would be hard letting go.

* * * * *

The twins both took evening sights on their first day at sea. They got six sights between them. Five sights gave the same fix; one was off by a fraction of a nautical mile. They were disappointed in their DR plot; it was seven nautical miles off.

Cathy reported, "Captain, sir, our DR plot for the day was off by seven nautical miles."

The Captain replied, "That is good, continue the good work."

Cathy replied, "We are used to doing better than that in good weather, Captain, sir."

"You are on a sailing ship, not a huge steamship. We do not just steam along on a nice, straight, and steady course. Is all going well with the two of you?"

"Yes, sir, Captain, we are doing good."

The Captain had occasionally checked their plot and log entries. Each time, he said nothing, only nodding in approval. He was watching their work.

After dark, the Captain addressed Cathy, "Ensign, there is one lookout in the crow's nest, one lookout in the bow, two sailors on deck to tend and trim the sails, and one helmsman, keep them alert. If the wind or seas change, send someone below to wake the Sailing Master. I will be in my cabin. You have the watch. Wake me if needed."

Cathy responded, "Yes, sir." Her legs felt weak. This huge ship, five men, she was in charge and responsible. She thought of her situation. Being in charge was supposed to make one feel good, being important. But this was scary; what if she did something wrong? She determined to do her best.

Dotty came on deck. "What did the Captain say about out seven-mile error?"

"He said it was acceptable for a sailing ship."

"I will go get some sleep so I can relieve you in four hours." Looking around, Dotty asked, "Who is the officer on watch?"

Cathy answered, "I am the officer on watch. The Captain is in his cabin."

"Are you trying to fool me?"

"No, it is scary. Go get some rest. I will need you in four hours."

After a couple of hours, the First Mate came on deck and relieved Cathy.

Cathy asked him about the ship sailing with so few on deck. The *Bonnie Duffy* usually had more than this on watch. He told Cathy that in the trade winds, a ship could sail for days with no one having to do anything except man the helm. In a storm or sailing into the wind with little sea room, all hands would have to work hard for days. A sailor soon learned to get as much sleep as he can when he can. Cathy told him she had been around the Horn in a storm aboard the *Bonnie Duffy* and could not imagine it on a ship like this.

He held up his left hand. The ends of his two smallest fingers were missing. He said, "Rounding the Horn in the winter. They froze and broke off."

They spent three days on the same course with no sail change, only slight sail trimming. On the fourth morning, they were over three hundred miles south of their rhumb line. They came to a course of northeast by north. There was no sail change, but all the sails had to be retrimmed. Now they were on a beam reach, their fastest point of sailing, their speed increased to fourteen knots. The apparent wind was near abeam.

As the *Monterey* cut through the water, it could be felt and heard, there was a sizzling sound made by the hull and water. It was a little hard getting used to the sound and feel of the ship; they were accustomed to the ever-present sound and vibration of engines. Aboard the *Bonnie*, the constant throb of the engines became a reassuring thing. Any slight change was immediately noticed.

Both of the twins spent time out on the bow sprint. They agreed, lying face down, across the bow sprint stays, stretching their arms out made it felt like they were flying over the ocean. They agreed that it was scary and exciting to climb up the rigging the top yard arm. This was a whole new experience.

During their spare time, the twins practiced their Laido. The crew seemed to enjoy hanging onto a yard arms watching them. There was little entertainment aboard the *Monterey*. The Captain, with a laugh, said they would be an asset if they were attacked by pirates, though they would need steel swords, not wooden ones.

Dotty told the Captain that when they sailed near Madagascar, they posted extra watches for pirates and avoided other ships.

Cathy and Dotty were proficient and diligent in their duties, as well as adventurous. On occasions, the Captain would check their work, sometimes saying, "Keep up the good work."

Both of the twins spent time as the officer on watch for short periods. They learned to be mindful and tour the deck, checking to see that all on watch were alert and the ship was ship-shape. They were instructed that was part of their duty. All the sailors treated them with respect. None of the crew ever casually talked with them, and the new Ensigns were instructed that would be fraternizing. They were expected to give orders when necessary and not make friends of the crew. The other officers were friendly and helped them out with their many questions. The Captain and the other officers seemed to enjoy teaching them about sailing vessels. In fair weather, when sailing in the trade winds, there was a lot of time to learn, and some time to play. The crew was kept busy swabbing the deck, checking and repairing the caulking, as well as sewing sails and splicing and seizing lines. One morning, the sailors replaced several lines that were showing signs of deterioration.

On the fifth day, they had a couple of squall lines that required sail reefing and trimming. They had to do some maneuvering because of some erratic wind shifts that made the DR plot a challenge. They were proud of themselves. They stood fast as they were pelted by rain and the ocean spray; they did not get blown or washed overboard. They held fast to lines. Their DR plot were only six nautical miles off when they took their evening sights and got a good fix.

* * * * *

The SS *Bonnie Duffy* was only one day from port. Bonnie and Charlotte tallied up their voyage.

Six of the seven continents visited.

Six of the seven oceans sailed on.

Twenty-two countries and colonies visited.

Twenty-four ports of call.

One hundred sixty-two days.

49,686 nautical miles sailed.

Two endurance speed records set.

First ever circumnavigation by a Passenger Liner.

Averaged over 306 nautical miles a day.

Many new friends and goodwill made.

The SS *Bonnie Duffy* accomplished their goals, The Safest, Most Luxurious, Fastest, and Most Reliable Ship on the Seas." They also were profitable.

Tomorrow afternoon, they would arrive at home port, June 5, 1894.

Tonight, there would be a celebration. Some passengers would continue on, and some would disembark. A few passengers would become crew. Some crew would depart, and others would be signed on as crew.

At the party several toasts were given, to the SS *Bonnie Duffy*, to Smithfield Steamships, to the crew, to Bonnie Smithfield, to Mr. and Mrs. Frank Krupp, a.k.a. the Captain and Miss Charlotte.

After Bonnie's morning sights, she took her sextant with her. She donated her books to the ship's library, except the baby book. The twins had several of her books, which she did not expect back. By noon, Bonnie was all packed, a pile in her cabin.

Several crew members asked Bonnie to come with them. They escorted Bonnie to the ship's work shop and presented her with a gift. It was a large beautiful desk made from Australian white Cyprus. It was obvious they selected each piece of wood for its beautiful grain to match the grain of the adjoining piece. Bonnie sincerely hugged the two women carpenters that did most of the work. The desk was a one of a kind, a work of art. Again, Bonnie held back a tear. Bonnie did have a concern over the desk—her mother-in-law, fathers-in-law, and husband would be jealous and want it.

CHAPTER 22

Home Port

B onnie went to the bridge, which she felt was her duty station. She watched as they neared the dock. There was Joseph with an enormous bouquet of flowers. Bonnie heart pounded in her chest as she went to the top of the gangway. As it was lowered, Joseph jumped up on the gangway before it touched the dock and ran up toward Bonnie. Somehow the bouquet landed on the deck as they passionately embraced. Joseph's hug felt so good Bonnie felt like she was going to melt in his arms. Eventually, Bonnie composed herself and looked Joseph in the eyes.

"In New York in February, you gave me a gift. I hope you will share it with me?"

Joseph replied, "What did I give you, a night on the town?"

Bonnie took Joseph's hand and put it on her belly, saying, "A baby."

Joseph looked into Bonnie's eyes, and gradually, realization of what she said sunk in. His mouth slowly turned into a broad smile. He ran back down the gangway, shouting, "I am going to have a baby." At the bottom of the gangway, his senses partially returned to him and he ran back up the gangway, shouting, "I am going to be a father." Reaching Bonnie, he threw his arms around her, picked her up, and swung her about in a circle. Then Joseph's senses returned a little more and he put Bonnie down, deeply concerned that he had hurt her or the baby.

Bonnie felt a warm, secure, and loved feeling engulf her whole body. All her apprehension and fears evaporated. All was right in her world.

The World Circumnavigator medallions were brought by Mom and Dad; they arrived just in time as the passengers started to disembark, and Bonnie grabbed a few.

Except for Charlotte, Megan, Candida, and the Doctor, Bonnie had kept her condition a secret. Now Joseph wanted the whole world to know. "My lovely wife is with child. I am going to be a father." Mom and Dad seemed to be just as excited as Joseph. Mom actually cried and made a scene, hugging Bonnie in public. After Dad hugged Bonnie, he lit up a cigar, gave a cigar to Joseph, and enthusiastically shook his son's hand, congratulating him, telling him, "Good work, son." Bonnie looked around, and there was Samuel the photographer taking photographs of them.

Bonnie said, "Joseph, please give me a minute."

Bonnie went to Samuel, pulled him aside, and in a soft voice in his ear said, "I will give you a reasonable price for those photographs you just took. If you show them to anyone else, I will not hesitate. I will bloody my sword on your privates. We got a deal."

Samuel replied, "Deal, ma'am. Does that include the photographs I took of you and the Samurai and you practicing with your sword and whip?"

"Yes. Any photographs that might prove embarrassing to my family. I am sorry, but my family comes first."

"Yes, ma'am."

Bonnie returned to her family.

Joseph asked, "What was that all about?"

"I just bought some photographs for you to look at."

Joseph and Bonnie with the help of a porter had moved all her things to the mansion.

Joseph picked up Bonnie's Katana and was immediately told, "Please leave that alone for now. It is a very dangerous weapon, it requires training."

After dinner, Dad got his two antique swords and photograph of the volcano erupting; he was impressed. Dad looked at the fancy bronze sword, saying, "This is a sword fit for a general."

Bonnie said, "I was told a Mongol Warlord, very old. It is called a Dao. The other sword is a soldier's sword called a Jian, supposedly very old. It looks well used."

Dad replied, "Three wonderful gifts. If I put them on my office wall, people will not listen to me. They will be too busy admiring my treasures."

Mom got her two antique vases and examined them closely. "They are exquisite. They look old."

Bonnie informed Mom, "I was told, Song Dynasty."

Mom said, "They are fit for an Emperor's palace. My friends will be envious."

Joseph got his ship model of the *Golden Hind*. But he was more interested in Bonnie's belly.

After Bonnie had answered a barrage of questions, the conversation went to what Bonnie was now going to do. Mom insisted that she got lots of rest, and could help her out in the retail business if she got bored. Dad insisted that she was a valuable part of the shipping business and could help him out. Dad said that he had gotten a telegram from Hawaii, telling him how knowledgeable Bonnie was in the shipping business. Joseph wanted her to consult, part-time, in the ship-building business.

Bonnie felt some movement in her belly. She sat and smiled. She felt surrounded by love. She was wanted. She was a part of a wonderful family. Her journey over, she had arrived at her destination.

For the present she wanted to enjoy her family and complete some unfinished ship's business. Bonnie was concerned for two of her crew that had been voluntarily shanghaied.

* * * * *

After they retired, it was soon apparent that Bonnie had another problem. Joseph started treating her like she was fragile and could be easily broken. Bonnie decided to make her wants apparent and she led Joseph by the hand and pushed him into bed, crawled on top of him, and proceeded to physically molest him. At first, he protested.

Bonnie told him, "Shut up, I am not fragile and I want you."

When Bonnie was adamant, she got her way.

* * * * *

In the morning, Joseph was slow getting out of bed; he felt worn out.

Bonnie went to the kitchen looking for a cup of coffee.

Dad was already having coffee. "Good morning. You are up early. I thought you would be resting up today after your spectacular voyage."

"Good morning. I have some unfinished business I need to attend to."

Dad asked, "Do you ever slow down?"

Dad poured Bonnie a cup of coffee.

"Dad, when you have time I would like to talk to you. It is nothing bad, I feel I have been selected as a messenger and there are a few incidental things you should to know."

"Bonnie, you have my attention."

Bonnie explained, "I have had discussions with the Japanese, Russians, Germans, French, British, and others that we needed to talk about. I feel that somehow I have been placed in the middle of international concerns. I was actually asked to deliver messages to our government. The Japanese and Russians sincerely want to do business with Smithfield Steamship Company in ship construction. I do not understand how I got myself in this situation. Somehow I seem to always get myself in situations."

Dad said, "Bonnie, I did not want to discuss this in front of the rest of the family. I wanted to give you some time, but since you brought it up, we do need to talk. I have gotten some correspondence of concern. Let us go to the study for some privacy. Can you grab the coffeepot? You seem to have charmed many and have become very influential. Being influential is people believing you are. If the Japanese talk to you and listen to you, you are influential to them and to the people interested in Japan. It appears that a lot of people know that you are influential. You do realize influence is power. The question is, what are you going to do now?"

Bonnie replied, "I do not want power or influence. I am going to have a baby. Can I just give the messages I have and be done with all this? I did not do anything but listen to people, trying to make friends."

"I know I told you it was a good thing to make friends, but, Bonnie, you seem to have made quite the name for yourself. I do not know what to make of all this. I have gotten correspondence from the Imperial Japanese Navy, Russian Imperial Navy, British Admiralty, the naval staff of Kaiser Wilhelm II, the US Secretary of the Navy, and the US Secretary of State's staff. I do not know what you did, but a lot of people wonder what we are up to. I know it is not just you but that ship. I wanted to make the Smithfield name something special, there is an old saying, 'Careful what you wish for.' The people who work for the President want to know whom we are working with and what we are doing. I am not sure what to do now. I am not into politics. I am a businessman."

Bonnie said, "Just tell them the truth and tell them I will talk to them."

Dad gave Bonnie a stack of telegrams and other correspondence. "Here you go. Talk to them."

Joseph showed up. "What is going on?"

Dad said, "Joseph, sit down, I know I gave you the go-ahead to work with Mr. Edison and General Electric on electrical innovation in the marine market. Bonnie, show Joseph the letter from the staff of Kaiser Wilhelm II."

Joseph looked at the letter and said, "They want to buy generators with control panels, telephone systems, and hatch status indicator light panels. What is the problem?"

Dad replied, "The United States Navy does not have these innovative systems."

Bonnie stated, "USN Naval Commander Roberts is well aware of these innovations. He knows they are available to the US Navy."

"All right, Bonnie, what do I tell the US Secretary of the Navy?"

"Tell Secretary Hilary Herbert to talk to his representative Commander Roberts. Tell the Secretary that Smithfield Steamships will gladly work with the US Navy."

Dad said, "Bonnie, you explained it to the Secretary of the Navy. Now read the letter from the staff of the Admiral of the Imperial Russian Navy."

Bonnie read the letter. "They want to discuss us building them a world-class battleship. I told them it would have to be approved by the US Government. They want something really big. They want to intimidate the Japanese and the Germans."

Dad asked, "Do you have any idea what is involved in building a battleship?"

Bonnie answered, "If the HMS *Centurion* is an example, really thick steel fastened together very strongly with big guns. It does not need to be pretty or accommodating, just robust."

Dad asked, "Is that the British Battleship that you embarrassed?"

"Yes. We made friends with them in Perth and Hong Kong. The *Centurion* now sails out of Hong Kong and is the Flagship of the British China Station Fleet. We toured and had lunch upon the *Centurion* in Perth."

Dad said, "Telegram from the Minister of the Imperial Japanese Navy."

Bonnie replied, "Dad, this is addressed to me. It is from Saigo. He is just wishing me well. That reminds me, he wants to have a collaborative effort with Smithfield in building passenger ships and freighters. They have a real need for commercial ships. They are an island nation dependent on the sea. I think that we can have a mutually profitable relationship with them. I was thinking that a warehouse in Japan would expand your trade business. It could be a bargaining point."

Dad questioned, "You are on a first-name basis with the Minister of the Imperial Japanese Navy, and why is he asking about a Katana? What is a Katana?"

Bonnie replied "He was educated at Oxford and got his advanced degree at Harvard."

Dad again asked, "What is a Katana?"

"A Katana is the traditional sword of a Samurai warrior."

Joseph asked, "Is that the sword on your stand that you would not let me examine?"

Bonnie answered, "Yes, it and the Wakizashi were a gift to me from the people of the Japans. By tradition, they were presented to me by a Samurai."

Dad pulled a telegram from his vest pocket and handed it to Bonnie and said, "You handle this. It brings concern to me."

Joseph asked, "What is it?"

Bonnie read then answered, "The Assistant Secretary of the Department of State is coming in two days by train and wants a meeting. It asks if Commander Roberts can participate."

Dad asked, "Bonnie, can you please handle the meeting?"

Bonnie felt very uncomfortable in what she was being asked. "Only if you also attend. The telegram is addressed to you. It would be rude if you were not there."

Dad said, "Son, you sure have a wife that is special. Does she ever slow down?"

Joseph replied, "I am not complaining, but she wears me out."

Bonnie said, "Dad, I am really sorry. I did not try to bring you all this trouble. I tried to make friends. I did show off the *Bonnie Duffy*. I thought it would be good for business. Every time I wired you for advice, you told me my decision."

Joseph said, "Dad, I did hear you say to make friends."

Dad answered, "You are both right. I am concerned that things are getting out of hand. I have little experience dealing with governments. Bonnie, you seem to do well dealing with government officials. I would like your help. Governments and politicians concern me."

"Dad, I will do what I can. I will talk with them. I want you with me."

"Dealing with one government is a challenge. Now we must deal with almost every powerful country in the world. Bonnie, do you have any more surprises for us?"

"I brought two engineers from Japan to work at the shipyard. They were educated at Princeton and are officers in the Imperial

Japanese navy. And I would like to have a small office to put my desk."

As Bonnie left to get ready for the day, Joseph and his dad were arguing who would give Bonnie an office. Dad said that he was president so she would have an office next to his. Joseph claimed, as his wife, she would have an office next to his. Bonnie just smiled. She would let them fight it out.

* * * * *

Bonnie and Joseph went to the ship, and Joseph was introduced to his Japanese engineers. Bonnie and the engineers exchanged bows and a few words in Japanese that Joseph did not understand. He was not going to ask. They met up with Commander Roberts and his family, and Bonnie introduced them. The Commander was still staying on the ship. He also received a telegram telling him to meet with the Assistant Secretary of State. The Commander told Bonnie that Charlotte gave them permission to stay on the ship for a few days.

Charlotte, Candida, and Willa were working together, planning, to get the ship ready for its second circumnavigation.

Charlotte said, "The ship is almost booked up. We have more special-ticket sales for the second time around. Billy Frisco's articles are making us famous. Along with Samuel's photographs, we have more publicity than I can handle. Everybody that is anybody wants to be on a Smithfield cruise. Should we give Billy a free trip around again? He wants to go, but his employer does not want to pay his fare. He wants first class."

Bonnie said, "Thank goodness that is your problem now. You are the boss, not me. I have a new job now."

"What is your new job, cutting fruit up with a sword?"

"In two days, I have a meeting with the Assistant Secretary of State. Want to trade jobs?"

Charlotte responded, "I told you before, you handle the politics. You are sort of good at that. Maybe you should run for Governor, or President."

Bonnie smiled with a small laugh. "Love you too."

Joseph asked, "Tell me about cutting fruit up with a sword."

Bonnie said, "Practicing with my Katana I cut a pineapple in half."

Joseph said, "I would like to see that."

Bonnie answered, "No, you would not."

Charlotte then said, "I would like to see it again. It was really something, real terrifying.

Joseph asked, "You will show me."

With a little smirk, Bonnie replied, "Maybe."

* * * * *

Early afternoon, they were sailing north by east on a close reach. The apparent wind was from their port bow. They were working their way into the wind, sailing at 4 knots. Cathy and Dotty were both on duty, on this their last leg of their cruise. They had been lucky and got good morning fix. Cathy had done a noon-sun sight to verify their DR plot. At their present speed, they should make San Francisco at dusk. If the wind held, it was in their favor to sail into the harbor. If they did not make it into the bay by dusk, they would have an opposing tide that would make it near impossible to enter the bay, and they would have to wait till morning, when the tide would turn in their favor.

Dotty came up from below and shouted to the lookout in the crow's nest. "Land should soon be visible to the northeast.

The Captain asked, "Ensign, how does it look to make port before the tide turns?"

Dotty responded, "Sir, it looks real close."

The Captain asked, "Sailing Master, any suggestions?"

The Sailing Master answered, "Sir, if we could sail even a half-point more easterly, I could get a little more speed. Falling off the wind a bit."

Captain addressed Dotty, "Ensign, do we have any sea room for a more easterly course?"

Dotty responded, "I will check the chart, sir."

Shortly, she returned. "Captain, sir, if we sail one half-point more easterly, we will come close to Seal Rocks. We will be in waters that are only two fathoms deep."

The Captain asked, "Ensign, can you navigate us safely by the Seal Rocks?"

Dotty replied, "Captain, sir, it would be difficult. May I suggest we hold the present course for another fifteen minutes? That will give us a little more sea room."

Captain said, "Thank you, Ensign, we will hold our present course."

The Captain had recently looked at the charts and plot. He knew the situation. He was looking for alternatives, wanting to make port by dark. They could tack westward; that would give them more sea room, but it would take time and add distance to port. Captain Smith decided that if they could not make port by the time the tide turned against them, they would tack to sea and enter the port in the morning.

They had become a team, working together. The officer had confidence in each other and could communicate with each other. The twins had gained the confidence for the Captain and officers. They were as Captain Krupp said, proficient and conscientious. Their navigation was exemplary; they had been trained well. They had the makings of good commanding officers. Captain Smith knew that good officers and Navigators were in great demand, girls or not, papers or not would not stop these two good sailors. At sea, the Captain is in command, not the Commissioners and the papers they issued.

The crow's nest lookout shouted, "Land, four points off starboard bow."

As the land came visible to starboard, a couple of landmarks became visible to starboard. Cathy took bearings. Dotty plotted the bearing.

Dotty reported, "Captain, sir, DR plot verified. Suggest a course of north-northeast. That should keep us outside the ten-fathom line."

The Captain ordered, "Course north-northeast."

The helmsman repeated the order.

The sails were retrimmed, and the Sailing Master reported, "Sir, we have gained two knots."

In half an hour, Dotty reported, "Captain, sir, barring any delays and the wind holds, we should make the inner bay before we encounter the full outbound tide."

The Captain said, "Thank you, Ensign. Continue your bearings and inform me of any changes." He checked the plot, "Sailing Master, you have the bridge. I have some letters to write."

They made it through the straights and past Alcatraz Island before the full tide turned against them. Two tugs helped the Monterey to the Smithfield dock as the sun started to set. It was a good voyage—eight days, eleven hours. The twins were busy packing and trying to leave the aft cabin neat and orderly. They had been diligent on keeping everything in good order; it would not take them long. The Captain asked permission to enter, then he addressed the twins.

"The two of you are excellent Navigators and good officers that I can trust. I would like to offer both of you a fulltime position here on the *Monterey*. The pay will be scale. This is a good ship and a good crew."

The twins looked at each other for a moment. Both shook their heads.

Cathy said, "No, thank you, Captain, sir. This is a good ship and a good crew. You are a good Captain to serve under."

Dotty added, "Sir, we have a home on the SS *Bonnie Duffy*. Our sisters are there."

The Captain said, "If you change your minds, the offer is still open."

Cathy said, "Thank you for the experience. We like sailing ships. It was wonderful, Captain, sir."

The Captain nodded. "I like your uniforms with your initial and name on them. Without the initial I could not tell you two apart. Here are recommendations and your wages. Thank you for your services and good luck. Hopefully, I will have the pleasure of sailing with you again."

With a grin on his face, Captain Smith said, "You should get steel swords, in case of pirates."

The Captain got a real surprise, a hug from both of the twins. Not appropriate but appreciated.

* * * *

The other sisters had seen the *Monterey* coming into port. They went to the pier to greet their sisters and were invited aboard.

Annie said, "We missed you and were worrying about you. How was it on a sailing ship?"

Dotty said, "We are officers aboard this ship. Address us as officers."

Betty added, "Do not try to give us your garbage."

Dotty looked at Captain Smith, saluted, and said, "Permission to leave the ship, sir."

The Captain returned the salute and said, "Permission granted, Ensign Adams."

Cathy went through the same routine.

Once they were off the *Monterey*, getting help with their sea bags, Annie said, "If you two expect us to salute you, you can stick it up your little butts!"

Betty said, "That goes for me too."

Eavey added, "Me three."

Cathy declared, "You are just jealous."

Dotty stated, "We have letters of recommendation."

Cathy asked, "Did the Captain spell your name right, or are you still Ditty?"

Dotty looked at her letter. "He got it right. I am Dotty."

Annie said, "I like Ditty. It sounds better than Dotty."

Dotty replied, "Shove it up your big, fat butt."

Eavey said, "I want to hear everything. Was it fun?"

Dotty answered, "We cannot tell you everything."

Annie asked, "Why not?"

Cathy replied, "You would not believe us, and you would call us liars."

Betty asked, "Like what?"

Cathy turned around and pointed up to the top of the ship's rigging and said, "We climbed to the top yard arm under full sail in a twenty-four-knot wind."

Annie said, "You are right. I will not believe you."

Eavey asked, "Did you really climb all the way up there? That looks scary. Were you scared?"

Dotty answered, "It is not as bad as it looks once you get used to it. It is like oiling an engine the first time."

The letters of recommendation were simple and straightforward. Dotty read hers.

> Dotty Adams served aboard the sailing ship *Monterey* as an Ensign and Navigator from May 29, 1894 till June 6, 1894. Ensign Adam's service as an officer was exemplary. The Ensign's navigation skills are exceptional. I highly recommend Dotty Adams and believe Dotty Adams will be an asset to any ship she sails aboard.
>
> Captain Fredrick Smith of the Monterey

Annie, "Sounds really good, but I am still not going to salute you, little sister."

* * * * *

Bonnie spent the afternoon going over all the correspondences her father-in-law had given her. They were mainly inquiries, not any accusations. Bonnie collected her thoughts, trying to prepare herself for the inevitable questions that might be difficult to answer. Bonnie thought of all the information crammed in her head. She had talked with and listened to many people from many countries. Some were discreet conversations with influential people. Bonnie was putting all that she knew together. Every piece of correspondence Dad gave her, she understood and thought she could respond to in an intelligent manner. Bonnie felt confident that she could give the Assistant Secretary good answers to his questions. Bonnie realized that again she had gotten herself into a situation, though this time, she had a little confidence in herself.

That evening, Joseph got a melon from the kitchen and started to pester Bonnie to show him how she can cut it with a sword. This continued through dinner. He managed to get his mom and dad to join in.

Dad said, "You do know that you will not have any peace until you show us."

Bonnie realized she was a part of the family. She would have to behave as such and honor their request. Bonnie put on her plain white kimono and got her Katana. She went to the patio in the back of the mansion, placed the melon on top of a high service table, and asked her family to step back. Bonnie went through her ritual, meditating for a moment, becoming one with her Katana. She fastened the sword's scabbard to her sash and bowed. She then stood in her defensive stance, then in one smooth, continuous motion, drew her Katana and sliced the melon. By the time her family reacted, Bonnie was wiping off her blade as she replaced it in its scabbard. Bonnie stepped back and bowed. Then she picked up the melon and handed half to Joseph and the other half to Dad.

Mom spoke, "It was so fast I did not see what happened. That is amazing."

Joseph asked, "How did you learn to do that?"

"Two good instructors and practice."

Dad said, "That sword must be really sharp. The cut is clean. I am going to keep my swords on the wall and avoid you when you have a sword. I have read that a trained swordsman can take a man's head off with one blow. Now I believe it."

Bonnie asked, "Please, I would appreciate that you not tell people of my skill. I do not enjoy showing off."

* * * * *

In the morning, Bonnie and Joseph went to the *Bonnie Duffy* and checked up on the twins. They were happy they went and happy they were home. They showed Bonnie their recommendations. Bonnie told them to keep the navigation books; they might need them. Bonnie gave the sisters their fourth silver Commemorative medallion with her sincere thank-you for their service, which got Bonnie big hugs. The sisters liked hugs; Bonnie liked hugs too.

Bonnie went to Captain Krupp and asked for his advice. He agreed to write a recommendation for the twins. First Mate Adam Fitzpatrick agreed to write a recommendation. Now if she could get Dad to write a recommendation, it would be hard to deny the young ladies. It was not as much their age; it was their gender. There were thirteen-year-old boys that were junior officers and Navigators. It was traditional in the British and other navies. Captain J. R. Jellicoe RN was promoted to Midshipman at thirteen.

As Joseph and Bonnie was leaving, they were approached by the photographer, Samuel. He handed Bonnie a large thick envelope, saying, "Your photographs, ma'am."

Bonnie asked, "What do I owe you?"

Samuel said, "Special ticket around again with a cabin appropriate for a studio. I will put SS *Bonnie Duffy* on every photograph. Passage at no cost to me. I think photography is an appropriate ship service. Many passengers want photographs of their voyage."

Bonnie asked, "Is this all of the photographs of me and my family?"

Samuel, "There are other photographs of you in group settings during normal ship activities. Many people have bought copies of such things as the King Neptune ceremonies and everyday activities. I have tried to include a copy of the better ones in the envelope."

Bonnie said, "Have a good voyage. I will inform Charlotte."

Charlotte agreed that Samuel was an asset to the enjoyment of the ship's passengers. She agreed to assign him an adequate cabin, big enough for a modest studio.

That afternoon, Bonnie and Joseph went to the shipyard. It was good to see Rachael and Connie. They had started the superstructure of the next ship in the *Bonnie* series and were laying the keel for the third in the series. Bonnie and Joseph were shown the changes that were proposed for the interior, with some modifications to the exterior. Most of Bonnie's suggestions were taken in account. The casino would be enlarged, and the smoking lounge would be shrunk; it had only a little usage. A library-and-classroom combination would be added. A bridge and a bridge deck would be added just beneath the Captain's bridge and bridge-deck. The additional bridge and bridge deck would be used for training and passenger observation.

Joseph said, "Additional coal bunker capacity is being added. The cargo holds would be reduced in size, a compromise. Conveyors would be added for coal movement. The new boilers would be smaller, have powered stokers, and forced draft, making them more efficient with more steam available at a higher temperature. Newer engines were already installed that were more powerful and more efficient, including more efficient propellers. Other improvements would be added working with General Electric. Steam turbines would run the generators.

Bonnie said, "It will not be long and the Germans and British will have larger ships. After this ship, let us make an eight-hundred-foot or longer Luxury Liner."

Joseph said, "I thought you were going to have a baby and not get involved in ship building."

Bonnie replied, "It is just an idea. Can we make the third *Bonnie* class into a freighter? Without the accommodations, it can carry large loads. It would be a super freighter. I know I can sell several, that is, if Mr. Smithfield lets me and does not keep it for himself. I can also sell engines and boilers to the Japanese. What are their availability?"

Joseph, Bonnie, Rachel, and Connie spent the rest of the day putting ideas together on new ships.

After taking a long, hot bath, Bonnie found Joseph sitting with all the photographs strewn about on a table; he was closely examining one.

Bonnie asked, "What are you doing, looking at my photographs?"

Joseph said, "I heard you say, 'Buying you some photographs.'"

Bonnie pondered for a minute and answered, "I did say that."

In her robe, Bonnie put her arms around her husband's shoulders and looked over his shoulder, with her head against his, looking at what he was looking at. It was a side view of Bonnie in a plain white kimono, hair pinned back, with a serious look on her face looking forward, her right bare foot forward flat on the ground, her left bare foot in back of her on her toes, her legs partially bent, her arms stretched straight forward; extending in a line straight from her arms was a long, slightly curved sword.

"My wife, pure beauty in face, body, and form. Can I have this photograph?"

"Why that one? What are you going to do with it?"

"Put it on my desk. My wife, a beautiful lady to be respected."

"It is yours. I love you. Let's go to bed."

"Can I have the one of you and your bull whip?"

"Come to bed and we can negotiate about the photographs."

* * * * *

Midday the next day, Mr. Harvey Smithfield sent a carriage and ported to pick up the Assistant Secretary of State at the train station.

Bonnie said, "Dad, relax. It's no big deal."

Dad replied, "People do not take a train across the country for no big deal. I hate politics and politicians. They do not make anything—they just spend money and interfere in other people's business."

Dad had arranged for the presidential suite at the best hotel for the Assistant Secretary. Dad was deeply concerned, though he pretended he was not.

Edward F. Uhl arrived; after introductions, he asked for a drink. It was Single Malt. Dad joined in; Commander Roberts and Bonnie declined a drink. They sat in the library of the mansion in comfortable chairs.

Mr. Uhl said, "Mrs. Smithfield, I am glad that you are joining us. When I made my reservations, I was not sure that you would be back. You and your ship are all the talk in Washington. If I had to wait a few days here for your arrival, I would have."

Bonnie asked, "Mr. Uhl, how was your trip? You came a long way."

"Long? I am from Michigan and have never been west of the Mississippi before, although I have been to Europe and South America on ships. The scenery is beautiful. Lots of prairie and mountains. We truly have a grand country."

"The SS *Bonnie Duffy's* voyage is one for many record books. I have a letter from President Grover Cleveland for the Smithfield family."

Mr. Uhl read the letter.

> Smithfield Family of San Francisco:
>
> Job well done. The SS *Bonnie Duffy's* contribution to the United States prestige in immeasurable. You toured the world extending a hand in friendship, as well as showing the world that America is a strong industrialized country. Many countries are building fleets of war ships to impress others. The Smithfield's showed them up, with a non-armed vessel spreading good will at no expense to the government and no threat to others.
>
> I thank you. America thanks you.
>
> Grover Cleveland
> President of the United States of America.

Mr. Uhl handed the letter to Dad. It was handwritten on presidential stationery.

Dad said, "Thank you, Mr. Uhl, I did not expect this. I can only accept a little credit. Joseph and Bonnie talked me into this. At first, I was very skeptical of the venture, but Joseph and Bonnie can be very persuasive. If you get to know Bonnie and Joseph, you will understand. I believe Bonnie has some messages for you if you have the time to listen."

Mr. Uhl replied, "By all means, lately, the names *Bonnie Duffy* and *Mrs. Smithfield* are often heard in diplomatic circles. You have my undivided attention."

Bonnie said, "I would like to give you a message from the Minister of the Imperial Japanese Navy. They have a good trade relationship with the United States, and they wish to maintain that relationship and possible strengthen it. They respect the United States and respect the country's neutrality. They are asking that the United States continues with their neutrality and not get involved in any Asian conflict. They warn that many will want to involve the United States for their own benefit."

Mr. Uhl said, "We have received the same message from their Consulate, thank you."

"Mr. Uhl, I understand that you have some questions for me."

"That I do, Mrs. Smithfield. We have heard that you have talked with a lot of important people, and we though you might have some insight into the situation in China and Japan. There is a lot of concern of the situation in Asia. What can you tell me that might be of interest to our government?"

Bonnie responded, "Please, call me Bonnie."

"If you call me Ed."

Bonnie said, "There are a lot of countries involved. I think there will be war. The Japanese and Russians are both posturing and threatening each other."

Ed stated, "We are concerned the British will try to colonize China."

Bonnie answered, "The British are strengthening their Navy to protect their interests in China and Southeast Asia. They recently added one of their new battleship to their China Station Fleet. At the present, Great Britain, as well as Australia, are coming out of a depression and money is tight for them. Their armies are involved in conflicts in Egypt, Sudan, and South Africa. They have concerns of a rebellion in parts of India, keeping more troops unavailable. There are questions they do not have the ground forces for another ground war. Their Army is stretched thin. In Asia, the British are in a defensive mode. China does not have cohesive military force.

Example, in Shanghai, the British, Russian, Japanese, German, and several Chinese Warlords have a military presence. There is even a USN Cruiser stationed there as well as a detachment of US Marines stationed ashore. I am sure you are aware of those deployments. Everyone wants a presence but at this time are not willing to face the possible consequences of military action. There is an uneasy peace. Everyone is afraid to shoot and start a war. There seems to be a problem drawing up sides. All are watching each other. Even though the Chinese do not have a cohesive military, there are several Warlords in power. If someone tries to invade China, the fear is that the Warlords will put aside their differences and units, creating a formable military force. The Russians are presently negotiating with the Chines. They are allies, by mutual interests. The British are in a defensive mode trying to protect their interests. The British still rule the seas, and nobody wants to start a fight with them."

Ed asked, "Who do you think will go to war?"

"The Japanese and Russians."

"What makes you think that?"

Bonnie explained, "Japan is an island nation. They have few mineral resources. They are presently trying to industrialize. They want to take their place as a powerful nation. Presently, they rely on the United States for a lot of their mineral resourced. They buy a lot of American scrap metals. The British and their colonies are restricting the sales to Japan, and the Japanese feel like they are being squeezed. To their west are Korea and Manchuria, which have abundant mineral resources. They have traditionally tried to control that area and historically invaded and occupied the area for periods of time. They believe it should be part of Japan. The Russians are building their Trans-Siberian-Railroad. Their route takes them through part of Mongolia. The Chinese are granting an easement to the Russians for protection from the Japanese. The Japanese need the mineral resources, and the Russians want to protect their Asian interests and territory. The Japanese are building up their Navy. Commander Roberts has a lot of current photographs of their build up. The photographs were taken from the deck of the *Bonnie Duffy* a few weeks ago. Both the Japanese and Russian seemed to want me to know of their Naval buildup. The Russians are currently having the French build them large battleships. The British do not want to get involved as long as it does not affect their current interests. I personally believe that the British will stand back and let the Japanese and Russians beat each other up than step in. The Chinese do not have the will to get involved as long as their warlords are not attacked or threatened. Both the Japanese and Russians want to be friends with the United States and want to have a good trade relationship with the United States. It is a very complicated and dangerous situation."

Ed said, "That was probably the best briefing I ever got. Want a job with the State Department? What do you think the United States should do?"

Bonnie answered, "I have friends that are British, Japanese, and Russian. I do not want to see the United States get militarily involved. The Japanese understand for the United States to remain neutral, we will not be able to sell arms. I believe the Russians want the United States on their side, at least as a supplier. If the United States remains neutral, selling nonmilitary materials to both the Russians and the Japanese, the United States will be an economic winner. Let us not make enemies."

Ed said, "Sure I cannot persuade you to move to the capital? We need people that can talk, listen, learn from others, and see beyond the blustering."

Bonnie replied, "No, thank you. I am going to have a baby and want to settle down. Besides, my family will not let me go. They think they need me. Some of what I said can be verified by Commander Roberts. I am sure he has his own perspective that should be seriously considered. Commander Roberts is a good listener and representative of our country and an asset to the US Navy."

Commander Roberts said, "I concur with Bonnie. I did not have as much contact with the Japanese as Bonnie had, but I believe there is a strong likelihood of a war between the Russians and Japanese. I spent time with both the British and Russians that are stationed in the area. They are all building up their militaries and preparing for war. The British are trying to stay out of the upcoming conflict, at least at this point in time."

Ed looked at Bonnie. "What about the Germans and French?"

Bonnie looked at the Commander, motioning for his input.

The Commander said, "The Kaiser is trying to develop his own powerful Navy. They are presently building a Battleship that allegedly will be the biggest, fastest, and the best-armed ship on the seas. Also, they are building a Luxury Liner that will also be the biggest and fastest. I do not think they have the assets or inclination to be heavily involved in Asia at this time. They might sell arms to the highest bidder. Their efforts seem to be in building up their own military. The French are building battleships for the Russians. The French are also building a large fleet of heavily armed heavy cruisers for themselves. Their Naval strategy is a large quantity of maneuverable ships that will overwhelm a large battleship. My concerns are that in the future, the Germans and French will have a conflict, possibly dragging other European nations into their conflict."

Ed asked, "Bonnie, what do you think?"

Bonnie replied, "There are definitely concerns of European peace. There is a lot of animosity between them and a desire for dominance. There are desires for Empire building."

Ed asked, "Mr. Smithfield, what is your company policy?"

Mr. Smithfield replied, "The Smithfield companies have no desire in building or supplying arms to other nations. We are a US company and will aid our country in any way we can. We do have a worldwide supply network of commerce. We would like to have the privilege of supplying nonmilitary materials and goods to all nations, not an enemy of the United States, including commercial ships and materials to build and equip ships."

Ed responded, "Mr. Smithfield, currently, I can see no reason for the United States Government to have any problems with your company policy. If you would get into the arms market, that might be a problem. Although there are no current laws, it would be advisable to inform the State Department of any arms shipments. The Smithfield Companies are an asset to California and the nation. Bonnie, I will inform the President of your advice to remain neutral. How about another drink, and we can talk about something other than politics?"

Bonnie said, "One more issue that I think might be important. I think that Cuba is about to explode in a civil war to expel the Spanish control. There is a lot of hatred of the Spanish by everyday Cuban citizens as well as business owners. We were treated rudely and suspiciously by the Spanish administrators of Cuba. The Spanish seized all telegrams to the *Bonnie Duffy* and threatened the telegraph operators if they disclosed the seizures to us. Spanish administrators do not like Americans. The Cubans will welcome America's help in ousting the Spanish."

Dad filled Ed's glass and sat the bottle on the table between them.

Ed replied, "Are you sure that I cannot talk you into taking a job with the State Department? Concerns of Cuba and the Spanish are part of every cabinet meeting. We are watching the situation closely. What do you think about the Philippines?"

Bonnie said, "Ed, we did not go to the Philippines. The Australians warned us that they had concerns. We went to Port Moresby, Papua New Guinea, instead, and avoided the cannibals and head hunters instead of dealing with the Spanish."

Commander Roberts interjected, "The British have concerns about the Philippines. The Spanish are hated and a civil war is a real possibility."

Ed said, "You two seem to know more that my people that as supposed to be the experts. Can I send a man with the *Bonnie Duffy* on the next trip? He can go as a tourist."

Bonnie suggested, "I think that if you sent a congenial United States State Department Representative as an Ambassador of Goodwill, you would get more information and better results. Send them with their family. America is neutral. America wants to make friends."

Ed said, "That is a wonderful idea. I am sure the President will agree. It will go with his policies. Bonnie, you are an amazing lady."

Dad quipped, "She is also unstoppable."

Bonnie said, "Ed, just one more thing I would like to mention. New York City, especially their police, are corrupt. All seem to want bribes. It makes for an unpleasant experience.

Ed responded, "Many are aware of the problem. I will tell you a new police commissioner had been appointed. He is a very ambitious man that has a reputation for integrity. He promises to ride rough over the police in New York and clean them up."

Than they talked of the SS *Bonnie Duffy*, Bonnie invited all for a tour and dinner. The ship cargo was being unloaded, and many maintenance chores were being done. Charlotte was not happy; they were not prepared for a tour. Dad's presence kept her from showing her ire. They did the entire tour, engine room and all. Ed seemed to understand that they were preparing for another circumnavigation.

Captain Krupp and wife were asked to attend dinner with the group. The chefs put on an extra effort, and the Single Malt continued to be consumed.

Dad informed Charlotte to reserve a nice family cabin for a Goodwill Ambassador, from the United States State Department. It was decided they could board in San Diego or another port if they could not make San Francisco before departure.

Dad was happy the government was on his side.

On their way back to the mansion, Dad being happy, Bonnie made her requests. Joseph just listened, not wanting to be in the middle, thinking, *At least Mom is not here.*

"You need to make Charlotte Krupp your owner's representative."

"I cannot argue with that request, she is an exceptional lady. I still have not replaced her at the office. I miss her expertise."

"I need your support getting the sisters the recognition and opportunities they deserved."

Dad replied, "Girls do not become engineers or ship officers."

Bonnie responded, "Girls do become carpenters and architects. They can be a Queen. Nobody tells Victoria that she cannot rule a great nation. If a woman can be at the head of the ship of state, why not an officer on a ship's deck upon the sea? Two of the young ladies navigated your *Monterey* from Hawaii to San Francisco safely. Is that not worth something? As your shipping business grows you are going to need good Navigators, engineers, and officers."

Dad answered, "I will do what I can."

Bonnie requested, "One more thing, what was my salary while I was running your ship?"

"You got a free trip around-the-world. What more do you want? Besides, I heard Mr. Uhl. He said, 'You and your ship.' By his words, the SS *Bonnie Duffy* belongs to you."

Bonnie replied, "A thousand dollars a month sounds fair."

"Why are we having this discussion? Just write yourself a check. A thousand a month sounds good. I will put your name on the general account. You are unstoppable! Does anything ever slow you up?"

"Dad, I am sorry. Mom is right. I am rough around the edges. I just cannot help myself. My grandfather said it was the Irish Blood and Red Hair."

"Bonnie, you are a beautiful, charming, and a very intelligent woman. You are honest, straightforward, reliable, and at times, you can be intimidating. With you, what one sees and hears is what one gets. You have an uncanny ability that people that get to know you admire, trust, and respect you. You treat people like they are your friend. You are honest and open with them. You continue to amaze me. I believe that in a matter of hours, you made a friend of Mr. Uhl, the Assistant Secretary of State. You are a one of a kind. Never let anybody change you, not even me."

Bonnie tried to reply.

"I am not done yet. Let me finish. Please hear me out. Let us negotiate. I will do everything I can to get your girls the recognition they deserve if you help Joseph and me in our ship business. I can really use your advice and assistance in dealing with politicians and other business people. Deal?"

"If you stop flattering me and cease bragging about me, making me feel uncomfortable, I get enough of that from Joseph. Deal."

"You drive a hard bargain. Deal."

They shook hands on it.

Dad, "I think that making *Bonnie III* a cargo ship is an excellent idea. An eight-hundred-foot Luxury Liner will have to be discussed.

It will be very expensive. You do know that it is okay to slow down a bit. I want a healthy grandchild."

* * * * *

The twins had six recommendations: Captain Krupp, Captain Smith, First Mate Fitzpatrick, USN Commander Roberts, Mrs. Joseph Smithfield, and Mr. Harvey Smithfield, the President of Smithfield Companies.

Captain Krupp coached them, "Do not be intimidated by the Commissioners. They are likely to give you misleading questions. Give them answers like you are the Officer in Command, making the decisions for the safety of the ship and crew. It is not just about your skills and knowledge, it is also about character and strength. Be polite and respectful, but do not let them rattle you. Answer their questions like I am asking you, seeing what you have learned. Be confident in yourself and let it show you are Navigators."

Dotty Adams and Cathy Adams took and passed their written tests. Now they stood before three men, the US Merchant Marine Commissioners, Pacific District.

"Cathy Adams, I see that you have had experience aboard a steamship and a sailing vessel. What is the difference in the navigation of the two?"

"Sir, they both require diligence in detail no matter the weather, sea, or other conditions that might have to be dealt with. On a sailing ship, the wind has to be given more consideration, but wind must be considered on a steamship. Coal consumption is very important on a steamship."

"Dotty Adams, do you prefer to take evening or morning star sights or noon-sun sights?"

"Sir, a good Navigator gets every fix they can. If the weather turns foul, your last fix is where you navigate from. Bearing are also vital when one can be taken. A Navigator must use all tools available to them for the safety of the ship, crew, and passengers."

"Cathy Adams, why do you want to be a Navigator?"

"Sir, I am a Navigator. I would like your acknowledgement."

"Dotty Adams, why would I want to give a girl papers saying she is a Navigator and Officer?"

"Sir, a woman should get papers only if they are qualified."

"Cathy Adams, have you ever been scared at sea?"

"Yes, sir, I have been scared."

"What did you do when you were scared?"

"My duty, sir."

"Dotty Adams, what was the scariest moment for you at sea?"

"Sir, aboard the *Monterey*, climbing to the top yard arm of the main mast under full sail in the trade winds."

"Why did you do that?"

"Sir, to know that I could do it if duty required me to do it."

The Chairman asked, "Any other questions?"

The Third Commissioner said, "I see nothing in the rules and regulations that prohibits a woman from being a Navigator or Officer in the US Merchant Marine Regulations. Both candidates have fulfilled all the requirements for Navigator and Ensign."

The Second Commissioner said, "I see only two candidates who meet all the requirements. They both have several impressive recommendations, and they have experience under varying conditions."

The Chairman said, "All requirements met. Congratulations, Ensign, Navigator Cathy Adams, and Ensign, Navigator Dotty Adams. Pick up your papers from the clerk in a couple of hours. Good sailing."

As Cathy and Dotty waked out, they overheard one of the Commissioners say, "Word gets out about this, I wonder if we will still be Commissioners?"

Annie, Betty, and Eavey got their official apprenticeship indentures to be Merchant Marine Engineers with credit for time served. That did not require an interview; that would come later, to get their license after they completed their apprenticeships and passed their tests.

* * * * *

Walking back to the *Bonnie*, with papers in hand, the two new Ensigns passed a secondhand store. In the window display was two well used cavalry sabers. Shortly, they got a lot of stares. Two teenage girls walking down the street, dressed as sailors, looking like double vision, with sabers hanging from their belts. Now, neither had money for candy.

As Cathy and Dotty returned to the SS *Bonnie Duffy*, their three sisters lined up greeted them at the top of the gangway; they saluted the new Ensigns. The salute was returned.

Shortly, Captain Krupp showed up. "Ensign C. Adams, Ensign D. Adams, you are both out of uniform. Officers aboard my ship are required to dress appropriately for their rank. This is a passenger ship. Arms are not appropriate unless so ordered or required for training. Here are your new ship's papers, destroy your old papers. Report to the bridge at 0800 hours tomorrow for your orders. Orders understood."

The two Ensigns, as they saluted, in unison, replied, "Yes, sir, orders understood, Captain, sir."

The Captain returned their salute, saying, "Congratulations, welcome aboard."

* * * * *

Several evenings later, Joseph and Bonnie held hands, watching as the SS *Bonnie Duffy* sailed out of the bay into the open sea.

Joseph asked, "Bonnie, what are you going to do now?"

Bonnie replied, "Love you. Have our baby and love my family."

Joseph asked, "What else?"

Bonnie answered, "Help you and Dad out a little when you ask."

Joseph quipped, "A little when we ask? You are full of shit."

* * * * *

As published in the local paper, under Announcements on November 19, 1894.

Mr. and Mrs. Joseph Smithfield of San Francisco wish to announce the birth of two healthy sons, Harvey Joseph and Davis Joseph.

The End

Epilogue

Spring 1960, Cathy Davidson got on a Boeing 707 in Chicago heading for New York. She was going to see her brother graduate from the Merchant Marine Academy in Kings Point, New York. The flight was fully booked, so Cathy was upgraded to first-class. Cathy was seated in the aisle seat next to a distinguished elderly lady.

As soon as Cathy sit down and fastened her seatbelt, the lady next to her asked, "Where did you get that lovely charm bracelet?"

"It was my grandmother's. The story is that she got the charms while sailing on an ocean liner."

"The SS *Bonnie Duffy*."

"How did you know that? Or you have really good eyes."

"It is too presumptuous. What is your grandmother's name?"

"Cathy Davidson. I was named after her. She is deceased now."

"I am sorry to hear of your loss. Was your grandmother's maiden name Adams?"

"Yes. Did you know my grandmother?"

"When she was young. I should introduce myself. I am Bonnie Smithfield. My maiden name was Duffy. I never thought to make our commemorative medallions into a charm bracelet."

With a look of great astonishment, Cathy responded, "Mrs. Smithfield, you are a legend in my family. Since I was a small child, I have heard stories of you. Are my grandmother's stories true?"

"I do not know, I would have to hear the story. Tell me about your grandmother. We lost touch with each other after the Great War. Or should I say, World War I."

"When she was younger she never said much about herself. She was always interested in others. She did tell stories of you and her sisters. When she got old, she started to tell some of the wildest stories, and we thought it was her imagination, old age. After she died, we found a wooden box in the top back of her closet. In it were this bracelet, some old papers saying she was a ship's Officer and a Navigator, along with some faded pictures and crumbling newspaper clippings. There was a commendation from the Department of the Navy for heroism for saving lives during the Great War. Shamefully, we did not pay attention to her stories. Her stories are lost forever."

"Your grandmother was a special lady. She was a very feisty twelve-year-old when I first met her. I know that her twin sister, Dotty, died in an airplane crash, testing a new airplane.

"I will tell you one story about your grandmother. If I remember correctly, she was thirteen. She and her twin, Dotty, sailed on a four-mast Clipper Ship as Ensigns. They were the Navigators. The ship lost their Navigator and was short of officers. They sailed from Hawaii to San Francisco. I do not remember the ship's name. Captain Smith was the skipper. Captain Smith gave them reconditions that enabled then to get their Merchant Marine Licenses as Navigators and junior officers. They had previous experience as Navigator apprentices aboard the SS *Bonnie Duffy*, where your grandmother got your charms."

"When we found the Merchant Marine papers, we doubted them, because the dates would make her thirteen."

"I can assure you that those documents are legitimate. That was a different time. After two world wars it is insignificant now, but at the time, the SS *Bonnie Duffy* was special. Now I am an old lady with a lot of fond memories. Some of those fond memories are of your grandmother and her sisters. Tell me of your other great aunts?"

"The only one still alive is Eavey. She retired from the Merchant Marine Academy as a Professor of Electrical Engineering. Now she lives on Kodak Island, Alaska, with her husband. Now she writes historical novels about the turn of the century. Her stories are about ships, the people that serve on them, and the sea. I do not see her often."

"If you see Eavey, ask her about her days serving on the *Bonnie Duffy*. Ask her about her time with Thomas A. Edison. Mr. Edison gave her a little book that inspired her. What are you going to New York for?"

"My brother is graduating from the Merchant Marine Academy. I heard that Eavey will be there. I hope to hear some of her stories. Maybe she can explain the meaning of these charms? These charms are certainly unique."

"That is where I am going. They want to give me an award, probably for living so long. They are all full of shit."

DO#LUB

_ _ _ _ _ E

CPSIA information can be obtained
at www.ICGtesting.com
Printed in the USA
LVOW11s0151170418
573765LV00001B/106/P